The seven eyes of Ningauble the Wizard floated back to his hood as he reported to Fafhrd: "I have seen much, yet cannot explain all. The Gray Mouser is exactly twenty-five feet below the deepest cellar in the palace of Glipkerio Kistomerces. Even though twenty-four parts in twenty-five of him are dead, *he* is alive.

"Now about Lankhmar. She's been invaded, her walls breached everywhere and desperate fighting is going on in the streets, by a fierce host which outnumbers Lankhmar's inhabitants by fifty to one— and equipped with all modern weapons. Yet you can save the city."

"How?" demanded Fafhrd.

Ningauble shrugged. "You're a hero. You should know."

AUTHOR'S FOREWORD

The list below is the proper order of the six books in the saga of the Gray Mouser and Fafhrd, beginning with the one containing two tales of Fafhrd's and the Mouser's lives before their meeting and also the yarn of that definitive encounter:

That plural ''swords'' sounds a bit monotonous, yet it seemed wise to make a clear link between the six books, especially since Fafhrd and the Gray Mouser are undoubtedly the greatest swordsmen who ever lived, or will ever live, in any of the many universes—having their many adventures, encountering many other proficient swordsmen and most evil and clever villains, fierce beasts and supernatural monsters, wizards of the vastest sorcerous skill, and delectable girls a-plenty, some of the last having great wisdom and character.

—FRITZ LEIBER

THE SWORDS OF LANKHMAR

FRITZ LEIBER

SF

ace books

A Division of Charter Communications Inc.
A GROSSET & DUNLAP COMPANY
360 Park Avenue South
New York, New York 10010

THE SWORDS OF LANKHMAR

The map on pages vi and vii published
by courtesy of *Amra* magazine.

Cover painting by Jeff Jones

First Ace printing: January 1968
Second Ace printing: February 1974
Third Ace printing: June 1974
Fourth Ace printing: August 1979

4 6 8 0 9 7 5
Manufactured in the United States of America

AUTHOR'S NOTE:

Fafhrd and the Mouser are rogues through and through, though each has in him a lot of humanity and at least a diamond chip of the spirit of true adventure. They drink, they feast, they wench, they brawl, they steal, they gamble, and surely they hire out their swords to powers that are only a shade better, if that, than the villains. It strikes me (and something might be made of this) that Fafhrd and the Gray Mouser are almost at the opposite extreme from the heroes of Tolkien. My stuff is at least equally as fantastic as his, but it's an earthier sort of fantasy with a strong seasoning of "black fantasy"—or of black humor, to use the current phrase for something that was once called gallows' humor and goes back a long, long way. Though with their vitality, appetites, warm sympathies, and imagination, Fafhrd and the Mouser are anything but "sick" heroes.

One of the original motives for conceiving Fafhrd and the Mouser was to have a couple of fantasy heroes closer to true human stature than supermen like Conan and Tarzan and many another. In a way they're a mixture of Cabell and Eddison, if we must look for literary ancestors. Fafhrd and the Mouser have a touch of Jurgen's cynicism and anti-romanticism, but they go on boldly having adventures— one more roll of the dice with destiny and death. While the characters they most parallel in *The Worm Ouroboros* are Corund and Gro, yet I don't think they're touched with evil as those two, rather they're rogues in a decadent world where you have to be a rogue to survive; perhaps, in legendry, Robin Hood comes closest to them, though they're certainly a pair of lone-wolf Robin Hoods. . . .

FRITZ LEIBER

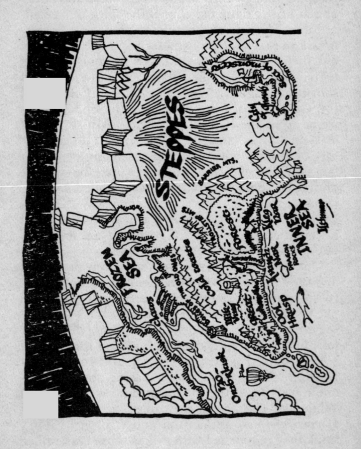

I

"I SEE WE'RE EXPECTED," the small man said, continuing to stroll toward the large open gate in the long, high, ancient wall. As if by chance, his hand brushed the hilt of his long, slim rapier.

"At over a bowshot distance how can you—" the big man began. "I get it. Bashabeck's orange headcloth. Stands out like a whore in church. And where Bashabeck is, his bullies are. You should have kept your dues to the Thieves Guild paid up."

"It's not so much the dues," the small man said. "It slipped my mind to split with them after the last job, when I lifted those eight diamonds from the Spider God's temple."

The big man sucked his tongue in disapproval. "I sometimes wonder why I associate with a faithless rogue like you."

The small man shrugged. "I was in a hurry. The Spider God was after me."

"Yes, I seem to recall he sucked the blood of your lookout man. You've got the diamonds to make the payoff now, of course?"

"My purse is as bulging as yours," the small man

1

asserted. "Which is exactly as much as a drunk's wineskin the morning after. Unless you're holding out on me, which I've long suspected. Incidentally, isn't that grossly fat man—the one between the two big-shouldered bravos—the keeper of the Silver Eel tavern?"

The big man squinted, nodded, then rocked his head disgustedly. "To make such a to-do over a brandy tab."

"Especially when it couldn't have been much more than a yard long," the small man agreed. "Of course there were those two full casks of brandy you smashed and set afire the last night you were brawling at the Eel."

"When the odds are ten to one against you in a tavern fight, you have to win by whatever methods come easiest to hand," the big man protested. "Which I'll grant you are apt at times to be a bit bizarre."

He squinted ahead again at the small crowd ranged around the square inside the open gate. After awhile he said, "I also make out Rivis Rightby the swordsmith . . . and just about all the other creditors any two men could have in Lankhmar. And each with his hired thug or three." He casually loosened in its scabbard his somewhat huge weapon, shaped like a rapier, but heavy almost as a broadsword. "Didn't you settle *any* of our bills before we left Lankhmar the last time? I was dead broke, of course, but you must have had money from all those earlier jobs for the Thieves Guild."

"I paid Nattick Nimblefingers in full for mending my cloak and for a new gray silk jerkin," the small man answered at once. He frowned. "There must have been others I paid—oh, I'm sure there were, but

I can't recall them at the moment. By the by, isn't that tall rangy wench—half behind the dainty man in black—one you were in trouble with? Her red hair stands out like a . . . like a bit of Hell. And those three other girls—each peering over her besworded pimp's shoulder like the first—weren't you in trouble with them also when we last left Lankhmar?"

"I don't know what you mean by trouble," the big man complained. "I rescued them from their protectors, who were abusing them dreadfully. Believe me, I trounced those protectors and the girls laughed. Thereafter I treated them like princesses."

"You did indeed—and spent all your cash and jewels on them, which is why you were broke. But one thing you didn't do for them: you didn't become their protector in turn. So they had to go back to their former protectors, which has made them justifiably angry at you."

"I should have become a pimp?" the big man objected. "Women!" Then, "I see a few of *your* girls in the crowd. Neglect to pay them off?"

"No, borrowed from them and forgot to return the money," the small man explained. "Hi-ho, it certainly appears that the welcoming committee is out in force."

"I told you we should have entered the city by the Grand Gate, where we'd have been lost in the numbers," the big man grumbled. "But no, I listened to you and came to this godforsaken End Gate."

"Wrong," the other said. "At the Grand Gate we wouldn't have been able to tell our foes from the bystanders. Here at least we know that everyone is against us, except for the Overlord's gate watch, and I'm not too sure of them—at the least they'll have been bribed to take no notice of our slaying."

"Why should they all be so hot to slay us?" the big man argued. "For all they know we may be coming home laden with rich treasures garnered from many a high adventure at the ends of the earth. Oh, I'll admit that three or four of them may also have a private grudge, but—"

"They can see we haven't a train of porters or heavily-laden mules," the small man interrupted reasonably. "In any case they know that after slaying us, they can pay themselves off from any treasure we may have and split the remainder. It's the rational procedure, which all civilized men follow."

"Civilization!" the big man snorted. "I sometimes wonder—"

"—why you ever climbed south over the Trollstep Mountains and got your beard trimmed and discovered that there were girls without hair on their chests," the small man finished for him. "Hey, I think our creditors and other haters have hired a third S besides swords and staves against us."

"Sorcery?"

The small man drew a coil of thin yellow wire from his pouch. He said, "Well, if those two graybeards in the second-story windows aren't wizards, they shouldn't scowl so ferociously. Besides, I can make out astrological symbols on the one's robe and see the glint of the other's wand."

They were close enough now to the End Gate that a sharp eye could guess at such details. The guardsmen in browned-iron mail leaned on their pikes impassively. The faces of those lining the small square beyond the gateway were impassive too, but grimly so, except for the girls, who smiled with venom and glee.

The big man said grumpily, "So they'll slay us by

spells and incantations. Failing which, they'll resort to cudgels and gizzard-cutters." He shook his head. "So much hate over a little cash. Lankhmarts are ingrates. They don't realize the tone we give their city, the excitement we provide."

The small man shrugged. "This time they're providing the excitement for us. Playing host, after a fashion." His fingers were deftly making a slipknot in one end of the pliant wire. His steps slowed a trifle. "Of course," he mused, "we don't have to return to Lankhmar."

The big man bristled. "Nonsense, we must! To turn back now would be cowardly. Besides, we've done everything else."

"There must be a few adventures left outside Lankhmar," the small man objected mildly, "if only little ones, suitable for cowards."

"Perhaps," the big man agreed, "but big or little, they all have a way of beginning in Lankhmar. Whatever are you up to with that wire?"

The small man had tightened the slipknot around the pommel of his rapier and let the wire trail behind him, flexible as a whip. "I've grounded my sword," he said. "Now any death-spell launched against me, striking my drawn sword first, will be discharged into the ground."

"Giving Mother Earth a tickle, eh? Watch out you don't trip over it." The warning seemed well-advised —the wire was fully a half score yards long.

"And don't you step on it. 'Tis a device Sheelba taught me."

"You and your swamp-rat wizard!" the big man mocked. "Why isn't he at your side now, making some spells for us?"

"Why isn't Ningauble at your side, doing the

same?" the small man counter-asked.

"He's too fat to travel." They were passing the blank-faced guardsmen. The atmosphere of menace in the square beyond thickened like a storm. Suddenly the big man grinned broadly at his comrade. "Let's not hurt any of them too seriously," he said in a somewhat loud voice. "We don't want our return to Lankhmar beclouded."

As they stepped into the open space walled by hostile faces, the storm broke without delay. The wizard in the star-symboled robe howled like a wolf and lifting his arms high above his head, threw them toward the small man with such force that one expected his hands to come off and fly through the air. They didn't, but a bolt of bluish fire, wraithlike in the sunlight, streamed from his out-flung fingers. The small man had drawn his rapier and pointed it at the wizard. The blue bolt crackled along the slim blade and then evidently did discharge itself into the ground, for he only felt a stinging thrill in his hand.

Rather unimaginatively the wizard repeated his tactics, with the same result, and then lifted his hands for a third bolt-hurling. By this time the small man had got the rhythm of the wizard's actions and just as the hands came down, he flipped the long wire so that it curled against the chests and faces of the bullies around the orange-turbaned Bashabeck. The blue stuff, whatever it was, went crackling into them from the wire and with a single screech each they fell down writhing.

Meanwhile the other sorcerer threw his wand at the big man, quickly following it with two more which he plucked from the air. The big man, his own out-size rapier drawn with surprising speed, awaited the first wand's arrival. Somewhat to his surprise, it had in flight the appearance of a silver-feathered hawk stooping with silver talons forward-pointing to strike. As he continued to watch it closely, its appearance changed to that of a silvery, long knife with this addition: that it had a silvery wing to either side.

Undaunted by this prodigy and playing the point of his great rapier as lightly as a fencing foil, the big man deftly deflected the first flying dagger so that it transfixed the shoulder of one of the bullies flanking the keeper of the Silver Eel. He treated the second and third flying dagger in the same fashion, so that two other of his foes were skewered painfully though unfatally.

They screeched too and collapsed, more from terror of such supernatural weapons than the actual severity of their wounds. Before they hit the cobbles, the big man had snatched a knife from his belt and hurled it left-handed at his sorcerous foe. Whether the graybeard was struck or barely managed to dodge, he at any rate dropped out of sight.

Meanwhile the other wizard, with continuing lack of imagination or perhaps mere stubbornness, directed a fourth bolt at the small man, who this time whipped upward the wire grounding his sword so that it snapped at the very window from which the blue bolt came. Whether it actually struck the wizard or only the window frame, there was a great crackling there and a bleating cry and that wizard dropped out of sight also.

It is to the credit of the assembled bullies and bravos that they hesitated hardly a heartbeat at this display of reflected death-spells, but urged on by their employers—and the pimps by their whores—they rushed in, lustily trampling the wounded and thrusting and slashing and clubbing with their various weapons. Of course, they had something of a fifty-to-two advantage; still, it took a certain courage.

The small man and the big man instantly placed themselves back to back and with lightning-like strokes stood off the first onset, seeking to jab as many faces and arms as they could rather than make the blows deep and mortal. The big man now had in his left hand a short-handled axe, with whose flat he rapped some skulls for variety, while the small man was supplementing his fiendishly pricking rapier with a long knife whose dartings were as swift as those of a cat's paw.

At first the greater number of the assaulters was a positive hindrance to them—they got into each other's way—while the greatest danger to the two fighting back-to-back was that they might be overwhelmed by the mere mass of their wounded foes, pushed forward enthusiastically by comrades behind. Then the battling got straightened out somewhat, and for awhile it looked as if the small and big man would have to use more deadly strokes—and perhaps nevertheless be cut down. The clash of tempered iron, the stamp of boots, the fighting-snarls from twisted lips, and the excited screeches of the girls added up to a great din, which made the gate guard look about nervously.

But then the lordly Bashabeck, who had at last deigned to take a hand, had an ear taken off and his collarbone on that side severed by a gentle swipe of the big man's axe, while the girls—their sense of romance touched—began to cheer on the outnumbered two, at which their pimps and bullies lost heart.

The attackers wavered on the verge of panic. There was a sudden blast of six trumpets from the widest street leading into the square. The great skirling sound was enough to shatter nerves already frayed. The attackers and their employers scattered in all other directions, the pimps dragging their fickle whores, while those who had been striken by the blue lightning and the winged daggers went crawling after them.

In a short time the square was empty, save for the two victors, the line of trumpeters in the street mouth, the line of guards outside the gateway now facing away from the square as if nothing at all had happened—and a hundred and more pairs of eyes as tiny and red-glinting black as wild cherries, which peered intently from between the grills of street drains and from various small holes in the walls and even from the rooftops. But who counts or even notices rats?—especially in a city as old and vermin-infested as Lankhmar.

The big man and the small man gazed about fiercely a bit longer. Then, regaining their breaths, they laughed uproariously, sheathed their weapons, and faced the trumpeters with a guarded yet relaxed curiosity.

The trumpeters wheeled to either side. A line of pikemen behind them executed the same movement, and there strode forward a venerable, clean-shaven, stern-visaged man in a black toga narrowly bordered with silver.

He raised his hand in a dignified salute. He said gravely, "I am chamberlain of Glipkerio Kistomerces, Overlord of Lankhmar, and here is my wand of authority." He produced a small silver wand tipped with a five-pointed bronze emblem in the form of a starfish.

The two men nodded slightly, as though to say,

"We accept your statement for what it's worth."

The chamberlain faced the big man. He drew a scroll from his toga, unrolled it, scanned it briefly, then looked up. "Are you Fafhrd the northern barbarian and brawler?"

The big man considered that for a bit, then said, "And if I am—"

The chamberlain turned toward the small man. He once more consulted his parchment. "And are you—your pardon, but it's written here—that mongrel and long-suspected burglar, cutpurse, swindler and assassin, the Gray Mouser?"

The small man fluffed his gray cape and said, "If it's any business of yours—well, he and I might be connected in some way."

As if those vaguest answers settled everything, the chamberlain rolled up his parchment with a snap and tucked it inside his toga. "Then my master wishes to see you. There is a service which you can render him, to your own considerable profit."

The Gray Mouser inquired, "If the all-powerful Glipkerio Kistomerces has need of us, why did he allow us to be assaulted and for all he might know slain by that company of hooligans who but now fled this place?"

The chamberlain answered, "If you were the sort of men who would allow yourselves to be murdered by such a mob, then you would not be the right men to handle the assignment, or fulfill the commission, which my master has in mind. But time presses. Follow me."

Fafhrd and the Gray Mouser looked at each other and after a moment they simultaneously shrugged, then nodded. Swaggering just a little, they fell in beside the chamberlain, the pikemen and trumpeters fell in behind them, and the cortege moved off the way it had come, leaving the square quite empty.

Except, of course, for the rats.

II

WITH THE motherly-generous west wind filling their brown triangular sails, the slim war galley and the five broad-beamed grain ships, two nights out of Lankhmar, coursed north in line ahead across the Inner Sea of the ancient world of Nehwon.

It was late afternoon of one of those mild blue days when sea and sky are the same hue, providing ir-refutable evidence for the hypothesis currently fa-vored by Lankhmar philosophers: that Nehwon is a giant bubble rising through the waters of eternity with continents, islands, and the great jewels that at night are the stars all orderly afloat on the bubble's inner surface.

On the afterdeck of the last grain ship, which was also the largest, the Gray Mouser spat a plum skin to leeward and boasted luxuriously, "Fat times in Lankhmar! Not one day returned to the City of the Black Toga after months away adventuring and we get this cushy job from the Overlord himself—and with an advance on pay too."

"I have an old distrust of cushy jobs," Fafhrd replied, yawning and pulling his fur-trimmed jerkin open wider so that the mild wind might trickle more fully through the tangled hair-field of his chest. "And we were rushed out of Lankhmar so quickly that we had not even time to pay our respects to the ladies. Nevertheless I must confess that we might have done worse. A full purse is the best ballast for any man-ship, especially one bearing letters of marque against ladies."

Ship's Master Slinoor looked back with hooded appraising eyes at the small lithe gray-clad man and his tall, more gaudily accoutered barbarian comrade. The master of *Squid* was a sleek black-robed man of middle years. He stood beside the two stocky black-tunicked bare-legged sailors who held steady the great high-arching tiller that guided *Squid*.

"How much do you two rogues really know of your cushy job?" Slinoor asked softly. "Or rather, how much did the arch-noble Glipkerio choose to tell you of the purpose and dark antecedents of this voyaging?" Two days of fortunate sailing seemed at last to have put the closed-mouthed ship's master in a mood to exchange confidences, or at least trade queries and lies.

From a bag of netted cord that hung by the taffrail, the Mouser speared a night-purple plum with the dirk he called Cat's Claw. Then he answered lightly, "This fleet bears a gift of grain from Overlord Glipkerio to Movarl of the Eight Cities in gratitude for Movarl's sweeping the Mingol pirates from the Inner Sea and mayhap diverting the steppe-dwelling Mingols from assaulting Lankhmar across the Sink-ing Land. Movarl needs grain for his hunter-farmers turned cityman-soldiers and especially to supply his army relieving his border city of Klelg Nar, which the

Mingols besiege. Fafhrd and I are, you might say, a small but mighty rearguard for the grain and for certain more delicate items of Glipkerio's gift."

"You mean those?" Slinoor bent a thumb toward the larboard rail.

Those were twelve large white rats distributed among four silver-barred cages. With their silky coats, pale-rimmed blue eyes and especially their short, arched upper lips and two huge upper incisors, they looked like a clique of haughty, bored, inbred aristocrats, and it was in a bored aristocratic fashion that they were staring at a scrawny black kitten which was perched with dug-in claws on the starboard rail, as if to get as far away from the rats as possible, and staring back at them most worriedly.

Fafhrd reached out and ran a finger down the black kitten's back. The kitten arched its spine, losing itself for a moment in sensuous delight, but then edged away and resumed its worried rat-peering—an activity shared by the two black-tunicked helmsmen, who seemed both resentful and fearful of the silver-caged afterdeck passengers.

The Mouser sucked plum juice from his fingers and flicked out his tongue-tip to neatly capture a drop that threatened to run down his chin. Then, "No, I mean not chiefly those high-bred gift-rats," he replied to Slinoor and kneeling lightly and unexpectedly and touching two fingers significantly to the scrubbed oak deck, he said, "I mean chiefly *she* who is below, who ousts you from your master's cabin, and who now insists that the gift-rats require sunlight and fresh air—which strikes me as a strange way of cosseting burrow-and-shadow-dwelling vermin."

Slinoor's cropped eyebrows rose. He came close

and whispered, "You think the Demoiselle Hisvet may not be merely the conductress of the rat-gift, but also herself part of Glipkerio's gift to Movarl? Why, she's the daughter of the greatest grain-merchant in Lankhmar, who's grown rich selling tawny corn to Glipkerio."

The Mouser smiled cryptically but said nothing.

Slinoor frowned, then whispered even lower, "True, I've heard the story that Hisvet has already been her father Hisvin's gift to Glipkerio to buy his patronage."

Fafhrd, who'd been trying to stroke the kitten again with no more success than to chase it up the aftermast, turned around at that. "Why, Hisvet's but a child," he said almost reprovingly. "A most prim and proper miss. I know not of Glipkerio, he seems decadent"—the word was not an insult in Lankhmar—"but surely Movarl, a Northerner albeit a forest man, likes only strong-beamed, ripe, complete women."

"Your own tastes, no doubt?" the Mouser remarked, gazing at Fafhrd with half-closed eyes. "No traffic with childlike women?"

Fafhrd blinked as if the Mouser had dug fingers in his side. Then he shrugged and said loudly, "What's so special about these rats? Do they do tricks?"

"Aye," Slinoor said distastefully. "They play at being men. They've been trained by Hisvet to dance to music, to drink from cups, hold tiny spears and swords, even fence. I've not seen it—nor would care to."

The picture struck the Mouser's fancy. He visioned himself small as a rat, dueling with rats who wore lace at their throats and wrists, slipping through the mazy tunnels of their underground cities, becoming a great connoisseur of cheese and smoked meats, perchance wooing a slim rat-queen and being surprised by her rat-king husband and having to dagger-fight him in the dark. Then he noted one of the white rats looking at him intently through the silver bars with a cold inhuman blue eye and suddenly his idea didn't seem amusing at all. He shivered in the sunlight.

Slinoor was saying, "It is not good for animals to try to be men." *Squid's* skipper gazed somberly at the silent white aristos. "Have you ever heard tell of the legend of—" he began, hesitated, then broke off, shaking his head as if deciding he had been about to say too much.

"A sail!" The call winged down thinly from the crow's nest. "A black sail to windward!"

"What manner of ship?" Slinoor shouted up.

"I know not, master. I see only sail top."

"Keep her under view, boy," Slinoor commanded.

"Under view it is, master."

Slinoor paced to the starboard rail and back.

"Movarl's sails are green," Fafhrd said thoughtfully.

Slinoor nodded. "Ilthmar's are white. The pirates' were red, mostly. Lankhmar's sails once were black, but now that color's only for funeral barges and they never venture out of sight of land. At least I've never known. . ."

The Mouser broke in with, "You spoke of dark antecedents of this voyaging. Why dark?"

Slinoor drew them back against the taffrail, away from the stocky helmsmen. Fafhrd ducked a little, passing under the arching tiller. They looked all three into the twisting wake, their heads bent together.

Slinoor said, "You've been out of Lankhmar. Did you know this is not the first gift-fleet of grain to Movarl?"

The Mouser nodded. "We'd been told there was another. Somehow lost. In a storm, I think. Glipkerio glossed over it."

"There were two," Slinoor said tersely. "Both lost. Without a living trace. There was no storm."

"What then?" Fafhrd asked, looking around as the rats chittered a little. "Pirates?"

"Movarl had already whipped the pirates east. Each of the two fleets was galley-guarded like ours. And each sailed off into fair weather with a good west wind." Slinoor smiled thinly. "Doubtless Glipkerio did not tell you of these matters for fear you might beg off. We sailors and the Lankhmarines obey for duty and the honor of the City, but of late Glipkerio's had trouble hiring the sort of special agents he likes to use for second bowstrings. He has brains of a sort, our overlord has, though he employs them mostly to dream of visiting other world bubbles in a great diving-bell or sealed metallic diving-ship, while he sits with trained girls watching trained rats and buys off Lankhmar's enemies with gold and repays Lankhmar's evermore-greedy friends with grain, not soldiers." Slinoor grunted. "Movarl grows most impatient, you know. He threatens, if the grain comes not, to recall his pirate patrol, league with the land-Mingols and set them at Lankhmar.

"Northerners, even though not snow-dwelling, league with Mingols?" Fafhrd objected. "Impossible!"

Slinoor looked at him. "I'll say just this, ice-eating Northerner. If I did not believe such a league both possible and likely—and Lankhmar thereby in dire

danger—I would never have sailed with this fleet,
honor and duty or no. Same's true of Lukeen, who
commands the galley. Nor do I think Glipkerio
would otherwise be sending to Movarl at Kvarch Nar
his noblest performing rats and dainty Hisvet.''

Fafhrd growled a little. "You say both fleets were
lost without a trace?" he asked incredulously.

Slinoor shook his head. "The first was. Of the second, some wreckage was sighted by an Ilthmar
trader Lankhmar-bound. The deck of only one grain
ship. It had been ripped off its hull, splinteringly—
how or by what, the Ilthmart dared not guess. Tied
to a fractured stretch of railing was the ship's master,
only hours dead. His face had been nibbled, his body
gnawed.''

"Fish?" the Mouser asked.

"Seabirds?" Fafhrd inquired.

"Dragons?" a third voice suggested, high,
breathless, and as merry as a schoolgirl's. The three
men turned around, Slinoor with guilty swiftness.

The Demoiselle Hisvet stood as tall as the Mouser,
but judging by her face, wrists, and ankles was considerably slenderer. Her face was delicate and taper-
chinned with small mouth and pouty upper lip that
lifted just enough to show a double dash of pearly
tooth. Her complexion was creamy pale except for
two spots of color high on her cheeks. Her straight
fine hair, which grew low on her forehead, was pure
white touched with silver and all drawn back
through a silver ring behind her neck, whence it hung
unbraided like a unicorn's tail. Her eyes had china
whites but darkly pink irises around the large black
pupils. Her body was enveloped and hidden by a
loose robe of violet silk except when the wind briefly
molded a flat curve of her girlish anatomy. There was

a violet hood, half thrown back. The sleeves were puffed but snug at the wrists. She was barefoot, her skin showing as creamy there as on her face, except for a tinge of pink about the toes.

She looked them all three one after another quickly in the eye. "You were whispering of the fleets that failed," she said accusingly. "Fie, Master Slinoor. We must all have courage."

"Aye," Fafhrd agreed, finding that a cue to his liking. "Even dragons need not daunt a brave man. I've often watched the sea monsters, crested, horned, and some two-headed, playing in the waves of outer ocean as they broke around the rocks sailors call the Claws. They were not to be feared, if a man remembered always to fix them with a commanding eye. They sported lustily together, the man dragons pursuing the woman dragons and going—" Here Fafhrd took a tremendous breath and then roared out so loudly and wailingly that the two helmsmen jumped—"*Hoongk! Hoongk!*"

"Fie, Swordsman Fafhrd," Hisvet said primly, a blush mantling her cheeks and forehead. "You are most indelicate. The sex of dragons—"

But Slinoor had whirled on Fafhrd, gripping his wrist and now crying, "Quiet, you monster-fool! Know you not we sail tonight by moonlight past the Dragon Rocks? You'll call them down on us!"

"There are no dragons in the Inner Sea," Fafhrd laughingly assured him.

"There's something that tears ships," Slinoor asserted stubbornly.

The Mouser took advantage of this brief interchange to move in on Hisvet, rapidly bowing thrice as he approached.

"We have missed the great pleasure of your company on deck, Demoiselle," he said suavely.

"Alas, sir, the sun mislikes me," she answered prettily. "Now his rays are mellowed as he prepared to submerge. Then too," she added with an equally pretty shudder, "these rough sailors—" She broke off as she saw that Fafhrd and the master of *Squid* had stopped their argument and returned to her. "Oh, I meant not you, dear Master Slinoor," she assured him, reaching out and almost touching his black robe.

"Would the Demoiselle fancy a sun-warmed, wind-cooled black plum of Sarheenmar?" the Mouser suggested, delicately sketching in the air with Cat's Claw.

"I know not." Hisvet said, eyeing the dirk's needlelike point. "I must be thinking of getting the White Shadows below before the evening's chill is upon us."

"True," Fafhrd agreed with a flattering laugh, realizing she must mean the white rats. "But 'twas most wise of you, Little Mistress, to let them spend the day on deck, where they surely cannot hanker so much to sport with the Black Shadows—I mean, of course, their black free commoner brothers, and slim delightful sisters, to be sure, hiding here and there in the hold."

"There are no rats on my ship, sportive or otherwise," Slinoor asserted instantly, his voice loud and angry. "Think you I run a rat-brothel? Your pardon, Demoiselle," he added quickly to Hisvet. "I mean, there are no common rats aboard *Squid*."

"Then yours is surely the first grain ship so blessed," Fafhrd told him with indulgent reasonableness.

The sun's vermilion disk touched the sea to the

west and flattened like a tangerine. Hisvet leaned
back against the taffrail under the arching tiller.
Fafhrd was to her right, the Mouser to her left with
the plums hanging just beyond him, near the silver
cages. Slinoor had moved haughtily forward to speak
to the helmsmen, or pretend to.

"I'll take that plum now, Dirksman Mouser," Hisvet said softly.

As the Mouser turned away in happy obedience
and with many a graceful gesture, delicately palpat-
ing the net bag to find the most tender fruit, Hisvet
stretched her right arm out sideways and without
looking once at Fafhrd slowly ran her spread-fingered hand through the hair on his chest, paused
when she reached the other side to grasp a fistful and
tweak it sharply, then trailed her fingers lightly back
across the hair she had ruffled.

Her hand came back to her just as the Mouser
turned around. She kissed the palm lingeringly, then
reached it across her body to take the black fruit from
the point of the Mouser's dirk. She sucked delicately
at the prick Cat's Claw had made and shivered.

"Fie, sir," she pouted. "You told me 'twould be
sun-warmed and 'tis not. Already all things grow
chilly with evening." She looked around her thoughtfully. "Why, Swordsman Fafhrd is all gooseflesh,"
she announced, then blushed and tapped her lips reprovingly. "Close your jerkin, sir. 'Twill save you
from catarrh and perchance from further embarrass-
ment a girl who is unused to any sight of manflesh
save in slaves."

"Here is a toastier plum," the Mouser called from
beside the bag. Hisvet smiled at him and lightly
tossed him back-handed the plum she'd sampled. He
dropped that overboard and tossed her the second

plum. She caught it deftly, lightly squeezed it, touched it to her lips, shook her head sadly though still smiling, and tossed back the plum. The Mouser, smiling gently too, caught it, dropped it overboard and tossed her a third. They played that way for some time. A shark following in the wake of the *Squid* got a stomachache.

The black kitten came single-footing back along the starboard rail with a sharp eye to larboard. Fafhrd seized it instantly as any good general does opportunity in the heat of battle.

"Have you seen the ship's catling, Little Mistress?" he called, crossing to Hisvet, the kitten almost hidden in his big hands. "Or perhaps we should call the *Squid* the catling's ship, for she adopted it, skipping by herself aboard just as we sailed. Here, Little Mistress. It feels sun-toasted now, warmer than any plum," and he reached the kitten out sitting on the palm of his right hand.

But Fafhrd had been forgetting the kitten's point of view. Its fur stood on end as it saw itself being carried toward the rats and now, as Hisvet stretched out her hand toward it, showing her upper teeth in a tiny smile and saying, "Poor little waif," the kitten hissed fiercely and raked out stiff armed with spread claws.

Hisvet drew back her hand with a gasp. Before Fafhrd could drop the kitten or bat it aside, it sprang to the top of his head and from there onto the highest point of the tiller.

The Mouser darted to Hisvet, crying meanwhile at Fafhrd, "Dolt! Lout! You knew the beast was half wild!" Then, to Hisvet, "Demoiselle! Are you hurt?"

Fafhrd struck angrily at the kitten and one of the

helmsmen came back to bat at it too, perhaps because he thought it improper for kittens to walk on the tiller. The kitten made a long leap to the starboard rail, slipped over it, and dangled by two claws above the curving water.

Hisvet was holding her hand away from the Mouser and he was saying, "Better let me examine it, Demoiselle. Even the slightest scratch from a filthy ship's cat can be dangerous," and she was saying, almost playfully, "No, Dirksman, I tell you it's nothing."

Fafhrd strode to the starboard rail, fully intending to flick the kitten overboard, but somehow when he came to do it he found he had instead cupped the kitten's rear in his hand and lifted it back on the rail. The kitten instantly sank its teeth deeply in the root of his thumb and fled up the aftermast. Fafhrd with difficulty suppressed a great yowl. Slinoor laughed.

"Nevertheless, I will examine it," the Mouser said masterfully and took Hisvet's hand by force. She let him hold it for a moment, then snatched it back and drawing herself up said frostily, "Dirksman, you forget yourself. Not even her own physician touches a Demoiselle of Lankhmar, he touches only the body of her maid, on which the Demoiselle points out her pains and symptoms. Leave me, Dirksman."

The Mouser stood huffily back against the taffrail. Fafhrd sucked the root of his thumb. Hisvet went and stood beside the Mouser. Without looking at him, she said softly, "You should have asked me to call my maid. She's quite pretty."

Only a fingernail clipping of red sun was left on the horizon. Slinoor addressed the crow's nest: "What of the black sail, boy?"

"She holds her distance, master," the cry came

back. "She courses on abreast of us."

The sun went under with a faint green flash. Hisvet bent her head sideways and kissed the Mouser on the neck, just under the ear. Her tongue tickled.

"Now I lose her, master," the crow's nest called. "There's mist to the northwest. And to the northeast . . . a small black cloud . . . like a black ship specked with light . . . that moves through the air. And now that fades too. All gone, master."

Hisvet straightened her head. Slinoor came toward them muttering, "The crow's nest sees too much." Hisvet shivered and said, "The White Shadows will take a chill. They're delicate, Dirksman." The Mouser breathed, "You are Ecstacy's White Shadow, Demoiselle," then strolled toward the silver cages, saying loudly for Slinoor's benefit, "Might we not be privileged to have a show of them, Demoiselle, tomorrow here on the afterdeck? 'Twould be wondrous instructive to watch you control them." He caressed the air over the cages and said, lying mightily, "My, they're fine handsome fellows." Actually he was peering apprehensively for any of the little spears and swords Slinoor had mentioned. The twelve rats looked up at him incuriously. One even seemed to yawn.

Slinoor said curtly, "I would advise against it, Demoiselle. The sailors have a mad fear and hatred of all rats. 'Twere best not to arouse it."

"But these are aristos," the Mouser objected, while Hisvet only repeated, "They'll take a chill."

Fafhrd, hearing this, took his hand out of his mouth and came hurrying to Hisvet, saying, "Little Mistress, may I carry them below? I'll be gentle as a Kleshite nurse." He lifted between thumb and third finger a cage with two rats in it. Hisvet rewarded him with a smile, saying, "I wish you would, gallant Swordsman. The common sailors handle them too roughly. But two cages are all you may safely carry. You'll need proper help." She gazed at the Mouser and Slinoor.

So Slinoor and the Mouser, the latter much to his distaste and apprehension, must each gingerly take up a silver cage, and Fafhrd two, and follow Hisvet to her cabin below the afterdeck. The Mouser could not forbear whispering privily to Fafhrd, "Oaf! To make rat-grooms of us! May you get rat-bites to match your cat-bite!" At the cabin door Hisvet's dark maid Frix received the cages, Hisvet thanked her three gallants most briefly and distantly and Frix closed the door against them. There was the muffled thud of a bar dropping across it and the jangle of a chain locking down the bar.

Darkness grew on the waters. A yellow lantern was lit and hoisted to the crow's nest. The black war galley *Shark,* its brown sail temporarily furled, came rowing back to fuss at *Clam,* next ahead of *Squid* in line, for being slow in getting up its masthead light, then dropped back by *Squid* while Lukeen and Slinoor exchanged shouts about a black sail and mist and ship-shaped small black clouds and the Dragon Rocks. Finally the galley went bustling ahead again with its Lankhmarines in browned-iron chain mail to take up its sailing station at the head of the column. The first stars twinkled, proof that the sun had not deserted through the waters of eternity to some other world bubble, but was swimming as he should back to the east under the ocean of the sky, errant rays from him lighting the floating star-jewels in his passage.

After moonrise that night Fafhrd and the Mouser

each found private occasion to go rapping at Hisvet's door, but neither profited greatly thereby. At Fafhrd's knock Hisvet herself opened the small grille set in the larger door, said swiftly, "Fie, for shame, Swordsman! Can't you see I'm undressing?" and closed it instantly. While when the Mouser asked softly for a moment with "Ecstacy's White Shadow," the merry face of the dark maid Frix appeared at the grille, saying, "My mistress bid me kiss my hand good night to you." Which she did and closed the grille.

Fafhrd, who had been spying, greeted the crestfallen Mouser with a sardonic, "Ecstacy's White Shadow!"

"Little Mistress!" the Mouser retorted scathingly.

"Black Plum of Sarheenmar!"

"Kleshite Nurse!"

Neither hero slept restfully that night and two-thirds through it the *Squid*'s gong began to sound at intervals, with the other ships' gongs replying or calling faintly. When at dawn's first blink the two came on deck, *Squid* was creeping through fog that hid the sail top. The two helmsmen were peering about jumpily, as if they expected to see ghosts. The sails were barely filled. Slinoor, his eyes dark-circled by fatigue and big with anxiety, explained tersely that the fog had not only slowed but disordered the grain fleet.

"That's *Tunny* next ahead of us. I can tell by her gong note. And beyond *Tunny*, *Carp*. Where's *Clam*? What's *Shark* about? And still not certainly past the Dragon Rocks! Not that I want to see 'em!"

"Do not some captains call them the Rat Rocks?" Fafhrd interposed. "From a rat-colony started there from a wreck?"

"Aye," Slinoor allowed and then grinning sourly

at the Mouser, observed, "Not the best day for a rat-show on the afterdeck, is it? Which is some good from this fog. I can't abide the lolling white brutes. Though but a dozen in number they remind me too much of the Thirteen. Have you ever heard tell of the legend of the Thirteen?"

"I have," Fafhrd said somberly. "A wise woman of the Cold Waste once told me that for each animal kind—wolves, bats, whales, it holds for all and each —there are always thirteen individuals having almost manlike (or demonlike!) wisdom and skill. Can you but find and master this inner circle, the Wise Woman said, then through them you can control all animals of that kind."

Slinoor looked narrowly at Fafhrd and said, "She was not an altogether stupid woman."

The Mouser wondered if for men also there was an inner circle of Thirteen.

The black kitten came ghosting along the deck out of the fog forward. It made toward Fafhrd with an eager mew, then hesitated, studying him dubiously.

"Take for example, cats," Fafhrd said with a grin. "Somewhere in Nehwon today, mayhap scattered but more likely banded together, are thirteen cats of superfeline sagacity, somehow sensing and controlling the destiny of all catkind."

"What's this one sensing now?" Slinoor demanded softly.

The black kitten was staring to larboard, sniffing. Suddenly its scrawny body stiffened, the hair rising along its back and its skimpy tail a-bush.

"Hoongk!"

Slinoor turned to Fafhrd with a curse, only to see the Northerner staring about shut-mouthed and startled. Clearly *he* had not bellowed.

III

Out of the fog to larboard came a green serpent's head big as a horse's, with white dagger teeth fencing red mouth horrendously agape. With dreadful swiftness it lunged low past Fafhrd on its endless yellow neck, its lower jaw loudly scraping the deck, and the white daggers clashed on the black kitten.

Or rather, on where the kitten had just been. For the latter seemed not so much to leap as to lift itself, by its tail perhaps, onto the starboard rail and thence vanished into the fog at the top of the aftermast in at most three more bounds.

The helmsmen raced each other forward. Slinoor and the Mouser threw themselves against the starboard taffrail, the unmanned tiller swinging slowly above them affording some sense of protection against the monster, which now lifted its nightmare head and swayed it this way and that, each time avoiding Fafhrd by inches. Apparently it was searching for the black kitten or more like it.

Fafhrd stood frozen, at first by sheer shock, then

28

by the thought that whatever part of him moved first would get snapped off.

Nevertheless he was about to jump for it—besides all else the monster's mere stench was horrible—when a second green dragon's head, four times as big as the first with teeth like scimitars, came looming out of the fog. Sitting commandingly atop this second head was a man dressed in orange and purple, like a herald of the Eastern Lands, with red boots, cape and helmet, the last with a blue window in it, seemingly of opaque glass.

There is a point of grotesquerie beyond which horror cannot go, but slips into delirium. Fafhrd had reached that point. He began to feel as if he were in an opium dream. Everything was unquestionably real, yet it had lost its power to horrify him acutely.

He noticed as the merest of quaint details that the two greenish yellow necks forked from a common trunk.

Besides, the gaudily garbed man or demon riding the larger head seemed very sure of himself, which might or might not be a good thing. Just now he was belaboring the smaller head, seemingly in rebuke, with a blunt-pointed, blunt-hooked pike he carried, and roaring out, either under or through his blue red helmet, a gibberish that might be rendered as:

*"Gottverdammter Ungeheuer!"**

The smaller head cringed away, whimpering like seventeen puppies. The man-demon whipped out a small book of pages and after consulting it twice (apparently he could see *out* through his blue window)

---

*"Goddam monster!" German is a language completely unknown in Nehwon.

called down in broken, outlandishly accented Lankhmarese, "What world is this, friend?"

Fafhrd had never before in his life heard that question asked, even by an awakening brandy guzzler. Nevertheless in his opium-dream mood he answered easily enough, "The world of Nehwon, oh sorcerer!"

*"Got set dank!"** the man-demon gibbered.

Fafhrd asked, "What world do *you* hail from?"

The question seemed to confound the man-demon. Hurriedly consulting his book, he replied, "Do you know about other worlds? Don't you believe the stars are only huge jewels?"

Fafhrd responded, "Any fool can see that the lights in the sky are jewels, but we are not simpletons, we know of other worlds. The Lankhmarts think they're bubbles in infinite waters. *I* believe we live in the jewel-ceilinged skull of a dead god. But doubtless there are other such skulls, the universe of universes being a great frosty battlefield."

The tiller, swinging as *Squid* wallowed with sail a-flap, bumped the lesser head, which twisted around and snapped at it, then shook splinters from its teeth.

"Tell the sorcerer to keep it off!" Slinoor shouted, cringing.

After more hurried page-flipping the man-demon called down, "Don't worry, the monster seems to eat only rats. I captured it by a small rocky island where many rats live. It mistook your small black ship's cat for a rat."

Still in his mood of opium-lucidity, Fafhrd called up, "Oh sorcerer, do you plan to conjure the monster to your own skull-world, or world-bubble?"

This question seemed doubly to confound and ex-

---

*Thank God!"

cite the man-demon. He appeared to think Fafhrd
must be a mind reader. With much frantic book-con-
sulting, he explained that he came from a world
called simply Tomorrow and that he was visiting
many worlds to collect monsters for some sort of
museum or zoo, which he called in his gibberish
*Hagenbeck's Zietgarten.** On this particular expedition
he had been seeking a monster that would be a reasonable facsimile of a wholly mythical six-headed
sea-monster that devoured men off the decks of ships
and was called Scylla by an ancient fantasy writer
named Homer.

"There never was a Lankhmar poet named Homer," muttered Slinoor.

"Doubtless he was a minor scribe of Quarmall or
the Eastern Lands," the Mouser told Slinoor reassur-
ingly. Then, grown less fearful of the two heads and
somewhat jealous of Fafhrd holding the center of the
stage, the Mouser leapt atop the taffrail and cried,
"Oh, sorcerer, with what spells will you conjure your
Little Scylla back to, or perhaps I should say ahead
to your Tomorrow bubble? I myself know somewhat
of witchcraft. Desist, vermin!" This last remark was
directed with a gesture of lordly contempt toward the
lesser head, which came questing curiously toward
the Mouser. Slinoor gripped the Mouser's ankle.

The man-demon reacted to the Mouser's question
by slapping himself on the side of his red helmet, as
though he'd forgotten something most important. He
hurriedly began to explain that he traveled between
worlds in a ship (or space-time engine, whatever that
might mean) that tended to float just above the water

*Literally, in German, "Hagenbeck's Time garden," apparently
derived from *Tiergarten*, which means animal-garden, or zoo.

—"a black ship with little lights and masts"—and
that the ship had floated away from him in another
fog a day ago while he'd been absorbed in taming the
newly captured sea-monster. Since then the man-demon, mounted on his now-docile monster, had been
fruitlessly searching for his lost vehicle.

The description awakened a memory in Slinoor,
who managed to nerve himself to explain audibly
that last sunset *Squid*'s crow's nest had sighted just
such a ship floating or flying to the northeast.

The man-demon was voluble in his thanks and after questioning Slinoor closely announced (rather to
everyone's relief) that he was now ready to turn his
search eastward with new hope.

"Probably I will never have the opportunity to re-
pay your courtesies," he said in parting. "But as you
drift through the waters of eternity at least carry with
you my name: Karl Treuherz of Hagenbeck's."

Hisvet, who had been listening from the middeck,
chose that moment to climb the short ladder that led
up to the afterdeck. She was wearing an ermine
smock and hood against the chilly fog.

As her silvery hair and pale lovely features rose
above the level of the afterdeck the smaller dragon's
head, which had been withdrawing decorously,
darted at her with the speed of a serpent striking.
Hisvet dropped. Woodwork rended loudly.

Backing off into the fog atop the larger and rather
benign-eyed head, Karl Treuherz gibbered as never
before and belabored the lesser head mercilessly as it
withdrew.

Then the two-headed monster with its orange-
and-purple mahout could be dimly seen moving
around *Squid*'s stern eastward into thicker fog, the
man-demon gibbering gentlier what might have been

an excuse and farewell: *"Es tut mir sehr leid! Aber dankeschoen, dankeschoen!"**

With a last gentle *"Hoongk!"* the man-demon dragon-dragon assemblage faded into the fog.

Fafhrd and the Mouser raced a tie to Hisvet's side, vaulting down over the splintered rail, only to have her scornfully reject their solicitude as she lifted herself from the oaken middeck, delicately rubbing her hip and limping for a step or two.

"Come not near me, Spoonmen," she said bitterly. "Shame it is when a Demoiselle must save herself from toothy perdition only by falling helter-skelter on that part of her which I would almost shame to show you on Frix. You are no gentle knights, else dragons' heads had littered the afterdeck. Fie, fie!"

Meanwhile patches of clear sky and water began to show to the west and the wind to freshen from the same quarter. Slinoor dashed forward, bawling for his bosun to chase the monster-scared sailors up from the forecastle before *Squid* did herself an injury.

Although there was yet little real danger of that, the Mouser stood by the tiller, Fafhrd looked to the mainsheet. Then Slinoor, hurrying back aft followed by a few pale sailors, sprang to the taffrail with a cry.

The fogbank was slowly rolling eastward. Clear water stretched to the western horizon. Two bowshots north of *Squid*, four other ships were emerging in a disordered cluster from the white wall: the war galley *Shark* and the grain ships *Tunny, Carp* and *Grouper*. The galley, moving rapidly under oars, was headed toward *Squid*.

But Slinoor was staring south. There, a scant

---

*It was: "I am so very sorry! But thank you, thank you so nicely!"

bowshot away, were two ships, the one standing clear of the fogbank, the other half hid in it.

The one in the clear was *Clam,* about to sink by the head, its gunwales awash. Its mainsail, somehow carried away, trailed brownly in the water. The empty deck was weirdly arched upward.

The fog-shrouded ship appeared to be a black cutter with a black sail.

Between the two ships, from *Clam* toward the cutter, moved a multitude of tiny, dark-headed ripples.

Fafhrd joined Slinoor. Without looking away, the latter said simply, "Rats!" Fafhrd's eyebrows rose.

The Mouser joined them, saying, *"Clam's* holed. The water swells the grain, which mightily forces up the deck."

Slinoor nodded and pointed toward the cutter. It was possible dimly to see tiny dark forms—rats surely!—climbing over its side from out of the water. "There's what gnawed holes in *Clam,"* Slinoor said.

Then Slinoor pointed between the ships, near the cutter. Among the last of the ripple-army was a white-headed one. A second later a small white form could be seen swiftly mounting the cutter's side. Slinoor said, "There's what commanded the hole-gnawers."

With a dull splintering rumble the arched deck of *Clam* burst upward, spewing brown.

"The grain!" Slinoor cried hollowly.

"Now you know what tears ships," the Mouser said.

The black cutter grew ghostlier, moving west now into the retreating fog.

The galley *Shark* went boiling past *Squid's* stern, its oars moving like the legs of a leaping centipede.

Lukeen shouted up, "Here's foul trickery! *Clam* was lured off in the night!"

The black cutter, winning its race with the eastward-rolling fog, vanished in whiteness.

The split-decked *Clam* nosed under with hardly a ripple and angled down into the black and salty depths, dragged by its leaden keel.

With war trumpet skirling, *Shark* drove into the white wall after the cutter.

Clam's masthead, cutting a little furrow in the swell, went under. All that was to be seen now on the waters south of *Squid* was a great spreading stain of tawny grain.

Slinoor turned grim-faced to his mate. "Enter the Demoiselle Hisvet's cabin, by force if need be," he commanded. "Count her white rats!"

Fafhrd and the Mouser looked at each other.

Three hours later the same four persons were assembled in Hisvet's cabin with the Demoiselle, Frix and Lukeen.

The cabin, low-ceilinged enough so that Fafhrd, Lukeen and the mate must move bent and tended to sit hunch-shouldered, was spacious for a grain ship, yet crowded by this company together with the caged rats and Hisvet's perfumed, silver-bound baggage piled on Slinoor's dark furniture and locked sea chests.

Three horn windows to the stern and louver slits to starboard and larboard let in a muted light.

Slinoor and Lukeen sat against the horn windows, behind a narrow table. Fafhrd occupied a cleared sea chest, the Mouser an upended cask. Between them were racked the four rat-cages, whose white-furred occupants seemed as quietly intent on the proceedings as any of the men. The Mouser amused himself by imagining what it would be like if the white rats were trying the men instead of the other way round. A row of blue-eyed white rats would make most formidable judges, already robed in ermine. He pictured them staring down mercilessly from very high seats at a tiny cringing Lukeen and Slinoor, round whom scuttled mouse pages and mouse clerks and behind whom stood rat pikemen in half armor holding fantastically barbed and curvy-bladed weapons.

The mate stood stooping by the open grille of the closed door, in part to see that no other sailors eavesdropped.

The Demoiselle Hisvet sat cross-legged on the swung-down sea-bed, her ermine smock decorously tucked under her knees, managing to look most distant and courtly even in this attitude. Now and again her right hand played with the dark wavy hair of Frix, who crouched on the deck at her knees.

Timbers creaked as *Squid* bowled north. Now and then the bare feet of the helmsmen could be heard faintly slithering on the afterdeck overhead. Around the small trapdoor-like hatches leading below and through the very crevices of the planking came the astringent, toastlike, all-pervasive odor of the grain.

Lukeen spoke. He was a lean, slant-shouldered, cordily muscled man almost as big as Fafhrd. His short coat of browned-iron mail over his simple black tunic was of the finest links. A golden band confined his dark hair and bound to his forehead the browned-iron five-pointed curvy-edged starfish emblem of Lankhmar.

"How do I know *Clam* was lured away?" Two hours before dawn I twice thought I heard *Shark*'s own gong-note in the distance, although I stood then beside *Shark*'s muffled gong. Three of my crew heard it too. 'Twas most eerie. Gentlemen, I know the gong-notes of Lankhmar war galleys and merchantmen better than I know my children's voices. This that we heard was so like *Shark*'s I never dreamed it might be that of another ship—I deemed it some ominous ghost-echo or trick of our minds and I thought no more about it as a matter for action. If I had only had the faintest suspicion. . . ."

Lukeen scowled bitterly, shaking his head, and continued, "Now I know the black cutter must carry a gong shaped to duplicate *Shark*'s note precisely. They used it, likely with someone mimicking my voice, to draw *Clam* out of line in the fog and get her far enough off so that the rat-horde, officered by the white one, could work its will on her without the crew's screams being heard. They must have gnawed twenty holes in her bottom for *Clam* to take on water so fast and the grain to swell so. Oh, they're far shrewder and more persevering than men, the little spade toothed fiends!"

"Midsea madness!" Fafhrd snorted in interruption. "Rats make men scream? And do away with them? Rats seize a ship and sink it? Rats officered and accepting discipline? Why this is the rankest superstition!"

"You're a fine one to talk of superstition and the impossible, Fafhrd," Slinoor shot at him, "when only this morning you talked with a masked and gibbering demon who rode a two-headed dragon."

Lukeen lifted his eyebrows at Slinoor. This was the first he'd heard of the Hagenbeck episode.

Fafhrd said, "That was travel between worlds. Another matter altogether. No superstition in it."

Slinoor responded skeptically. "I suppose there was no superstition in it either when you told me that you'd heard from the Wise Woman about the Thirteen?"

Fafhrd laughed. "Why, I never believed one word the Wise Woman ever told me. She was a witchy old fool. I recounted her nonsense merely as a curiosity."

Slinoor eyed Fafhrd with slit-eyed incredulity, then said to Lukeen, "Continue."

"There's little more to tell," the latter said. "I saw the rat-battalions swimming from *Clam* to the black cutter. I saw, as you did, their white officer." This with a glare at Fafhrd. "Thereafter I fruitlessly hunted the black cutter two hours in the fog until cramp took my rowers. If I'd found her, I'd not boarded her but thrown fire into her! Aye, and stood off the rats with burning oil on the waters if they tried again to change ships! Aye, and laughed as the furred murderers fried!"

"Just so," Slinoor said with finality. "And what, in your judgment, Commander Lukeen, should we do now?"

"Sink the white archfiends in their cages," Lukeen answered instantly, "before they officer the rape of more ships, or our sailors go mad with fear."

This brought an instant icy retort from Hisvet. "You'll have to sink me first, silver-weighted, oh Commander!"

Lukeen's gaze moved past her to a scatter of big-eared silver unguent jars and several looped heavy silver chains on a shelf by the bed. "That too is not impossible, Demoiselle," he said, smiling hardly.

"There's not one shred of proof against her!" Fafhrd exploded. "Little Mistress, the man is mad."

"No proof?" Lukeen roared. "There were twelve

white rats yesterday. Now there are eleven." He
waved a hand at the stacked cages and their blue-
eyed haughty occupants. "You've all counted them.
Who else but this devilish Demoiselle sent the white
officer to direct the sharp-toothed gnawers and
killers that destroyed *Clam?* What more proof do you
want?"

"Yes, indeed!" the Mouser interjected in a high
vibrant voice that commanded attention. "There is
proof aplenty . . . *if* there were twelve rats in the four
cages yesterday." Then he added casually but very
clearly, "It is my recollection that there were elev-
en."

Slinoor stared at the Mouser as though he couldn't
believe his ears. "You lie!" he said. "What's more,
you lie senselessly. Why, you and Fafhrd and I all
spoke of there being twelve white rats!"

The Mouser shook his head. "Fafhrd and I said no
word about the exact number of rats. *You* said there
were a dozen," he informed Slinoor. "Not twelve, but
. . . a dozen I assumed you were using the expression
as a round number, an approximation." The Mouser
snapped his fingers. "Now I remember that when
you said a dozen I became idly curious and counted
the rats. And got eleven. But it seemed to me too
trifling a matter to dispute."

"No, there were twelve rats yesterday," Slinoor asserted solemnly and with great conviction. "You're
mistaken, Gray Mouser."

"I'll believe my friend Slinoor before a dozen of
you," Lukeen put in.

"True, friends should stick together," the Mouser
said with an approving smile. "Yesterday I counted
Glipkerio's gift-rats and got eleven. Ship's Master
Slinoor, any man may be mistaken in his recollec-

tions from time to time. Let's analyze this. Twelve white rats divided by four silver cages equals three to a cage. Now let me see . . . I have it! There was a time yesterday when between us, we surely counted the rats—when we carried them down to this cabin. How many were in the cage you carried, Slinoor?"

"Three," the latter said instantly.

"And three in mine," the Mouser said.

"And three in each of the other two," Lukeen put in impatiently. "We waste time!"

"We certainly do," Slinoor agreed strongly, nodding.

"Wait!" said the Mouser, lifting a point-fingered hand. "There was a moment when all of us must have noticed how many rats there were in one of the cages Fafhrd carried—when he first lifted it up, speaking the while to Hisvet. Visualize it. He lifted it like this." The Mouser touched his thumb to his third finger. "How many rats were in that cage, Slinoor?"

Slinoor frowned deeply. "Two," he said, adding instantly, "and four in the other."

"You said three in each just now," the Mouser reminded him.

"I did not!" Slinoor denied. "Lukeen said that, not I."

"Yes, but you nodded, agreeing with him," the Mouser said, his raised eyebrows the very emblem of innocent truthseeking.

"I agreed with him only that we wasted time," Slinoor said. "And we do." Just the same a little of the frown lingered between his eyes and his voice had lost its edge of utter certainty.

"I see," the Mouser said doubtfully. By stages he had begun to play the part of an attorney elucidating a case in court, striding about and frowning most professionally. Now he shot a sudden question: "Fafhrd, how many rats did you carry?"

"Five," boldly answered the Northerner, whose mathematics were not of the sharpest, but who'd had plenty time to count surreptitiously on his fingers and to think about what the Mouser was up to. "Two in one cage, three in the other."

"A feeble falsehood!" Lukeen scoffed. "The base barbarian would swear to anything to win a smile from the Demoiselle, who has him fawning."

"That's a foul lie!" Fafhrd roared, springing up and fetching his head such a great hollow thump on a deck beam that he clapped both hands to it and crouched in dizzy agony.

"Sit down, Fafhrd, before I ask you to apologize to the deck!" the Mouser commanded with heartless harshness. "This is solemn civilized court, no barbarous brawling session! Let's see—three and three and five make . . . eleven. Demoiselle Hisvet!" He pointed an accusing finger straight between her red-irised eyes and demanded most sternly, "How many white rats did you bring aboard *Squid?* The truth now and nothing but the truth!"

"Eleven," she answered demurely. "La, but I'm joyed someone at last had the wit to ask me."

"That I know's not true!" Slinoor said abruptly, his brow once more clear. "Why didn't I think of it before?—'twould have saved us all this bother of questions and counting. I have in this very cabin Glipkerio's letter of commission to me. In it he speaks verbatim of entrusting to me the Demoiselle Hisvet, daughter of Hisvin, and twelve witty white rats. Wait, I'll get it out and prove it to your faces!"

"No need, Ship's Master," Hisvet interposed. "I

saw the letter writ and can testify to the perfect truth of your quotations. But most sadly, between the sending of the letter and my boarding of *Squid,* poor Tchy was gobbled up by Glippy's giant boarhound Bimbat." She touched a slim finger to the corner of her eye and sniffed. "Poor Tchy, he was the most winsome of the twelve. 'Twas why I kept to my cabin the first two days." Each time she spoke the name Tchy, the eleven caged rats chittered mournfully.

"Is it Glippy you call our overlord?" Slinoor ejaculated, genuinely shocked. "Oh shameless one!"

"Aye, watch your language, Demoiselle," the Mouser warned severely, maintaining to the hilt his new role of austere inquisitor. "Any familiar relationship between you and our overlord the archnoble Glipkerio Kistomerces does not come within the province of this court."

"She lies like a shrewd subtle witch!" Lukeen asserted angrily. "Thumbscrew or rack, or perchance just a pale arm twisted high behind her back would get the truth from her fast enough!"

Hisvet turned and looked at him proudly. "I accept your challenge, Commander," she said evenly, laying her right hand on her maid's dark head. "Frix, reach out your naked hand, or whatever other part of you the brave gentleman wishes to torture." The dark maid straightened her back. Her face was impassive, lips firmly pressed together, though her eyes searched around wildly. Hisvet continued to Slinoor and Lukeen, "If you know any Lankhmar law at all, you know that a virgin of the rank of Demoiselle is tortured only in the person of her maid, who proves by her steadfastness under extreme pain the innocence of her mistress."

"What did I tell you about her?" Lukeen demanded of them all. "Subtle is too gross a term for her spiderwebby sleights!" He glared at Hisvet and said scornfully, his mouth a-twist, "Virgin!"

Hisvet smiled with cold long-suffering. Fafhrd flushed and although still holding his battered head, barely refrained from leaping up again. Lukeen looked at him with amusement, secure in his knowledge that he could bait Fafhrd at will and that the barbarian lacked the civilized wit to insult him deeply in return.

Fafhrd stared thoughtfully at Lukeen from under his capping hands. Then he said, "Yes, you're brave enough in armor, with your threats against girls and your hot imaginings of torture, but if you were without armor and had to prove your manhood with just one brave girl alone, you'd fall like a worm!"

Lukeen shot up enraged and got himself such a clout from a deck beam that he squeaked shudderingly and swayed. Nevertheless he gripped blindly for his sword at his side. Slinoor grasped that wrist and pulled him down into his seat.

"Govern yourself, Commander," Slinoor implored sternly, seeming to grow in resolution as the rest quarreled and quibbled. "Fafhrd, no more dagger words. Gray Mouser, this is not your court but mine and we are not met to split the hairs of high law but to meet a present peril. Here and now this grain fleet is in grave danger. Our very lives are risked. Much more than that, Lankhmar's in danger if Movarl gets not his gift-grain at this third sending. Last night *Clam* was foully murdered. Tonight it may be *Grouper* or *Squid, Shark* even, or no less than all our ships. The first two fleets went warned and well guarded, yet suffered only total perdition."

He paused to let that sink in. Then, "Mouser,

you've roused some small doubts in my mind by your
eleven-twelving. But small doubts are nothing where
home lives and home cities are in peril. For the safety
of the fleet and of Lankhmar we'll sink the white rats
forthwith and keep close watch on the Demoiselle
Hisvet to the very docks of Kvarch Nar."

"Right!" the Mouser cried approvingly, getting in
ahead of Hisvet. But then he instantly added, with
the air of sudden brilliant inspiration, *"Or . . . better
yet . . .* appoint Fafhrd and myself to keep unending
watch not only on Hisvet but also on the eleven white
rats. That way we don't spoil Glipkerio's gift and risk
offending Movarl."

"I'd trust no one's mere watching of the rats.
They're too tricksy," Slinoor informed him. "The
Demoiselle I intend to put on *Shark,* where she'll be
more closely guarded. The grain is what Movarl
wants, not the rats. He doesn't know about them, so
can't be angered at not getting them."

"But he does know about them," Hisvet interjected. "Glipkerio and Movarl exchange weekly letters by albatross-post. La, but Nehwon grows
smaller each year, Ship's Master—ships are snails
compared to the great winging mail-birds. Glipkerio
wrote of the rats to Movarl, who expressed great delight at the prospective gift and intense anticipation
of watching the White Shadows perform. Along with
myself," she added, demurely bending her head.

"Also," the Mouser put in rapidly, "I must firmly
oppose—most regretfully, Slinoor—the transfer of
Hisvet to another ship. Fafhrd's and my commission
from Glipkerio, which I can produce at any time,
states in clearest words that we are to attend the Demoiselle at all times outside her private quarters. He
makes us wholly responsible for her safety—and also

for that of the White Shadows, which creatures our overlord states, again in clearest writing, that he prizes beyond their weight in jewels."

"You can attend her in *Shark*," Slinoor told the Mouser curtly.

"I'll not have the barbarian on my ship!" Lukeen rasped, still squinting from the pain of his clout.

"I'd scorn to board such a tricked-out rowboat or oar-worm," Fafhrd shot back at him, voicing the common barbarian contempt for galleys.

"*Also*," the Mouser cut in again, loudly, with an admonitory gesture at Fafhrd, "it is my duty as a friend to warn you, Slinoor, that in your reckless threats against the White Shadows and the Demoiselle herself, you risk incurring the heaviest displeasure not only of our overlord but also of the most powerful grain-merchant in Lankhmar."

Slinoor answered most simply, "I think only of the City and the grain fleet. You know that," but Lukeen, fuming, spat out a "Hah!" and said scornfully, "The Gray Fool has not grasped that it is Hisvet's very father Hisvin who is behind the rat-sinkings, since he thereby grows rich with the extra nation's-ransoms of grain he sells Glipkerio!"

"Quiet, Lukeen!" Slinoor commanded apprehensively. "This dubious guesswork of yours has no place here."

"Guesswork? Mine?" Lukeen exploded. "It was *your* suggestion, Slinoor—Yes, and that Hisvin plots Glipkerio's overthrow—Aye, and even that he's in league with the Mingols! Let's speak truth for once!"

"Then speak it for yourself alone, Commander," Slinoor said most sober-sharply. "I fear the blow's disordered your brain. Gray Mouser, you're a man of sense," he appealed. "Can you not understand my one overriding concern? We're alone with mass murder on the high seas. We must take measures against it. Oh, will none of you show some simple wit?"

"La, and I will, Ship's Master, since you ask it," Hisvet said brightly, rising to her knees on the sea-bed as she turned toward Slinoor. Sunlight striking through a louver shimmered on her silver hair and gleamed from the silver ring confining it. "I'm but a girl, unused to problems of war and rapine, yet I have an all-explaining simple thought that I have waited in vain to hear voiced by one of you gentlemen, wise in the ways of violence.

"Last night a ship was slain. You hang the crime on rats—small beasties which would leave a sinking ship in any case, which often have a few whites among them, and which only by the wildest stretch of imagination are picturable as killing an entire crew and vanishing their bodies. To fill the great gaps in this weird theory you make me a sinister rat-queen, who can work black miracles, and now even, it seems, create my poor doting daddy an all-powerful rat-emperor.

"Yet this morning you met a ship's murderer if there ever was one and let him go honking off un-challenged. La, but the man-demon even confessed he'd been seeking a multi-headed monster that would snatch living men from a ship's deck and de-vour them. Surely he lied when he said his this-world foundling ate small fry only, for it struck at me to devour me—and might earlier have snapped up any of you, except it was sated!

"For what is more likely than that the two-head long-neck dragon ate all *Clam*'s sailors off her deck, snaking them out of the forecastle and hold, if they fled there, like sweetmeats from a compartmented comfit-box, and then scratched holes in *Clam*'s planking? Or perhaps more likely still, that *Clam* tore out her bottom on the Dragon Rocks in the fog and at the same time met the sea-dragon? These are sober possibilities, gentlemen, apparent even to a soft girl and asking no mind-stretch at all."

This startling speech brought forth an excited medley of reactions. Simultaneously the Mouser applauded, "A gem of princess-wit, Demoiselle; oh you'd make a rare strategist." Fafhrd said stoutly, "Most lucid, Little Mistress, yet Karl Treuherz seemed to me an honest demon." Frix told them proudly, "My mistress outthinks you all." The mate at the door goggled at Hisvet and made the sign of the starfish. Lukeen snarled, "She conveniently forgets the black cutter," while Slinoor cried them all down with, "Rat-queen you say jestingly? Rat-queen you are!"

As the others grew silent at that dire accusation, Slinoor gazing grimly fearful at Hisvet, continued rapidly, "The Demoiselle has recalled to me by her speech the worst point against her. Karl Treuherz said his dragon, living by the Rat Rocks, ate only rats. It made no move to gobble us several men, though it had every chance, yet when Hisvet appeared it struck at her at once. It knew her true race."

Slinoor's voice went shudderingly low. "Thirteen rats with the minds of men rule the whole rat race. That's ancient wisdom from Lankhmar's wisest seers. Eleven are these silver-furred silent sharpies, hearing our every word. The twelfth celebrates in the black cutter his conquest of *Clam*. The thirteenth"—

and he pointed finger—"is the silver-haired, red-eyed Demoiselle herself!"

Lukeen slithered to his feet at that, crying, "Oh most shrewdly reasoned, Slinoor! And why does she wear such modest shrouding garb except to hide further evidence of the dread kinship? Let me but strip off that cloaking ermine smock and I'll show you a white-furred body and ten small black dugs instead of proper maiden breasts!"

As he came snaking around the table toward His-vet, Fafhrd sprang up, also cautiously, and pinned Lukeen's arms to his sides in a bear-hug, calling, "Nay, and you touch her, you die!"

Meantime Frix cried, "The dragon was sated with *Clam*'s crew, as my mistress told you. It wanted no more coarse-fibered men, but eagerly seized at my dainty-fleshed darling for a dessert mouthful!"

Lukeen wrenched around until his black eyes glared into Fafhrd's green ones inches away. "Oh most foul barbarian!" he grated. "I forego rank and dignity and challenge you this instant to a bout of quarterstaves on middeck. I'll prove Hisvet's taint on you by trial of battle. That is, if you dare face civilized combat, you great stinking ape!" And he spat full in Fafhrd's taunting face.

Fafhrd's only reaction was to smile a great smile through the spittle running gummily down his cheek, while maintaining his grip of Lukeen and wary lookout for a bite at his own nose.

Thereafter, challenge having been given and accepted, there was naught for even the head-shaking, heaven-glancing Slinoor to do but hurry preparation for the combat or duel, so that it might be fought before sunset and leave some daylight for taking sober measures for the fleet's safety in the approaching dark of night.

As Slinoor, the Mouser and mate came around them, Fafhrd released Lukeen, who scornfully averting his gaze instantly went on deck to summon a squad of his marines from *Shark* to second him and see fair play. Slinoor conferred with his mate and other officers. The Mouser, after a word with Fafhrd, slipped forward and could be seen gossiping industriously with *Squid*'s bosun and the common members of her crew down to cook and cabin boy. Occasionally something might have passed rapidly from the Mouser's hand to that of the sailor with whom he spoke.

IV

DESPITE Slinoor's urging, the sun was dropping
down the western sky before *Squid*'s gongsman beat
the rapid brassy tattoo that signalized the imminence
of combat. The sky was clear to the west and overhead, but the sinister fogbank still rested a
Lankhmar league (twenty bowshots) to the east, par-
alleling the northward course of the fleet and looking
almost as solid and dazzling as a glacier wall in the
sun's crosswise rays. Most mysteriously neither hot
sun nor west wind dissipated it.

Black-suited, brown-mailed and brown-helmeted
marines facing aft made a wall across *Squid* to either
side of the mainmast. They held their spears horizon-
tal and crosswise at arm's-length down, making an
additional low fence. Black-tunicked sailors peered
between their shoulders and boots, or sat with their
own brown legs a-dangle on the larboard side of the
foredeck, where the great sail did not cut off their
view. A few perched in the rigging.

The damaged rail had been stripped away from

the break in the afterdeck and there around the bare aftermast sat the three judges: Slinoor, the Mouser, and Lukeen's sergeant. Around them, mostly to larboard of the two helmsmen, were grouped *Squid*'s officers and certain officers of the other ship on whose presence the Mouser had stubbornly insisted, though it had meant time-consuming ferrying by ship's boat.

Hisvet and Frix were in the cabin with the door shut. The Demoiselle had wanted to watch the duel through the open door or even from the afterdeck, but Lukeen had protested that this would make it easier for her to work an evil spell on him, and the judges had ruled for Lukeen. However the grille was open and now and again the sun's rays twinkled on a peering eye or silvered fingernail.

Between the dark spear-wall of marines and the afterdeck stretched a great square of white oaken deck, empty save for the crane-fittings and like fixed gear and level except for the main hatch, which made a central square of deck a hand's span above the rest. Each corner of the larger square was marked off by a black-chalked quarter circle. Either contestant stepping inside a quarter circle after the duel began (or springing on the rail or grasping the rigging or falling over the side) would at once forfeit the match.

In the forward larboard quarter circle stood Lukeen in black shirt and hose, still wearing his gold-banded starfish emblem. By him was his second, his own hawkfaced lieutenant. With his right hand Lukeen gripped his quarterstaff, a heavy wand of close-grained oak as tall as himself and thick as Hisvet's wrist. Raising it above his head he twirled it till it hummed. He smiled fiendishly.

In the after starboard quarter circle, next to the cabin door, were Fafhrd and his second, the mate of

Carp, a grossly fat man with a touch of the Mingol in his sallow features. The Mouser could not be judge and second both, and he and Fafhrd had diced more than once with *Carp*'s mate in the old days at Lankhmar—losing money to him, too, which at least indicated that he might be resourceful.

Fafhrd took from him now his own quarterstaff, gripping it cross-handed near one end. He made a few slow practice passes with it through the air, then handed it back to *Carp*'s mate and stripped off his jerkin.

Lukeen's marines sniggered to each other at the Northerner handling a quarterstaff as if it were a two-handed broadsword, but when Fafhrd bared his hairy chest *Squid*'s sailors set up a rousing cheer and when Lukeen commented loudly to his second, "What did I tell you? A great hairy-pelted ape, beyond question," and spun his staff again, the sailors booed him lustily.

"Strange," Slinoor commented in a low voice. "I had thought Lukeen to be popular among the sailors."

Lukeen's sergeant looked around incredulously at that remark. The Mouser only shrugged. Slinoor continued to him, "If the sailors knew your comrade fought on the side of rats, they'd not cheer him." The Mouser only smiled.

The gong sounded again.

Slinoor rose and spoke loudly: "A bout at quarterstaves with no breathing spells! Commander Lukeen seeks to prove on the overlord's mercenary Fafhrd certain allegations against a Demoiselle of Lankhmar. First man struck senseless or at mercy of his foe loses. Prepare!"

Two ship's boys went skipping across the

middeck, scattering handfuls of white sand.

Sitting, Slinoor remarked to the Mouser, "A pox on this footling duel! It delays our action against Hisvet and the rats. Lukeen was a fool to bridle at the barbarian. Still, when he's drubbed him, there'll be time enough."

The Mouser lifted an eyebrow. Slinoor said lightly, "Oh didn't you know? Lukeen will win; that's certain," while the sergeant, nodding soberly, confirmed, "The Commander's a master of staves. 'Tis no game for barbarians."

The gong sounded a third time.

Lukeen sprang nimbly across the chalk and onto the hatch, crying, "Ho, hairy ape! Art ready to double-kiss the oak?—first my staff, then the deck?"

Fafhrd came shambling out, gripping his wand most awkwardly and responding, "Your spit has poisoned my left eye, Lukeen, but I see some civilized target with my right."

Lukeen dashed at him joyously then, feinting at elbow and head, then rapidly striking with the other end of his staff at Fafhrd's knee to tumble or lame him.

Fafhrd, abruptly switching to conventional stance and grip, parried the blow and swung a lightning riposte at Lukeen's jaw.

Lukeen got his staff up in time so that the blow hit only his cheek glancingly, but he was unsettled by it and thereafter Fafhrd was upon him, driving him back in a hail of barely-parried blows while the sailors cheered.

Slinoor and the sergeant gaped wide-eyed, but the Mouser only knotted his fingers, muttering, "Not so fast, Fafhrd."

Then, as Fafhrd prepared to end it all, he

stumbled stepping off the hatch, which changed his swift blow to the head into a slow blow at the ankles. Lukeen leaped up so that Fafhrd's staff passed under his feet, and while he was still in the air rapped Fafhrd on the head.

The sailors groaned. The marines cheered once, growlingly.

The unfooted blow was not of the heaviest, none-theless it three-quarters stunned Fafhrd and now it was his turn to be driven back under a pelting shower of swipes. For several moments there was no sound but the rutch of soft-soled boots on sanded oak and the rapid dry musical *bong* of staff meeting staff.

When Fafhrd came suddenly to his full senses he was falling away from a wicked swing. A glimpse of black by his heel told him that his next inevitable backward step would carry him inside his own quarter circle.

Swift as thought he thrust far behind him with his staff. Its end struck deck, then stopped against the cabin wall, and Fafhrd heaved himself forward with it, away from the chalk line, ducking and lunging to the side to escape Lukeen's blows while his staff could not protect him.

The sailors screamed with excitement. The judges and officers on the afterdeck kneeled like dice-players, peering over the edge.

Fafhrd had to lift his left arm to guard his head. He took a blow on the elbow and his left arm dropped limp to his side. Thereafter he had to handle his staff like a broadsword indeed, swinging it one-handed in whistling parries and strokes.

Lukeen hung back, playing more cautiously now, knowing Fafhrd's one wrist must tire sooner than his two. He'd aim a few rapid blows at Fafhrd, then prance back.

Barely parrying the third of these attacks, Fafhrd riposted recklessly, not with a proper swinging blow, but simply gripping the end of his staff and lunging. The combined length of Fafhrd and his staff overtook Lukeen's retreat and the tip of Fafhrd's staff poked him low in the chest, just on the nerve spot.

Lukeen's jaw dropped, his mouth stayed open wide, and he wavered. Fafhrd smartly rapped his staff out of his fingers and as it clattered down, toppled Lukeen to the deck with a second almost casual prod.

The sailors cheered themselves hoarse. The marines growled surlily and one cried, "Foul!" Lukeen's second knelt by him, glaring at Fafhrd. *Carp*'s mate danced a ponderous jig up to Fafhrd and wafted the wand out of his hands. On the afterdeck *Squid*'s officers were glum, though those of the other grain ships seemed strangely jubilant. The Mouser gripped Slinoor's elbow, urging, "Cry Fafhrd victor," while the sergeant frowned prodigiously, hand to temple, saying, "Well, there's nothing I know of in the *rules* . . ."

At that moment the cabin door opened and Hisvet stepped out, wearing a long scarlet, scarlet-hooded silk robe.

The Mouser, sensing climax, sprang to starboard, where *Squid*'s gong hung, snatched the striker from the gongsman and clanged it wildly.

Squid grew silent. Then there were pointings and questioning cries as Hisvet was seen. She put a silver recorder to her lips and began to dance dreamily toward Fafhrd, softly whistling with her recorder a high haunting tune of seven notes in a minor key. From somewhere tiny tuned bells accompanied it tinklingly. Then Hisvet swung to one side, facing Fafhrd as she moved around him, and the questioning cries changed to ones of wonder and astonishment and the sailors came crowding as far aft as they could and swinging through the rigging, as the procession became visible that Hisvet headed.

It consisted of eleven white rats walking in single file on their hind legs and wearing little scarlet robes and caps. The first four carried in each forepaw clusters of tiny silver bells which they shook rhythmically. The next five bore on their shoulders, hanging down between them a little, a double length of looped gleaming silver chain—they were very like five sailors lugging an anchor chain. The last two each bore slantwise a slim silver wand as tall as himself as he walked erect, tail curving high.

The first four halted side by side in rank facing Fafhrd and tinkling their bells to Hisvet's piping.

The next five marched on steadily to Fafhrd's right foot. There their leader paused, looked up at Fafhrd's face with upraised paw, and squeaked three times. Then, gripping his end of the chain in one paw, he used his other three to climb Fafhrd's boot. Imitated by his four fellows, he then carefully climbed Fafhrd's trousers and hairy chest.

Fafhrd stared down at the mounting chain and scarlet-robed rats without moving a muscle, except to frown faintly as tiny paws unavoidably tweaked clumps of his chest-hair.

The first rat mounted to Fafhrd's right shoulder and moved behind his back to his left shoulder, the four other rats following in order and never letting slip the chain.

When all five rats were standing on Fafhrd's shoulders, they lifted one strand of the silver chain and brought it forward over his head, most dexterously. Meanwhile he was looking straight ahead at Hisvet, who had completely circled him and now stood piping behind the bell-tinklers.

The five rats dropped the strand, so that the chain hung in a gleaming oval down Fafhrd's chest. At the same instant each rat lifted his scarlet cap as high above his head as his foreleg would reach.

Someone cried, "Victor!"

The five rats swung down their caps and again lifted them high, and as if from one throat all the sailors and most of the marines and officers cried in a great shout: "*Victor!*"

The five rats led two more cheers for Fafhrd, the men aboard *Squid* obeying as if hypnotized—though whether by some magic power or simply by the wonder and appropriateness of the rats' behavior, it was hard to tell.

Hisvet finished her piping with a merry flourish and the two rats with silver wands scurried up onto the afterdeck and standing at the foot of the aftermast where all might see, began to drub away at each other in most authentic quarterstaff style, their wands flashing in the sunlight and chiming sweetly when they clashed. The silence broke in rounds of exclamation and laughter. The five rats scampered down Fafhrd and returned with the bell-tinklers to cluster around the hem of Hisvet's skirt. Mouser and several officers were leaping down from the afterdeck to wring Fafhrd's good hand or clap his back. The marines had much ado to hold back the sailors, who were offering each other bets on which rat would be the winner in this new bout.

Fafhrd, fingering his chain, remarked to the
Mouser, "Strange that the sailors were with me from
the start," and under cover of the hubbub the
Mouser smilingly explained, "I gave them money to
bet on you against the marines. Likewise I dropped
some hints and made some loans for the same
purpose to the officers of the other ships—a fighter
can't have too big a claque. Also I started the story
going round that the whiteys are anti-rat rats,
trained exterminators of their own kind, sample of
Glipkerio's latest device for the safety of the grain
fleets—sailors eat up such tosh."

"Did you first cry victor?" Fafhrd asked.

The Mouser grinned. "A judge take sides? In *civilized* combat? Oh, I was prepared to, but 'twasn't
needful."

At that moment Fafhrd felt a small tug at his
trousers and looking down saw that the black kitten
had bravely approached through the forest of legs
and was now climbing him purposefully. Touched at
this further display of animal homage, Fafhrd
rumbled gently as the kitten reached his belt, "Decided to heal our quarrel, eh, small black one?" At
that the kitten sprang up his chest, sunk his little
claws in Fafhrd's bare shoulder and, glaring like a
black hangman, raked Fafhrd bloodily across the
jaw, then sprang by way of a couple of startled heads
to the mainsail and rapidly climbed its concave taut
brown curve. Someone threw a belaying pin at the
small black blot, but it was negligently aimed and
the kitten safely reached the mast-top.

"I forswear all cats!" Fafhrd cried angrily, dabbl-
ing at his chin. "Henceforth rats are my favored
beasties."

"Most properly spoken, Swordsman!" Hisvet

called gaily from her own circle of admirers, continuing, "I will be pleased by your company and the Dirksman's at dinner in my cabin an hour past sunset. We'll conform to the very letter of Slinoor's stricture that I be closely watched and the White Shadows too." She whistled a little call on her silver recorder and swept back into her cabin with the nine rats close at her heels. The quarterstaving scarlet-robed pair on the afterdeck broke off their drubbing with neither victorious and scampered after her, the crowd parting to make way for them admiringly.

Slinoor, hurrying forward, paused to watch. *Squid*'s skipper was a man deeply bemused. Somewhere in the last half hour the white rats had been transformed from eerie poison-toothed monsters threatening the fleet into popular, clever, harmless animal-mountebanks, whom *Squid*'s sailors appeared to regard as a band of white mascots. Slinoor seemed to be seeking unsuccessfully but unceasingly to decipher how and why.

Lukeen, still looking very pale, followed the last of his disgruntled marines (their purses lighter by many a silver smerduk, for they had been coaxed into offering odds) over the side into *Shark*'s long dinghy, brushing off Slinoor when *Squid*'s skipper would have conferred with him.

Slinoor vented his chagrin by harshly commanding his sailors to leave off their disorderly milling and frisking, but they obeyed him right cheerily, skipping to their proper stations with the happiest of sailor smirks. Those passing the Mouser winked at him and surreptitiously touched their forelocks. *Squid* bowled smartly northward a half bowshot astern of *Tunny*, as she'd been doing throughout the duel, only now she began to cleave the blue water a little more

swiftly yet as the west wind freshened and her after
sail was broken out. In fact, the fleet began to sail so
swiftly now that *Shark*'s dinghy couldn't make the
head of the line, although Lukeen could be noted bul-
lying his marine-oarsmen into back-cracking efforts,
and the dinghy had finally come to signal *Shark*
herself to come back and pick her up—which the war
galley achieved only with difficulty, rolling danger-
ously in the mounting seas and taking until sunset,
oars helping sails, to return to the head of the line.

"*He*'ll not be eager to come to *Squid*'s help tonight,
or much able to either," Fafhrd commented to the
Mouser where they stood by the larboard middeck
rail. There had been no open break between them
and Slinoor, but they were inclined to leave him the
afterdeck, where he stood beyond the helmsmen in
bent-head converse with his three officers, who had
all lost money on Lukeen and had been sticking close
to their skipper ever since.

"Not still expecting *that* sort of peril tonight, are
you, Fafhrd?" the Mouser asked with a soft laugh.
"We're far past the Rat Rocks."

Fafhrd shrugged and said frowningly, "Perhaps
we've gone just a shade too far in endorsing the rats."

"Perhaps," the Mouser agreed. "But then their
charming mistress is worth a fib and false stamp or
two, aye and more than that, eh, Fafhrd?"

"She's a brave sweet lass," Fafhrd said carefully.

"Aye, and her maid too," the Mouser said brightly. "I noted Frix peering at you adoringly from the
cabin entryway after your victory. A most voluptuous
wench. Some men might well prefer the maid to the
mistress in this instance. Fafhrd?"

Without looking around at the Mouser, the Northerner shook his head.

The Mouser studied Fafhrd, wondering if it were politic to make a certain proposal he had in mind. He was not quite certain of the full nature of Fafhrd's feelings toward Hisvet. He knew the Northerner was a goatish man enough and had yesterday seemed quite obsessed with the love-making they'd missed in Lankhmar, yet he also knew that his comrade had a variable romantic streak that was sometimes thin as a thread yet sometimes grew into a silken ribbon leagues wide in which armies might stumble and be lost.

On the afterdeck Slinoor was now conferring most earnestly with the cook, presumably (the Mouser decided) about Hisvet's (and his own and Fafhrd's) dinner. The thought of Slinoor having to go to so much trouble about the pleasures of three persons who today had thoroughly thwarted him made the Mouser grin and somehow also nerved him to take the uncertain step he'd been contemplating.

"Fafhrd," he whispered, "I'll dice you for Hisvet's favors."

"Why, Hisvet's but a girl—" Fafhrd began in accents of rebuke, then cut off abruptly and closed his eyes in thought. When he opened them, they were regarding the Mouser with a large smile.

"No," Fafhrd said softly, "for truly I think this Hisvet is so balky and fantastic a miss it will take both our most heartfelt and cunning efforts to persuade her to aught. And, after that, who knows? Dicing for such a girl's favors were like betting when a Lankhmar night-lily will open and whether to north or south."

The Mouser chuckled and lovingly dug Fafhrd in the ribs, saying, "There's my shrewd true comrade!"

Fafhrd looked at the Mouser with sudden dark

suspicions. "Now don't go trying to get me drunk tonight," he warned, "or sifting opium in my drink."

"Hah, you know me better than that, Fafhrd," the Mouser said with laughing reproach.

"I certainly do," Fafhrd agreed sardonically.

Again the sun went under with a green flash, indicating crystal clear air to the west, though the strange fogbank, now an ominous dark wall, still paralleled their course a league or so to the east.

The cook, crying, "My mutton!" went racing forward past them toward the galley, whence a deliciously spicy aroma was wafting.

"We've an hour to kill," the Mouser said. "Come on, Fafhrd. On our way to board *Squid* I bought a little jar of wine of Quarmall at the Silver Eel. It's still sealed."

From just overhead in the rat-lines, the black kitten hissed down at them in angry menace or perhaps warning.

V

TWO HOURS LATER the Demoiselle Hisvet offered to the Mouser, "A golden rilk for your thoughts, Dirksman."

She was on the swung-down sea-bed once more, half reclining. The long table, now laden with tempting viands and tall silver wine cups, had been placed against the bed. Fafhrd sat across from Hisvet, the empty silver cages behind him, while the Mouser was at the stern end of the table. Frix served them all from the door forward, where she took the trays from the cook's boys without giving them so much as a peep inside. She had a small brazier there for keeping hot such items as required it and she tasted each dish and set it aside for a while before serving it. Thick dark pink candles in silver sconces shed a pale light.

The white rats crouched in rather disorderly fashion around a little table of their own set on the floor near the wall between the sea-bed and the door, just aft of one of the trapdoors opening down into the grain-redolent hold. They wore little black jackets open at the front and little black belts around their

middles. They seemed more to play with than eat the
bits of food Frix set before them on their three or four
little silver plates and they did not lift their small
bowls to drink their wine-tinted water but rather
lapped at them and that not very industriously. One
or two would always be scampering up onto the bed
to be with Hisvet, which made them most difficult to
count, even for Fafhrd, who had the best view. Sometimes he got eleven, sometimes ten. At intervals one
of them would stand up on the pink coverlet by
Hisvet's knees and chitter at her in cadences so like
those of human speech that Fafhrd and the Mouser
would have to chuckle.

"Dreamy Dirksman, two rilks for your thoughts!"
Hisvet repeated, upping her offer. "And most im-
modestly I'll wager a third rilk they are of me."

The Mouser smiled and lifted his eyebrows. He
was feeling very light-headed and a bit uneasy, chiefly because contrary to his intentions he had been
drinking much more than Fafhrd. Frix had just
served them the main dish, a masterly yellow curry
heavy with dark-tasting spices and originally appear-
ing with "Victor" pricked on it with black capers.
Fafhrd was devouring it manfully, though not
voraciously, the Mouser was going at it more slowly,
while Hisvet all evening had merely toyed with her
food.

"I'll take your two rilks, White Princess," the
Mouser replied airily, "for I'll need one to pay the
wager you've just won and the other to fee you for
telling me *what* I was thinking of you."

"You'll not keep my second rilk long, Dirksman,"
Hisvet said merrily, "for as you thought of me you
were looking not at my face, but most impudently
somewhat lower. You were thinking of those some-

what nasty suspicions Lukeen voiced this day about my secretest person. Confess it now, you were!''

The Mouser could only hang his head a little and shrug helplessly, for she had most truly divined his thoughts. Hisvet laughed and frowned at him in mock anger, saying, "Oh, you are most indelicate minded, Dirksman. Yet at least you can see that Frix, though indubitably mammalian, is not fronted like a she-rat.''

This statement was undeniably true, for Hisvet's maid was all dark smooth skin except where black silk scarves narrowly circled her slim body at breasts and hips. Silver net tightly confined her black hair and there were many plain silver bracelets on each wrist. Yet although garbed like a slave, Frix did not seem one tonight, but rather a lady-companion who expertly played at being slave, serving them all with perfect yet laughing, wholly unservile obedience.

Hisvet, by contrast, was wearing another of her long smocks, this of black silk edged with black lace, with a lace-edged hood half thrown back. Her silvery white hair was dressed high on her head in great smooth swelling sweeps. Regarding her across the table, Fafhrd said, "I am certain that the Demoiselle would be no less than completely beautiful to us in whatever shape she chose to present herself to the world—wholly human or somewhat otherwise.''

''Now that was most gallantly spoken, Swordsman,'' Hisvet said with a somewhat breathless laugh. "I must reward you for it. Come to me, Frix.'' As the slim maid bent close to her, Hisvet yet twined her white hands round the dark waist and imprinted a sweet slow kiss on Frix's lips. Then she looked up and gave a little tap on the shoulder to Frix, who moved smiling around the table and, half kneeling by Fafhrd, kissed him as she had been kissed. He received the token graciously, without unmannerly excitement, yet when Frix would have drawn back, prolonged the kiss, explaining a bit thickly when he released her: "Somewhat extra to return to the sender, perchance." She grinned at him saucily and went to her serving table by the door, saying, "I must first chop the rats their meat, naughty barbarian." While Hisvet discoursed, "Don't seek too much, Bold Swordsman. That was in any case but a small proxy reward for a small gallant speech. A reward with the mouth for words spoken with the mouth. To reward you for drubbing Lukeen and vindicating my honor were a more serious matter altogether, not to be entered on lightly. I'll think of it."

At this point the Mouser, who just had to be saying something but whose fuddled brain was momentarily empty of suitably venturesome yet courteous wit, called out to Frix, "Why chop you the rats their mutton, dusky minx? 'Twould be rare sport to see them slice it for themselves." Frix only wrinkled her nose at him, but Hisvet expounded gravely, "Only Skwee carves with any great skill. The others might hurt themselves, particularly with the meat shifting about in the slippery curry. Frix, reserve a single chunk for Skwee to display us his ability. Chop the rest fine. Skwee!" she called, setting her voice high. "Skwee-skwee-skwee!"

A tall rat sprang onto the bed and stood dutifully before her with forelegs folded across his chest. Hisvet instructed him, then took from a silver box behind her a most tiny carving set of knife, steel and fork in joined treble scabbard and tied it carefully to his belt. Then Skwee bowed low to her and sprang nimbly down to the rats' table.

The Mouser watched the little scene with clouded and heavy-lidded wonder, feeling that he was falling under some sort of spell. At times thick shadows crossed the cabin; at times Skwee grew tall as Hisvet or perhaps it was Hisvet tiny as Skwee. And then the Mouser grew small as Skwee, too, and ran under the bed and fell into a chute that darkly swiftly slid him, not into a dark hold of sacked or loose delicious grain, but into the dark spacious low-ceilinged pleasance of a subterranean rat-metropolis, lit by phosphorus, where robed and long-skirted rats whose hoods hid their long faces moved about mysteriously, where rat-swords clashed behind the next pillar and rat-money chinked, where lewd female rats danced in their fur for a fee, where masked rat-spies and rat-informers lurked, where everyone—every-furry-one—was cringingly conscious of the omniscient overlordship of a supernally powerful Council of Thirteen, and where a rat-Mouser sought everywhere a slim rat-princess named Hisvet-sur-Hisvin.

The Mouser woke from his dinnerdream with a jerk. Somehow he'd surely drunk even more cups than he'd counted, he told himself haltingly. Skwee, he saw, had returned to the rats' table and was standing before the yellow chunk Frix had set on the silver platter at Skwee's end. With the other rats watching him, Skwee drew forth knife and steel with a flourish. The Mouser roused himself more fully with another jerk and shake and was inspired to say, "Ah, were I but a rat, White Princess, so that I might come as close to you, serving you!"

The Demoiselle Hisvet cried, "A tribute indeed!" and laughed with delight, showing—it appeared to the Mouser—a slim pink tongue half splotched with blue and an inner mouth similarly pied. Then she said rather soberly, "Have a care what you wish, for some wishes have been granted," but at once continued gaily, "nevertheless, 'twas most gallantly said, Dirksman. I must reward you. Frix, sit at my ride side here."

The Mouser could not see what passed between them, for Hisvet's loosely smocked form hid Frix from him, but the merry eyes of the maid peered steadily at him over Hisvet's shoulder, twinkling like the black silk. Hisvet seemed to be whispering into Frix's ear while nuzzling it playfully.

Meanwhile there commenced the faintest of high *skirrings* as Skwee rapidly clashed steel and knife together, sharpening the latter. The Mouser could barely see the rat's head and shoulders and the tiny glimmer of flashing metal over the larger table intervening. He felt the urge to stand and move closer to observe the prodigy—and perchance glimpse something of the interesting activities of Hisvet and Frix—but he was held fast by a great lethargy, whether of wine or sensuous anticipation or pure magic he could not tell.

He had one great worry—that Fafhrd would out with a cleverer compliment than his own, one so much cleverer that it might even divert Frix's mission to him. But then he noted that Fafhrd's chin had fallen to his chest, and there came to his ears along with the silvery *klirring* the barbarian's gently rumbling snores.

The Mouser's first reaction was pure wicked relief. He remembered gloatingly past times he'd gamboled with generous, gay girls while his comrade snored sodden. Fafhrd must after all have been sneaking many extra swigs or whole drinks!

Frix jerked and giggled immoderately. Hisvet continued to whisper in her ear while Frix giggled and cooed again from time to time, continuing to watch the Mouser impishly.

Skwee scabbarded the steel with a tiny *clash*, drew the fork with a flourish, plunged it into the yellow-coated meat-chunk, big as a roast for him, and began to carve most dexterously.

Frix rose at last, received her tap from Hisvet, and headed around the table, smiling the while at the Mouser.

Skwee up with a paper-thin tiny slice of mutton on his fork and flapped it this way and that for all to see, then brought it close to his muzzle for a sniff and a taste.

The Mouser in his dreamy slump felt a sudden twinge of apprehension. It had occurred to him that Fafhrd simply couldn't have sneaked *that* much extra wine. Why, the Northerner hadn't been out of his sight the past two hours. Of course blows on the head sometimes had a delayed effect.

All the same his first reaction was pure angry jeal-ousy when Frix paused beside Fafhrd and leaned over his shoulder and looked in his forward-tipped face.

Just then there came a great squeak of outrage and alarm from Skwee and the white rat sprang up onto the bed, still holding carving knife and fork with the mutton slice dangling from it.

From under eyelids that persisted in drooping low-er and lower, the Mouser watched Skwee gesticulate with his tiny implements, as he chittered dramati-cally to Hisvet in most man-like cadences, and finally lift the petal of mutton to her lips with an accusing squeak.

Then, coming faintly through the chittering, the

Mouser heard a host of stealthy footsteps crossing the middeck, converging on the cabin. He tried to call Hisvet's attention to it, but found his lips and tongue numb and unobedient to his will.

Frix suddenly grasped the hair of Fafhrd's forehead and jerked his head up and back. The Northerner's jaw hung slackly, his eyes fell open, showing only whites.

There was a gentle rapping at the door, exactly the same as the cook's boys had made delivering the earlier courses.

A look passed between Hisvet and Frix. The latter dropped Fafhrd's head, darted to the door, slammed the bar across it and locked the bar with the chain (the grille already being shut) just as something (a man's shoulder, it sounded) thudded heavily against the thick panels.

That thudding continued and a few heartbeats later became much more sharply ponderous, as if a spare mast-section were being swung like a battering ram against the door, which yielded visibly at each blow.

The Mouser realized at last, much against his will, that something was happening that he ought to do something about. He made a great effort to shake off his lethargy and spring up.

He found he could not even twitch a finger. In fact it was all he could do to keep his eyes from closing altogether and watch through lash-blurred slits as Hisvet, Frix and the rats spun into a whirlwind of silent activity.

Frix jammed her serving table against the jolting door and began to pile other furniture against it.

Hisvet dragged out from behind the sea-bed various dark long boxes and began to unlock them. As

fast as she threw them open the white rats helped
themselves to the small blued-iron weapons they contained: swords, spears, even most wicked-looking
blued-iron crossbows with belted cannisters of darts.
They took more weapons than they could effectively
use themselves. Skwee hurriedly put on a black-
plumed helmet that fitted down over his furry cheeks.
The number of rats busy around the boxes was ten—
that much the Mouser noted clearly.

A split appeared in the middle of the piled door.
Nevertheless Frix sprang away from there to the
starboard trapdoor leading to the hold and heaved it
up. Hisvet threw herself on the floor toward it and
thrust her head down into the dark square hole.

There was something terribly animal-like about
the movements of the two women. It may have been
only the cramped quarters and the low ceiling, but it
seemed to the Mouser that they moved by preference
on all fours.

All the while Fafhrd's chest-sunk head kept lifting
very slowly and then falling with a jerk as he went on
snoring.

Hisvet sprang up and waved on the ten white rats.
Led by Skwee, they trooped down through the hatch,
their blued-iron weapons flashing and once or twice
clashing, and were gone in a twinkling. Frix grabbed
dark garments out of a curtained niche. Hisvet
caught her by the wrist and thrust the maid ahead of
her down the trap and then descended herself. Before
pulling the hatch down above her, she took a last
look around the cabin. As her red eyes gazed briefly
at the Mouser, it seemed to him that her forehead
and cheeks were grown over with silky white hair,
but that may well have been a combination of
eyelash-blur and her own disordered hair streaming

and streaking down across her face.

The cabin door split and a man's length of thick mast boomed through, overturning the bolstering table and scattering the furniture set on and against it. After the mast-end came piling in three apprehensive sailors followed by Slinoor, holding a cutlass low, and Slinoor's starsman (navigation officer) with a crossbow at the cock.

Slinoor pressed ahead a little and surveyed the scene swiftly yet intently, then said, "Our poppy-dust curry has taken Glipkerio's two lust-besotted rogues, but Hisvet's hid with her nymphy slave-girl. The rats are out of their cages. Search, sailors! Starsman, cover us!"

Gingerly at first, but soon in a rush, the sailors searched the cabin, tumbling the empty boxes and jerking the quilts and mattress off the sea-bed and swinging it up to see beneath, heaving chests away from walls and flinging open the unlocked ones, sweeping Hisvet's wardrobe in great silken armfuls out of the curtained niches in which it had been hanging.

The Mouser again made a mighty effort to speak or move, with no more success than to widen his blurred eye-slits a little. A sailor louted into him and he helplessly collapsed sideways against an arm of his chair without quite falling out of it. Fafhrd got a shove behind and slumped face-down on the table in a dish of stewed plums, his great arms outsweeping unconsciously, upsetting cups and scattering plates.

The starsman kept crossbow trained on each new space uncovered. Slinoor watched with eagle eye, flipping aside silken fripperies with his cutlass point and using it to overset the rats' table, peering the while narrowly.

"There's where the vermin feasted like men," he observed disgustedly. "The curry was set before them. Would they had gorged themselves senseless on it."

"Likely they were the ones to note the drug even through the masking spices of the curry, and warn the women," the starsman put in. "Rats are prodigiously wise to poisons."

As it became apparent neither girls nor rats were in the cabin, Slinoor cried with angry anxiety, "They can't have escaped to the deck—there's the sky-trap locked below besides our guard above. The mate's party bars the after hold. Perchance the stern-lights —"

But just then the Mouser heard one of the horn windows behind him being opened and *Squid*'s armsmaster call from there, "Naught came this way. Where are they, captain?"

"Ask someone wittier than I," Slinoor tossed him sourly. "Certain they're not here."

"Would that these two could speak," the starsman wished, indicating the Mouser and Fafhrd.

"No," Slinoor said dourly. "They'd just lie. Cover the larboard trap to the hold. I'll have it up and speak to the mate."

Just then footsteps came hurrying across the middeck and *Squid*'s mate with blood-streaked face entered by the broken door, half dragging and half supporting a sailor who seemed to be holding a thin stick to his own bloody cheek.

"Why have you left the hold?" Slinoor demanded of the first. "You should be with your party below."

"Rats ambushed us on our way to the after hold," the mate gasped. "There were dozens of blacks led by a white, some armed like men. The sword of a beam-hanger almost cut my eye across. Two foamy-mouthed springers dashed out our lamp. 'Twere pure folly to have gone on in the dark. There's scarce a man of my party not bitten, slashed or jabbed. I left them guarding the foreway to the hold. They say their wounds are poisoned and talk of nailing down the hatch.''

"Oh monstrous cowardice!" Slinoor cried. "You've spoiled my trap that would have scotched them at the start. Now all's to do and difficult. Oh scarelings! Daunted by rats!"

"I tell you they were armed!" the mate protested and then, swinging the sailor forward, "Here's my proof with a spearlet in his cheek.''

"Don't drag her out, captain, sir," the sailor begged as Slinoor moved to examine his face. " 'Tis poisoned too, I wot.''

"Hold still, boy," Slinoor commanded. "And take your hands away—I've got it firm. The point's near the skin. I'll drive it out forward so the barbs don't catch. Pinion his arms, mate. Don't move your face, boy, or you'll be hurt worse. If it's poisoned, it must come out the faster. There!''

The sailor squeaked. Fresh blood rilled down his cheek.

" 'Tis a nasty needle indeed," Slinoor commended, inspecting the bloody point. "Doesn't look poisoned. Mate, gently cut off the shaft aft of the wound, draw out the rest forward.''

"Here's further proof, most wicked," said the starsman, who'd been picking about in the litter. He handed Slinoor a tiny crossbow.

Slinoor held it up before him. In the pale candlelight it gleamed bluely, while the skipper's dark-circled eyes were like agates.

"Here's evil's soul," he cried. "Perchance 'twas well you were ambushed in the hold. 'Twill teach each mariner to hate and fear all rats again, like a good grain-sailor should. And now by a swift certain killing of all rats on *Squid* wipe out today's traitorous foolery, when you clapped for rats and let rats lead your cheers, seduced by a scarlet girl and bribed by that most misnamed Mouser."

The Mouser, still paralyzed and perforce watching Slinoor aslant as Slinoor pointed at him, had to admit it was a well-turned reference to himself.

"First off," Slinoor said, "drag those two rogues on deck. Truss them to mast or rail. I'll not have them waking to botch my victory."

"Shall I up with a trap and loose a dart in the after hold?" the starsman asked eagerly.

"You should know better," was all Slinoor answered.

"Shall I gong for the galley and run up a red lamp?" the mate suggested.

Slinoor was silent two heartbeats, then said, "No. This is *Squid*'s fight to wipe out today's shame. Besides, Lukeen's a hothead butcher. Forget I said that, gentlemen, but it is so."

"Yet we'd be safer with the galley standing by," the mate ventured to continue. "Even now the rats may be gnawing holes in us."

"That's unlikely with the Rat-Queen below," Slinoor retorted. "Speed's what will save us and not standby ships. Now hearken close. Guard well all ways to the hold. Keep traps and hatches shut. Rouse the off watch. Arm every man. Gather on middeck all we can spare from sailing. Move!"

The Mouser wished Slinoor hadn't said "Move!" quite so vehemently, for the two sailors instantly

grabbed his ankles and dragged him most enthusiastically out of the littered cabin and across the
middeck, his head bumping a bit. True, he couldn't
feel the bumps, only hear them.

To the west the sky was a quarter globe of stars, to
the east a mass of fog below the thinner mist above,
with the gibbous moon shining through the latter like
a pale misshapen silver ghost-lamp. The wind had
slackened. *Squid* sailed smoothly.

One sailor held the Mouser against the mainmast,
facing aft, while the other looped rope around him.
As the sailors bound him with his arms flat to his
sides, the Mouser felt a tickle in his throat and life
returning to his tongue, but he decided not to try to
speak just yet. Slinoor in his present mood might order him gagged.

The Mouser's next divertisement was watching
Fafhrd dragged out by four sailors and bound
lengthwise, facing inboard with head aft and higher
than feet, to the larboard rail. It was quite a comic
performance, but the Northerner snored through it.

Sailors began to gather then on middeck, some
palely silent but most quipping in low voices. Pikes
and cutlasses gave them courage. Some carried nets
and long sharp-tined forks. Even the cook came with
a great cleaver, which he hefted playfully at the
Mouser.

"Struck dumb with admiration of my sleepy curry,
eh?"

Meanwhile the Mouser found he could move his
fingers. No one had bothered to disarm him, but
Cat's Claw was unfortunately fixed far too high on
his left side for either hand to touch, let alone get out
of its scabbard. He felt the hem of his tunic until he
touched, through the cloth, a rather small flat round

object thinner along one edge than the other. Gripping it by the thick edge through the cloth, he began to scrape with the thin edge at the fabric confining it.

The sailors crowded aft as Slinoor emerged from the cabin with his officers and began to issue low-voiced orders. The Mouser caught, "Slay Hisvet or her maid on sight. They're not women but were-rats or worse," and then the last of Slinoor's orders: "Poise your parties below the hatch or trap by which you enter. When you hear the bosun's whistle, move!"

The effect of this "Move!" was rather spoiled by a tiny *twing* and the arms-master clapping his hand to his eye and screaming. There was a flurry of movement among the sailors. Cutlasses struck at a pale form that scurried along the deck. For an instant a rat with a crossbow in his forepaws was silhouetted on the starboard rail against the moon-pale mist. Then the starsman's crossbow twanged and the dart winging with exceptional accuracy or luck knocked the rat off the rail into the sea.

"That was a whitey, lads!" Slinoor cried. "A good omen!"

Thereafter there was some confusion, but it was quickly settled, especially when it was discovered that the arm's-master had not been struck in the eye but only near it, and the beweaponed parties moved off, one into the cabin, two forward past the mainmast, leaving on deck a skeleton crew of four.

The fabric the Mouser had been scraping parted and he most carefully eased out of the shredded hem an iron tik (the Lankhmar coin of least value) with half its edge honed to razor sharpness and began to slice with it in tiny strokes at the nearest loop of the line binding him. He looked hopefully toward

Fafhrd, but the latter's head still hung at a senseless angle.

A whistle sounded faintly, followed some ten breaths later by a louder one from another part of the hold, it seemed. Then muffled shouts began to come in flurries, there were two screams, something thumped the deck from below, and a sailor swinging a rat squeaking in a net dashed past the Mouser.

The Mouser's fingers told him he was almost through the first loop. Leaving it joined by a few threads, he began to slice at the next loop, bending his wrist acutely to do it.

An explosion shook the deck, stinging the Mouser's feet. He could not conjecture its nature and sawed furiously with his sharpened coin. The skeleton crew cried out and one of the helmsmen fled forward but the other stuck by the tiller. Somehow the gong clanged once, though no one was by it.

Then *Squid*'s sailors began to pour up out of the hold, half of them without weapons and frantic with fear. They milled about. The Mouser could hear sailors dragging *Squid*'s boats, which were forward of the mainmast, to the ship's side. The Mouser gathered that the sailors had fared most evilly below, assaulted by battalions of black rats, confused by false whistles, slashed and jabbed from dark corners, stung by darts, two struck in the eye and blinded. What had completed their rout was that, coming to a hold of unsacked grain, they'd found the air above it choked with grain dust from the recent churnings and scatterings of a horde of rats, and Frix had thrown in fire from beyond, exploding the stuff and knocking them off their feet though not setting fire to the ship.

At the same time as the panic-stricken sailors, there also came on deck another group, noted only by the Mouser—a most quiet and orderly file of black rats that went climbing around him up the mainmast. The Mouser weighed crying an alarm, although he wouldn't have wagered a tik on his chances of survival with hysterical be-cutlassed sailors rat-slashing all around him.

In any case his decision was made for him in the negative by Skwee, who climbed on his left shoulder just then. Holding on by a lock of the Mouser's hair, Skwee leaned out in front of him, staring into the Mouser's left eye with his own two wally blue ones under his black-plumed silver helmet. Skwee touched pale paw to his buck-toothed lips, enjoining silence, then patted the little sword at his side and jerked his rat-thumb across his rat-throat to indicate the penalty for silence broken. Thereafter he retired into the shadows by the Mouser's ear, presumably to watch the routed sailors and wave on and command his own company—and keep close to the Mouser's jugular vein. The Mouser kept sawing with his coin.

The starsman came aft followed by three sailors with two white lanterns apiece. Skwee crowded back closer between the Mouser and the mast, but touched the cold flat of his sword to the Mouser's neck, just under the ear, as a reminder. The Mouser remembered Hisvet's kiss. With a frown at the Mouser the starsman avoided the mainmast and had the sailors hang their lanterns to the aftermast and the crane fittings and the forward range of the afterdeck, fussing about the exact positions. He asserted in a high babble that light was the perfect military defense and counter-weapon, and talked wildly of light-entrenchments and light palisades, and was just about to set the sailors hunting more lamps, when Slinoor limped out of the cabin bloody-fore-headed and looked around.

"Courage, lads," Slinoor shouted hoarsely. "On deck we're still masters. Let down the boats orderly, lads, we'll need 'em to fetch the marines. Run up the red lamp! You there, gong the alarm!"

Someone responded, "The gong's gone overboard. The ropes that hung it—gnawed!"

At the same time thickening waves of fog came out of the east, shrouding *Squid* in deadly moonlit silver. A sailor moaned. It was a strange fog that seemed to increase rather than diminish the amount of light cast by the moon and the starsman's lantern. Colors stood out, yet soon there were only white walls beyond the *Squid*'s rails.

Slinoor ordered, "Get up the spare gong! Cook, let's have your biggest kettles, lids and pots—anything to beat an alarm!"

There were two splashing thumps as *Squid*'s boats hit the water.

Someone screamed agonizingly in the cabin.

Then two things happened together. The mainsail parted from the mast, falling to starboard like a cathedral ceiling in a gale, its lines and ties to the mast gnawed loose or sawed by tiny swords. It floated darkly on the water, dragging the boom wide. *Squid* lurched to starboard.

At the same time a horde of black rats spewed out of the cabin door and came pouring over the taffrail, the latter presumably by way of the stern lights. They rushed at the humans in waves, springing with equal force and resolution whether they landed on pike points or tooth-clinging to noses and throats.

The sailors broke and made for the boats, rats landing on their backs and nipping at their heels. The officers fled too. Slinoor was carried along, crying for a last stand. Skwee out with his sword on the Mouser's shoulder and bravely waved on his suicidal soldiery, chittering high, then leaped down to follow in their rear. Four white rats armed with crossbows knelt on the crane fittings and began to crank, load and fire with great efficiency.

Splashings began, first two and three, then what sounded like a half dozen together, mixed with screams. The Mouser twisted his head around and from the corner of his eye saw the last two of *Squid*'s sailors leap over the side. Straining a little further around yet, he saw Slinoor clutch to his chest two rats that worried him and follow the sailors. The four white-furred arbalesters leaped down from the crane fittings and raced toward a new firing position on the prow. Hoarse human cries came up from the water and faded off. Silence fell on *Squid* like the fog, broken only by the inevitable chitterings—and those few now.

When the Mouser turned his head aft again, Hisvet was standing before him. She was dressed in close-fitting black leather from neck to elbows and knees, looking most like a slim boy, and she wore a black leather helmet fitting down over her temples and cheeks like Skwee's silver one, her white hair streaming down in a tail behind making her plume. A slim dagger was scabbarded on her left hip.

"Dear, dear Dirksman," she said softly, smiling with her little mouth, "you at least do not desert me," and she reached out and almost brushed his cheek with her fingers. Then, "Bound!" she said, seeming to see the rope for the first time and drawing back her hand. "We must remedy that, Dirksman."

"I would be most grateful, White Princess," the Mouser said humbly. Nevertheless, he did not let go his sharpened coin, which although somewhat dulled had now sliced almost halfway through a third loop.

"We must remedy that," Hisvet repeated a little absently, her gaze straying beyond the Mouser. "But my fingers are too soft and unskilled to deal with such mighty knots as I see. Frix will release you. Now I must hear Skwee's report on the afterdeck. Skwee-skwee-skwee!"

As she turned and walked aft the Mouser saw that her hair all went through a silver-ringed hole in the back top of her black helmet. Skwee came running past the Mouser and when he had almost caught up with Hisvet he took position to her right and three rat-paces behind her, strutting with forepaw on sword-hilt and head held high, like a captain-general behind his empress.

As the Mouser resumed his weary sawing of the third loop, he looked at Fafhrd bound to the rail and saw that the black kitten was crouched fur-on-end on Fafhrd's neck and slowly raking his cheek with the spread claws of a forepaw while the Northerner still snored garglingly. The the kitten dipped its head and bit Fafhrd's ear. Fafhrd groaned piteously, but then came another of the gargling snores. The kitten resumed its cheek-raking. Two rats, one white, one black, walked by and the kitten wailed at them softly yet direly. The rats stopped and stared, then scurried straight toward the afterdeck, presumably to report the unwholesome condition to Skwee or Hisvet.

The Mouser decided to burst loose without more ado, but just then the four white arbalesters came back dragging a brass cage of frightened cheeping wrens the Mouser remembered seeing hanging by a sailor's bunk in the forecastle. They stopped by the crane fittings again and started a wren-shoot. They'd release one of the tiny terrified flutterers, then as it winged off bring it down with a well-aimed dart—at distances up to five and six yards, never missing. Once or twice one of them would glance at the Mouser narrowly and touch the dart's point.

Frix stepped down the ladder from the afterdeck. She was now dressed like her mistress, except she had no helmet, only the tight silver hairnet, though the silver rings were gone from her wrists.

"Lady Frix!" the Mouser called in a light voice, almost gaily. It was hard to say how one should speak on a ship manned by rats, but a high voice seemed indicated.

She came toward him smiling, but, "Frix will do better," she said. "Lady is such a corset title."

"Frix then," the Mouser called, "on your way would you scare that black witch cat from our poppy-sodden friend? He'll rake out my comrade's eye."

Frix looked sideways to see what the Mouser meant, but still kept stepping toward him.

"I never interfere with another person's pleasures or pains, since it's hard to be certain which are which," she informed him, coming close. "I only carry out my mistress' directives. Now she bids me tell you be patient and of good cheer. Your trials will soon be over. And this withal she sends you as a re-membrancer." Lifting her mouth, she kissed the Mouser softly on each upper eyelid.

The Mouser said, "That's the kiss with which the green priestess of Djil seals the eyes of those departing this world."

"Is it?" Frix asked softly.

"Aye, 'tis," the Mouser said with a little shudder, continuing briskly, "So now undo me these knots,

Frix, which is something your mistress has directed.
And then perchance give me a livelier smack—after
I've looked to Fafhrd."

"I only carry out the directives of my mistress' own
mouth," Frix said, shaking her head a little sadly.
"She said nothing to me about untying knots. But
doubtless she will direct me to loose you shortly."

"Doubtless," the Mouser agreed, a little glumly,
forbearing to saw with his coin at the third loop while
Frix watched him. If he could but sever at once three
loops, he told himself, he might be able to shake off
the remaining ones in a not impossibly large number
of heartbeats.

As if on cue, Hisvet stepped lightly down from the
afterdeck and hastened to them.

"Dear mistress, do you bid me undo the Dirksman
his knots?" Frix asked at once, almost as if she
wanted to be told to.

"I will attend to matters here," Hisvet replied hurriedly. "Go you to the afterdeck, Frix, and harken
and watch for my father. He delays overlong this
night." She also ordered the white crossbow-rats,
who'd winged their last wren, to retire to the afterdeck.

VI

After Frix and the rats had gone, Hisvet gazed at the Mouser for the space of a score of heartbeats, frowning just a little, studying him deeply with her red-irised eyes.

Finally she said with a sigh, "I wish I could be certain."

"Certain of what, White Princessship?" the Mouser asked.

"Certain that you love me truly," she answered softly yet downrightly, as if he surely knew. "Many men—aye and women too and demons and beasts—have told me they loved me truly, but truly I think none of them loved me for myself (save Frix, whose happiness is in being a shadow) but only because I was young or beautiful or a Demoiselle of Lankhmar or dreadfully clever or had a rich father or was dowered with power, being blood-related to the rats, which is a certain sign of power in more worlds than Nehwon. Do you truly love me for myself, Gray Mouser?"

"I love you most truly indeed, Shadow Princess,"

the Mouser said with hardly an instant's hesitation.
"Truly I love you for yourself alone, Hisvet. I love you
more dearly than aught else in Nehwon—aye, and in
all other worlds too and heaven and hell besides."

Just then Fafhrd, cruelly clawed or bit by the kitten,
let off a most piteous groan indeed with a dreadful
high note in it, and the Mouser said impulsively,
"Dear Princess, first chase me that were-cat from my
large friend, for I fear it will be blinding and death's
bane, and then we shall discourse of our great loves
to the end of eternity."

"*That* is what I mean," Hisvet said softly and reproachfully. "If you loved me truly for myself, Gray
Mouser, you would not care a feather if your closest
friend or your wife or mother or child were tortured
and done to death before your eyes, so long as my
eyes were upon you and I touched you with my fingertips. With my kisses on your lips and my slim
hands playing about you, my whole person accepting
and welcoming you, you could watch your large
friend there scratched to blindness and death by a
cat—or mayhap eaten alive by rats—and be utterly
content. I have touched few things in this world,
Gray Mouser. I have touched no man, or male demon or larger male beast, save by the proxy of Frix.
Remember that, Gray Mouser."

"To be sure, Dear Light of my Life!" the Mouser
replied most spiritedly, certain now of the sort of self-
adoring madness with which he had to deal, since he
had a touch of the same mania and so was well-ac-
quainted with it. "Let the barbarian bleed to death
by pinpricks! Let the cat have his eyes! Let the rats
banquet on him to his bones! What skills it while we
trade sweet words and caresses, discoursing to each
other with our entire bodies and our whole souls!"

Meanwhile, however, he had started to saw again

most fiercely with his now-dulled coin, unmindful of
Hisvet's eyes upon him. It joyed him to feel Cat's
Claw lying against his ribs.

"That's spoken like my own true Mouser," Hisvet
said with most melting tenderness, brushing her fingers so close to his cheek that he could feel the tiny
chill zephyr of their passage. Then, turning, she
called, "Holla, Frix! Send to me Skwee and the
White Company. Each may bring with him two
black comrades of his own choice. I have somewhat
of a reward for them, somewhat of a special treat.
Skwee! Skwee-skwee-skwee!"

What would have happened then, both instantly
and ultimately, is impossible to say, for at that moment Frix hailed, "Ahoy!" into the fog and called
happily down, "A black sail! Oh Blessed Demoiselle,
it is your father!"

Out of the pearly fog to starboard came the
shark's-fin triangle of the upper portion of a black
sail, running alongside *Squid* aft of the dragging
brown mainsail. Two boathooks, a small ship's
length apart, came up and clamped down on the
starboard middeck rail while the black sail flapped.
Frix came running lightly forward and secured to the
rail midway between the boathooks the top of a rope
ladder next heaved up from the black cutter (for surely this must be that dire craft, the Mouser thought).

Then up the ladder and over the rail came nimbly
an old man of Lankhmar dressed all in black leather
and on his left shoulder a white rat clinging with
right forepaw to a cheekflap of his black leather cap.
He was followed swiftly by two lean bald Mingols
with faces yellow-brown as old lemons, each
shoulder bearing a large black rat that steadied itself
by a yellow ear.

At that moment, most coincidentally, Fafhrd groaned again, more loudly, and opened his eyes and cried out in the faraway moan of an opium-dreamer, "Millions of black monkeys! Take him off, I say! 'Tis a black fiend of hell torments me! Take him off!"

At that the black kitten raised up, stretched out its small evil face, and bit Fafhrd on the nose. Disregarding this interruption, Hisvet threw up her hand at the newcomers and cried clearly, "Greetings, oh Co-commander my Father! Greetings, peerless rat-captain Grig! *Clam* is conquered by you, now *Squid* by me, and this very night, after small business of my own attended to, shall see the perdition of all this final fleet. Then it's Movarl estranged, the Mingols across the Sinking Land, Glipkerio hurled down, and the rats ruling Lankhmar under my overlordship and yours!"

The Mouser, sawing ceaselessly at the third loop, chanced to note Skwee's muzzle at that moment. The small white captain had come down from the afterdeck at Hisvet's summoning along with eight white comrades, two bandaged, and now he shot Hisvet a silent look that seemed to say there might be doubts about the last item of her boast, once the rats ruled Lankhmar.

Hisvet's father Hisvin had a long-nosed, much wrinkled face patched by a week of white, old-man's beard, and he seemed permanently stooped far over, yet he moved most briskly for all that, taking very rapid little shuffling steps.

Now he answered his daughter's bragging speech with a petulant sideways flirt of his black glove close to his chest and a little impatient "Tsk-tsk!" of disapproval, then went circling the deck at his odd scuttling gait while the Mingols waited by the ladder-top. Hisvin circled by Fafhrd and his black tormenter ("Tsk-tsk!") and by the Mouser (another "Tsk!") and stopping in front of Hisvet said rapid and fumingly, still crouched over, jogging a bit from foot to foot, "Here's confusion indeed tonight! You catsing and romancing with bound men!—I know, I know! The moon coming through too much! (I'll have my astrologer's liver!) *Shark* oaring like a mad cuttlefish through the foggy white! A black balloon with little lights scudding above the waves! And but now ere we found you, a vast sea monster swimming about in circles with a gibbering demon on his head—it came sniffing at us as if we were dinner, but we evaded it!

"Daughter, you and your maid and your little people must into the cutter at once with us, pausing only to slay these two and leave a suicide squad of gnawers to sink *Squid!*"

"Yeth, think *Thquid!*" the Mouser could have sworn he heard the rat on Hisvin's shoulder lisp shrilly in Lankhmarese.

"Sink *Squid?*" Hisvet questioned. "The plan was to slip her to Ilthmar with a Mingol skeleton crew and there sell her cargo."

"Plans change!" Hisvin snapped. "Daughter, if we're not off this ship in forty breaths, *Shark* will ram us by pure excess of blundering energy or the monster with the clown-clad mad mahout will eat us up as we drift here helpless. Give orders to Skwee! Then out with your knife and cut me those two fools' throats! Quick, quick!"

"But, Daddy," Hisvet objected, "I had something quite different in mind for them. Not death, at least not altogether. Something far more artistic, even loving—"

"I give you thirty breaths each to torture ere you slay them!" Hisvin conceded. "Thirty breaths and not one more, mind you! I know your somethings!"

"Dad, don't be crude! Among new friends! *Why* must you always give people a wrong impression of me? I won't endure it longer!"

"Chat-chat-chat! You pother and pose more than your rat-mother."

"But I tell you I won't endure it. This time we're going to do things *my* way for a change!"

"Hist-hist!" her father commanded, stooping still lower and cupping hand to left ear, while his white rat Grig imitated his gesture on the other side.

Faintly through the fog came a gibbering. "*Gottverdammter Nebel! Freunde, wo sind Sie?*"*

"'Tis the gibberer!" Hisvin cried under his breath. "The monster will be upon us! Quick, daughter, out with your knife and slay, or I'll have my Mingols dispatch them!"

Hisvet lifted her hand against that villainous possibility. Her proudly plumed head literally bent to the inevitable.

"I'll do it," she said. "Skwee, give me your crossbow. Load with silver."

The white rat-captain folded his forelegs across his chest and chittered at her with a note of demand.

"No, you can't have him," she said sharply. "You can't have either of them. They're mine now."

Another curt chitter from Skwee.

"Very well, your people may have the small black one. Now quick with your crossbow or I'll curse you! Remember, only a smooth silver dart."

---

*"Goddam fog! Friends, where are you?" Evidently Karl Treuherz Lankhmarese dictionary was unavailable to him at the moment.

Hisvin had scuttled to his Mingols and now he went around in a little circle, almost spitting. Frix, smiling, glided to him and touched his arm but he shook away from her with an angry flirt.

Skwee was fumbling into his cannister rat-frantically. His eight comrades were fanning out across the deck toward Fafhrd and the black kitten, which leaped down now in front of Fafhrd, snarling defiance.

Fafhrd himself was looking about bloody-faced but at last lucid-eyed, drinking in the desperate situation, poppy-languor banished by nose-bite.

Just then there came another gibber through the fog, *"Gottverdammter Nirgendswelt!"**

Fafhrd's bloodshot eyes widened and brightened with a great inspiration. Bracing himself against his bonds, he inflated his mighty chest.

"Hoongk!" he bellowed. *"Hoongk!"*

Out of the fog came eager answer, growing each time louder: "Hoongk! *Hoongk! Hoongk!"*

Seven of the eight white rats that had crossed the deck now returned carrying stretched between them the still-snarling black kitten, spread-eagled on its back, one to each paw and ear while the seventh tried to master but was shaken from side to side by the whipping tail. The eighth came hobbling behind on three legs, shoulder paralyzed by a deep-stabbing cat-bite.

From cabin and forecastle and all corners of the deck, the black rats scurried in to watch gloatingly their traditional enemy mastered and delivered to torment, until the middeck was thick with their bloaty dark forms.

Hisvin cracked a command at his Mingols. Each

---

*"Goddam Nowhere-World!"

drew a wavy-edged knife. One headed for Fafhrd, the other for the Mouser. Black rats hid their feet.

Skwee dumped his tiny darts on the deck. His paw closed on a palely gleaming one and he slapped it in his crossbow, which he hurriedly handed up toward his mistress. She lifted it in her right hand toward Fafhrd, but just then the Mingol moving toward the Mouser crossed in front of her, his kreese point-first before him. She shifted crossbow to left hand, whipped out her dagger and darted ahead of the Mingol.

Meanwhile the Mouser had snapped the three cut loops with one surge. The others still confined him loosely at ankles and throat, but he reached across his body, drew Cat's Claw and slashed out at the Mingol as Hisvet shouldered the yellow man aside.

The dirk sliced her pale cheek from jaw to nose.

The other Mingol, advancing his kreese toward Fafhrd's throat, abruptly dropped to the deck and began to roll back across it, the black rats squeaking and snapping at him in surprise.

"*Hoongk!*"

A great green dragon's head had loomed from the moon-mist over the larboard rail just at the spot where Fafhrd was tied. Strings of slaver trailed on the Northerner from the dagger-toothed jaws.

Like a ponderous jack-in-the-box, the red-mawed head dipped and drove forward, lower jaw rasping the oaken deck and sweeping up from a swath of black rats three rats wide. The jaws crunched together on their great squealing mouthful inches from the rolling Mingol's head. Then the green head swayed aloft and a horrid swelling traveled down the green-ish yellow neck.

But even as it poised there for a second strike, it shrank in size by comparison with what now appeared out of the mist after it—a second green dragon's head fourfold larger and fantastically crested in red, orange and purple (for at first sight the rider seemed to be part of the monster). This head now drove forward as if it were that of the father of all dragons, sweeping up a black-rat swath twice as wide as had the first and topping off its monster gobble with the two white rats behind the rat-carried black kitten.

It ended its first strike so suddenly (perhaps to avoid eating the kitten) that its parti-colored rider, who'd been waving his pike futilely, was hurled forward off its green head. The rider sailed low past the mainmast, knocking aside the Mingol striking at the Mouser, and skidded across the deck into the starboard rail.

The white rats let go of the kitten, which raced for the mainmast.

Then the two green heads, famished by their two days of small fishy pickings since their last real meal at the Rat Rocks, began methodically to sweep *Squid's* deck clean of rats, avoiding humans for the most part, though not very carefully. And the rats, huddled in their mobs, did little to evade this dreadful mowing. Perhaps in their straining toward world-dominion they had grown just human and civilized enough to experience imaginative, unhelpful, freezing panic and to have acquired something of humanity's talent for inviting and enduring destruction. Perhaps they looked on the dragons' heads as the twin red maws of war and hell, into which they must throw themselves willy-nilly. At all events they were swept up by dozens and scores. All but three of the white rats were among those engulfed.

Meanwhile the larger people aboard *Squid* faced up variously to the drastically altered situation.

Old Hisvin shook his fist and spat in the larger
dragon's face when after its first gargantuan swallow
it came questing toward him, as if trying to decide
whether this bent black thing were (ugh!) a very
queer man or (yum!) a very large rat. But when the
stinking apparition kept coming on, Hisvin rolled
deftly over the rail as if into bed and swiftly climbed
down the rope ladder, fairly chittering in consternation, while Grig clung for dear life to the back of the
black leather collar.

Hisvin's two Mingols picked themselves up and
followed him, vowing to get back to their cozy cold
steppes as soon as Mingolly possible.

Fafhrd and Karl Treuherz watched the melee from
opposite sides of the middeck, the one bound by
ropes, the other by out-wearied astonishment.

Skwee and a white rat named Siss ran over the
heads of their packed apathetic black fellows and
hopped on the starboard rail. There they looked
back. Siss blinked in horror. But Skwee, his black-
plumed helmet pushed down over his left eye, menaced with his little sword and chittered defiance.

Frix ran to Hisvet and urged her to the starboard
rail. As they neared the head of the rope ladder,
Skwee went down it to make way for his empress,
dragging Siss with him. Just then Hisvet turned like
someone in a dream. The smaller dragon's head
drove toward her viciously. Frix sprang in the way,
arms wide, smiling, a little like a ballet dancer taking
a curtain call. Perhaps it was the suddenness or
seeming aggressiveness of her move that made the
dragon sheer off, fangs clashing. The two girls
climbed the rail.

Hisvet turned again, Cat's Claw's cut a bold red
line across her face, and sighted her crossbow at the

Mouser. There was the faintest silvery flash. Hisvet tossed the crossbow in the black sea and followed Frix down the ladder. The boathooks let go, the flapping black sail filled, and the black cutter faded into the mist.

The Mouser felt a little sting in his left temple, but he forgot it while whirling the last loops from his shoulders and ankles. Then he ran across the deck, disregarding the green heads lazily searching for last rat morsels, and cut Fafhrd's bonds.

All the rest of that night the two adventurers conversed with Karl Treuherz, telling each other fabulous things about each other's worlds, while Scylla's sated daughter slowly circled *Squid,* first one head sleeping and then the other. Talking was slow and uncertain work, even with the aid of the little Lankhmarese-German German-Lankhmarese Dictionary for Space-Time and Inter-Cosmic Travelers, and neither party really believed a great deal of the other's tales, yet pretended to for friendship's sake.

"Do all men dress as grandly as you do in Tomorrow?" Fafhrd once asked, admiring the German's purple and orange garb.

"No, Hagenbeck just has his employees do it, to spread his time zoo's fame," Karl Treuherz explained.

The last of the mist vanished just before dawn and they saw, silhouetted against the sea silvered by the sinking gibbous moon, the black ship of Karl Treuherz hovering not a bowshot west of *Squid,* its little lights twinkling softly.

The German shouted for joy, summoned his sleepy monster by thwacking his pike against the rail, swung astride the larger head, and swam off calling after him, *"Auf Wiedersehen!"*

Fafhrd had learned just enough Gibberish during the night to know this meant, "Until we meet again."

When the monster and the German had swum below it, the space-time engine descended, somehow engulfing them. Then a little later the black ship vanished.

"It dove into the infinite waters toward Karl's Tomorrow bubble," the Gray Mouser affirmed confidently. "By Ning and by Sheel, the German's a master magician!"

Fafhrd blinked, frowned, and then simply shrugged.

The black kitten rubbed his ankle. Fafhrd lifted it gently to eye level, saying, "I wonder, kitten, if you're one of the Cat's Thirteen or else their small agent, sent to wake me when waking was needful?" The kitten smiled solemnly into Fafhrd's cruelly scratched and bitten face and purred.

Clear gray dawn spread across the waters of the Inner Sea, showing them first *Squid*'s two boats crowded with men and Slinoor sitting dejected in the stern of the nearer but standing with uplifted hand as he recognized the figures of the Mouser and Fafhrd; next Lukeen's war galley *Shark* and the three other grain ships *Tunny*, *Carp* and *Grouper;* lastly, small on the northern horizon, the green sails of two dragon-ships of Movarl.

The Mouser, running his left hand back through his hair, felt a short, straight, rounded ridge in his temple under the skin. He knew it was Hisvet's smooth silver dart, there to stay.

VII

Fafhrd awoke consumed by thirst and amorous yearning, and with a certainty that it was late afternoon. He knew where he was and, in a general way, what had been happening, but his memory for the past half day or so was at the moment foggy. His situation was that of a man who stands on a patch of ground with mountains sharp-etched all around, but the middle distance hidden by a white sea of ground-mist.

He was in leafy Kvarch Nar, chief of the Eight so-called Cities—truly, none of them could compare with Lankhmar, the only city worth the name on the Inner Sea. And he was in his room in the straggling, low, unwalled, yet shapely wooden palace of Movarl. Four days ago the Mouser had sailed for Lankhmar aboard *Squid* with a cargo of lumber which the thrifty Slinoor had shipped, to report to Glipkerio the safe delivery of four-fifths of the grain, the eerie treacheries of Hisvin and Hisvet, and the whole mad adventure. Fafhrd, however, had chosen to remain a while in Kvarch Nar, for to him it was a fun-place, not least because he had found a fun-loving, handsome girl there, one Hrenlet.

More particularly, Fafhrd was snug abed but feeling somewhat constricted—clearly he had not taken off his boots or any other of his clothing or even unbelted his short-ax, the blade of which, fortunately covered by its thick leather sheath, stuck into his side. Yet he was also filled with a sense of glorious achievement—why, he wasn't yet sure, but it was a grand feeling.

Without opening his eyes or moving any part of him the thickness of a Lankhmar penny a century old, he oriented himself. To his left, within easy arm-reach on a stout night table would be a large pewter flagon of light wine. Even now he could sense, he thought, its coolth. Good.

To his right, within even easier reach, Hrenlet. He could feel her radiant warmth and hear her snoring —very loudly, in fact.

Or was it Hrenlet for certain?—or at any rate *only* Hrenlet? She had been very merry last night before he went to the gaming table, playfully threatening to introduce him intimately to a red-haired and hot-blooded female cousin of hers from Ool Hrusp, where they had great wealth in cattle. Could it be that . . .? At any rate, good too, or even better.

While under his downy thick pillows— Ah, there was the explanation for his ever-mounting sense of glory! Late last night he had cleaned them all out of every golden Lankhmarian rilk, every golden Kvarch Nar gront, every golden coin from the Eastern Lands, Quarmall, or elsewhere! Yes, he remembered it well now: he had taken them all—and at the simple game of sixes and seven, where the banker wins if he matches the number of coins the player holds in his fist; those Eight-City fools didn't realize they tried to make their fists big when they held six golden coins and tightened them when they held seven. Yes, he had turned all their pockets and pouches inside out—and at the end he had crazily matched a quarter of his winnings against an oddly engraved slim tin whistle supposed to have magical properties . . . and won that too! And then saluted them all and reeled off happily, well-ballasted by gold like a treasure galleon, to bed and Hrenlet. Had he had Hrenlet? He wasn't sure.

Fafhrd permitted himself a dry-throated, raspy yawn. Was ever man so fortunate? At his left hand, wine. At his right a beauteous girl, or more likely two, since there was a sweet strong farm-smell coming to him under the sheets; and what is juicier than a farmer's (or cattleman's) redhead daughter? While under his pillows— He twisted his head and neck luxuriously; he couldn't quite feel the tight-bulging bag of golden coins—the pillows were many and thick—but he could imagine it.

He tried to recall why he had made that last hare-brained successful wager. The curly-bearded braggart had claimed he had the slim tin whistle of a wise woman and that it summoned thirteen helpful beasts of some sort—and this had recalled to Fafhrd the wise woman who had told him in his youth that each sort of animal has its governing thirteen—and so his sentimentality had been awakened—and he had wanted to get the whistle as a present for the Gray Mouser, who doted on the little props of magic—yes, that was it!

Eyes still shut, Fafhrd plotted his course of action. He suddenly stretched out his left arm blind and without any groping fastened it on the pewter flagon

—it was even bedewed!—and drained half of it—
nectar!—and set it back.

Then with his right hand he stroked the girl—
Hrenlet, or her cousin?—from shoulder to haunch.

She was covered with short bristly fur and, at his
amorous touch, she mooed!

Fafhrd wide-popped his eyes and jackknifed up in
the bed, so that sunlight, striking low through the
small unglazed window, drenched him yellowly and
made a myriad wonder of the hand-polished woods
paneling the room, their grains an infinitely varied
arabesque. Beside him, pillowed as thickly as he was
—and possibly drugged—was a large, long-eared,
pink-nostriled auburn calf. Suddenly he could feel
her hooves through his boots, and drew the latter
abruptly back. Beyond her was no girl—or even other calf—at all.

He dove his right hand under his pillows. His fingers touched the familiar double-stitched leather of
his pouch, but instead of being ridgy and taut with
gold pieces, it was, except for one thin cylinder—that
tin whistle—flat as an unleavened Sarheenmar pan-
cake.

He flung back the bedclothes so that they bellied
high and wild in the air, like a sail torn loose in a
squall. Thrusting the burgled purse under his belt,
he vaulted out of bed, snatched up his long-sword by
its furry scabbard—he intended it for spanking
purposes—and dashed through the heavy double
drapes out the door, pausing only to dump down his
throat the last of the wine.

Despite his fury at Hrenlet, he had to admit, as he
hurriedly quaffed, that she had dealt honestly with
him up to a point: his bed-comrade was female, red-
haired, indubitably from the farm and—for a calf—

beauteous, while her now-alarmed mooing had nevertheless a throaty amorous quality.

The common-room was another wonder of polished wood—Movarl's kingdom was so young that its forests were still its chief wealth. Most of the windows showed green leaves close beyond. From walls and ceiling jutted fantastic demons and winged warrior-maidens all wood-carved. Here and there against the wall leaned beautifully polished bows and spears. A wide doorway led out to a narrow courtyard where a bay stallion moved restlessly under an irregular green roof. The city of Kvarch Nar had twenty times as many mighty trees as homes.

About the common-room lounged a dozen men clad in green and brown, drinking wine, playing at board-games, and conversing. They were dark-bearded brawny fellows, a little shorter—though not much—than Fafhrd.

Fafhrd instantly noted that they were the identical fellows whom he had stripped of their gold-pieces at last night's play. And this tempted him—hot with rage and fired by gulped wine—into a near-fatal indiscretion.

"Where is that thieving, misbegotten Hrenlet?" he roared, shaking his scabbarded sword above his head. "She's stolen from under my pillows all my winnings!"

Instantly the twelve sprang to their feet, hands gripping sword hilts. The burliest took a step toward Fafhrd, saying icily, "You dare suggest that a noble maiden of Kvarch Nar shared your bed, barbarian?"

Fafhrd realized his mistake. His liaison with Hrenlet, though obvious to all, had never before been remarked on, because the women of the Eight Cities are revered by their men and may do what they wish,

no matter how licentious. But woe betide the out-
lander who puts this into words.

Yet Fafhrd's rage still drove him beyond reason.
"Noble?" he cried. "She's a liar and a whore! Her
arms are two white snakes, a-crawl 'neath the
blankets—for gold, not man-flesh! Despite which,
she's also a shepherd of lusts and pastures her flock
between my sheets!"

A dozen swords came screeching out of their scabbards at that and there was a rush. Fafhrd grew
logical, almost too late. There seemed only one
chance of survival left. He sprinted straight for the
big door, parrying with his still-scabbarded sword
the hasty blows of Movarl's henchmen, raced across
the courtyard, vaulted into the saddle of the bay, and
kicked him into a gallop.

He risked one backward look as the bay's iron-
shod hooves began to strike sparks from the flinty
narrow forest road. He was rewarded by a vivid
glimpse of his yellow-haired Hrenlet leaning bare-
armed in her shift from an upper window and laughing heartily.

A half-dozen arrows whirred viciously around him
and he devoted himself to getting more speed from
the bay. He was three leagues along the winding
road to Klelg Nar, which runs east through the thick
forest close to the coast of the Inner Sea, when he
decided that the whole business had been a trick,
worked by last night's losers in league with Hrenlet,
to regain their gold—and perhaps one of them his
girl—and that the arrows had been deliberately
winged to miss.

He drew up the bay and listened. He could hear no
pursuit. That pretty well confirmed it.

Yet there was no turning back now. Even Movarl

could hardly protect him after he had spoken the words he had of a Lankhmar lady.

There were no ports between Kvarch Nar and Klelg Nar. He would have to ride at least that far around the Inner Sea, somehow evading the Mingols besieging Klelg Nar, if he were to get back to Lankhmar and his share of Glipkerio's reward for bringing all the grain ships save *Clam* safe to port. It was most irksome.

Yet he still could not really hate Hrenlet. This horse was a stout one and there was a big saddlebag of food balancing a large canteen of wine. Besides, its reddish hue delightfully echoed that of the calf. A rough joke, but a good one.

Also, he couldn't deny that Hrenlet had been magnificent between the sheets—a superior sort of slim unfurred cow, and witty too.

He dipped in his pancake-flat pouch and examined the tin whistle, which aside from memories was now his sole spoil from Kvarch Nar. It had down one side of it a string of undecipherable characters and down the other the figure of a slim feline beast couchant. He grinned widely, shaking his head. What a fool was a drunken gambler! He made to toss it away, then remembered the Mouser and returned it to his pouch.

He touched the bay with his heels and cantered on toward Klelg Nar, whistling an eerie but quickening Mingol march.

Nehwon—a vast bubble leaping up forever through the waters of eternity. Like airy champagne . . . or, to certain moralists, like a globe of stinking gas from the slimiest, most worm-infested marsh.

Lankhmar—a continent firm-seated on the solid

watery inside of the bubble called Nehwon. With mountains, hills, towns, plains, a crooked coastline, deserts, lakes, marshes too, and grainfields—especially grainfields, source of the continent's wealth, to either side of the Hlal, greatest of rivers.

And on the continent's northern tip, on the east bank of the Hlal, mistress of the grainfields and their wealth, the City of Lankhmar, oldest in the world. Lankhmar, thick-walled against barbarians and beasts, thick-floored against creepers and crawlers and gnawers.

At the south of the City of Lankhmar, the Grain Gate, its twenty-foot thickness and thirty-foot width often echoing with the creak of ox-drawn wagons bringing in Lankhmar's tawny, dry, edible treasure. Also the Grand Gate, larger still and more glorious, and the smaller End Gate. Then the South Barracks with its black-clad soldiery, the Rich Men's Quarter, the Park of Pleasure and the Plaza of Dark Delights. Next Whore Street and the streets of other crafts. Beyond those, crossing the city from the Marsh Gate to the docks, the Street of the Gods, with its many flamboyantly soaring fanes of the Gods *in* Lankhmar and its single squat black temple of the Gods *of* Lankhmar—more like an ancient tomb except for its tall, square, eternally silent bell-tower. Then the slums and the windowless homes of the nobles; the great grain-towers, like a giant's forest of house-thick tree-trunks chopped off evenly. Finally, facing the Inner Sea to the north and the Hlal to the west, the North Barracks, and on a hill of solid, sea-sculptured rock, the Citadel and the Rainbow Palace of Glipkerio Kistomerces.

An adolescent serving maid balancing on her close-shaven head with aid of a silver coronet-ring a large tray of sweetmeats and brimming silver goblets,

strode like a tightrope walker into a green-tiled antechamber of the Blue Audience Chamber of that palace. She wore black leather collars around her neck,
wrists, and slender waist. Light silver chains a little
shorter than her forearms tied her wrist-collars to her
waist-collar—it was Glipkerio's whim that no maid's
finger should touch his food or even its tray and that
every maid's balance be perfect. Aside from her collars she was unclothed, while aside from her short-
clipped eyelashes, she was entirely shaven—another
of the fantastic monarch's dainty whims, that no hair
should drop in his soup. She looked like a doll before
it is dressed, its wig affixed, and its eyebrows painted
on.

The sea-hued tiles lining the chamber were hex-
agonal and big as the palm of a large hand. Most
were plain, but here and there were ones figured with
sea creatures: a mollusk, a cod, an octopus, a sea
horse.

The maid was almost halfway to the narrow, curtained archway leading to the Blue Audience
Chamber when her gaze became fixed on a tile in the
floor a long stride from the archway ahead but somewhat to the left. It was figured with a sea lion. It
lifted the breadth of a thumb, like a little trapdoor,
and eyes with a jetty gleam a finger-joint apart
peered out at her.

She shook from toes to head, but her tight-bitten
lips uttered no sound. The goblets chinked faintly, the
tray began to slide, but she got her head under its
center again with a swift sidewise ducking movement, and then began to go with long fearful steps
around the horrid tile as far as she could to the right,
so that the edge of the tray was hardly a finger's-
breadth from the wall.

Just under the edge of the tray, as if that were a

porch-roof, a plain green tile in the wall opened like a door and a rat's black face thrust out with spade-teeth bared.

The maid leaped convulsively away, still in utter silence. The tray left her head. She tried to get under it. The floortile clattered open wide and a long-bodied black rat came undulating out. The tray struck the dodging maid's shoulder, she strained toward it futilely with her short-chained hands, then it struck the floor with a nerve-shattering clangor and all the spilled goblets rang.

As the silver reverberations died, there was else only the rapid soft *thump* of her bare feet running back the way she had come. One goblet rolled a last turn. Then there was desert stillness in the green antechamber.

Two hundred heartbeats later, it was broken by another muted thudding of bare feet, this time those of a party returning the way the maid had run. There entered first, watchful-eyed, two shaven-headed, white-smocked, browny cooks, each armed with a cleaver in one hand and a long toasting-fork in the other. Second, two naked and shaven kitchen boys, bearing many wet and dry rags and a broom of black feathers. After them, the maid, her silver chains gathered in her hands, so that they would not chink from her trembling. Behind her, a monstrously fat woman in a dress of thick black wool that went to her redoubled chins and plump knuckles and hid her surely monstrous feet and ankles. Her black hair was dressed in a great round beehive stuck through and through with long black-headed pins, so that it was as if she bore a prickly planet on her head. This appeared to be the case, for her puffed face was weighted with a world of sullenness and hate. Her black eyes peered stern and all-distrustful from between folds of fat, while a sparse black moustache, like the ghost of a black centipede, crossed her upper lip. Around her vast belly, she wore a broad leather belt from which hung at intervals keys, thongs, chains, and whips. The kitchen boys believed she had deliberately grown mountain-fat to keep them from clinking together and so warn them when she came a-spying.

Now the fat kitchen-queen and palace mistress stared shrewdly around the antechamber, then spread her humpy palms, glaring at the maid. Not one green tile was displaced.

In like dumb-show, the maid nodded vehemently, pointing from her waist at the tile figured with a sea lion, then threaded tremblingly forward between the spilled stuff and touched it with her toe.

One of the cooks quickly knelt and gently thumped it and the surrounding tiles with a knuckle. Each time the faint sound was equally solid. He tried to get the tines of his fork under the sea lion tile from every side and failed.

The maid ran to the wall where the other glazed door had opened and searched the bare tiles frantically, her slim hands tugging uselessly. The other cook thumped the tiles she indicated without getting a hollow sound.

The glare of the palace mistress changed from suspicion to certainty. She advanced on the maid like a storm cloud, her eyes its lightning, and suddenly thrusting out her two ham-like arms, snapped a thong to a silver ring in the maid's collar. That snap was the loudest sound yet.

The maid shook her head wildly three times. Her trembling increased, then suddenly stopped altogether. As the palace mistress led her back the way they had come, she drooped her head and shoulders, and at the first vindictive downward jerk dropped to her hands and knees and padded rapidly, dog-fashion.

Under the watchful eyes of one of the cooks, the kitchen boys began swiftly to clean up the mess, wrapping each goblet in a rag ere they laid it on the platter, lest it chink. Their gazes kept darting fearfully about at the myriad tiles.

The Gray Mouser, standing on *Squid*'s gently-dipping prow, sighted the soaring Citadel of Lankhmar through the dispersing fog. Beyond it to the east there soon came into view the square-topped minarets of the Overlord's palace, each finished in stone of different hue, and to the south the dun granaries like vast smokestacks. He hailed the first sea-wherry he saw to *Squid*'s side. With the black kitten spitting at him reproachfully, and against Slinoor's command—but before Slinoor could decide to have him forcibly restrained—he slid down the long boathook with which the prow wherryman had caught hold of *Squid*'s rail. Landing lightly in the wherry, he gave an approving shoulder-pat to the astonished hookholder, then commanded, promising a fat fee, that he be rowed with all speed to the palace dock. The hook was shipped, the Mouser wove his way to the slender craft's stern, the three wherrymen out-oared and the craft raced east over the silty water, brown with mud from the Hlal.

The Mouser called consolingly back to Slinoor, "Never fear, I will make a marvelous report to Glipkerio, praising you to the skies—and even Lukeen to the height of a low raincloud!"

Then he faced forward, faintly smiling and frowning at once in thought. He was somewhat sorry he had had to desert Fafhrd, who had been immersed in an apparently endless drinking and dicing bout with Movarl's toughest henchmen when *Squid* had sailed from Kvarch Nar—the great oafs died of wine and their losses each dawn, but were reborn in the late afternoon with thirst restored and money-pouches miraculously refilled.

But he was even more pleased that now he alone would bear to Glipkerio Movarl's thanks for the four shiploads of grain and be able all by himself to tell the wondrous tale of the dragon, the rats, and their human masters—or colleagues. By the time Fafhrd got back from Kvarch Nar, broken-pursed and likely broken-pated too, the Mouser would be occupying a fine apartment in Glipkerio's palace and be able subtly to irk his large comrade by offering him hospitalities and favors.

He wondered idly where Hisvin and Hisvet and their small entourage were now. Perhaps in Sarheenmar, or more likely Ilthmar, or already lurching by camel-train from that city to some retreat in the Eastern Lands, to be well away from Glipkerio's and Movarl's vengeance. Unwilled, his left hand rose to his temple, gently fingering the tiny straight ridge there. Truly, at this already dreamy distance, he could not hate Hisvet or the brave proxy-creature Frix. Surely Hisvet's vicious threats had been in part a kind of love-play. He did not doubt that some part of her yearned for him. Besides, he had marked her far worse than she had marked him. Well, perhaps he would meet her again some year in some far corner of the world.

These foolishly forgiving and forgetting thoughts of the Mouser were in part due, he knew himself, to his present taut yearning for any acceptable girl.

Kvarch Nar under Movarl had proved a strait-laced
city, by the Mouser's standards, and during his brief
stay the one erring girl encountered—one Hrenlet—
had chosen to err with Fafhrd. Well, Hrenlet had
been something of a giantess, albeit slender, and now
he was in Lankhmar, where he knew a dozen score
spots to ease his tautness.

The silty-brown water gave way abruptly to deep
green. The sea-wherry passed beyond the outflow of
the Hlal and was darting along atop the Lankhmar
Deep, which dove down sheer-walled and bottomless
at the very foot of the wave-pitted great rock on
which stood the citadel and the palace. And now the
wherrymen had to row out around a strange obstruc-
tion: a copper chute wide as a man is tall that,
braced by great brazen beams, angled down from a
porch of the palace almost to the surface of the sea.
The Mouser wondered if the whimmy Glipkerio had
taken up aquatic sports during his absence. Or perhaps this was a new way of disposing of unsatisfac-
tory servants and slaves—sliding them suitably
weighted into the sea. Then he noted a spindle-
shaped vehicle (if it was that) thrice as long as a man
and made of some dull gray metal poised at the top
of the chute. A puzzle.

The Mouser dearly loved puzzles, if only to
elaborate on them rather than solve them, but he had
no time for this one. The wherry had drawn up at the
royal wharf, and he was haughtily exhibiting to the
clamoring eunuchs and guards his starfish-
emblemed courier's ring from Glipkerio and his
parchment sealed with the cross-sworded seal of
Movarl.

The latter seemed to impress the palace-fry most.
He was swiftly bowed across the dock, mounted a

dizzily tall, gaily-painted wooden stair, and found himself in Glipkerio's audience chamber—a glorious sea-fronting blue-tiled room, each large triangular tile bearing a fishy emblem in bas-relief.

The room was huge despite the blue curtains dividing it now into two halves. A pair of naked and shaven pages bowed to the Mouser and parted the curtains for him. Their sinuous silent movements against that blue background made him think of mermen. He stepped through the narrow triangular opening—to be greeted by a rather distant but imperious "Hush!"

Since the hissing command came from the puckered lips of Glipkerio himself and since one of the beanpole monarch's hand-long skinny fingers now rose and crossed those lips, the Mouser stopped dead. With a fainter hiss the blue curtains fell together behind him.

It was a strange and most startling scene that presented itself. The Mouser's heart missed a beat—mostly in self-outrage that his imagination had completely missed the weird possibility that was now staged before him.

Three broad archways led out onto a porch on which rested the pointy-ended gray vehicle he had noted balanced at the top of the chute. Now he could see a hinged manhole toward its out-jutting bow.

At the near end of the room was a large, thick-bottomed, close-barred cage containing at least a score of black rats, which chittered and wove around each other ceaselessly and sometimes clattered the bars menacingly.

At the far end of the sea-blue room, near the circular stair leading up into the palace's tallest minaret, Glipkerio had risen in excitement from his golden audience couch shaped like a seashell. The fantastic overlord stood a head higher than Fafhrd, but was thin as a starved Mingol. His black toga made him look like a funeral cypress. Perhaps to off-set this dismal effect, he wore a wreath of small violet flowers around his blond head, the hair of which clustered in golden ringlets.

Close beside him, scarce half his height, hanging weightlessly on his arm like an elf and dressed in a loose robe of pale blonde silk, was Hisvet. The Mouser's dagger-cut, stretching from her left nostril to her jaw, was still a pink line and would have given her a sardonic expression, except that now as her gaze swung to the Mouser she smiled most prettily.

Standing almost midway between the audience couch and the caged rats was Hisvet's father Hisvin. His skinny frame was wrapped in a black toga, but he still wore his tight black leather cap with its long cheek-flaps. His gaze was fixed fiercely on the caged rats and he was weaving his bony fingers at them hypnotically.

"Gnawers dark from deep below . . ." he began to incant in a voice that whistled with age yet was authoritatively strident.

At that instant a naked young servant maid appeared through a narrow archway near the audience couch, bearing on her shaven head a great silver tray laden with goblets and temptingly-mounded silver plates. Her wrists were chained to her waist, while a fine silver chain between her narrow black anklets prevented her from taking steps more than twice as long as her narrow pink-toed feet.

Without a "Hush!" this time, Glipkerio raised a narrow long palm to her and once again put a long, skinny finger to his lips. The slim maid's movements ceased imperceptibly and she stood silent as a birch tree on a windless day.

The Mouser was about to say, "Puissant Overlord, this is evilest enchantment. You are consorting with your dearest enemies!"—but at that instant Hisvet smiled at him again and he felt a frighteningly delicious tingling run down his cheek and gums from the silver dart in his left temple to his tongue, inhibiting speech.

Hisvin recommended in his commanding Lankhmarese that bore the faintest trace of an Ilthmar lisp and reminded the Mouser of the lisping rat Grig:

> "Gnawers dark from deep below,
> To ratty grave you now must go!
> Blear each eye and drag each tail!
> Fur fall off and heartbeat fail!"

All the black rats crowded to the farthest side of their cage from Hisvin, chittering and squeaking as if in maddest terror. Most of them were on their hind feet, clawing toward the bars like a panicky human crowd.

The old man, now swiftly weaving his fingers in a most complex, mysterious pattern, continued relentlessly:

> "Blur your eyesight, stop your breath!—
> By corrupting spell of Death!
> Your brains are cheese, your life is fled!
> Spin once around and drop down dead!"

And the black rats did just that—spinning like amateur actors both to ease and dramatize their falls, yet falling most convincingly all the same with varying *plops* onto the cage floor or each other and lying stiff and still with furry eyelids a-droop and hairless tails slack and sharp-nailed feet thrust stiffly up.

There was a curious slow-paced slappy clapping
as Glipkerio applauded with his narrow hands which
were long as human feet. Then the beanpole
monarch hurried to the cage with strides so lengthy
that the lower two-thirds of his toga looked like the
silhouette of a tent. Hisvet skipped merrily at his
side, while Hisvin came circling swiftly.

"Didst see that wonder, Gray Mouser?" Glipkerio
demanded in piping voice, waving his courier closer.
"There is a plague of rats in Lankhmar. You, who
might from your name be expected to protect us,
have returned somewhat tardily. But—bless the
Black-Boned Gods!—my redoubtable servant Hisvin
and his incomparable sorcerer-apprentice daughter
Hisvet, having conquered the rats which menaced
the grain fleet, hastened back in good time to take
measures against our local rat-plague—magical
measures which will surely be successful, as has now
been fully demonstrated."

At this point the fantastical overlord reached a
long thin naked arm from under his toga and
chucked the Mouser under the chin, much to the
latter's distaste, though he concealed it. "Hisvin and
Hisvet even tell me," Glipkerio remarked with a fluty
chuckle, "that they suspected *you* for awhile of being
in league with the rats—as who would not from your
gray garb and small crouchy figure?—and kept you
tied. But all's well that ends well and I forgive you."

The Mouser began a most polemical refutation
and accusation—but only in his mind, for he heard
himself saying, "Here, Milord, is an urgent missive
from the King of the Eight Cities. By the by, there
was a dragon—"

"Oh, that two-headed dragon!" Glipkerio interrupted with another piping chuckle and a roguish

finger-wave. He thrust the parchment into the breast of his toga without even glancing at the seal. "Movarl has informed me by albatross post of the strange mass delusion in my fleet. Hisvin and Hisvet, master psychologists both, confirm this. Sailors are a woefully superstitious lot, Gray Mouser, and 'tis evident their fancies are more furiously contagious than I suspected—for even you were infected! I would have expected it of your barbarian mate—Favner? Fafrah?—or even of Slinoor and Lukeen—for what are captains but jumped-up sailors?—but you, who are at least sleazily civilized . . . However, I forgive you that too! Oh, what a mercy that wise Hisvin here thought to keep watch on the fleet in his cutter!"

The Mouser realized he was nodding—and that Hisvet and, in his wrinkle-lipped fashion, Hisvin were smiling archly. He looked down at the piled stiff rats in their theatrical death-throes. Issek take 'em, but their droopy-lidded eyes even looked whitely glazed!

"Their fur hasn't fallen off," he criticized mildly.

"You are too literal," Glipkerio told him with a laugh. "You don't comprehend poetic license."

"Or the devices of humano-animal suggestion," Hisvin added solemnly.

The Mouser trod hard—and, he thought, surreptitiously—on a long tail that drooped from the cage bottom to the tiled floor. There was no atom of response.

But Hisvin noted and lightly clicked a fingernail. The Mouser fancied there was a slight stirring deep in the ratpile. Suddenly a nauseous stink sprang from the cage. Glipkerio gulped. Hisvet delicately pinched her pale nostrils between thumb and ring-finger.

"You had some question about the efficacy of my

spell?" Hisvin asked the Mouser most civilly.

"Aren't the rats corrupting rather fast?" the Mouser asked. It occurred to him that there might have been a tight-sealed sliding door in the floor of the cage and a dozen long-dead rats or merely a well-rotted steak in the thick bottom beneath.

"Hisvin kills 'em doubly dead," Glipkerio asserted somewhat feebly, pressing his long hand to his narrow stomach. "All processes of decay are accelerated!"

Hisvin waved hurriedly and pointed toward an open window beyond the archways to the porch. A brawny yellow Mingol in black loincloth sprang from where he squatted in a corner, heaved up the cage, and ran with it to dump it in the sea. The Mouser followed him. Elbowing the Mingol aside with a shrewd dig at the short ribs and leaning far out, supporting himself with his other hand reaching up and gripping the tiled window-side, the Mouser saw the cage tumbling down the sheer wall and sea-eaten rock, the stiff rats tumbling about in it, and fall with a white splash into the blue waters.

At the same instant he felt Hisvet, who had rapidly followed him, press closely with her silken side against his from armpit to ankle bone.

The Mouser thought he made out small dark shapes leaving the cage and swimming strongly underwater toward the rock as the iron rat-prison sank down and down.

Hisvet breathed in his ear, "Tonight when the evening star goes to bed. The Plaza of Dark Delight. The grove of closet trees."

Turning swiftly back, Hisvin's delicate daughter commanded the black-collared, silver-chained maid, "Light wine of Ilthmar for his Majesty! Then serve us others."

Glipkerio gulped down a goblet of sparkling color-less ferment and turned a shade less green. The Mouser selected a goblet of darker, more potent stuff and also a black-edged tender beef cutlet from the great silver tray as the maid dropped gracefully to both knees while keeping her slender upper body per-fectly erect.

As she rose with an effortless-seeming undulation and moved mincingly toward Hisvin, the short steps enforced by her silver ankles-chain, the Mouser noted that although her front had been innocent of both raiment and ornamentation, her naked back was crisscrossed diamond-wise by a design of evenly-spaced pink lines from nape to heels.

Then he realized that these were not narrow strokes painted on, but the weals of a whiplashing. So stout Samanda was maintaining her artistic dis-ciplines! The unspoken torment-conspiracy between the lath-thin effeminate Glipkerio and the bladder-fat palace mistress was both psychologically instruc-tive and disgusting. The Mouser wondered what the maid's offense had been. He also pictured Samanda sputtering through her singing black woolen garb in a huge white-hot oven—or sliding with a leaden weight on her knee-thick ankles down the copper chute outside the porch.

Glipkerio was saying to Hisvin, "So it is only need-ful to lure out all the rats into the streets and speak your spell at them?"

"Most true, O sapient Majesty," Hisvin assured him, "though we must delay a little, until the stars have sailed to their most potent stations in the ocean of the sky. Only then will my magic slay rats at a distance. I'll speak my spell from the blue minaret and slay them all."

"I hope those stars will set all canvas and make

best speed," Glipkerio said, worry momentarily
clouding the childish delight in his long, low-browed
face. "My people have begun to fret at me to do
something to disperse the rats or fight 'em back into
their holes. Which will interfere with luring them
forth, don't you think?"

"Don't trouble your mighty brain with that
worry," Hisvin reassured him. "The rats are not easily scared. Take measures against them in so far as
you're urged to. Meanwhile, tell your council you
have an all-powerful weapon in reserve."

The Mouser suggested, "Why not have a thousand
pages memorize Hisvin's deadly incantation and
shout it down the ratholes? The rats, being underground, won't be able to tell that the stars are in the
wrong place."

Glipkerio objected, "Ah, but it is necessary that
the tiny beasts also see Hisvin's finger-weaving. You
do not understand these refinements, Mouser. You
have delivered Movarl's missive. Leave us.

"But mark this," he added, fluttering his black
toga, his yellow-irised eyes like angry gold coins in
his narrow head. "I have forgiven you once your delays, Small Gray Man, and your dragon-delusions
and your doubts of Hisvin's magical might. But I
shall not forgive a second time. Never mention such
matters again."

The Mouser bowed and made his way out. As he
passed the statuesque maid with crisscrossed back,
he whispered, "Your name?"

"Reetha," she breathed.

Hisvet came rustling past to dip up a silver forkful
of caviar, Reetha automatically dropping to her
knees.

"Dark delights," Hisvin's daughter murmured

and rolled the tiny black fish eggs between her bee-stung upper lip and pink and blue tongue.

When the Mouser was gone, Glipkerio bent down to Hisvin, until his figure somewhat resembled a black gibbet. "A word in your ear," he whispered. "The rats sometimes make even me . . . well, nervous."

"They are most fearsome beasties," Hisvin agreed somberly, "who might daunt even the gods."

Fafhrd spurred south along the stony sea-road that led from Klelg Nar to Sarheenmar and which was squeezed between steep, rocky mountains and the Inner Sea. The sea's dark swells peaked up blackly as they neared shore and burst with unending crashes a few yards below the road, which was dank and slippery with their spray. Overhead pressed low dark clouds which seemed less water vapor than the smoke of volcanoes or burning cities.

The Northerner was leaner—he had sweated and burned away weight—and his face was grim, his eyes red-shot and red-rimmed from dust, his hair dulled with it. He rode a tall, powerful, gaunt-ribbed gray mare with dangerous eyes, also red-shot—a beast looking as cursed as the landscape they traversed.

He had traded the bay with the Mingols for this mount, and despite its ill temper got the best of the bargain, for the bay had been redly gasping out its life from a lance thrust at the time of the trade. Approaching Klelg Nar along the forest road, he had spied three spider-thin Mingols preparing to rape slender twin sisters. He had managed to thwart this cruel and unaesthetic enterprise because he had given the Mingols no time to use their bows, only the lance, while their short narrow scimitars had been no

match for Gray-wand. When the last of the three had
gone down, sputtering curses and blood, Fafhrd had
turned to the identically-clad girls, only to discover
that he had rescued but one—a Mingol had mean-
heartedly cut the other's throat before turning his
scimitar on Fafhrd. Thereafter Fafhrd had mastered
one of the tethered Mingol horses despite its fiendish
biting and kicking. The surviving girl had revealed
among her other shriekings that her family might
still be alive among the defenders of Klelg Nar, so
Fafhrd had swung her up on his saddlebow despite
her frantic struggles and efforts to bite. When she
quieted somewhat, he had been stirred by her slim
sprawly limbs so close and her lemur-large eyes and
her repeated assertion, reinforced by horrendous
maidenly curses and quaint childhood slang, that all
men without exception were hairy beasts, this with a
sneer at Fafhrd's luxuriously furred chest. But although tempted to amorousness he had restrained
himself out of consideration for her coltish youth—
she seemed scarce twelve, though tall for her age—
and recent bereavement. Yet when he had returned
her to her not very grateful and strangely suspicious
family, she had replied to his courteous promise to
return in a year or two with a wrinkling of her snub
nose and a sardonic flirt of her blue eyes and slim
shoulders, leaving Fafhrd somewhat doubtful of his
wisdom in sparing her his wooing and also saving her
in the first place. Yet he had gained a fresh mount
and a tough Mingol bow with its quiver of darts.

Klelg Nar was the scene of bitter house-to-house
and tree-to-tree street fighting, while Mingol
campfires glowed in a semicircle to the east every
night. To his dismay Fafhrd had learned that for
weeks there had not been a ship in Klelg Nar's har-
bor, of which the Mingols held half the perimeter.

They had not fired the city because wood was wealth to the lean dwellers of the treeless steppes—in fact, their slaves dismantled and plucked apart houses as soon as won and the precious planks and lovely carvings were instantly carted off east, or more often dragged on travoises.

So despite the rumor that a branch of the Mingol horde had bent south, Fafhrd had set off in that direction on his vicious-tempered mount, somewhat tamed by the whip and morsels of honeycomb. And now it seemed from the smoke adrift above the sea-road that the Mingols might not have spared Sarheenmar from the torch as they had Klelg Nar. It also began to seem certain that the Mingols had taken Sarheenmar, from the evidence of the wild-eyed, desperate, ragged, dust-caked refugees who began to crowd the road in their flight north, forcing Fafhrd to tour now and again up the hillside, to save them from his new mount's savage hooves. He questioned a few of the refugees, but they were incoherent with terror, babbling as wildly as if he sought to waken them from nightmare. Fafhrd nodded to himself—he knew the Mingol penchant for torture.

But then a disordered troop of Mingol cavalry had come galloping along in the same direction as the escaping Sarheenmarts. Their horses were lathered with sweat and their skinny faces contorted by terror. They appeared not to see Fafhrd, let alone consider attacking him, while it seemed not from malice but panic that they rode down such refugees as got in their way.

Fafhrd's face grew grim and frowning as he cantered on, still against the gibbering stream, wondering what horror would daunt Mingol and Sarheenmart alike.

* * *

Black rats kept showing themselves in Lankhmar
by day—not stealing or biting, squealing or scurrying, but only showing themselves. They peered from
drains and new-gnawed holes, they sat in window
slits, they crouched indoors as calmly and confident-
eyed as cats—and as often, proportionately, in
milady's boudoir as in the tenement-cells of the poor.

Whenever they were noted, there was a gasping
and thin shrieking, a rush of footsteps, and a hurling
of black pots, begemmed bracelets, knives, rocks,
chessmen, or whatever else might be handy. But
often it was a time before the rats were noted, so
serene and at home they seemed.

Some trotted sedately amidst the ankles and
swaying black togas of the crowds on the tiled or cobbled streets, like pet dwarf dogs, causing sharp human eddies when they were recognized. Five sat like
black, bright-eyed bottles on a top shelf in the store
of the wealthiest grocer in Lankhmar, until they were
spied for what they were and hysterically pelted with
clumpy spice-roots, weighty Hrusp nuts, and even
jars of caviar, whereupon they made their leisurely
exit through a splinter-edged rat doorway which had
not been in the back of the shelf the day before.
Among the black marble sculptures lining the walls
of the Temple of the Beasts, another dozen posed
two-legged like carvings until the climax of the ritual,
when they took up a fife-like squeaking and began a
slow, sure-foot weaving through the niches. Beside
the blind beggar Naph, three curled on the curb,
mistaken for his soot-dirty rucksack, until a thief
tried to steal it. Another reposed on the jeweled
cushion of the pet black marmoset of Elakeria, niece
of the overlord and a most lush devourer of lovers,
until she absently reached out a plump hand to

stroke the beastie and her nail-gilded fingers encountered not velvet fur, but short and bristly.

During floods and outbreaks of the dread Black Sickness, rats had in remembered times invaded the streets and dwellings of Lankhmar, but then they had raced and dodged or staggered in curves, never moved with their present impudent deliberation.

Their behavior made old folks and storytellers and thin-bearded squinting scholars fearfully recall the fables that there had once been a humped city of rats large as men where imperial Lankhmar had now stood for three-score centuries; that rats had once had a language and government of their own and a single empire stretching to the borders of the unknown world, coexistent with man's cities but more unified; and that beneath the stoutly mortared stones of Lankhmar, far below their customary burrowings and any delvings of man, there was a low-ceilinged rodent metropolis with streets and homes and glowlights all its own and granaries stuffed with stolen grain.

Now it seemed as if the rats owned not only that legendary sub-metropolitan rodent Lankhmar, but Lankhmar above ground as well, they stood and sat and moved so arrogantly.

The sailors from *Squid,* prepared to awe their sea-tavern cronies and get many free drinks with their tales of the horrid rat-attack on their ship, found Lankhmar interested only in its own rat plague. They were filled with chagrin and fear. Some of them returned for refuge to *Squid,* where the starsman's light-defenses had been renewed and both Slinoor and the black kitten worriedly paced the poop.

VIII

Glipkerio Kistomerces ordered tapers lit while the sunset glow still flared in his lofty sea-footed banquet hall. Yet the beanpole monarch seemed very merry as with many a giggle and whinnying laugh he assured his grave, nervous councillors that he had a secret weapon to scotch the rats at the peak of their insolent invasion and that Lankhmar would be rid of them well before the next full moon. He scoffed at his wrinkle-faced Captain General, Olegnya Mingolsbane, who would have him summon troops from the outlying cities and towns to deal with the furry attackers. He seemed unmindful of the faint patterings that came from behind the gorgeously figured draperies whenever a lull in the conversation and clink of eating tools let it be heard, or of the occasional small, hunchbacked, four-footed shadow cast by the tapers' light. As the long banquet went its bibulous course, he seemed to grow more merry and carefree yet—*fey*, some whispered in their partners' ears. But twice his right hand shook as he lifted his tall-stemmed wine glass, while beneath the table his ropy left fingers quivered continuously, and he had doubled his long skinny legs and hooked the heels of his gilded boots over a silver rung of his chair to keep his feet off the floor.

Outdoors the rising moon, gibbous and waning, showed small, low, humped shapes moving along each roof-ridge of the city, except those on the Street of the Gods, both the many temples of the Gods *in* Lankhmar and the grimy cornices of the temple of the Gods *of* Lankhmar and its tall, square bell-tower which never issued chimes.

The Gray Mouser scuffed moodily up and down the pale sandy path that curved around the grove of perfumy closet trees. Each tree was like a huge, up-ended, hemispherical basket, its bottom and sides formed by the thin, resilient, closely-spaced branches which, weighted with dark green leaves and pure white blooms, curved widely out and down, so that the interior was a single bell-shaped, leaf-and-flower-walled room, most private. Fire-beetles and glow-wasps and night-bees supping at the closet flowers dimly outlined each natural tent with their pale, winking, golden and violet and pinkish lights.

From within two or three of the softly iridescent bowers already came the faint murmurings of lovers, or perhaps, the Mouser thought with a vicious stab of the mind, of thieves who had chosen one of these innocent and traditionally hallowed privacies to plot the night's maraudings. Younger or on another night, the Mouser would have eavesdropped on the second class of privacy-seekers, in order to loot their chosen victims ahead of them. But now he had other rats to roast.

High tenements to the east hid the moon, so that

beyond the twinkling twilight of the closet trees, the
rest of the Plaza of Dark Delights was almost gropingly black, except where some small dim sheen
marked store or stand, or ghostly flames and
charcoal glow showed hot food and drink available,
or where some courtesan rhythmically swung her
tiny scarlet lantern as she sauntered.

Those last lights mightily irked the Mouser at the
moment, though there had been times when they had
drawn him as the closet bloom does the night-bee
and twice they had jogged redly through his dreams
as he had sailed home in *Squid*. But several most em-
barrassing visits this afternoon—first to fashionable
female friendlets, then to the city's most titillating
brothels—had demonstrated to him that his manhood, which he had felt so ravenously a-leap in
Kvarch Nar and aboard *Squid,* was limply dead except—he first surmised, now rather desperately
hoped—where Hisvet was concerned. Every time he
had embraced a girl this disastrous half-day, the slim
triangular face of Hisvin's daughter had got ghostily
in the way, making the visage of his companion of the
moment dull and gross by comparison, while from
the tiny silver dart in his temple a feeling of sick
boredom and unjoyful satiety had radiated through
all his flesh.

Reflected from his flesh, this feeling filled his
mind. He was dully aware that the rats, despite the
great losses they had suffered aboard *Squid*, threatened Lankhmar. Rats were deterred even less than
men by numerical losses and made them up more
readily. And Lankhmar was a city for which he felt
some small affection, as of a man for a very large pet.
Yet the rats menacing it had, whether from Hisvet's
training or some deeper source, an intelligence and

organization that was eerily frightening. Even now he could imagine troops of black rats footing it unseen across the lawns and along the paths of the Plaza beyond the closet trees' glow, encircling him in a great ambush, rank on black rank.

He was aware too that he had lost whatever small trust the fickle Glipkerio had ever had in him and that Hisvin and Hisvet, after their seemingly total defeat, had turned the tables on him and must be opposed and defeated once again, just as Glipkerio's favor must be re-won.

But Hisvet, far from being an enemy to be beaten, was the girl to whom he was in thrall, the only being who could restore him to his rightful, calculating, selfish self. He touched with his fingertips the little ridge the silver dart made in his temple. It would be the work of a moment to squeeze it out point-first through its thin covering of skin. But he had a dread of what would happen then: he might not lose only his bored satiety, but the juice of all feeling, or even life itself. Besides, he didn't want to give up his silver link with Hisvet.

A tiny treading on the gravel of the path, a very faint rutching that was nevertheless more than that of one pair of footsteps, made him look up. Two slim nuns in the black robes of the Gods *of* Lankhmar and in the customary narrow, jutting hoods which left faces totally shadowed were approaching him, long-sleeved arm in arm.

He had known courtesans in the Plaza of Dark Delights to adopt almost any garb to inflame the senses of their customers, new or old, and capture or recapture their interest: the torn smock of a beggar girl, the hose and short jerkin and close-cropped hair of a page, the beads and bangles of a slave-girl of the

Eastern Lands, the fine chain mail and visored
helmet and slim sword of a fighting prince from those
same areas of Nehwon, the rustling greenery of a
wood nymph, the green or purplish weeds of a sea
nymph, the prim dress of a schoolgirl, the em-
broidered garb of a priestess of any of the Gods *in*
Lankhmar—the folk of the City of the Black Toga
are rarely or never disturbed by blasphemies com-
mitted against such gods, since there are thousands
of them, and easily replaced.

But there was one dress that no courtesan would
dare counterfeit: the simple, straight-falling black
robes and hood of a nun of the Gods *of* Lankhmar.

And yet . . .

A dozen yards short of him, the two slim black
figures turned off the path toward the nearest closet
tree. One parted its rustling, pendant branches,
black sleeve hanging from her arm like a bat's wing.
The other slipped inside. The first swiftly followed
her, but not before her hood had slipped back a little,
showing for an instant by a wasp's violet pulse the
smiling face of Frix.

The Mouser's heart leaped. So did he.

As the Mouser arrived inside the bower amid an
explosion of dislodged white blooms, as if the tree
herself were throwing flowers to welcome him, the
two slim black figures faced around toward him and
dropped back their hoods. The same as he had last
seen it aboard *Squid,* Frix's dark hair was confined by
a silver net. The smile still curved her lips, though
her gaze was distant and grave. But Hisvet's hair was
itself a silver-blonde wonder, her lips pouted entic-
ingly, as if blowing him a kiss, while her gaze danced
all over his person with naughty merriment.

She moved toward him a step.

With a happy roaring shout only he could hear, blood rushed through the Mouser's arteries toward his center, reviving his limp manhood in a mere moment, as a magically summoned genie offhandedly builds a tower.

The Mouser imitated his blood, rushing blindly to Hisvet and clapping his arms around her.

But with a concerted movement like a half circling in a swift dance, the two girls had changed places, so that it was Frix he found himself embracing, and with cheek pressed to cheek, for at the last moment she had swayed her head aside.

The Mouser would have disengaged himself then, murmuring courteous and indeed almost sincere excuses, for through her robe Frix's body felt slimly enticing and most interestingly embossed, except that at that instant Hisvet leaned her head over Frix's shoulder and tipping her elfin face sideways, planted her half-parted lips on the Mouser's mouth, which instantly began to imitate that of the industrious bee sipping nectar.

It seemed to him that he was in the Seventh Heaven, which is reserved for only the most youthful and beauteous of the gods.

When at last Hisvet removed her lips from his, keeping her face so close that the fresh scar Cat's Claw had made was a blue-edged pink ribbon from magnificent nostril to velvet-rounded slender jaw, it was instantly to murmur to him, "Rejoice, delicious Dirksman, for you have kissed with your own the actual lips of a Demoiselle of Lankhmar, which is a familiarity almost beyond imagining, and you have kissed *my* lips, an intimacy which passeth all understanding. And now, Dirksman, embrace Frix closely whilst I preoccupy your eyes and solace your face,

which is truly the noblest area of the skin, the very
soul's vizard. It is demeaning work for me, to be sure,
as if a goddess should scrub and anoint with oil a
common soldier's dirty boot, yet know that I do it
right gladly."

Meanwhile Frix's slim fingers were unbuckling his
ratskin belt. With the faintest slither and tiniest
double *thunk,* it slipped with Scalpel and Cat's Claw
to the springy close-cropped turf bleached almost
white by the closet tree's perpetual shade.

"Remember, your eyes on *me* only," Hisvet whispered with the faintest yet firmest note of reproach.
"I remain unjealous of Frix only so long as you disregard her utterly."

Though the light was still velvet soft, it seemed
brighter inside the closet tree's bower than without.
Perhaps the gibbous moon had risen. Perhaps the
glimmer of the nectar-supping fire-beetles and glow-
wasps and night-bees was concentrated here. A few
of them circled lazily inside the bower, winking on
and off like flirtatious gem moons.

The Mouser clapped his arms more tightly around
Frix's slim waist, meanwhile murmuring to Hisvet,
"Oh, White Princess . . . Oh, icy directress of desire
. . . Oh, frosty goddess of the erotic . . . Oh, satanic
virgin . . ." as she all the while planted tiny kisses on
his eyelids and cheeks and free ear, and raked them
with the long silvery lashes of her blinking eyes, so
that the plant of love was tenderly cultivated and
grew and grew. The Mouser sought to return these
favors, but she stopped his mouth with hers. As his
tongue caressed her teeth, he noted that her two center front incisors were somewhat overlarge, but in his
infatuated state this difference seemed only one more
point of beauty. Why even if Hisvet turned out to

have some of the appurtenances of a dragon or a
giant white spider—or a rat, for that matter—he
would love and cosset them each and all. Even if
there lifted over her head from behind the joint-
masted white moist sting of a scorpion, he would
honor it with a loving kiss—well, he mightn't go
quite so far as that, he decided abruptly . . . still and
on the other hand, he almost might, for at that instant Hisvet's eyelashes tickled the ridge of skin over
the silver dart in his temple.

This was ecstasy indeed, he assured himself. It
seemed to him that he was now in the Ninth and
topmost Heaven, where a few select heroes luxuriate
and dream and submit themselves to almost unen-
durable pleasures, at whiles glancing down with lazy
amusement at all the gods toiling at their sparrow-
watching and incense-sniffing and destiny-directing
on the many tiers below.

The Mouser might never have known what happened next—and it might have been a direly different
happening too—if it had not been that, never satis-
fied even with the most supreme ecstasy, he decided
once more to disobey Hisvet's explicit injunction and
steal a glance at Frix. Up to this moment he had been
obediently disregarding her with eye and ear, but
now it occurred to him that it would twist the
launching cords of the catapult of pleasure a notch
tighter if he observed both faces of his—after a fashion—two-headed light-of-love.

So when Hisvet once again nuzzled his outside ear
with her slender pink and blue tongue and while he
encouraged her to keep at it with small twistings of
his head and moanings of delight, he rolled his eyes
in the other direction, gazing surreptitiously at the
face of Frix.

His first thought was that she had her neck bent at
an angle that could hardly be anything but uncom-
fortable, to keep her head quite out of the way of the
Mouser's and her mistress'. His second thought was
that although her cheeks were passionately inflamed
and her perfumy breath was panting through her
yawn-slack lips, her gaze was coolly sad, distantly
melancholy, and fixed on something worlds away,
perhaps a chess game in which she and the Mouser
and even Hisvet were less than pawns, perhaps a
scene from an unimaginably remote childhood, perhaps—

Or perhaps she was watching something a little
closer than that, something behind him and not quite
worlds away—

Although it discourteously took his ear away from
Hisvet's maddening tongue, he rolled his whole head
in the direction he had his eyeballs and glancing over
shoulder saw, blackly outlined against the pale
pulsating wall of closet-blooms, the edge of a
crouching silhouette with half-outstretched arm and
something gleaming blue-gray at the end of that.

Instantly the Mouser crouched himself, rudely
drawing back from Frix, and then half spun around,
flailing out backhanded with his left hand, which had
an instant earlier embraced Hisvet's maid.

It was a blow barely in time and of necessity im-
perfectly aimed. As the back of his left fist crashed
against the lean wrist of the ocher hand holding the
knife, he felt the sting of its point in his forearm. But
then his right fist smashed into the Mingol's face,
stirring it at least for a moment from its taut-skinned
impassiveness.

As the snugly black-clad figure staggered backward under the impact, it seemed to divide in two,

like some creature of slime reproducing itself, as a second dagger-armed Mingol circled from behind the first and moved toward the Mouser, who was snatching up his belt and its pendant scabbards with a curse, drawing his dirk Cat's Claw, because the pommel of that weapon came first to his hand.

Frix, who still stood dreamily in her black draperies, was saying in a husky, faraway voice, "Alarums and excursions. Enter two Mingols," while behind her Hisvet was exclaiming petulantly, "Oh, my accursed, spoilsport father! He always ruins my most aesthetic creations in the realms of delight, whether from some vile and most unfatherly jealousy, or from—"

By now the first Mingol had recovered and the two rushed warily toward the Mouser, flickering their knives ahead of their slit-eyed yellow faces as they came in. The Mouser, Cat's Claw poised a little ahead of his chest, drove them back with a sudden swishing swing of his belt held in his other hand. The weighted scabbard of his sword Scalpel took one of them in the ear, so that he winced in pain. Now would be the time to leap forward and finish them— with a single dagger-thrust apiece if he were lucky.

But the Mouser didn't. He had no way of knowing that these Mingols were the only two, or whether Hisvet and Frix might not leave off their playacting —if it had been altogether that—and leap upon him with knives of their own as he attacked his lean black assassins. Moreover, his left arm was dripping blood and he could not yet tell how bad that wound was. Finally, it was being borne in reluctantly on his proud mind that he was faced with dangers which might be a mite too much for even his great cunning, that he was blundering about in a situation he did

not wholly understand, that he had even now,
drunken-sensed, risked his very life against an admittedly unusual ecstacy, that he dared not depend
longer on fickle luck, and that—especially in the
absence of brawny Fafhrd—he badly needed wise
counsel.

In two heartbeats he had turned his back on his
assailants, darted past a somewhat startled-looking
Frix and Hisvet, and burst out through the branchy
wall of the closet-bower amidst a second and even
larger explosion of white blooms.

Five heartbeats more and as he scurried north
across the Plaza of Dark Delights in the light of the
new-risen moon, he had buckled on his belt and
withdrawn from a small pouch pendant on it a bandage which he began deftly to wrap tightly about his
wound.

Five more heartbeats and he was hastening
through a narrow cobbled alleyway that led in the
direction of the Marsh Gate.

For he had decided that, much as he hated to admit it to himself, the time had come when he must
venture across the treacherous, malodorous Great
Salt Marsh and seek the advice of his sorcerous mentor, Sheelba of the Eyeless Face.

Fafhrd spurred his tall gray mare south through
the burning streets of Sarheenmar, since no road led
around that city fronted by the Inner Sea and backed
by desert mountains. Through those latter dry,
craggy hills the only trail led east to the land-locked
desert-grit Sea of Monsters, by which stood the lonely City of Ghouls, avoided by all other men.

It was smoke-clouded night and the sole light was
that of the flames gushing in streamers and roaring

sheets from the roofs, doors, and windows of buildings once noted for their coolness, firing their thick
walls of dried-clay bricks to red heat and a beauteous, rippling porcelain-like gloss where they did
not melt and topple entirely.

Though the wide street was empty, Fafhrd's
bloodshot eyes were watchful in his haggard, smoke-
stained, sweat-riveted face. He had loosened his
sword in its scabbard and his short-ax in its wide
sheath, strung his Mingol bow and held it ready in
his left hand, and slung the quiver of its arrows high
behind his right shoulder. His lightened saddlebag
and half-full canteen thumped against his mount's
ribs, while his flat pouch, still empty except for the
ridiculous tin whistle, flapped about.

For a wonder the mare was not panicked by the
fire all around. Fafhrd had heard that the Mingols,
by stark-real tests, inured their horses to all manner
of horrors almost as sternly as they did themselves,
slaying without mercy those who still quailed on the
seventh attempt of a beast or the second of a man.

Yet now Fafhrd's mount suddenly stopped dead,
just short of a narrow side street, snorting her
lathered nostrils and glaring her great eyes more wild
and bloodshot than Fafhrd's. Heel-thuds on her ribs
would not put her in motion again, so Fafhrd dis-
mounted and began to drag her forward by brute
force down the center of the smoke-swirled, flame-
walled street.

Then there came rushing from around the burning
corner ahead what looked at first glance to be a gang
of exceptionally tall and skinny red-litten skeletons,
each wearing a skimpy harness and brandishing in
either bony hand a short tapering double-edged
needle-pointed sword.

After an instant's shock, Fafhrd realized these must be Ghouls, whose flesh and inner organs, he had heard—with much skepticism, but now no longer—were transparent except where the skin became sallowly or rosily translucent on the genital organs and on the lips and small breasts of their women.

It was said also that they ate only flesh, human by preference, and that it was strange indeed to watch the raw gobbets they gulped course down and churn within the bars of their ribs, gradually turning to mush and fading from sight as their sightless blood assimilated and transformed the food—granting that a mere normal man might ever have opportunity to watch Ghouls feast without becoming a supply of gobbets himself.

Fafhrd was filled with dread, but also indignation, that he, clearly a neutral in a Ghoul-Sarheenmart-Mingol war, should be thus ambushed—for now the leading skeleton hurled his right-hand sword and Fafhrd had to weave swiftly aside as it came cartwheeling through the smoky air.

Whipping his hand over shoulder, he set arrow to bow and dropped the foremost Ghoul with a shot that transfixed his ribs just to the left of his breastbone. Somewhat to his surprise, he discovered that having a skeleton for foe and target made it easier to aim for a vital part. Now as the Ghouls approached closer, uttering horrendous warshrieks, he noted the flame-light glinting here and there from their glassy hides and realized that even counting their flesh as solid, they were an exceptionally skinny, though rangy, folk.

He brought down two more of his charging foes, the last with a dart into a black eye socket, then dropped his bow, whirled out short-ax and sword, and made a long lunge with the latter as the four remaining Ghouls, their speed unchecked, were upon him.

Graywand took a Ghoul under the chin, jolting him to a dying stop. It was weird to see the skeleton collapse without rattle of bone. The short-ax next licked out, decapitating another enemy, whose glassy-fleshed skull went spinning off, but whose torso, louting forward, drenched the Northerner's ax-hand with invisible, warm, silky fluid.

These grisly events gave the third Ghoul time to run around his stricken comrades and get in on Fafhrd a thrust which, fortunately coming from above, glanced off his left ribs without wounding him deeply.

The long smarting sword-slice, however, turned Fafhrd's indignation wholly to fury and he smote that Ghoul so deeply in the skull that the short-ax stuck and was jerked from Fafhrd's hand. His fury became an almost blinding red rage, not lacking sexual undertones, so that when he noted that the fourth and last Ghoul carried pale breasts on her white ribs like two roses pinned there, he knocked the weapons from her hands with short disarming sword-swipes as she came darting toward him; then as she faltered stretched her full-length on the road with a left-handed punch to her jaw.

. He stood panting, closely eyeing the scattered skeletons for sign of movement—there was none—and glaring all about for evidence of other parties of Ghouls. None also.

The horror-inured gray mare had hardly shifted an ironshod hoof during the melee. Now she tossed her gaunt head, writhed back her black lips from her huge teeth and whinnied snickeringly.

Sheathing Graywand, Fafhrd knelt warily by the female skeleton and pressed two fingers into the invisible flesh under the hinges of her jaw. He felt a slow pulse. Without ceremony he hoisted her by the waist. She weighed a little more than he anticipated so that her slenderness surprised him as did also the resilience and smooth texture of her invisible skin. Cold-headedly leashing his hot vengeful impulses, he dumped her over his saddlebow so that her legs dangled on one side and her trunk on the other. The mare glared back over shoulder and again lip-writhingly bared her yellowish teeth, but did no more than that.

Fafhrd bandaged his wound, rocked his hand-ax from its bony trap and sheathed it, gathered up his bow, mounted the mare and cantered on down the fire-fenced street through the wreaths of smoke and swirls of stinging sparks. He was constantly peering for more ambushes, yet glancing down once he found himself disconcerted that there should appear to be a bare white pelvic girdle on his saddlebow, just a fantastically-finned large loose bony knot to the eyes, even though hitched on either side by misty sinews and other cloudy gristle to the balance of a skeleton. After a bit he slung his strung bow over her left shoulder and rested his left hand on the slim warm invisible buttocks, to reassure himself there was a woman there.

The rats were looting by night in Lankhmar. Everywhere in the age-old city they were pilfering, and not only food. They filched the greenish bent brass coins off a dead carter's eyes and the platinum-set nose, ear and lip jewels from the triply locked gem chest of Glipkerio's wraith-thin aunt, gnawing in the thick oak a postern door neat as a fairy tale. The wealthiest grocer lost all his husked Hrusp nuts, gray caviar from sea-sundered Ool Plerns, dried larks' hearts, strength-imparting tiger meal, sugar-dusted ghostfingers, and ambrosia wafers, while less costly dainties were untouched. Rare parchments were taken from the Great Library, including original deeds to the sewerage and tunneling rights under the most ancient parts of the city. Sweetmeats vanished from beside tables, toys from princes' nurseries, tidbits from gold-inlaid silver appetizer trays, and flinty grain from horses' feedbags. Bracelets were unhooked from the wrists of embracing lovers, the pouches and snugly-flapped pockets of crossbow-armed rat watchers were picked, and from under the noses of cats and ferrets their food was stolen.

Ominous touch, the rats gnawed nothing except where it was needful to make entries, they left no dirty, clawed tracks or fluted toothmarks, and they befouled nothing, but left their dark droppings in neat pyramids, as if taking an absent owner's care for a house they might decide to occupy permanently.

The most cunning traps were set, subtle poisons laid out invitingly, ratholes stoppered with leaden plugs and brazen plates, candles lit in dark corners, unwinking watch kept in every likely spot. All to no avail.

Shiversomely, the rats showed a human sagacity in many of their actions. Of their few doorways discovered, some looked sawed rather than gnawed, the sawed-out part being replaced like a little door. They swung by cords of their own to dainties hung from ceilings for safety, and a few terrified witnesses claimed to have seen them hurling such cords over their hanging places like bolas, or even shooting them there attached to the darts of tiny crossbows. They seemed to practice a division of labor, some acting as lookouts, others as leaders and guards, others as skilled breakers and mechanics, still others as mere burden-bearers docile to the squeak of command.

Worst of all, the humans who heard their rare squeakings and chitterings claimed they were not mere animal noises, but the language of Lankhmar, though spoken so swiftly and pitched so high that it was generally impossible to follow.

Lankhmar's fears grew. Prophecies were recalled that a dark conqueror commanding a countless horde of cruel followers who aped the manners of civilization but were brutes *and wore dirty furs,* would some day seize the city. This had been thought to refer to the Mingols, but it could be construed as designating the rats.

Even fat Samanda was inwardly terrorized by the depredation of the overlord's pantries and food lockers, and by a ceaseless invisible pattering. She had all the maids and pages routed from their cots two hours before dawn and in the cavernous kitchen and before the roaring fireplace, big enough to roast two beefs and heat two dozen ovens, she conducted a mass interrogation and whipping to quiet her nerves and divert her thoughts from the real culprits. Looking like slim copper statues in the orange light each shaven victim stood, bent, knelt or lay flat before Samanda, as directed, and endured her or his artistically laid-on welting, afterwards kissing the black hem of Samanda's skirt or gently patting her face and neck with a lily-white towel, chilled with ice water and wrung out, for the ogress plied her whip until the sweat trickled down from the black sphere of her hair and dripped in beads from her moustache. Slender Reetha was lashed once more, but she had a revenge by slipping a fistful of finely ground white pepper into the icy basin when she returned the towel to it; true, this resulted in a quadrupling of the next victim's punishment, but when one achieves revenge, the innocent perforce suffer.

The spectacle was watched by a select audience of white-smocked cooks and grinning barbers, of whom not a few were needed to shave the palace's army of servants. They guffawed and giggled appreciatively. It was also observed by Glipkerio from behind curtains in a gallery. The beanpole overlord was entranced and his aristocratically long nerves as much soothed as Samanda's—until he noted in the kitchen's topmost gloomy shelves the hundreds of paired pinpoints of the eyes of uninvited onlookers. He raced back to his well-guarded private chambers with his black toga flapping like a sail torn loose in a squall from a tall-masted yacht. Oh, he thought, if only Hisvin would work his master spell! But the old grain-merchant and sorcerer had told him that one planet was not quite yet in the proper configuration to reinforce his magic. Events in Lankhmar had begun to look like a race between some star and the rats. Well, if worse came to worst, Glipkerio told himself, at once giggling and panting in his swirly flight, he had an infallible way of escaping from Lankhmar and Nehwon too, and winning his way to some other world, where he would doubtless quickly be proclaimed monarch of all or at any rate an ample principality to begin with—he was a very reasonable overlord, Glipkerio felt—and thereby have some small solace for the loss of Lankhmar.

IX

Sheelba of the Eyeless Face reached into the hut
without turning his hooded head and swiftly found a
small object and held it forth.

"Here is your answer to Lankhmar's Rat Plague,"
he said in a voice deep, hollow, rapid and grating as
round stones thudding together in a moderate surf.
"Solve that problem, you solve all."

Gazing from more than a yard below, the Gray
Mouser saw silhouetted against the paling sky a
small squat bottle pinched between the black fabric
of the overlong sleeve of Sheelba, who chose never to
show his fingers, if they were that. Silvery dawnlight
shivered through the bottle's crystal stopper.

The Mouser was not impressed. He was bone-
weary and be-mired from armpit to boots, which were
now sunk ankle-deep in sucking muck and sinking deeper all the time. His coarse gray silks were be-
slimed and ripped, he feared, beyond the most cunning tailor's repair. His scratched skin, where it was
dry, was scaled with the Marsh's itching muddy salt.
The bandaged wound in his left arm ached and

burned. And now his neck had begun to ache too, from having to peer craningly upward.

All around him stretched the dismal reaches of the Great Salt Marsh, acres of knife-edged sea grass hiding treacherous creeks and deadly sink-holes and pimpled with low hummocks crowded with twisted, dwarfed thorn trees and bloated prickly cactuses. While its animal population ran a noxious gamut from sea leeches, giant worms, poison eels and water cobras to saw-beaked, low-flapping cadaver birds and far-leaping, claw-footed salt-spiders.

Sheelba's hut was a black dome about as big as the closet-tree bower in which the Mouser had last evening endured ecstacy and attempted assassination. It stood above the Marsh on five crooked poles or legs, four spaced evenly around its rim, the fifth central. Each leg was footed with a round plate big as a cutlassman's shield, concave upward, and apparently envenomed, for ringing each was a small collection of corpses of the Marsh's deadly fauna.

The hut had a single doorway, low and top-rounded as a burrow entrance. In it now Sheelba lay, chin on bent left elbow, if either of those were those, stretching out the squat bottle and seeming to peer down at the Mouser, unmindful of the illogicality of one called the Eyeless peering. Yet despite the sky-rim now pinkening to the east, the Mouser could see no hint of face of any sort in the deep hood, only midnight dark. Wearily and for perhaps the thousandth time, the Mouser wondered if Sheelba were called the Eyeless because he was blind in the ordinary way, or had only leathery skin between nostrils and pate, or was skull-headed, or perhaps had quivering antennae where eyes should be. The speculation gave him no shiver of fear, he was too angry and fatigued—and the squat bottle still didn't impress him.

Batting aside a springing salt-spider with the back of his gauntleted hand, the Mouser called upward, "That's a mighty small jug to hold poison for all the rats of Lankhmar. Hola, you in the black bag there, aren't you going to invite me up for a drink, a bite, and a dry-out? I'll curse you otherwise with spells I've unbeknownst stolen from you!"

"I'm not your mother, mistress, or nurse, but your wizard!" Sheelba retorted in his harsh hollow sea-voice. "Cease your childish threats and stiffen your back, small gray one!"

That last seemed the ultimate and crushing indignity to the Mouser with his stiff neck and straining spine. He thought bitterly of the sinew-punishing, skin-smarting night he'd just spent. He'd left Lankhmar by the Marsh Gate, to the frightened amazement of the guards, who had strongly advised against solo Marsh sorties even by day. Then he'd followed the twisty causeway by moonlight to the lightning-blasted but still towering gray Seahawk Tree. There after long peering he'd spotted Sheelba's hut by a pulsing blue glow coming from its low doorway, and plunged boldly toward it through the swordish sea grass. Then had come nightmare. Deep creeks and thorny hummocks had appeared where he didn't expect them and he had speedily lost his usually infallible sense of direction. The small blue glow had winked out and finally reappeared far to his right, then seemed to draw near and recede bafflingly time after time. He had realized he must be walking in circles around it and guessed that Sheelba had cast a dizzying enchantment on the area, perhaps to ensure against interruption while working some particularly toilsome and heinous magic. Only after twice almost perishing in quicksands and being stalked by a long-legged marsh leopard with blue-glinting eyes which the Mouser once mistook for the hut, because the beast seemed to have a habit of winking, had he at last reached his destination as the stars were dimming.

Thereafter he had poured out, or rather up, to Sheelba all his recent vexations, suggesting suitable solutions for each problem: a love potion for Hisvet, friendship potions for Frix and Hisvin, a patron potion for Glipkerio, a Mingol-repellent ointment, a black albatross to seek out Fafhrd and tell him to hurry home, and perhaps something to use against the rats, too. Now he was being offered only the last.

He rotated his head writhingly to unkink his neck, flicked a sea cobra away with Scalpel's scabbard-tip, then gazed up sourly at the little bottle.

"How am I supposed to administer it?" he demanded. "A drop down each rathole? Or do I spoon it into selected rats and release them? I warn you that if it contains seeds of the Black Sickness, I will send all Lankhmar to extirpate you from the Marsh."

"None of those," Sheelba grated contemptuously. "You find a spot where rats are foregathered. Then you drink it yourself."

The Mouser's eyebrows lifted. After a bit he asked, "What will that do? Give me an evil eye for rats, so my glance strikes them dead? Make me clairvoyant, so I can spy out their chief nests through solid earth and rock? Or wondrously increase my cunning and mental powers?" he added, though truth to tell, he somewhat doubted if the last were possible to any great degree.

"Something like all those," Sheelba retorted care-lessly, nodding his hood. "It will put you on the right footing to cope with the situation. It will give you a power to deal with rats and deal death to them too, which no complete man has ever possessed on earth before. Here." He let go the bottle. The Mouser caught it. Sheelba added instantly, "The effects of the potion last but nine hours, to the exact pulse-beat, which I reckon at a tenth of a million to the day, so see that all your work be finished in three-eighths that time. Do not fail to report to me at once thereafter all the circumstances of your adventure. And now farewell. Do not follow me."

Sheelba withdrew inside his hut, which instantly bent its legs and by ones and twos lifted its shield-like feet with sucking *plops* and walked away—somewhat ponderously at first, but then more swiftly, footing it like a great black beetle or water bug, its platters fair-ly skidding on the mashed-down sea grass.

The Mouser gazed after it with fury and amaze-ment. Now he understood why the hut had been so elusive, and what had *not* gone wrong with his sense of direction, and why the tall Seahawk Tree was no longer anywhere in sight. The wizard had led him a long chase last night, and doubtless a merry one from Sheelba's viewpoint.

And when it occurred to the bone-tired, be-mired Mouser that Sheelba could readily now have trans-ported him to the vicinity of the Marsh Gate in his traveling hut, he was minded to peg at the departing vehicular dwelling the lousy little bottle he'd got.

Instead he knotted a length of bandage tightly around the small black container, top to bottom, to make sure the stopper didn't come out, put the bottle in the midst of his pouch, and carefully retightened

and tied the pouch's thong. He promised himself that
if the potion did not solve his problems, he would
make Sheelba feel that the whole city of Lankhmar
had lifted up on myriad stout legs and come trampling across the Great Salt Marsh to pash the wizard in
his hut. Then with a great effort he pulled his feet one
after the other out of the muck into which he'd sunk
almost knee-deep, pried a couple of pulsing sea slugs
off his left boot with Cat's Claw, used the same dagger to slay by slashing a giant worm tightening
around his right ankle, drank the last stinging sup of
wine in his wine-flask, tossed that away, and set out
toward the tiny towers of Lankhmar, now dimly visible in the smoky west, directly under the sinking,
fading gibbous moon.

The rats were harming in Lankhmar, inflicting
pain and wounds. Dogs came howling to their masters to have needle-like darts taken out of their faces.
Cats crawled into hiding to wait it out while rat-bites
festered and healed. Ferrets were found squealing in
rat-traps that bruised flesh and broke bones.
Elakeria's black marmoset almost drowned in the
oiled and perfumed water of his mistress' deep,
slippery-sided silver bathtub, into which the spidery-
armed pet had somehow been driven, befouling the
water in his fear.

Rat-nips on the face brought sleepers screamingly
awake, sometimes to see a small black form scuttling
across the blanket and leaping from the bed. Beautiful or merely terrified women took to wearing while
they slept full masks of silver filigree or tough leather.
Most households, highest to humblest, slept by
candlelight and in shifts, so that there were always
watchers. A shortage of candles developed, while

lamps and lanterns were priced almost out of sight. Strollers had their ankles bitten; most streets showed only a few hurrying figures, while alleys were deserted. Only the Street of the Gods, which stretched from the Marsh Gate to the granaries on the Hlal, was free of rats, in consequence of which it and its temples were crammed with worshipers rich and poor, credulous and hitherto atheist, praying for relief from the Rat Plague to the ten hundred and one Gods *in* Lankhmar and even to the dire and aloof Gods *of* Lankhmar, whose bell-towered, ever-locked temple stood at the granaries-end of the street, opposite the narrow house of Hisvin the grain-merchant.

In frantic reprisal, ratholes were flooded, sometimes with poisoned water. Fumes of burning phosphorous and sulfur were pumped down them with bellows. By order of the Supreme Council and with the oddly ambivalent approval of Glipkerio, who kept chattering about his secret weapons, professional rat-catchers were summoned en masse from the grainfields to the south and from those to the west, across the river Hlal. By command of Olegnya Mingolsbane, acting without consultation with his overlord, regiments of black-clad soldiers were rushed at the double from Tovilyis, Kartishla, even Land's End, and issued on the way weapons and items of uniform which puzzled them mightily and made them sneer more than ever at their quartermasters and at the effete and fantasy-minded Lankhmar military bureaucracy: long-handled three-tined forks, throwing balls pierced with many double-ended slim spikes, lead-weighted throwing nets, sickles, heavy leather gauntlets and bag-masks of the same material.

Where *Squid* was docked at the towering granaries near the end of the Street of the Gods, waiting fresh cargo, Slinoor paced the deck nervously and ordered smooth copper disks more than a yard across set midway up each mooring cable, to baffle any rat creeping up them. The black kitten stayed mostly at the mast-top, worriedly a-peer at the city and descending only to scavenge meals. No wharf-cats came sniffing aboard *Squid* or were to be seen prowling the docks.

In a green-tiled room in the Rainbow Palace of Glipkerio Kistomerces, and in the midst of a circle of fork-armed pages and guardsmen officers with bared dirks and small one-hand crossbows at the cock, Hisvin sought to cope with the hysteria of Lankhmar's beanpole monarch, whom a half-dozen slim naked serving maids were simultaneously brow-stroking, finger-fondling, toe-kissing, plying with wine and black opium pills tiny as poppy seeds, and otherwise hopefully soothing.

Twisting away from his delightful ministrants, who moderated but did not cease their attentions, Glipkerio bleated petulantly, "Hisvin, Hisvin, you must hurry things. My people mutter at me. My Council and Captain General take measures over my head. There are even slavering mad-dog whispers of supplanting me on my seashell throne, as by my idiot cousin Radomix Kistomerces-Null. Hisvin, you've got your rats in the streets by day and night now, all set to be blasted by your incantations. When, oh when, is that planet of yours going to reach its proper spot on the starry stage so you can recite and finger-weave your rat-deadly magic? What's delaying it, Hisvin? I command that planet to move faster! Else I will send a naval expedition across the unknown Outer Sea to sink it!"

The skinny, round-shouldered grain-merchant sorrowfully sucked in his cheeks beneath the flaps of his black leather cap, raised his beady eyes ceilingward, and in general made a most pious face.

"Alas, my brave overlord," he said, "that star's course may not yet be predicted with absolute certainty. It will soon arrive at its spot, never fear, but exactly how soon the most learned astrologer cannot foretell. Benign waves urge it forward, then a malign sky-swell drives it back. It is in the eye of a celestial storm. As an iceberg-huge jewel floating in the blue waters of the heavens, it is subject to their currents and ragings. Recall also what I've told you of your traitorous courier, the Gray Mouser, who it now appears is in league with powerful witch doctors and fetish-men working against us."

Nervously plucking at his black toga and slapping away with his long flappy fingers the pink hand of a maid who sought to rearrange the garment, Glipkerio spat out peevishly, "Now the Mouser. Now the stars. What sort of impotent sorcerer are you? Methinks the rats rule the stars as well as the streets and corridors of Lankhmar."

Reetha, who was the rebuffed maid, uttered a soundless philosophic sigh and softly as a mouse inserted her slapped hand under her overlord's toga and began most gently to scratch his stomach, meanwhile occupying her mind with a vision of herself girdled in three leather loops with Samanda's keys, thongs, chains, and whips, while the blubbery palace mistress knelt naked and quaking before her.

Hisvin intoned, "Against that pernicious thought, I present you with a most powerful palindrome: Rats live on no evil star. Recite it with lips and mind when your warlike eagerness to come to final grips with your furry foes makes you melancholy, oh most courageous commander in chief."

"You give me words; I ask for action," Glipkerio complained.

"I will send my daughter Hisvet to attend you. She has now disciplined into instructive erotic capers a new dozen of silver-caged white rats."

"Rats, rats, rats! Do you seek to drive me mad?" Glipkerio squeaked angrily.

"I will at once order her to destroy her harmless pets, good scholars though they be," Hisvin answered smoothly, bowing very low so that he could make a nasty face unseen. "Then, your overlordship wishing, she shall come to soothe your battle-strung nerves with mystic rhythms learned in the Eastern Lands. While her maid Frix is skilled in subtle massages known only to her and to certain practitioners in Quarmall, Kokgnab, and Klesh."

Glipkerio lifted his shoulders, pouted his lips, and uttered a little grunt midway between indifference and unwilling satisfaction.

At that instant, a half-dozen of the officers and pages crouched together and directed their gazes and weapons at a doorway in which had appeared a little low shadow.

At the same moment, her mind overly absorbed and excited by the imagined squeals and groans of Samanda forced to crawl about the kitchen floor by jerks of her globe-dressed black hair and by jabs of the long pins taken from it, Reetha inadvertently tweaked a tuft of body hair which her gently scratching fingers had encountered.

Her monarch writhed as if stabbed and uttered a thin, piercing shriek.

A dwarf white cat had trotted nervously into the

doorway, looking back over shoulder with nervous pink eyes, and now when Glipkerio screamed, disappeared as if batted by an unseen broom.

Glipkerio gasped, then shook a pointing finger under Reetha's nose. It was all she could do not to snap with her teeth at the soft, perfumed object, which looked as long and loathsome to her as the white caterpillar of a giant moon moth.

"Report yourself to Samanda!" he commanded. "Describe to her in full detail your offense. Tell her to inform me beforehand of your hour of punishment."

Against his own rule, Hisvin permitted himself a small, veiled expression of his contempt for his overlord's wits. In his solemn professional voice he said, "For best effect, recite my palindrome backwards, letter by letter."

The Mouser snored peacefully on a thick mattress in a small bedroom above the shop of Nattick Nimblefingers the tailor, who was furiously at work below cleaning and mending the Mouser's clothing and accouterments. One full and one half-empty wine-jug rested on the floor by the mattress, while under the Mouser's pillow, clenched in his left fist for greater security, was the small black bottle he'd got from Sheelba.

It had been high noon when he had finally climbed out of the Great Salt Marsh and trudged through the Marsh Gate, utterly spent. Nattick had provided him with a bath, wine and a bed—and what sense of security the Mouser could get from harboring with an old slum friend.

Now he slept the sleep of exhaustion, his mind just

beginning to be tickled by dreams of the glory that
would be his when, under the eyes of Glipkerio, he
would prove himself Hisvin's superior at blasting
rats. His dreams did not take account of the fact that
Hisvin could hardly be counted a blaster of rats, but
rather their ally—unless the wily grain-merchant
had decided it was time to change sides.

Fafhrd, stretched out in a grassy hilltop hollow lit
by moonlight and campfire, was conversing with a
long-limbed recumbent skeleton named Kreeshkra,
but whom he now mostly addressed by the pet name
Bonny Bones. It was a moderately strange sight, yet
one to touch the hearts of imaginative lovers and enemies of racial discrimination in all the many universes.

The somewhat oddly-matched pair regarded each
other tenderly. Fafhrd's curly, rather abundant body
hair against his pale skin, where his loosened jerkin
revealed it, was charmingly counterpointed by the
curving glints of campfire reflected here and there
from Kreeshkra's skin against the background of her
ivory bones. Like two scarlet minnows joined head
and tail, her mobile lips played or lay quivering side
by side, alternately revealing and hiding her pearly
front teeth. Her breasts mounted on her rib cage
were like the stem-halves of pears, shading from
palest pink to scarlet.

Fafhrd thoughtfully gazed back and forth between
these colorful adornments.

"Why?" he asked finally.

Her laughter rippled like glass chimes. "Dear stupid Mud Man!" she said in her outlandishly-ac-
cented Lankhmarese. "Girls who are not Ghouls—
all your previous women, I suppose, may they be

chopped to still-sentient raw bits in Hell!—draw attention to their points of attraction by concealing them with rich fabric or precious metals. We, who are transparent-fleshed and scorn all raiment, must go about it another way, employing cosmetics."

Fafhrd chuckled lazily in answer. He was now looking back and forth between his dear white-ribbed companion and the moon seen through the smooth, pale gray branches of the dead thorn tree on the rim of the hollow, and finding a wondrous content in *that* counterpoint. He thought how strange it was, though really not so much, that his feelings toward Kreeshkra had changed so swiftly. Last night, when she had revived from her knockout a mile or so beyond burning Sarheenmar, he had been ready to ravage and slay her, but she had comported herself with such courage and later proven herself such a spirited and sympathetic companion, and possessed of a ready wit, though somewhat dry, as befitted a skeleton, that when the pink rim of dawn had added itself to and then drunk the city's flames, it had seemed the natural thing that she should ride pillion behind him as he resumed his journey south. Indeed, he'd thought, such a comrade might daunt without fight the brigands who swarmed around Ilthmar and thought Ghouls a myth. He had offered her bread, which she refused, and wine, which she drank sparingly. Toward evening his arrow had brought down a desert antelope and they had feasted well, she devouring her portion raw. It was true what they said about Ghoulish digestion. Fafhrd had at first been bothered because she seemed to hold no grudge on behalf of her slain fellows and he suspected that she might be employing her extreme amiability to put him off guard and then slay him, but he had later decided that life or its loss was likely accounted no great matter by Ghouls, who looked so much like skeletons to begin with.

The gray Mingol mare, tethered to the thorn tree on the hollow's rim, threw up her head and nickered.

A mile or more overhead in the windy dark, a bat slipped from the back of a strongly winging black albatross and fluttered earthward like an animate large black leaf.

Fafhrd reached out an arm and ran his fingers through Kreeshkra's invisible, shoulder-length hair. "Bonny Bones," he asked, "why do you call me Mud Man?"

She answered tranquilly, "All your kind seem mud to us, whose flesh is as sparkling clear as running water in a brook untroubled by man or rains. Bones are beautiful. They are made to be seen." She reached out skeleton-seeming soft-touching hand and played with the hair on his chest, then went on seriously, staring toward the stars. "We Ghouls have such an aesthetic distaste for mud-flesh that we consider it a sacred duty to transform it to crystal-flesh by devouring it. Not yours, at least not tonight, Mud Man," she added, sharply tweaking a copper ringlet.

He lightly captured her wrist. "So your love for me is most unnatural, at least by Ghoulish standards," he said with a touch of argumentiveness.

"If you say so, master," she answered with a sardonic, mock-submissive note.

"I stand, or rather lie, corrected," Fafhrd murmured. "I'm the lucky one, whatever your motives and whatever name we give them." His voice became clearer again. "Tell me, Bonny Bones, how in the world did you ever come to learn Lankhmarese?"

"Stupid, *stupid* Mud Man," she replied indulgent-
ly. "Why, 'tis our native tongue"—and here her
voice grew dreamy—"deriving from those ages a
millennium and more ago when Lankhmar's empire
stretched from Quarmall to the Trollstep Mountains
and from Earth's End to the Sea of Monsters, when
Kvarch Nar was Hwarshmar and we lonely Ghouls
alley-and-graveyard thieves only. We had another
language, but Lankhmarese was easier."

He returned her hand to her side, to plant his own
beyond her and stare down into her black eye
sockets. She whimpered faintly and ran her fingers
lightly down his sides. Fighting impulse for the moment, he said, "Tell me, Bonny Bones, how do you
manage to *see* anything when light goes right through
you? Do you see with the inside of the back of your
skull?"

"Questions, questions, questions," she complained moaningly.

"I only want to become less stupid," he explained
humbly.

"But I *like* you to be stupid," she answered with a
sigh. Then raising up on her elbow so that she faced
the still blazing campfire—the thorn tree's dense
wood burnt slowly and fiercely—she said, "Look
closely into my eyes. No, without getting between
them and the fire. Can you see a small rainbow in
each? That's where light is refracted to the seeing
part of my brain, and a very tiny real image formed
there."

Fafhrd agreed he could see twin rainbows, then
went on eagerly, "Don't stop looking at the fire yet;
I want to show you something." He made a cylinder
of one hand and held an end of the cylinder to her
nearest eye, then clapped his fingers, held tightly to-

gether, against the other end. "There!" he said.
"You can see the fire glow through the edges of my
fingers, can't you? So I'm part transparent. I'm part
crystal, at least."

"I can, I can," she assured him with singsong
weariness. She looked away from his hands and the
fire at his face and hairy chest. "But I *like* you to be
mud," she said. She put her hands on his shoulders.
"Come, darling, be dirtiest mud."

He gazed down at the moonlit pearl-toothed skull
and blackest eye sockets in each of which a faint
opalescent moonbow showed, and he remembered
how a wisewoman of the North had once told him
and the Mouser that they were both in love with
Death. Well, she'd been right, at least about himself,
Fafhrd had to confess now, as Kreeshkra's arms
began to tug at him.

At that instant there sounded a thin whistle, so
high as to be almost inaudible, yet piercing the ear
like a needle finer than a hair. Fafhrd jerked around,
Kreeshkra swiftly lifted her head, and they noted
that they were being watched not only by the Mingol
mare, but also with upside-down eyes by a black bat
which hung from a high gray twig of the thorn tree.

Filled with premonition, Fafhrd pointed a fore-
finger at the dangling black flier, which instantly
fluttered down to the fleshly perch presented. Fafhrd
drew off its leg a tiny black roll of parchment springy
as thinnest tempered iron, waved the flutterer back
to its first perch, and unrolling the black parchment
and holding it close to the firelight and his eyes close
to it, read the following missive writ in a white script:

*Mouser in direst danger. Also Lankhmar. Consult
Ningauble of the Seven Eyes. Speed of the essence.
Don't lose the tin whistle.*

The signature was a tiny unfeatured oval, which Fafhrd knew to be one of the sigils of Sheelba of the Eyeless Face.

White jaw resting on folded white knuckles, Kreeshkra watched the Northerner from her inscrutable black eye pits as he buckled on his sword.

"You're leaving me," she asserted in a flat voice.

"Yes, Bonny Bones, I must ride south like the wind," Fafhrd admitted hurriedly. "A lifelong comrade's in immense peril."

"A man, of course," she divined with the same tonelessness. "Even Ghoulish men save their greatest love for their male swordmates."

"It's a different sort of love," Fafhrd started to argue as he untied the mare from the thorn tree, feeling at the flat pouch hanging from the saddlebow, to make sure it still held the thin tin cylinder. Then, more practically, "There's still half the antelope to give you strength for your trudge home—and it's uncooked too."

"So you assume my people are eaters of carrion, and that half a dead antelope is a proper measure of what I mean to you?"

"Well, I'd always heard that Ghouls . . . and no, of course, I'm not trying to *pay* you. . . . Look here, Bonny Bones—I won't argue with you, you're much too good at it. Suffice it that I must course like the lonely thunderbolt to Lankhmar, pausing only to consult my master sorcerer. I couldn't take you—or anyone!—on that journey."

Kreeshkra looked around curiously. "Who asked to go? The bat?"

Fafhrd bit his lip, then said, "Here, take my hunting knife," and when she made no reply, laid it by her hand. "Can you shoot an arrow?"

The skeleton girl observed to some invisible listener, "Next the Mud Mad will be asking if I can slice a liver. Oh well, I should doubtless have tired of him in another night and on pretext of kissing his neck, bit through the great artery under his ear, and drunk his blood and devoured his carrion mud-flesh, leaving only his stupid brain, for fear of contaminating and making imbecilic my own."

Abstaining from speech, Fafhrd laid the Mingol bow and its quiver of arrows beside the hunting knife. Then he knelt for a farewell kiss, but at the last instant the Ghoul turned her head so that his lips found only her cold cheek.

As he stood up, he said, "Believe it or not, I'll come back and find you."

"You won't do either," she assured him, "and I shan't be anywhere."

"Nevertheless I will hunt you down," he said. He had untethered the mare and stood beside it. "For you have given me the weirdest and most wondrous ecstacy of any woman in the world."

Looking out into the night, the Ghoulish girl said, "Congratulations, Kreeshkra. Your gift to humanity: freakish thrills. Make like a thunderbolt, Mud Man. I dote on thrills too."

Fafhrd shut his lips, gazed at her a moment longer. Then as he whirled about him his cloak, the bat fluttered to it and hung there.

Kreeshkra nodded her head. "I said the bat." Fafhrd mounted the mare and cantered down the hillside.

Kreeshkra sprang up, snatched the bow and arrow, ran to the rim of the grassy saucer and drew a bead on Fafhrd's back, held it for three heartbeats, then turned abruptly and winged the arrow at the thorn tree. It lodged quivering in the center of the gray trunk.

Fafhrd glanced quickly around at the *snap, whir, tchunk!* A skeleton arm was waving him goodbye and continued to do so until he reached the road at the foot of the slope, where he urged the mare into a long-striding lope.

On the hilltop Kreeshkra stood in thought for two breaths. Then from her belt she detached something invisible, which she dropped in the center of the dying campfire.

There was a sputtering and a shower of sparks, when a bright blue flame shot straight up a dozen yards and burnt for as many heartbeats before it died. Kreeshkra's bones looked like blued iron, her glinting glassy flesh like scraps of tropic night-sky, but there was none to see this beauty.

Fafhrd watched the needlelike flare over shoulder as he sped rockingly along and he frowned into the wind.

The rats were murdering in Lankhmar that night. Cats died by swiftly sped crossbow darts that punctured slit-pupiled eye to lodge in brain. Poison set out for rats was cunningly secreted in goblets of dogs' dinners. Elakeria's marmoset died crucified to the head of the sandalwood bed of that plump wanton, just opposite her ceiling-tall mirror of daily-polished silver. Babies were bitten to death in their cradles. A few big folk were stung by deep-burrowing darts smeared with a black stuff and died in convulsions after hours of agony. Many drank to still their fears, but the unwatched dead-drunk bled to death from neat cuts that tapped arteries. Glipkerio's aunt, who was also Elakeria's mother, strangled in a

noose hung over a dark steep stairs made slippery
by spilled oil. A venturesome harlot was overrun in
the Plaza of Dark Delights and eaten alive while no
one heeded her screams.

So tricky were some of the traps the rats set and by
circumstantial evidence so deft their wielding of their
weapons, that many folk began to insist that some of
them, especially the rare and elusive albinos, had on
their forelegs tiny clawed hands rather than paws,
while there were many reports of rats running on
their hind legs.

Ferrets were driven in droves down ratholes. None
returned. Eerily bag-headed, brown-uniformed soldiers rushed about in squads, searching in vain for
targets for their new and much-touted weapons. The
deepest wells in the city were deliberately poisoned,
on the assumption that the city of rats went as deep
and tapped those wells for its water supply. Burning
brimstone was recklessly poured into ratholes and
soldiers had to be detached from their primary duty
to fight the resultant fires.

An exodus begun by day continued by night from
the city, by yacht, barge, rowboat, and raft, also
south by cart, carriage, or afoot through the Grain
Gate and even east through the Marsh Gate, until
bloodily checked by command of Glipkerio, advised
by Hisvin and by the city's stiff-necked and ancient
Captain General, Olegnya Mingolsbane. Lukeen's
war galley was one of the several which rounded up
the fleeing civilian vessels and returned them to their
docks—that is, all but the most gold-heavy, bribe-
capable yachts. Shortly afterwards, rumor spread
fast as news of a new sin, that there was a conspiracy
to assassinate Glipkerio and set on his throne his
widely-admired and studious pauper cousin,

Radomix Kistomerces-Null, who was known to keep seventeen pet cats. A striking force of plainclothes constables and Lankhmarines was sent from the Rainbow Palace through the torchlit dark to seize Radomix, but he was warned in time and lost himself and his cats in the slums, where he and they had many friends, both human and feline.

As the night of terror grew older at snail's pace, the streets emptied of civilian human traffic and grew peculiarly silent and dark, since all cellars and many ground floors had been abandoned and locked, barred, and barricaded from above. Only the Street of the Gods was still crowded, where the rats still had made no assault and where comfort of a sort was to be had against fears. Elsewhere the only sounds were the quick, nervous tramp of squads of constables and soldiers on night guard and patterings and chitterings that grew ever more bold and numerous.

Reetha lay stretched before the great kitchen fire, trying to ignore Samanda sitting in her huge palace mistress' chair and inspecting her whips, rods, paddles, and other instruments of correction, sometimes suddenly whishing one through the air. A very long thin chain confined Reetha by her neck collar to a large, recessed, iron ring-bolt in the kitchen's tiled floor near the center of the room. Occasionally Samanda would eye her thoughtfully, and whenever the bell tolled the half hour, she'd order the girl to stand to attention and perhaps perform some trifling chore, such as filling Samanda's wine-tankard. Yet still she never struck the girl, nor so far as Reetha knew, had sent message to Glipkerio apprising him of the time of his maid's correction.

Reetha realized that she was being deliberately

subjected to the torment of punishment deferred and
tried to lose her mind in sleep and fantasies. But
sleep, the few times she achieved it, brought nightmares and made more shockful the half-hourly
wakenings, while fantasies of lording it cruelly over
Samanda rang too hollow in her present situation.
She tried to romance, but the material she had to
work with was thin. Among other scraps, there was
the smallish, gray-clad swordsman who had asked
her her name the day she had been whipped for
being scared by rats into dropping her tray. He at
least had been courteous and had seemed to regard
her as more than an animated serving tray, but surely he had long since forgotten her.

Without warning, the thought flashed across her
mind that if she could lure Samanda close, she might
if she were swift enough be able to strangle her with
the slack of her chain—but this thought only set her
trembling. In the end she was driven to a count of her
blessings, such as that at least she had no hair to be
pulled or set afire.

The Gray Mouser woke an hour past midnight
feeling fit and ready for action. His bandaged
wound didn't bother him, though his left forearm
was still somewhat stiff. But since he could not
favorably contact Glipkerio before daylight, and
having no mind to work Sheelba's anti-rat magic
except in the overlord's admiring presence, he decided to put himself to sleep again with the remaining wine.

Operating silently, so as not to disturb Nattick
Nimblefingers, whom he heard snoring tiredly on a
pallet near him, he rather rapidly finished off the half
jug and then began more meditatively to suck on the
full one. Yet drowsiness, let alone sleep, perversely

refused to come. Instead the more that he drank, the more tinglingly alive he became, until at last with a shrug and a smile he took up Scalpel and Cat's Claw with never a clink and stole downstairs.

There a horn-shielded lamp burning low showed his clothes and accouterments all orderly lying on Nattick's clean worktable. His boots and other leather had been brushed and scrubbed and then re-suppled with neat's-foot oil, and his gray silk tunic and cloak washed, dried, and neatly mended, each new seam and patch interlocked and double-stitched. With a little wave of thanks at the ceiling, he rapidly dressed himself, lifted one of the two large oil-filmed identical keys from their secret hook, un-locked the door, drew it open on its well-greased hinges, slipped into the night and locked the door behind him.

He stood in deep shadow. Moonlight impartially silvered the age-worn walls opposite and their stains and the tight-shuttered little windows and the low, shut doors above the footstep-hollowed stone thresholds and the worn-down cobbles and the bronze-edged drain-slits and the scattered garbage and trash. The street was silent and empty either way to where it curved out of sight. So, he thought, must look the City of Ghouls by night, except that there, there were supposed to be skeletons slipping about on narrow ridgy ivory feet with somehow never a *clack* or *click*.

Moving like a great cat, he stepped out of the shad-ows. The swollen but deformed moon peered down at him almost blindingly over Nattick's scolloped roof-ridge. Then he was himself part of the silvered world, padding at a swift, long-striding walk on his spongy-soled boots along Cheap Street's center to-ward its curve-hidden intersections with the Street of the Thinkers and the Street of the Gods. Whore Street paralleled Cheap Street to the left and Carter Street and Wall Street to the right, all four following the curving Marsh Wall beyond Wall Street.

At first the silence was unbroken. When the Mouser moved like a cat, he made no more noise. Then he began to hear it—a tiny pattering, almost like a first flurry of small raindrops, or the first breath of a storm through a small-leafed tree. He paused and looked around. The pattering stopped. His eyes searched the shadows and discerned nothing except two close-set glints in the trash that might have been water-drops or rubies—or something.

He set out again. At once the pattering was resumed, only now there was more of it, as if the storm were about to break. He quickened his stride a little, and then all of a sudden they were upon him: two ragged lines of small low silvered shapes rushing out of the shadows to his right and from behind the trash-heaps and out of the drain-slits to his left and a few even squeezing under the scoop-thresholded doors.

He began to run skippingly and much faster than his foes, Scalpel striking out like a silver toad's tongue to pink one after another of them in a vital part, as if he were some fantastic trash collector and the rats animate small rubbish. They continued to close on him from ahead, but most he outran and the rest he skewered. The wine he'd bibbed giving him complete confidence, it became almost a dance—a dance of death with the rats figuring as humanity and he their grisly gray overlord, armed with rapier instead of scythe.

Shadows and silvered wall switched sides as the street curved. A larger rat got past Scalpel and sprang for his waist, but he deftly flicked it past him on Cat's Claw's point while his sword thrust through two more. Never in his life, he told himself gleefully, had he been so truly and literally the Gray Mouser, decimating a mouser's natural prey.

Then something whirred past his nose like an angry wasp, and everything changed. He recalled in a vivid flash the supremely strange night of decision aboard *Squid,* which had become almost a fantasy-memory to him, and the crossbow rats and Skwee with sword at his jugular, and he realized fully for the first time in Lankhmar that he was not dealing with ordinary or even extraordinary rats, but with an alien and hostile culture of intelligent beings, small to be sure, but perhaps more clever and surely more prolific and murder-bent than even men.

Leaving off skipping, he ran as fast as he could, slashing out repeatedly with Scalpel, but thrusting his dirk in his belt and grabbing in his pouch for Sheelba's black bottle.

It wasn't there. With sinking heart and a self-curse, he remembered that, wine-bemused, he'd left it under his pillow at Nattick's.

He shot past the black Street of the Thinkers with its taller buildings shutting out the moon. More rats poured out. His boot squished down on one and he almost slipped. Two more steel wasps buzzed past his face and—he'd never have believed it from another's lips—a small blue-flaming arrow. He raced past the lightless long wall of the building housing the Thieves' Guild, thinking chiefly of making more speed and hardly at all of rat-slashing.

Then almost at once, Cheap Street curving more sharply, there were bright lights ahead of him and many people, and a few strides later he was among them and the rats all gone.

He bought from a street vendor a small tankard of charcoal-heated ale to occupy the time while his dread and gasping faded. When his dry throat had been warmly and bitterly wetted, he gazed east two squares down the Street of the Gods to the Marsh Gate and then west more glittering blocks than he could clearly see.

It seemed to him that all Lankhmar was gathered here tonight by light of flaring torch and lamp and horn-shielded candle—and pole-lofted flare—praying and strolling, moaning and drinking, munching, and whispering fearful gossip. He wondered why the rats had spared this street only. Were they even more afraid of men's gods than men were?

At the Marsh Gate end of the Street of the Gods were only the hutments of the newest, poorest, and most slum-suited Gods *in* Lankhmar. Indeed most of the congregation here were mere curb-side gatherings about some scrawny hermit or leather-skinned death-skinny priest come from the deserts of the Eastern Lands.

The Mouser turned the other way and began a slow and twisty stroll through the hush-voiced mob, here greeting an old acquaintance, there purchasing a cup of wine or a noggin of spirits from a street seller, for the Lankhmarts believe that religion and minds half-fuddled, or at least drink-soothed, go nicely together.

Despite momentary temptation, he successfully got by the intersection with Whore Street, tapping the dart in his temple to remind himself that erotic experience would end in futility. Although Whore Street itself was dark, the girls young and old were out in force tonight, doing their business in the shadowed porticos, workmanlike providing man's third most potent banishment of fears after prayers and wine.

The farther he got from the Marsh Gate, the wealthier and more richly served became the Gods *in* Lankhmar whose establishments he passed— churches and temples now, some even with silver-chased pillars and priests with golden chains and gold-worked vestments. From the open doors came rich yellow light and heady incense and the drone of chanted curses and prayers—all against the rats, so far as the Mouser could make them out.

Yet the rats were not altogether absent from the Street of the Gods, he began to note. Tiny black heads peered down from the roofs now and again, while more than once he saw close-set amber-red eyes behind the grill of a drain in the curb.

But by now he had taken aboard enough wine and spirits not to be troubled by such trifles, despite his recent fright, and his memory wandered off to the strange season, years ago, when Fafhrd had been the penniless, shaven acolyte of Bwadres, sole priest of Issek of the Jug, and he himself had been lieutenant to the racketeer Pulg, who preyed on all priests and prayerful folk.

He returned to his complete senses near the Hlal end of the Street of the Gods, where the temples are all golden-doored and their spires shoot sky-high and the priests' robes are rainbow expanses of jewels. Around him was a throng of folk almost as richly clad, and now through a break in it he suddenly perceived, under green velvet hood and high-piled, silver-woven black hair, the merry-melancholy face of Frix with dark eyes upon him. Something pale brown and small and irregularly shaped dropped noiselessly from her hand to the pavement, here of ceramic bricks morticed with brass. Then she turned and was gone. He rushed after her, snatching up the small square of ball-crumpled parchment she'd dropped, but two aristos and their courtesans and a merchant in cloth of gold got shoulderingly in his way, and when he had broken free of them, resolutely curbing his wine-fired temper to avoid a duel, and got out of the press, no hooded green velvet robe was to be seen, or any woman in any guise looking remotely like Frix.

He smoothed the crumpled parchment and read it by the light of a low-swinging, horn-paned oil street lamp.

> *Be of hero-like patience and courage.*
> *Your dearest desire will be fulfilled*
> *beyond your daringest expectations,*
> *and all enchantments lifted.*
>
> > *Hisvet*

He looked up and discovered he was past the last luxuriously gleaming, soaring temple of the Gods *in* Lankhmar and facing the lightless low square fane with its silent square bell-tower of the Gods *of* Lankhmar, those brown-boned, black-togaed ancestor-dieties, whom the Lankhmarts never gather to worship, yet fear and revere in their inmost sleeping minds beyond the sum of all the other gods and devils in Nehwon.

The excitement engendered in him by Hisvet's note momentarily extinguished by that sight, the Mouser moved forward from the last street lamp until he stood in the lightless street facing the lightless low temple. There crowded into his liquored compassless mind all he had ever heard of the dread Gods *of* Lankhmar: They cared not for priests, or wealth, or even worshipers. They were content with their dingy temple *so long as they were not disturbed*. And in a world where practically all other gods, including all the Gods *in* Lankhmar, seemed to desire naught but more worshipers, more wealth, more news of themselves to be dissipated to the ends of the world, this was most unusual and even sinister. They emerged only when Lankhmar was in direct peril—and even then not always—they rescued and then they chastised—not Lankhmar's foes but her folks—and after that they retired as swiftly as possible to their dismal fane and rotting beds.

There were no rat-shapes on the roof of *that* temple, or in the shadows crowding thick around it.

With a shudder the Mouser turned his back on it, and there across the street, shouldered by the great dim cylinders of the granaries and backgrounded by Glipkerio's palace with its rainbow minarets pastel in the moonlight, was the narrow, dark-stoned house of Hisvin the grain-merchant. Only one window in the top floor showed light.

The wild desires roused in the Mouser by Hisvet's note flared up again and he was mightily tempted to climb that window, however smooth and holdless looked the unadorned sooty stone wall, but common sense got the better of wild desire in him despite the fire of wine. After all, Hisvet had writ "patience" before "courage."

With a sigh and a shrug he turned back toward the brightly lit section of the Street of the Gods, gave most of the coins in his pouch to a mincing, be-jeweled slave-girl for a small crystal flask of rare white brandy from the walled tray hung from her shoulders just below her naked breasts, took one swig of the icily fiery stuff, and was by that swig emboldened to cut down pitch-black Nun Street, intending to go a square beyond the Street of the Thinkers and by way of Crafts Street, weave home to Cheap Street and Nattick's.

Aboard *Squid*, curled up in the crow's nest, the black kitten writhed and whimpered in his sleep as though racked by the nightmares of a full-grown cat, or even a tiger.

X

___

Fafhrd stole a lamb at dawn and broke into a corn-
field north of Ilthmar to provide breakfast for himself
and his mount. The thick chops, broiled or at least
well-scorched on a thick green twig over a small fire,
were delicious, but the mare as she chomped grimly
eyed her new master with what seemed to him quali-
fied approval, as if to say, "I'll eat this corn, though
it is soft, milky, and effeminate truck compared to the
flinty Mingol grain on which they raised me and
grew my stern courage, which comes of grinding the
teeth."

They finished their repast, but made off hurriedly
when outraged shepherds and farmers came hooting
at them through the tall green field. A stone slung by
a shepherd who'd probably brained a few dozen
wolves in his day, whizzed close above Fafhrd's
ducked head. He attempted no reprisal, but galloped
out of range, then reined in to an amble to give himself time to think before passing through Ilthmar,
around which no roads led, and the squatty towers of
which were already visible ahead, glinting deceptive-

ly golden in the new-minted rays of the fresh sun.

Ilthmar, fronting the Inner Sea somewhat north of the Sinking Land which led west to Lankhmar, was an ill, treacherous, money-minded city. Though nearest Lankhmar, it stood at the crossroads of the known world, roughly equidistant from the desert-guarded Eastern Lands, the forested Land of the Eight Cities, and the steppes, where traveled about the great tent-city of the merciless Mingols. And being so situated, it forever sought by guile or secret force to levy toll on all travelers. Its land-pirates and sea-brigands, who split their take with its unruly governing barons, were widely feared, yet the great powers could never permit one of themselves to dominate such a strategic point, so Ilthmar maintained the independence of a middleman, albeit a most thievish and untrustworthy one.

Central location, where the gossip of all Nehwon crossed tracks along with the world's travelers, was surely also the reason why Ningauble of the Seven Eyes had located himself in a mazy, enchantment-guarded cave at the foot of the little mountains south of Ilthmar.

Fafhrd saw no signs of Mingol raiding, which did not entirely please him. An alarmed Ilthmar would be easier to slip through than an Ilthmar pretending to laze in the sun, but with pig-eyes ever a-watch for booty. He wished now he'd brought Kreeshkra with him, as he'd earlier planned. Her terrifying bones would have been a surer guarantee of safe transit than a passport from the King of the East stamped in gold-sifted wax with his famed Behemoth Seal. What a fool, either to dote or to flee, a man was about a woman new-bedded! He wished also that he had not given her his bow, or rather that he'd had two bows.

However, he was three-quarters of the way through the trash-paved city with its bedbug inns and smiling little taverns of resinous wine, more often than not laced with opium for the unwary, before trouble pounced. A great gaudy caravan rousing itself for its homeward journey to the Eastern Lands doubtless attracted attention from him. The only decor of the mean buildings around him was the emblem of Ilthmar's rat-god, endlessly repeated.

The trouble came two blocks beyond the caravan and consisted of seven scarred and pockmarked rogues, all clad in black boots, tight black trousers and jerkins and black cloaks with hoods thrown back to show close-fitting black skullcaps. One moment the street seemed clear, the next all seven were around him, menacing with their wickedly saw-toothed swords and other weapons, and demanding he dismount.

One made to seize the mare's bridle near the bit. That was definitely a mistake. She reared and put an iron-shod hoof past his guard and into his skull as neatly as a duelist. Fafhrd drew Graywand and at the end of the drawing stroke slashed through the throat of the nearest black brigand. Coming down on her forehooves the mare lashed out a hind one and ruined the guts of an unchivalrous fellow preparing to launch a short javelin at Fafhrd's back. Then horse and rider were galloping away at a pace that at the southern outskirts of the city took them past Ilthmar's baronial guard before those slightly more respectable, iron-clad brigands could get set to stop them.

A half league beyond, Fafhrd looked back. There was no sign as yet of pursuit, but he was hardly re-assured. He knew his Ilthmar brigands. They were stickers. Fired now by revenge-lust as well as loot-hunger, the four remaining black rogues would doubtless soon be on his trail. And this time they'd have arrows or at least more javelins, and use them at a respectful distance. He began to scan the slopes ahead for the tricky, almost unmarked path leading to Ningauble's underground dwelling.

Glipkerio Kistomerces found the meeting of the Council of Emergency almost more than he could bear. It was nothing more than the Inner Council plus the War Council, which overlapped in membership, these two being augmented by a few additional notables, including Hisvin, who had said nothing so far, though his small black-irised eyes were watchful. But all the others, waving their toga-winged arms for emphasis, did nothing but talk, talk, talk about the rats, rats, rats!

The beanpole overlord, who did not look tall when seated, since all his height was in his legs, had long since dropped his hands below the tabletop to hide the jittery way they were weaving like a nest of nervous white snakes, but perhaps because of this he had now developed a violent facial tic which jolted his wreath of daffodils down over his eyes every thirteenth breath he drew—he had been counting and found the number decidedly ominous.

Besides this, he had lunched only hurriedly and meagerly and—worse—not watched a page or maid being whipped or even slapped since before breakfast, so that his long nerves, finer drawn than those of other men by reason of his superior aristocracy and great length of limb, were in a most wretched state. It was all of yesterday, he recalled, that he had sent that one mincing maid to Samanda for punishment and still had got no word from his overbearing palace mistress. Glipkerio knew well enough the torment of punishment deferred, but in this case it seemed to have turned into a torment of pleasure deferred—for himself. The beastly fat woman should have more imagination! Why, oh why, he asked himself, was it only that watching a whipping could soothe him? He was a man greatly abused by destiny.

Now some black-togaed idiot was listing out nine arguments for feeing the entire priesthood of Ilthmar's rat-god to come to Lankhmar and make propitiating prayers. Glipkerio had grown so nervously impatient that he was exasperated even by the fulsome compliments to himself with which each speaker lengthily prefaced his speech, and whenever a speaker paused more than a moment for breath or effect, he had taken to quickly saying "Yes," or "No," at random, hoping this would speed things up, but it appeared to be working out the other way. Olegnya Mingolsbane had still to speak and he was the most boring, lengthiest, and self-infatuated talker of them all.

A page approached him and kneeled, holding respectfully out a scrap of dirty parchment twice folded and sealed with candle grease. He snatched it, glancing at Samanda's unmistakably large and thick-whorled thumbprint in the sooty grease, and tore it open and read the black scrawl.

> She shall be lashed with white-hot wires
> on the stroke of three. Do not be tardy, little
> overlord, for I shall not wait for you.

Glipkerio sprang up, his thoughts for the moment concerned only with whether it was the half-hour or three-quarter hour after two o'clock he had last heard strike.

Waving the refolded note at his council—or perhaps it was only that his hand was wildly a-twitch—he said in one breath, glaring defiantly as he did so, "Important news of my secret weapon! I must closet me at once with its sender," and without waiting for reactions, but with a final tic so violent it jolted his daffodil wreath forward to rest on his nose, Lankhmar's overlord dashed through a silver-chased purple-wood arch out of the Council Chamber.

Hisvin slid out of his chair with a curt, thin-lipped bow to the council and went scuttling after him as fast as if he had wheels under his toga rather than feet. He caught up with Glipkerio in the corridor, laid firm hand on the skinny elbow high as his black-capped skull and after a quick glance ahead and back for eavesdroppers, called up softly yet stirringly, "Rejoice, oh mighty mind that is Lankhmar's very brain, for the lagging planet has at last arrived at his proper station, made rendezvous with his starry fleet, and tonight I speak my spell that shall save your city from the rats!"

"What's that? Oh yes. Good, oh good," the other responded, seeking chiefly to break loose from Hisvin's grasp, though meanwhile pushing back his yellow wreath so it was once more atop his blond-ringleted narrow skull. "But now I must rush me to—"

"She will stand and wait for her thrashing," Hisvin hissed with naked contempt. "I said that tonight at the stroke of twelve I speak my spell that shall save Lankhmar from the rats, and save your overlord's throne too, which you must certainly lose before dawn if we beat not the rats tonight."

"But that's just the point, she *won't* wait," Glipkerio responded with agonizing agitation. "It's *twelve*, you say? But that can't be. It's not yet three!—surely?"

"Oh wisest and most patient one, master of time and the waters of space," Hisvin growled obsequiously, a-tiptoe. Then he dug his nails into Glipkerio's arm and said slowly, marking each word, "I said that tonight's the night. My demonic intelligencers assure me the rats plan to hold off this evening, to lull the city's wariness, then make a grand assault at midnight. To make sure they're all in the streets and stay there while I recite my noxious spell from this palace's tallest minaret, you must an hour beforehand order all soldiers to the South Barracks and your constables too. Tell Captain General Olegnya you wish him to deliver them a morale-building address—the old fool won't be able to resist that bait. Do . . . you . . . understand . . . me . . . my . . . overlord?"

"Yes, yes, oh yes!" Glipkerio babbled eagerly, grimacing at the pain of Hisvin's grip, yet not angered but thinking only of getting loose. "Eleven o'clock tonight . . . all soldiers and constables off streets . . . oration by Olegnya. And now, please, Hisvin, I must rush me to—"

"—to see a maid thrashed," Hisvin finished for him flatly. Again the fingernails dug. "Expect me infallibly at a quarter to midnight in your Blue Audience Chamber, whence I shall climb the Blue Minaret to speak my spell. You yourself *must* be there—and with a corps of your pages to carry a message of reassurance to your people. See that they are provided with wands of authority. I will bring my daughter and her maid to mollify you—and also a company of my Mingol slaves to supplement your pages if need be. There'd best be wands for them too. Also—"

"Yes, yes, dear Hisvin," Glipkerio cut in, his babbling growing desperate. "I'm very grateful . . . Frix and Hisvet, they're good ones . . . I'll remember all . . . quarter to midnight . . . Blue Chamber . . . pages . . . wands . . . wands for Mingols. And now I must rush me—"

"Also," Hisvin continued implacably, his fingernails like a spiked trap. *"Beware of the Gray Mouser!* Set your guards on the watch for him! And now . . . be off to your flagellatory pastimes," he added lightly, loosing his horny nails from Glipkerio's arm.

Massaging the dents they'd made, hardly yet realizing he was free, Glipkerio babbled on, "Ah yes, the Mouser—bad, bad! But the rest . . . good, good! Enormous thanks, Hisvin! And now I *must* rush me—" And he turned away with a lunging, improbably long step.

"—to see a maid—" Hisvin couldn't resist repeating.

As if the words stung him between the shoulders, Glipkerio turned back at that and interrupted with some spirit. "To attend to business of highest importance! I have other secret weapons than yours, old man—and other sorcerors too!" And then he was swift-striding off again, black toga at extremest stretch.

Cupping bony hand to wrinkled lips, Hisvin cried after him sweetly, "I hope your business writhes prettily and screams most soothingly, brave overlord!"

The Gray Mouser showed his courier's ring to the guards at the opal-tiled land entry of the palace. He half expected it not to work. Hisvin had had two days to poison silly Glip's mind against him. And indeed there were sidewise glances and a wait long enough for the Mouser to feel the full strength of his hang-over and to swear he'd never drink so much, so mixed again. And to marvel too at his stupidity and good luck in venturing last night into the dark, rat-infested streets and getting back silly-drunk to Nattick's through some of the darkest of them without stagger-ing into a second rat-ambush. Ah well, at least he'd found Sheelba's black vial safe at Nattick's, resisted the impulse to drink it while tipsy, and he'd got that heartening, titillating note from Hisvet. As soon as his business was finished here, he must hie himself straight to Hisvin's house and—

A guard returned from somewhere and nodded sourly. He was passed inside.

From the sneer-lipped third butler, who was an old gossip friend of the Mouser, he learned that Lankhmar's overlord was with his Emergency Coun-cil, which now included Hisvin. He resisted the gran-diose impulse to show off his Sheelban rat-magic before the notables of Lankhmar and in the presence of his chief sorcerous rival, though he did confidently pat the black vial in his pouch. After all, he needed a spot where rats were foregathered for the thing to work and he needed Glipkerio alone best to work on *him*. So he strolled into the dim mazy lower corridors of the palace to waste an hour and eavesdrop or chat as opportunity afforded.

As generally happened when he killed time, the Mouser soon found himself headed for the kitchen. Though he dearly detested Samanda, he made a point of slyly courting her, because he knew her power in the palace and liked her stuffed mushrooms and mulled wine.

The plain-tiled yet spotless corridors he now trav-ersed were empty. It was the slack half hour when

dinner has been washed up and supper mostly not
begun, and every weary servitor who can flops on a
cot or the floor. Also, the menace of the rats doubtless discouraged wanderings of servant and master
alike. Once he thought he heard a faint boot-tramp
behind him, but it faded when he looked back, and
no one appeared. By the time he had begun to smell
foods and fire and pots and soap and dishwater and
floorwater, the silence had become almost eerie.
Then somewhere a bell harshly knelled three times
and from ahead, "Get out!" was suddenly roared in
Samanda's harsh voice. The Mouser shrank back despite himself. A leather curtain bellied a score of
paces ahead of him and three kitchen boys and a
maid came hurrying silently into the corridor, their
bare feet making no sound on the tiles. In the light
filtering down from the tiny, high windows they
looked like waxen mannikins as they filed swiftly past
him. Though they avoided him, they seemed not to
see him. Or perhaps that was only some whip-in-
grained "Eyes front!" discipline.

As silently as they—who couldn't even make the
noise of a hair dropping, since this morning's barber-
ing had left them none—the Mouser hurried forward
and put his eye to the slit in the leather curtains.

The four other doorways to the kitchen, even the
one in the gallery, also had their curtains drawn. The
great hot room had only two occupants. Fat Samanda, perspiring in her black wool dress and under the
prickly plum pudding of her piled black hair, was
heating in the whitely blazing fireplace the seven
wire lashes of a long-handled whip. She drew it forth
a little. The strands glowed dull red. She thrust it
back. Her sparse, sweat-beaded black moustache
lengthened and shed its salt rain in a smile as her

tiny, fat-pillowed eyes fed on Reetha, who stood with arms straight down her sides and chin high, almost in the room's center, half faced away from the blaze. The serving maid wore only her black leather collar. The diamond stripe patterns of her last whippings still showed faintly down her back.

"Stand straighter, my pet," Samanda cooed like a cow. "Or would it be easier if your wrists were roped to a beam and your ankles to the ring-bolt in the cellar door?"

Now the dry stink of dirty floorwater was strongest in the Mouser's nostrils. Glancing down and to one side through his slit, he noted a large wooden pail filled almost to the brim with a mop's huge soggy head, lapped around by gray, soap-foamy water.

Samanda inspected the seven wires again. They glowed bright red. "Now," she said. "Brace yourself, my poppet."

Slipping through the curtain and snatching up the mop by its thick, splintery handle, the Mouser raced at Samanda, holding the mop's huge, dripping Medusa-head between their faces in hopes that she would not be able to identify her assailant. As the fiery wires hissed faintly through the air, he took her square in the face with a big smack and a gray splash, so that she was driven back a yard before she tripped on a long grilling-fork and fell backwards on her hinder fat-cushions.

Leaving the mop lying on her face with its handle neatly down her front, the Mouser whirled around, noting as he did a watery yellow eye in the nearest curtain slit and also the last red winking out of the wires lying midway between the fireplace and Reetha, still stiffly erect and with eyes squeezed shut and muscles taut against the red-hot blow.

He grabbed her arm at its pit, she screamed with
amazement and pent tension, but he ignored this and
hurried her toward the doorway by which he had entered, then stopped short at the tramp of many boots
just beyond it. He rushed the girl in turn toward the
two other leather-curtained doorways that hadn't an
eye in their slits. More boots tramping. He sped back
to the room's center, still firmly gripping Reetha.

Samanda, still on her back, had pushed the mop
away and was frantically wiping her eyes with her
pudgy fingers and squealing from soap-smart and
rage.

The watery yellow eye was joined by its partner as
Glipkerio strode in, daffodil wreath awry, black toga
a-flap, and to either side of him a guardsman presenting toward the Mouser the gleaming brown-steel
blade of a pike, while close behind came more
guardsmen. Still others, pikes ready, filled the other
three doorways and even appeared in the gallery.

Waving long white fingers at the Mouser,
Glipkerio hissed, "Oh most false Gray Mouser! Hisvin has hinted you work against me and now I catch
you at it!"

The Mouser squatted suddenly on his hams and
heaved muscle-crackingly with both hands on a big
recessed iron ring-bolt. A thick square trapdoor
made of heavy wood topped with tile, came up on its
hinges. "Down!" he commanded Reetha, who
obeyed with commendably cool-headed alacrity. The
Mouser followed hunched at her heels, and let drop
the trapdoor. It slammed down just in time to catch
the blades of two pikes thrust at him, and presumably lever them with a jerk from their wielders'
hands. Admirable wedges those tapering browned-
iron blades would make to keep the trapdoor shut,

the Mouser told himself.

Now he was in absolute darkness, but an earlier glance had shown him the shape and length of the stone stairs and an empty flagstoned area below abutting a niter-stained wall. Once again grasping Reetha's upper arm, he guided her down the stairs and across the gritty floor to within a couple of yards of the unseen wall. Then he let go the girl and felt in his pouch for flint, steel, his tinderbox, and a short thick-wicked candle.

From above came a muffled crack. Doubtless a pike-pole breaking as someone sought to rock out the trapped blade. Then someone commanded a muffled, "Heave!" The Mouser grinned in the dark, thinking how that would wedge the browned-iron wedges tighter.

Tiny sparks showered, a ghostly flame rose from a corner of the tinderbox, a tiny round flame like a golden pillbug with a sapphire center appeared at the tip of the candle's wick and began to swell. The Mouser snapped shut the tinderbox and held up the candle beside his head. Its flame suddenly flared big and bright. The next instant Reetha's arms were clamped around his neck and she was gasping in dry-mouthed terror against his ear.

Surrounding them on three sides and backing them against the ancient stone wall with its pale crystalline splotches, were a dozen ranks of silent rats formed in a semicircle about a spear-length away—hundreds, nay thousands of blackest long-tails, and more pouring out to join them from a score of ratholes in the base of the walls in the long cellar, which was piled here and there with barrels, casks, and grain-sacks.

The Mouser suddenly grinned, thrust tinderbox,

steel, and flint back in his pouch and felt there for
something else.

Meanwhile he noted a tall, narrow rathole just by
them, newly gnawed—or perhaps chiseled and pick-
axed, to judge from the fragments of mortar and tiny
shards of stone scattered in front of it. No rats came
from it, but he kept a wary eye on it.

The Mouser found Sheelba's squat black bottle,
pried the bandage off it, and withdrew its crystal
stopper.

The dull-brained louts in the kitchen overhead
were pounding on the trapdoor now—another useless assault!

The rats still poured from the holes and in such
numbers that they threatened to become a humpy
black carpet covering the whole floor of the cellar except for the tiny area where Reetha clung to the
Mouser.

His grin widened. He set the bottle to his lips, took
an experimental sip, thoughtfully rolled it on his
tongue, then upended the vial and let its faintly bitter
contents gurgle into his mouth and down his throat.

Reetha, unlinking her arms, said a little reproachfully, "I could use some wine too."

The Mouser raised his eyebrows happily at her
and explained, "Not wine. Magic!" Had not her
own eyebrows been shaven, they would have risen in
puzzlement. He gave her a wink, tossed the bottle
aside, and confidently awaited the emergence of his
anti-rat powers, whatever they might be.

From above came the groan of metal and the slow
cracking of tough wood. Now they were going about
it the right way, with pry-bars. Likely the trap would
open just in time for Glipkerio to witness the Mouser

vanquishing the rat army. Everything was timing itself perfectly.

The black sea of hitherto silent rats began to toss and wave and from it came an angry chittering and a clashing of tiny teeth. Better and better!—this war-like show would put some life into their defeat.

He idly noted that he was standing in the center of a large, gray-bordered splotch of pinkish slime he must have overlooked before in his haste and excitement. He had never seen a cellar-mold quite like it.

His eyeballs seemed to him to swell and burn a little and suddenly he felt in himself the powers of a god. He looked up at Reetha to warn her not to be frightened at anything that might happen—say his flesh glowing with a golden light or two bright scarlet beams flashing from his eyes to shrivel rats or heat them to popping.

Then he was asking himself, *"Up* at Reetha?"

The pinkish splotch had become a large puddle lapping slimily over the soles of his boots.

There was a splintering. Light spilled down from the kitchen on the crowded rats.

The Mouser gawked at them horror-struck. They were as big as cats! No, black wolves! No, furry black men on all fours! He clutched at Reetha . . . and found himself vainly seeking to encircle with his arms a smooth white calf thick as a temple pillar. He gazed up at Reetha's amazed and fear-struck giant face two stories above. There echoed evilly in his ears Sheelba's carelessly spoken, fiendishly ambiguous: ". . . put you on the right footing to cope with the situation . . ." Oh yes indeed!

The slime-puddle and its gray border had grown wider still and he was in it up to his ankles.

He clung to Reetha's leg a moment longer with the faint and ungracious hope that since his weapons and his clothing, which touched him, had shrunk with him, she might shrink too at his touch. He would at least have a companion. Perhaps to his credit, it did not occur to him to yell, "Pick me up!"

The only thing that happened was that an almost inaudibly deep voice thundered down at him from Reetha's mouth, big as a red-edged shield, "What are you doing? I'm scared. Start the magic!"

The Mouser jumped away from the fleshly pillar, splashing the nasty pink stuff and almost slipping in it, and whipped out his sword Scalpel. It was just a shade bigger than a needle for mending sails. While the candle, which he still held in his left hand, was the proper size to light a small room in a doll's house.

There was loud, confused, multiple padding and claw-clicking, chittering war cries blasted his ears, and he saw the huge black rats stampeding him from three sides, kicking up the gray border in puffs as if it were a powder and then splashing the pink slime and sending ripples across it.

Reetha, terror-struck, watched her inexplicably diminished rescuer spin around, leap over a shard of rock, land in a pink splash, and brandishing his tiny sword before him, shielding his doll's candle with his cloak, and ducking his head, rush into the rathole behind her and so vanish. Racing rats brushed her ankles and snapped at each other, to be first down the hole after the Mouser. Elsewhere the rat horde was swiftly disappearing down the other holes. But one rat stayed long enough to nip her foot.

Her nerve snapped. Her first footsteps splattering pink slime and gray dust, she shrieked and ran, rats dodging from under her feet, and dashed up the steps, clawed her way past several wide-eyed guardsmen into the kitchen, and sank sobbing and panting on the tiles. Samanda snapped a chain on her collar.

Fafhrd, his arms joined in a circle above and before his head to avoid skull-bump from rocky outcrops and also the unexpected brushings on face of cobwebs and wraithlike fingers and filmy wings, at last saw a jaggedly circular green glow ahead. Soon he emerged from the black tunnel into a large and many entranced cavern somewhat lit at the center of its rocky floor by a green fire which was being replenished with thin blood-red logs by two skinny, raggedy-tunicked, sharp-eyed boys, who looked like typical street urchins of Lankhmar or Ilthmar, or any other decadent city. One had a puckered scar under his left eye. On the other side of the fire from them sat on low wide stone an obscenely fat figure so well cloaked and hooded that not a speck of his face or hands were visible. He was sorting out a large pile of parchment scraps and potsherds, pinching hold of them through the dark fabric of his overlong, dangling sleeves, and scanning them close-sightedly, almost putting them inside his hood.

"Welcome, my Gentle Son," he called to Fafhrd in a voice like a quavering sweet flute. "What happy chance brings you here?"

"*You* know!" Fafhrd said harshly, striding forward until he was glaring across the leaping green flames at the black oval defined by the forward edge of the hood. "How am I to save the Mouser? What's with Lankhmar? And why, in the name of all the gods of death and destruction, is the tin whistle so important?"

"You speak in riddles, Gentle Son," the fluty voice

responded soothingly, as its owner went on sorting
his scraps. "What tin whistle? What peril's the
Mouser in now?—reckless youth! And what *is* with
Lankhmar?"

Fafhrd let loose a flood of curses, which rattled im-
potently among the stalactites overhead. Then he
jerked free from his pouch the tiny black oblong of
Sheelba's message and held it forward between finger and thumb that shook with rage. "Look, Know-
nothing One: I dumped a lovely girl to answer this
and now—"

But the hooded figure had whistled warblingly and
at that signal the black bat, which Fafhrd had forgot,
launched itself from his shoulder, snatched with
sharp teeth the black note from his finger-grip, and
fluttered past the green flames to land on the
paunchy one's sleeve-hidden hand, or 'tentacle, or
whatever it was. The whatever-it-was conveyed to
hood-mouth the bat, who obligingly fluttered inside
and vanished in the coally dark there.

There followed a squeaky, unintelligible, hood-
muffled dialogue while Fafhrd sat his fists on his hips
and fumed. The two skinny boys gave him sly grins
and whispered together impudently, their bright eyes
never leaving him. At last the fluty voice called,
"Now it's crystal clear to me, Oh Patient Son.
Sheelba of the Eyeless Face and I have been on the
outs—a bit of a wizardly bicker—and now he seeks
to mend fences with this. Well, well, well, first ad-
vances by Sheelba. Ho-ho-ho!"

"Very funny," Fafhrd growled. "Haste's the mar-
row of our confab. The Sinking Land came up, shed-
ding its waters, as I entered your caves. My swift but
jaded mount crops your stingy grass outside. I must
leave within the half hour if I am to cross the Sinking

Land before it resubmerges. *What do I do about the Mouser, Lankhmar, and the tin whistle?*"

"But, Gentle Son, I know nothing about those things," the other replied artlessly. " 'Tis only Sheelba's motives are air-clear to me. Oh, ho, to think that he— Wait, wait now, Fafhrd! Don't rattle the stalactites again. I've ensorcled them against falling, but there are no spells in the universe which a big fellow can't sometimes break through. I'll advise you, never fear. But I must first clairvoy. Scatter on the golden dust, boys—thriftily now, don't waste it, 'tis worth ten times its weight in diamond unpowdered."

The two urchins each dipped into a bag beside them and threw into the feet of the green flames a glittering golden swirl. Instantly the flames darkened, though leaping high as ever and sending off no soot. Watching them in the now almost night-dark cavern, Fafhrd thought he could make out the transitory, ever-distorting shadows of twisty towers, ugly trees, tall hunchbacked men, low-shouldered beasts, beautiful wax women melting, and the like, but nothing was clear or even hinted at a story.

Then from the obese warlock's hood came toward the darkened fire two greenish ovals, each with a vertical black streak like the jewel cat's eye. A half yard out of the hood they paused and held steady. They were speedily joined by two more which both diverged and went farther. Then came a single one arching up over the fire until one would have thought it was in great danger of sizzling. Lastly, two which floated in opposite directions almost impossibly far around the fire and then hooked in to observe it from points near Fafhrd.

The voice fluted sagely: "It is always best to look

at a problem from all sides.''

Fafhrd drew his shoulders together and repressed a shudder. It never failed to be disconcerting to watch Ningauble send forth his Seven Eyes on their apparently indefinitely extensible eyestalks. Especially on occasions when he'd been coy as a virgin in a bathrobe about keeping them hidden.

So much time passed that Fafhrd began to snap his fingers with impatience, softly at first, then more crackingly. He'd given up looking at the flames. They never held anything but the tantalizing, churning shadows.

At last the green eyes floated back into the hood, like a mystic fleet returning to post. The flames turned bright green again, and Ningauble said, "Gentle Son, I now understand your problem and its answer. In part, I have seen much, yet cannot explain all. The Gray Mouser, now. He's exactly twenty-five feet below the deepest cellar in the palace of Glipkerio Kistomerces. But he's not buried there, or even dead—though about twenty-four parts in twenty-five of him *are* dead, in the cellar I mentioned. But *he* is alive.''

"But *how?*" Fafhrd almost gawked, spreading his spread-fingered hands.

"I haven't the faintest idea. He's surrounded by enemies but near him are two friends—of a sort. Now about Lankhmar, that's clearer. She's been invaded, her walls breached everywhere and desperate fighting going on in the streets, by a fierce host which outnumbers Lankhmar's inhabitants by . . . my goodness . . . fifty to one—and equipped with all modern weapons.

"Yet you can save the city, you can turn the tide of battle—this part came through very clearly—if you only hasten to the temple of the Gods *of* Lankhmar and climb its bell-tower and ring the chimes there, which have been silent for uncounted centuries. Presumably to rouse those gods. But that's only my guess."

"I don't like the idea of having anything to do with that dusty crew," Fafhrd complained. "From what I've heard of them, they're more like walking mummies than true gods—and even more dry-spirited and unloving, being sifted through like sand with poisonous senile whims."

Ningauble shrugged his cloaked, bulbous shoulders. "I thought you were a brave man, addicted to deeds of derring-do."

Fafhrd cursed sardonically, then demanded, "But even if I should go clang those rusty bells, how can Lankhmar hold out until then with her walls breached and the odds fifty to one against her?"

"I'd like to know that myself ," Ningauble assured him.

"And how do I get to the temple when the streets are crammed with warfare?"

Ningauble shrugged once again. "You're a hero. You should know."

"Well then, the tin whistle?" Fafhrd grated.

"You know, I didn't get a thing on the tin whistle. Sorry about that. Do you have it with you? Might I look at it?"

Grumbling, Fafhrd extracted it from his flat pouch, and brought it around the fire.

"Have you ever blown it?" Ningauble asked.

"No," Fafhrd said with surprise, lifting it to his lips.

"Don't!" Ningauble squeaked. "Not on any account! Never blow a strange whistle. It might summon things far worse even than savage mastiffs or the police. Here, give it to me."

He pinched it away from Fafhrd with a double fold of animated sleeve and held it close to his hood, revolving it clockwise and counterclockwise, finally serpentinely gliding out four of his eyes and subjecting it to their massed scrutiny at thumbnail distance.

At last he withdrew his eyes, sighed, and said, "Well . . . I'm not sure. But there are thirteen characters in the inscription—I couldn't decipher 'em, mind you, but there *are* thirteen. Now if you take that fact in conjunction with the slim couchant feline figure on the other side . . . Well, I think you blow this whistle to summon the War Cats. Mind you, that's only a deduction, and one of several steps, each uncertain."

"Who are the War Cats?" Fafhrd asked.

Ningauble writhed his fat shoulders and neck under their garments. "I've never been quite certain. But putting together various rumors and legends— oh yes, and some cave drawings north of the Cold Waste and south of Quarmall—I have arrived at the tentative conclusion that they are a military aristocracy of all the feline tribes, a bloodthirsty Inner Circle of thirteen members—in short, a dozen and one ailuric berserkers. I would assume—provisionally only, mind you—that they would appear when summoned, as perhaps by this whistle, and instantly assault whatever creature or creatures, beast or man, that seemed to threaten the feline tribes. So I would advise you not to blow it except in the presence of enemies of cats more worthy of attack than yourself, for I suppose you have slain a few tigers and leopards in your day. Here, take it."

Fafhrd snatched and pouched it, demanding, "But

by God's ice-rimmed skull, when *am* I to blow it? How can the Mouser be two parts in fifty alive when buried eight yards deep? What vast, fifty-to-one host can have assaulted Lankhmar without months of rumors and reports of their approach? What fleets could carry—"

"No more questions!" Ningauble interposed shrilly. "Your half hour is up. If you are to beat the Sinking Land and be in time to save the city, you must gallop at once for Lankhmar. Now no more words."

Fafhrd raved for a while longer, but Ningauble maintained a stubborn silence, so Fafhrd gave him a last thundering curse, which brought down a small stalactite that narrowly missed bashing his brains out, and departed, ignoring the urchins' maddening grins.

Outside the caves, he mounted the Mingol mare and cantered, followed by hoof-raised dust-cloud, down the sun-yellowed, dryly rustling slope toward the mile-wide westward-leading isthmus of dark brown rock, salt-filmed and here and there sea-puddled, that was the Sinking Land. Southward gleamed the placid blue waters of the Sea of the East, northward the restless gray waters of the Inner Sea and the glinting squat towers of Ilthmar. Also northward he noted four small dust-clouds like his own coming down the Ilthmar road, which he had earlier traveled himself. Almost surely and just as he'd guessed, the four black brigands were after him at last, hot to revenge their three slain or at least woefully damaged fellow-rogues. He narrowed his eyes and nudged the gray mare to a lively lope.

XI

THE MOUSER was hurrying against a marked moist cool draft through a vast, low-ceilinged concourse close-pillared like a mine with upended bricks and sections of pike-haft and broom-handle, and lit by caged fire-beetles and glow-worms and an occasional sputtering torch held by a rat-page in jacket and short trews lighting the way for some masked person or persons of quality. A few jewel-decked or monstrously fat rat-folk, likewise masked, traveled in litters carried by two or four squat, muscular, nearly naked rats. A limping, aged rat carrying two sacks which twitched a little from the inside was removing dim, weary fire-beetles from their cages and replacing them with fresh bright ones. The Mouser hastened along on tiptoe with knees permanently bent, body hunched forward, and chin out-thrust. It made his legs in particular ache abominably, but it gave him, he hoped, the general silhouette and gait of a rat walking two-legged. His entire head was covered by a cylindrical mask cut from the bottom of his cloak, provided with eye-holes only, and which, stiffened by a wire which had previously stiffened the scabbard of Scalpel, thrust down several inches below his chin to give the impression that it covered a rat's long snout.

He worried what would happen if someone came close enough and were sufficiently observant to note that his mask and cloak too of course were made of tiny ratskins closely stitched together. He hoped that rats were plagued by proportionately tinier rats, though he hadn't noted any tiny ratholes so far; after all, there was the proverb about little bugs having littler bugs, and so on; at any rate he could claim in a pinch that he came from a distant rat-city where such was the case. To keep the curious and watchful at a distance he hovered his gauntleted hands a-twitch above the pommels of Scalpel and Cat's Claw, and chittered angrily or muttered such odd oaths as "All rat-catchers fry!" or "By candle-fat and bacon-rind!" in Lankhmarese, for now that he had ears small and quick enough to hear, he knew that the language was spoken underground, and especially well by the aristos of these lower levels. And what more natural than that rats, who were parasites on man's farms and ships and cities, should copy his language along with many other items of his habits and culture? He had already noted other solitary armed rats—bravos or berserkers, presumably—who behaved in the irritable and dangerous manner he now put on.

His escape from the cellar-rats had been achieved by his own cool-headedness and his pursuers' blundering eagerness, which had made them fight to be first, so that the tunnel had been briefly blocked behind him. His candle had been most helpful in his descent of the first sharply down-angling, rough-hewn, then rough-digged passages, where he had made his way by sliding and leaping, checking himself on a rocky outcropping or by digging heel into dirt only when his speed became so great as to threaten a disastrous fall. The first rough-pillared concourse had also been pitchdark, almost. There he had quickly thrown his cloak over his face to the eyes, for his candle had shown him numerous rats, most of them going naked on all fours, but a few of them hunchedly erect and wearing rough dark clothing, if only a pair of trews or a jacket or slouch hat or smock, or a belt for a short-bladed hanger. Some of these had carried pickax or shovel or pry-bar over shoulder. And there had been one rat fully clothed in black, armed with sword and dagger and wearing a silver-edged full-face vizard—at least the Mouser had assumed it was a rat.

He had taken the first passage leading down— there had been regular steps now, hewn in rock or cut in gravel—and had paused at a turn in the stairs by a curious though stenchful alcove. It contained the first he had seen of the fire-beetle lamps and also a half-dozen small compartments, each closed by a door that left space below and above. After a moment's hesitation he had darted into one which showed no black hind paws or boots below and securely hooking the door behind him, had instantly and rapidly begun to fabricate his ratskin mask. His instinctive assumption about the function of the compartments was confirmed by a large two-handled basket half full of rat droppings and a bucket of stinking urine. After his long-chinned vizard had been made and donned, he had shaken out his candle, pouched it, and then relieved himself, at last permitting himself to wonder in amazement that all his clothes and belongings had been reduced in size proportionately with his body. Ah, he told himself, that

would account for the wide gray border of the pink
puddle which had appeared around his boots in the
cellar above. When he'd been sorcerously shrunken,
the excess motes or atomies of his flesh, blood, and
bones had been shed downward to make the pink
pool, while those of his gray clothing and tempered
iron weapons had sifted away to make up the pool's
gray border, which had been powdery rather than
slimy, of course, because metal or fabric contains little or no liquid compared to flesh. It had occurred to
him that there must be twenty times as much of the
Mouser by weight in that poor abused pink pool o-
verhead as there was in his present rat-small form,
and for a moment he had felt a sentimental sadness.

Finishing his business, he had prepared to continue his downward course when there had come the
descending clatter of paw- and boot-steps, quickly
followed by a banging on the door of his compartment.

Without hesitation he had unhooked the door and
opened it with a jerk. Facing him close there had
been the black-clad, black-and-silver-masked rat he
had seen on the level above, and behind him three
bare-faced rats with drawn hangers that looked and
probably were sharper than gross human fingers
could ever hone.

After the first glance, the Mouser had looked lower
than his pursuers' faces, for fear the color and shape
and especially the placing of his eyes might give him
away.

The vizarded one had said swiftly and clearly in
excellent Lankhmarese, "Have you seen or heard
anyone come down the stairs?—in particular an
armed human magically reduced to decent and normal size?"

Again without hesitation the Mouser had chittered

most angrily, and roughly shouldering his questioner
and the others aside, had spat out, "Idiots! Opium-
chewers! Nibblers of hemp! Out of my way!"

On the stairs he had paused to look back briefly,
snarl loudly and contemptuously, "No, of course
not!" and then gone down the stairs with dignity,
though taking them two at a time.

The next level had shown no rats in sight and been
redolent of grain. He had noted bins of wheat,
barley, millet, kombo, and wild rice from the River
Tilth. A good place to hide—perhaps. But what
could he gain by hiding?

The next level—the third down—had been full of
military clatter and rank with rat-stink. He had
noted rat pikemen drilling in bronze cuirasses and
helmets and another squad being instructed in the
crossbow, while still others crowded around a table
where routes on a great map were being pointed out.
He had lingered even a shorter time there.

Midway down each stairs had been a compartmented nook like the first he'd used. He had
docketed away in his mind this information.

Refreshingly clean, moist air had poured out of the
fourth level, it had been more brightly lit, and most
of the rats strolling in it had been richly dressed and
masked. He had turned into it at once, walking
against the moist breeze, since that might well come
from the outer world and mark a route of escape, and
he had continued with angry chitters and curses to
play his impulsively assumed role of crotchety, half-
mad rat-bravo or rogue-rat.

In fact, he found himself trying so hard to be a
convincing rat that without volition his eyes now followed with leering interest a small mincing she-rat in
pink silk and pearls—mask as well as dress—who led

on a leash what he took at first to be a baby rat and then realized was a dwarfish, well-groomed, fear-eyed mouse; and also an imperiously tall ratess in dark green silk sewn over with ruby chips and holding in one hand a whip and in the other the short leashes of two fierce-eyed, quick-breathing shrews that looked as big as mastiffs and were doubtless even more bloodthirsty.

Still looking lustfully at this striking proud creature as she passed him with green, be-rubied mask tilted high, he ran into a slow-gaited, portly rat robed and masked in ermine, which looked extremely coarse-haired now, and wearing about his neck a long gold chain and about his aldermanic waist a gold-studded belt, from which hung a heavy bag that chinked dulcetly at the Mouser's jolting impact.

Snapping a "Your pardon, merchant!" at the wheezingly chittering fellow, the Mouser strode on without backward glance. He grinned conceitedly under his mask. These rats were easy to befool!—and perhaps reduction in size had sharpened finer his own sharp wits.

He was tempted for an instant to turn back and lure off and rob the fat fellow, but realized at once that in the human world the chinking goldpieces would be smaller than sequins.

This thought set his mind on a problem which had been obscurely terrifying him ever since he had plunged into the rat-world. Sheelba had said the effects of the potion would last for nine hours. Then presumably the Mouser would resume his normal size as swiftly as he had lost it. To have that happen in a burrow or even in the foot-and-a-half-high, pillar-studden concourse would be disastrous—it made him wince to think of it.

Now, the Mouser had no intention of staying anything like nine hours in the rat-world. On the other hand, he didn't exactly want to escape at once. Dodging around in Lankhmar like a nimbly animate gray doll for half a night didn't appeal to him—it would be shame-making even if, or perhaps especially if while doll-size he had to report his important intelligences about the rat-world to Glipkerio and Olegnya Mingolsbane—with Hisvet watching perhaps. Besides, his mind was already afire with schemes to assassinate the rats' king, if they had one, or foil their obvious project of conquest in some even more spectacular fashion on their home ground. He felt a peculiarly great self-confidence and had not realized yet that it was because he was fully as tall as the taller rats around, as tall as Fafhrd, relatively, and no longer the smallish man he had been all his life.

However, there was always the possibility that by some unforeseeable ill fortune he might be unmasked, captured, and imprisoned in a tiny cell. A panicking thought.

But even more unnerving was the basic problem of time. Did it move faster for the rats, or slower? He had the impression that life and all its processes moved at a quicker tempo down here. But was that true? Did he now clearly hear the rat-Lankhmarese, which had previously sounded like squeaks, because his ears were quicker, or merely smaller, or because most of a rat's voice was pitched too high for human ears to hear, or even because rats spoke Lankhmarese only in their burrows? He surreptitiously felt his pulse. It seemed the same as always. But mightn't it be greatly speeded up equally, so that he noted no difference? Sheelba had said something about a day being a tenth of a million pulsebeats.

Was that rat or human pulse? Were rat-hours so short that nine of them might pass in a hundred or so human minutes? Almost he was tempted to rush up the first stairs he saw. No, wait . . . if the timing was by pulse and his pulse seemed normal, then wouldn't he have one normal Mouser-sleep to work in down here? It was truly most confusing. "Out upon it all, by cat-gut sausages and roasted dog's eyes!" he heard himself curse with sincerity.

Several things at any rate were clear. Before he dared idle or nap, let alone sleep, he must discover some way of measuring down here the passage of time in the aboveground world. Also, to get at the truth about rat-night and day, he must swiftly learn about rodent sleeping habits. For some reason his mind jumped back to the tall ratess with the brace of straining shrews. But that was ridiculous, he told himself. There was sleeping and sleeping, and that one had very little if anything to do with the other.

He came out of his thought-trance to realize fully what his senses had for some time been telling him: that the strollers had become fewer, the breeze more damp and cool and fresh, and sea-odorous too, and the pillars ahead natural rock, while through the doorways chiseled between them shone a yellowish light, not bright yet twinkling and quite unlike that of the fire-beetles, glow-wasps, and tiny torches.

He passed a marble doorway and noted white marble steps going down from it. Then he stepped between two of the rocky pillars and halted on the rim of a wonder-place.

It was a roughly circular natural rock cave many rats high and many more long and wide, and filled with faintly rippling seawater which transmitted a mild flood of yellowish light that came through a

great wide hole, underwater by about the length of a
rat's-pike, in the other end of the glitter-ceilinged
cavern. All around this sea lake, about two rat-pikes
above the water, went the rather narrow rock road,
looking in part natural, in part chiseled and pick-
axed, on which he now stood. At its distant end, in
the shadows above the great underwater hole, he
could dimly make out the forms and gleaming weapons of a half-dozen or so motionless rats, evidently on
guard duty.

As the Mouser watched, the yellow light became
yellower still, and he realized it must be the light of
later afternoon, surely the afternoon of the day in
which he had entered the rat-world. Since sunset was
at six o'clock and he had entered the rat-world after
three, he had spent fewer than three of his nine
hours. Most important, he had linked the passage of
time in the rat-world with that in the big world—and
was somewhat startled at the relief he felt.

He recalled too the "dead" rats which had seemed
to swim away from the cage dropped from the palace
window into the Inner Sea after Hisvin's demonstra-
tion of his deathspell. They might very well have
swum underwater into this very cavern, or another
like it.

It also came to him that he had discovered the secret of the damp breeze. He knew the tide was rising
now, an hour or so short of full, and in rising it drove
the cave-trapped air through the concourse. At low
tide the great hole would be in part above water, allowing the cavern air to be refreshed from outside. A
rather clever if intermittent ventilation system. Perhaps some of these rats were a bit more ingenious
than he had given them credit for.

At that instant there came a light, inhuman touch

on his right shoulder. Turning around, he saw stepping back from him with naked rapier held a little to one side the black-masked black-clad rat who had disturbed him in the privy.

"What's the meaning of this?" he chitteringly blustered. "By God's hairless tail, why am I catted and ferreted?—you black dog!"

In far less ratlike Lankhmarese than the Mouser's, the other asked quietly, "What are you doing in a restricted area? I must ask you to unmask, sir."

"Unmask? I'll see the color of your liver first, mousling!" the Mouser ranted wildly. It would never do, he knew, to change character now.

"Must I call in my underlings to unmask you by force?" the other inquired in the same soft, deadly voice. "But it is not necessary. Your reluctance to unmask is final confirmation of my deduction that you are indeed the magically shrunken human come as a spy into Lankhmar Below."

"That opium specter again?" the Mouser raved, dropping his hand to Scalpel's hilt. "Begone, mad mouse dipped in ink, before I cut you to collops!"

"Your threats and brags are alike useless, sir," the other answered with a low and humorous laugh. "You wonder how I became certain of your identity? I suppose you think you were very clever. Actually you gave yourself away more than once. First, by relieving yourself in that jakes where I first encountered you. Your dung was of a different shape, color, consistency, and odor than that of my compatriots. You should have sought out a water-privy. Second, although you did try to shadow your eyes, the eye-holes in your mask are too squintingly close together, as are all human eyes. Third, your boots are clearly made to fit human rather than rodent feet, though you have the small sense to talk on your toes to ape our legs and gait."

The Mouser noted that the other's black boots had far tinier soles than his own and were of soft leather both below and above the big ankle-bend.

The other continued, "And from the very first I knew you must be an utter stranger, else you would never have dared shoulder aside and insult the many times proven greatest duelist and fastest sword in all Lankhmar Below."

With black-gloved left paw the other whipped off his silver-trimmed mask, revealing upstanding oval ears and long furry black face and huge, protuberant, wide-spaced black eyes. Baring his great white incisors in a lordly smirk and bringing his mask across his chest in a curt, sardonic bow, he finished, "Svivomilo, at your service."

At least now the Mouser understood the vast vanity—great almost as his own!—which had led his pursuer to leave his underlings behind in the concourse while he came on alone to make the arrest. Whipping out simultaneously Scalpel and Cat's Claw, purposely not pausing to unmask, the Mouser made his most rapid advance, ending in a tremendous lunge at the neck. It seemed to him that he had never before in his life moved as swiftly—small size certainly had its points.

There was a flash and a clash and Scalpel was deflected—by Svivomilo's dagger drawn with lightning speed. And then Svivomilo's rapier was on the offensive and the Mouser barely avoiding it by rapid parries with both his weapons and by backing off perilously along the water's brink. Now his involuntary thought was that his opponent had had a much longer time than he of being small and practicing the swiftness it allowed, while his mask interfered with his vision and if it slipped a little would blind him altogether. Yet Svivomilo's incessant attacks gave him no time to whip it off. With sudden desperation he lunged forward himself, managing to get a bind with Scalpel on the rapier that momentarily took both weapons out of the fight, and an instant later lashed out with Cat's Claw at Svivomilo's dagger-stabbing wrist, and by accurate eye and good fortune cut its inner tendons.

Then as Svivomilo hesitated and sprang back, the Mouser disengaged Scalpel and launched it in another sinew-straining, long lunge, thrice dipping his point just under Svivomilo's double and then circle parries, and finally drove its point on in a slicing thrust that went through the rat's neck and ended grating against the vertebra there.

Scarlet blood pouring over the black lace at Svivomilo's throat and down his chest, and with only one short, bubbling, suffocated gasp, for the Mouser's thrust had severed windpipe as well as arteries, the rightly boastful but foolishly reckless duelist pitched forward on his face and lay writhing.

The Mouser made the mistake of trying to sheathe his bloodied sword, forgetting that Scalpel's scabbard was no longer wire-stiffened, which made the action difficult. He cursed the scabbard, limp as Svivomilo's now nerveless tail.

Four cuirassed and helmeted rats with pikes at the ready appeared at two of the rocky doorways. Brandishing his red-dripping sword and gleaming dirk, the Mouser raced through an untenanted doorway and with a chittering scream to clear the way ahead of him, sprinted across the concourse to the marble doorway he'd noted earlier, and plunged down the white stairway.

The unusual nook in the turn of the stairs held

only three compartments, each with a silver-fitted
door of ivory. Into the central one there was going a
white-booted rat wearing a voluminous white cloak
and hood and bearing in his white-gloved right hand
an ivory staff with a large sapphire set in its top.

Without an instant's pause the Mouser ended his
plunging descent with a dash into the nook. He
hurled ahead of him the white-cloaked rat and
slammed and hooked fast behind them the ivory
door.

Recovering himself, the Mouser's victim turned
and with outraged dignity and brandished staff demanded through his white mask set with diamonds,
"Who dareth dithturb with rude thcufflingth Counthillor Grig of the Inner Thircle of Thirteen?
Mithcreant!"

While a part of the Mouser's brain was realizing
that this was the lisping white rat he had seen aboard
Squid sitting on Hisvin's shoulder, his eyes were informing him that this compartment held not a box
for droppings, but a raised silver toilet seat, up
through which came the sound and odor of rushing
seawater. It must be one of the water-privies
Svivomilo had mentioned.

Dropping Scalpel, the Mouser threw back Grig's
hood, dragged off his mask over his head, tripped the
sputtering councillor and forced his head down
against the far side of the privy's silver rim, and then
with Cat's Claw cut Grig's furry white throat almost
from ratty ear to ear, so that his blood gushed down
into the rushing water below. As soon as his victim's
writhings stilled, the Mouser drew off Grig's white
cloak and hood, taking great care that no blood got
on them.

At that moment he heard the booted footsteps of

several persons coming down the stairs. Operating with demonic speed, the Mouser placed Scalpel, the ivory staff, and the white mask and hood and cloak behind the seat of the privy, then hoisted the dead body so that it sat on the same, and himself stood crouching on the silver rim, facing the hooked door and holding the limp trunk erect. Then he silently prayed with great sincerity to Issek of the Jug, the first god he could think of, the one whom Fafhrd had once served.

Wavy and hooked browned-iron pike-blades gleamed above the doorways. The two to either side were slammed open. Then after a pause, during which he hoped someone had peered under the central door just enough to note the white boots, there came a light rapping, and then a respectful voice inquiring, "Your pardon, Nobility, but have you recently seen anything of a person in gray with cloak and mask of finest gray fur, and armed with rapier and dagger?"

The Mouser answered in a voice which he tried to make calm and dignifiedly benign, "I have theen nothing, thir. About thicty breathth ago I heard thomeone clattering at thpeed down the thtairth."

"Our humblest thanks, Nobility," the questioner responded, and the booted footsteps continued rapidly down toward the fifth level.

The Mouser let off a long soft sigh and chopped short his prayer. Then he set swiftly to work, for he knew he had a considerable task ahead of him, some of it most grisly. He wiped off and scabbarded Scalpel and Cat's Claw. Then he examined his victim's cloak, hood, and mask, discovering almost no blood on them, and set them aside. He noted that the cloak could be fastened down the front with ivory

buttons. Then he dragged off Grig's tall boots of
whitest suede and tried them on his own legs.
Though their softness helped, they fitted
abominably, the sole covering little more than the
area under his toes. Still, this would keep him reminded to maintain a rat's gait at all times. He also
tried on Grig's long white gloves, which fitted worse,
if that were possible. Still, he could wear them. His
own boots and gauntlets he tucked securely over his
gray belt.

Next he undressed Grig and dropped his garments
one by one into the water, retaining only a razor-
sharp ivory-and-gold-fitted dagger, a number of
small parchment scrolls, Grig's undershirt, and a
double-ended purse filled with gold coins struck with
a rat's head on one side, circled by a wreath of wheat,
and on the other a complex maze (tunnels?) and a
numeral followed by the initials *S. F. L. B.* "Since
the Founding of Lankhmar Below?" he hazarded
brilliantly. He hung the purse over his belt, fixed the
dagger to it by a gold hook on its ivory sheath, and
thrust the scrolls unscanned into his own pouch.

Then with a grunt of distaste he rolled up his
sleeves and using the ivory-handled dagger, pro-
ceeded to dismember the furry corpse into pieces
small enough to force through the silver rim so that
they splashed into the water and were carried away.

This horrid task at last accomplished, he made a
careful search for blood splatters, wiped them up
with Grig's undershirt, used it to polish the silver
rim, then dropped it after the other stuff.

Still not giving himself a pause, he pulled on again
the white suede boots, donned the white cloak, which
was of finest wool, and buttoned it all the way down
the front, thrusting his arms through the slits in the

cloak to either side. Then he put on the mask, discovered that he had to use the dagger to extend narrowly the eye-slits at their inner ends to be able to see at all with his own close-set human eyes. After that he tied on the hood, throwing it as far forward as practicable to hide the mask's mutilations and his lack of be-furred rat ears. Finally he drew on the long, ill-fitting white gloves.

It was well that he had worked as speedily as he had, allowing himself no time for rest, for now there came booted footsteps up the stairs and the nastily hooked pike-blades a-wave again, while below the door of his compartment there appeared typically crooked rat-boots of fine black leather embossed with golden scroll-work.

There was a sharper knocking and a grating voice, polite yet peremptory, said, "Your pardon, Councillor. This is Hreest. As Lieutenant Warden of the Fifth Level, I must ask you to open the door. You have been closeted a long while in there, and I must assure myself that the spy we seek is not holding a knife at your throat."

The Mouser coughed, took up the sapphire-headed ivory staff, drew wide the door and majestically strode forth with a slight hobble. Resuming with tired legs the aching, tip-toe rat-gait had given him a sudden torturing cramp in his left calf.

The pike-rats knelt. The fancy-booted rat, whose black clothes, mask, gauntlets and rapier-scabbard were also covered with fine-lined golden arabesques, dropped back two steps.

Directing only a brief gaze at him, the Mouser said coolly, "You dare dithturb and hathten Counthillor Grig at hith eliminathionth? Well, perhapth your reathonth are good enough. Perhapth."

Hreest swept off his wide-brimmed hat plumed
with the breast-feathers of black canaries. "I am certain they are, Nobility. There is loose in Lankhmar
Below a human spy, magically changed to our size.
He has already murdered that skillful if unruly and
conceited swordsman Svivomilo."

"Thorry newth indeed!" the Mouser lisped.
"Thearch out thith thpy at onthe! Thpare no ecth-
penthe in men or effort. I will inform the Counthil,
Hreetht, if you have not."

And while Hreest's voice followed him with ratly
apologies, thanks, and reassurances, the Mouser
stepped regally down the white marble stairs, his
limp hardly noticeable due to the grateful support
afforded by his ivory staff. The sapphire in its top
twinkled like the blue star Ashsha. He felt like a king.

Fafhrd rode west through the gathering twilight,
the iron-shod hooves of the Mingol mare striking
sparks from the flinty substance of the Sinking Land.
The sparks were becoming faintly visible, just as
were a few of the largest stars. The road, mere hoof
dints, was becoming hard to discern. To north and
south, the Inner Sea and the Sea of the East were
sullen gray expanses, the former wave-flecked. And
now finally, against the last dirty pink ribbon of sunset fringing the west, he made out the wavery black
line of squat trees and towering cactuses that marked
the beginning of the Great Salt Marsh.

It was a welcome sight, yet Fafhrd was frowning
deeply—two vertical furrows springing up from the
inside end of either eyebrow.

The left furrow, you might say, was for what followed him. Taking an unhurried look over shoulder,
he saw that the four riders whom he had first

glimpsed coming down the Sarheenmar road were now only a bowshot and a half behind him. Their horses were black and they wore great black cloaks and hoods. He knew now to a certainty they were his four black Ilthmar brigands. And Ilthmar land-pirates hungry only for loot, let alone vengeance, had been known to pursue their prey to the very Marsh Gate of Lankhmar.

The right furrow, which was deepest, was for an almost imperceptible tilt, south lifting above north, in the ragged black horizon ahead. That this was actually a slight tilting of the Sinking Land in the opposite direction was proven when the Mingol mare took a lurch to the left. Fafhrd harshly kicked his mount into a gallop. It would be a near thing whether he reached the Marsh causeway before he was engulfed.

Lankhmar philosophers believe that the Sinking Land is a vast long shield, concave underneath, of hard-topped rock so porous below that it is exactly the same weight as water. Volcanic gases from the roots of the Ilthmar Mountains and also mephitic vapors from the incredibly deep-rooted and yeasty Great Salt Marsh gradually fill the concavity and lift the huge shield above the surface of the seas. But then an instability develops, due to the greater density of the shield's topping. The shield begins to rock. The supporting gasses and vapors escape in great alternate belches through the waters to north and south. Then the shield sinks somewhat below the waves and the whole slow, rhythmic process begins again.

So it was that the tilting told Fafhrd that the Sinking Land was once more about to submerge. And now the tilt had increased so much that he had to

pull a little on the mare's right bridle to keep her to
the road. Looking back over right shoulder, he saw
that the four black horsemen were also coming on
faster, in fact somewhat faster than he.

As his gaze returned to his goal of safety, the
Marsh, he saw the near waters of the Inner Sea shoot
upward in a line of gray, foamy geysers—the first escape of vapors—while the waters of the Sea of the
East drew suddenly closer.

Then very slowly the rock beneath him began to
tilt in the opposite direction, until at last he was pulling on the mare's left bridle to keep her to the road.
He was very glad she was a Mingol beast, trained to
ignore any and all unnaturalness, even earthquake.

And now it was the still waters of the Sea of the
East that exploded upward in a long, dirty, bubbling
fence of escaping gas, while the waters of the Inner
Sea came foaming almost to the road.

Yet the Marsh was very close. He could make out
individual thorn trees and cactuses and thickets of
giant sea-grass outlined against the now utterly bled
west. And then he saw straight ahead a gap that—
pray Issek!—would be the causeway.

Sparks sped whitely from under the mare's iron
shoes. The beast's breath rasped.

But now there was a new disquieting change in the
landscape, though a very slight one. Almost imperceptibly, the whole Great Salt Marsh was beginning to rise.

The Sinking Land was beginning its periodic sub-
mergence.

From either side, from north and south, gray walls
were converging on him—the foam-fronted raging
waters of the Inner Sea and the Sea of the East
rushing to sink the great stone shield now its gaseous
support was gone.

A black barrier a yard high loomed just ahead. Fafhrd leaned low in the saddle, nudging the mare's flanks with his heels, and with a great long leap the mare lifted them the needed yard and found them firm footing again, and with never a pause galloped on unchangingly, except that now instead of clashing sharply against rock, the iron shoes struck mutedly on the tight-packed gravel of the causeway.

From behind them came a mounting, rumbling, snarling roar that suddenly rose to a crashing climax. Fafhrd looked back and saw a great starburst of waters—not gray now, but ghostly white in the remaining light from the west—where the waves of the Inner Sea had met the rollers of the Sea of the East exactly at the road.

He was about to look forward again and slow his mount, when out of that pale, churny explosion there appeared a black horse and rider, then another, then a third. But no more—the fourth had evidently been engulfed. The hair lifted on his back at the thought of the leaps the three other beasts had made with their black riders, and he cursed the Mingol mare to make more speed, knowing that kind words went unheard by her.

XII

LANKHMAR READIED herself for another night of terror as shadows lengthened toward infinity and the sunlight turned deep orange. Her inhabitants were not reassured by the lessening number of murderous rats in the streets; they smelled the electric calm before the storm and they barricaded themselves in upper stories as they had the night gone by. Soldiers and constables, according to their individual characters, grinned with relief or griped at bureaucracy's inanities when they got the news that they were to repair to the Southern Barracks one hour before midnight to be harangued by Olegnya Mingolsbane, who was reputed to make the longest and most tedious spittle-spraying speeches of any Captain General in Nehwon's history, and to stink with the sourness of near-senility besides that.

Aboard *Squid*, Slinoor gave orders for lights to burn all night and an all-hands watch to be kept. While the black kitten, forsaking the crow's nest, paced the rail nearest the docks, from time to time uttering an anxious mew and eyeing the dark streets as if with mingled temptation and dread.

For awhile Glipkerio soothed his nerves by observing the subtle torturing of Reetha, designed chiefly to fray her nerves rather than her flesh, and by auditing her hours-long questioning by well-trained inquisitors, who sought to hammer from her the admission that the Gray Mouser was leader of the rats —as his shrinking to rat-size seemed surely to prove —and also force her to divulge a veritable handbook of information on the Mouser's magical methods and sorcerous strategems. The girl truly entranced Glipkerio: she reacted to threats, evil teasings, and relatively minor pain in such a lively, unwearying way.

But after awhile he nonetheless grew bored and had a light supper served him in the sunset's red glow on his seaporch outside the Blue Audience Chamber and beside the head of the great copper chute where balanced the great leaden spindle, which he reached out and touched from time to time for reassurance. He hadn't lied to Hisvin, he told himself smugly; he *did* have at least one other secret weapon, albeit it wasn't a weapon of offense, but rather the ultimate opposite. Pray, though, he wouldn't have to use it! Hisvin had promised that at midnight he would work his spell against the assaulting rats, and thus far Hisvin had never failed—had he not conquered the rats of the grain fleet?—while his daughter and her maid had ways of soothing Glipkerio that amazingly did not involve whippings. He had seen with his own eyes Hisvin slay rats with his spell—while on his own part he had arranged for all soldiers and police to be in the South Barracks at midnight listening to that tiresome Olegnya Mingolsbane. He had done his part, he told himself; Hisvin would do his; and at midnight his troubles and vexations would be done.

But it was such a long time until midnight! Once more boredom engulfed the black-togaed, purple-pansy coroneted, beanpole monarch, and he began to think wistfully of whips and Reetha. Beyond all other men, he mused, an overlord, burdened by administration and ceremonies, had no time for even the most homely hobbies and innocent diversions.

Reetha's questioners, meanwhile, gave up for the day and left her in Samanda's charge, who from time to time described gloatingly to the girl the various all-out thrashings and other torments the palace mistress would visit on her as soon as her namby-pamby inquisitors were through with her. The much-abused maid sought to comfort herself with the thought that her madcap gray rescuer might somehow regain his proper size and return to work again her escape. Surely, and despite all the nasty insinuations she had endured, the Gray Mouser was rat-size against his will. She recalled the many fairy tales she had heard of lizard- and frog-princes restored to handsomeness and proper height by a maiden's loving kiss, and despite her miseries, her eyebrowless eyes grew dreamy.

The Mouser squinted through Grig's notched mask at the glorious Council Chamber and the other members of the Supreme Thirteen. Already the scene had become oppressively familiar to him, and he was damnably tired of lisping. Nevertheless, he gathered himself for a supreme effort, which at least was one that tickled his wits.

His coming here had been simplicity itself, and inevitability too. Upon reaching the Fifth Level after parting with Hreest and his pike-rats, rat-pages had fallen in beside him at the foot of the white marble stairs, and a rat-chamberlain had gone solemnly before him, ringing an engraved silver bell which probably once had tinkled from the ankle of a temple dancer in the Street of the Gods in the world above. Thus, footing it grandly himself with the aid of his sapphire-topped ivory staff, though still hobbling a little, he had been wordlessly conducted into the Council Chamber and to the very chair which he now occupied.

The chamber was low but vast, pillared by golden and silver candlesticks doubtless pilfered from palaces and churches overhead. Among them were a few of what looked like jeweled scepters of office and maces of command. In the background, toward the distant walls and half hid by the pillars, were grouped rat-pikemen, waiters, and other servants, litter-bearers with their vehicles, and the like.

The chamber was lit by golden and silver cages of fire-beetles and night-bees and glow-wasps large as eagles, and so many of them that the pulsing of their light was barely apparent. The Mouser had decided that if it became necessary to create a diversion, he would loose some of the glow-wasps.

Within a central circle of particularly costly pillars was set a great round table, about which sat evenly spaced the Thirteen, all masked and clad in white hoods and robes, from which white-gloved rat-hands emerged.

Opposite the Mouser and on a slightly higher chair sat Skwee, well remembered from the time he had crouched on the Mouser's shoulder threatening to sever the artery under his ear. On Skwee's right sat Siss, while on his left was a taciturn rat whom the rest addressed as Lord Null. Alone of the Thirteen, this grumpy Lord Null was clad in robe, hood, mask, and gloves of black. There was something hauntingly familiar about him, perhaps because the hue of his garb recalled to the Mouser Svivomilo and also Hreest.

The remaining nine rats were clearly apprentice members, promoted to fill the gaps in the Circle of Thirteen left by the white rats slain aboard *Squid,* for they never spoke and when questions were voted, only bobbingly agreed with the majority opinion among Skwee, Siss, Lord Null, and Grig—that is, the Mouser—or if that opinion were split two to two, abstained.

The entire tabletop was hidden by a circular map of what appeared to be well-tanned and buffed human skin, the most delicate and finely pored. The map itself was nothing but innumerable dots: golden, silver, red and black, and thick as fly-specks in the stall of a slum fruit-merchant. At first the Mouser had been able to think of nothing but some eerie, dense starfield. Then it had been revealed to him, by the references the others made to it, that it was nothing more or less than a map of all the ratholes in Lankhmar!

At first this knowledge hadn't made the map come to life for the Mouser. But then gradually he had begun to see in the apparently randomly clustered and twisty-trailed dots the outlines of at least the principal buildings and streets of Lankhmar. Of course, the whole plot of the city was reversed, because viewed from below instead of above.

The golden dots, it had turned out, stood for ratholes unknown to humans and used by rats; the red, for holes known to humans yet still used by rats; the silver, for holes unknown to humans, but not currently employed by the dwellers underneath; while the black dots designated the holes known to humans and avoided by the rodents of Lankhmar Below.

During the entire council session, three slim female rat-pages silently went about, changing the color of ratholes and even dotting in new ones, according to information whispered them by rat-pages, who ceaselessly came and went on equally silent paws. For this purpose, the three females used rat-tail brushes each made of a single, stiffened horsehair frayed at the tip, which they employed most dexterously, and each had slung in a rack at the waist four ink-pots of the appropriate colors.

What the Mouser had learned during the council session had been, simply yet horribly, the all-over plan for the grand assault on Lankhmar Above, which was to take place a half-hour before this very midnight: detailed information about the disposition of pike companies, crossbow detachments, dagger groups, poison-weapon brigades, incendiaries, lone assassins, child-killers, panic-rats, stink-rats, genital-snappers and breast-biters and other berserkers, setters of man-traps such as trip-cords and needle-sharp caltrops and strangling nooses, artillery brigades which would carry up piecemeal larger weapons to be assembled above ground, until his brain could no longer hold all the data.

He had also learned that the principal attacks were to be made on the South Barracks and especially on the Street of the Gods, hitherto spared.

Finally he learned that the aim of the rats was not to exterminate humans or drive them from Lankhmar, but to force an unconditional surrender from Glipkerio and enslave the overlord's subjects by that agreement and a continuing terror so that

Lankhmar would go on as always about its pleasures
and business, buying and selling, birthing and dying,
sending out of ships and caravans, gathering of grain
—especially grain!—but ruled by the rats.

Fortunately all this briefing had been done by
Skwee and Siss. Nothing had been asked of the
Mouser—that is, Grig—or of Lord Null, except to
supply opinions on knotty problems and lead in the
voting. This had also provided the Mouser with time
to devise ways and means of throwing a cat into the
rats' plans.

Finally the briefing was done and Skwee asked
around the table for ideas to improve the grand assault—not as if he expected to get any.

But at this point the Mouser rose up—somewhat
crippled, since Grig's damnably ill-fitting rat-boots
were still giving him the cramp—and taking up his
ivory staff laid its tip unerringly on a cluster of silver
dots at the west end of the Street of Gods.

"Why ith no aththault made here?" he demanded.
"I thuggetht that at the height of the battle, a party
of ratth clad in black togath iththue from the temple
of the Godth *of* Lankhmar. Thith will convinthe the
humanth ath nothing elthe that their very godth—
the godth of their thity—have turned againtht them
—been tranthformed, in fact, to ratth!"

He swallowed hard down his raw, wearied throat.
Why the devil had Grig had to have a lisp?

His suggestion appeared for a moment to stupify
the other members of the Council. Then Siss said,
wonderingly, admiringly, enviously, and as if against
his will, "I never thought of that."

Skwee said, "The temple of the Gods *of* Lankhmar
has long been avoided by man and rat alike, as you
well know, Grig. Nevertheless . . ."

Lord Null said peevishly, "I am against it. Why meddle with the unknown? The humans of Lankhmar fear and avoid the temple of their city's gods. So should we."

The Mouser glared at the black-robed rat through his mask slits. "Are we mithe or ratth?" he demanded. "Or are we even cowardly, thuperthtitiouth men? Where ith your ratly courage, Lord Null? Or thovereign, thkeptical, ratly reathon? My thratagem will cow the humanth and prove forever the thuperior bravery of ratth! Thkwee! Thith! Ith it not tho?"

The matter was put to a vote. Lord Null voted nay, Siss and the Mouser and—after a pause—Skwee voted aye, the other nine bobbed, and so Operation Black Toga, as Skwee christened it, was hastily added to the battle plans.

"We have over four hours in which to organize it," Skwee reminded his nervous colleagues.

The Mouser grinned behind his mask. He had a feeling that the Gods *of* Lankhmar, if ever roused, would side with the city's human inhabitants. Or would they!—he wondered belatedly.

In any case, his business and desire now was to get out of the Council Chamber as soon as possible. A stratagem instantly suggested itself to him. He waved to a page.

"Thummon a litter," he commanded. "Thith deliberathion hath tired me. I feel faint and am troubled by leg cramp. I will go for a thhort while to my home and wife to retht me."

Skwee looked around at him. "Wife?" the white rat asked incredulously.

Instantly the Mouser answered, "Ith it any buthineth of yourth if it ith my whim to call my mithtreth my wife?"

Skwee still eyed him for a bit, then shrugged.

The litter arrived almost immediately, borne by
two very brawny, half-naked rats. The Mouser rolled
into it gratefully, laying his ivory staff beside him,
commanded "To my home!" and waved a gentle
goodbye to Skwee and Lord Null as he was carried
joggingly off. He felt himself at the moment to be the
most brilliant mind in the whole universe and
thoroughly deserving of a rest, even in a rat burrow.
He reminded himself he had at least four hours to go
before Sheelba's spell wore off and he became once
more human size. He'd done his best for Lankhmar,
now he must think of himself. He lazily wondered
what the comforts of a rat home would be like. He
must sample them before escaping above ground. It
really had been a damnably tiring council session after all that had gone before.

Skwee turned to Lord Null as the litter disappeared by stages beyond the pillars and said through
his be-diamonded white mask, "So Grig has a mistress, the old misogynist! Perhaps it's she who has
quickened his mind to such new brilliancies as Operation Black Toga."

"I still don't like that one, though you outvoted me
and I must go along," chittered the other irritably
from behind his black vizard. "There's too much un-
certainty tonight. The final battle about to be joined.
A magically transformed human spy reported in
Lankhmar Below. The change in Grig's character.
That rabid mouse running widdershins a-foam at the
jaws, outside the Council Chamber, and which
squeaked thrice when you slew him. The un-
customary buzzing of the night-bees in Siss' cham-

bers. And now this new operation adopted on the spur of the moment—"

Skwee clapped Lord Null on the shoulder in friendly fashion. "You're distraught tonight, comrade, and see omens in every night-bug," he said. "Grig at all events had one most sound notion. We all could do with a little rest and refreshment. Especially you before your all-important mission. Come."

And turning the table over to Siss, he and Lord Null went to a curtained alcove just off the Council Chamber, Skwee ordering on the way that food and drink be brought them.

When the curtains were closed behind them, Skwee seated himself in one of the two chairs beside the small table there and took off his mask. In the pulsing violet light of the three silver-caged glow-wasps illuminating the alcove, his long, white-furred, blue-eyed snout looked remarkably sinister.

"To think," he said, "that tomorrow my people will be masters of Lankhmar Above. For millenia we rats have planned and built, tunneled and studied and striven, and now in less than six hours—it's worth a drink! Which reminds me, comrade, isn't it time for your medicinal draught?"

Lord Null hissed with consternation, prepared to lift his black mask distractedly, dipped his black-gloved right fore-member into his pouch, and came up with a tiny white vial.

"Stop!" Skwee commanded with some horror, capturing the black-gloved wrist with a sudden grab. "If you should drink *that one* now—!"

"I *am* nervous tonight, nervous to flusteration," the other admitted, returning the white vial to his pouch and coming up with a black one. Before draining its contents, he lifted his black mask entirely. The face behind was not a rat's, but the seamed and beady-eyed visage, rat-small, of Hisvin the grain-merchant.

The black draught swallowed, he appeared to experience relief and easement of tension. The worry lines in his face were replaced by those of thought.

"Who is Grig's mistress, Skwee?" he speculated suddenly. "No common slut, I'll swear, or vanity-puffed courtesan."

Skwee shrugged his hunchy shoulders and said cynically, "The more brilliant the enchanted male, the stupider the enchanting female."

"No!" Hisvin said impatiently. "I sense a brilliant and rapacious mind here that is not Grig's. He was ambitious once, you know, sought your position, then his fires sank to coals glowing through wintery ash."

"That's true," Skwee agreed thoughtfully.

"Who has blown him alight again?" Hisvin demanded, now with anxious suspicion. "*Who* is his mistress, Skwee?"

Fafhrd pulled up the Mingol mare before that iron-hearted beast should topple from exhaustion— and had trouble doing it, so resolute unto death was the grim creature. Yet once stopped, he felt her legs giving under her and he dropped quickly from the saddle lest she collapse from his weight. She was lathered with sweat, her head hung between her trembling forelegs, and her slatted ribs worked like a bellows as she gasped whistlingly.

He rested his hand lightly on her shaking shoulders. She never could have made Lankhmar, he knew. They were less than halfway across the Great Salt Marsh.

Low moonlight, striking from behind, washed with

a faint gold the gravel of the causeway road and yellowly touched the tops of thorn tree and cactus, but could not yet slant down to the Marsh's sea-grassed floor and black bottoms.

Save for the hum and crackle of insects and the calls of night birds, the moonlight-brushed area was silent—yet would not be so for long, Fafhrd knew with a shudder.

Ever since the preternatural emergence of the three black riders from the crash of waves over the Sinking Land and their drumming unshakable pursuit of him through the deepening night, he had been less and less able to think of them as mere vengeful Ilthmar brigands, and more and more conceived them as a supernatural black trinity of death. For miles now, besides, something huge and long-legged and lurching, though never distinctly seen, had been pursuing him through the Marsh, keeping pace with him at the distance of a spear cast. Some giant familiar or obedient djinn of the black horsemen seemed most likely.

His fears had so worked on him that Fafhrd had finally put the mare to her extremest gallop, outdistancing the hoof-noise of the pursuit, though with no effect on the lurching shape and with the inevitable present result. He drew Graywand and faced back toward the new-risen gibbous moon.

Then very faintly he began to hear it: the muted rhythmic drumming of hooves on gravel. They were coming.

At the same moment, from the deep shadows where the giant familiar should be, he heard the Gray Mouser call hoarsely, "This way, Fafhrd! Toward the blue light. Lead your mount. Make it swift!"

Grinning even as the hairs lifted on his neck,
Fafhrd looked south and saw a shaped blue glow, like
a round-topped, smallish, blue-lit window in the
blackness of the Marsh. He plunged down the
causeway's slanting south side toward it, pulling the
mare after him, and found underfoot a low ridge of
firm ground rather than mud. He moved ahead
eagerly through the dark, digging in his heels and
leaning forward as he dragged his spent mount. The
blue window looked a little above his head now. The
drumming coming up from the east was louder.

"Shake a leg, Lazybones!" he heard the Mouser
call in the same rasping tones. The Gray One must
have caught a cold from the Marsh's damp or—the
Fates forfend!—a fever from its miasmas.

"Tether your mount to the thorn stump," the
Mouser continued gruffly. "There's food for her
there and a water pool. Then come up. Speed,
speed!"

Fafhrd obeyed without word or waste motion, for
the drumming had become very loud.

As he leaped and caught hold of the blue window's
bottom and drew himself up to it, the blue glow went
out. He scrambled inside onto the reed-carpeted
floor of whatever it was and swiftly squirmed around
so he was looking back the way he'd come.

The Mingol mare was invisible in the dark below.
The causeway's top glowed faintly in the moonlight.

Then round a cluster of thorn trees came speeding
the three black riders, the drumming of the twelve
hooves thunderous now. Fafhrd thought he could
make out a fiendish phosphorescent glow around the
nostrils and eyes of the tall black horses and he could
faintly discern the black cloaks and hoods of the
riders streaming in the wind of their speed. With

never a pause they passed the point where he'd left the causeway and vanished behind another thorn grove to the west. He let out a long-held breath.

"Now get away from the door and brace yourself," a voice that wasn't the Mouser's at all grated over his shoulder. "I've got to be there to pilot this rig."

The hairs that had just lain down on Fafhrd's neck erected themselves again. He had more than once heard the rock-harsh voice of Sheelba of the Eyeless Face, though never seen, let alone entered, his fabulous hut. He swiftly hitched himself to one side, back against wall. Something smooth and round and cool touched the back of his neck. A wall-hung skull, it almost had to be.

A black figure crawled into the space he'd just vacated. Dimly silhouetted in the doorway, its edge touched by moonlight, he saw a black cowl.

"Where's the Mouser?" Fafhrd asked with a wheeze in his voice.

The hut gave a violent lurch. Fafhrd grabbed gropingly for and luckily found two wall posts.

"In trouble. *Deep*-down trouble," Sheelba answered curtly. "I did his voice to make you jump lively. As soon as you've fulfilled whatever geas Ningauble has laid upon you—bells, isn't it?—you must go instantly to his aid."

The hut gave a second lurch and a third, then began to rock and pitch somewhat like a ship, but in a swift rhythm and more joltingly, as if one were in a howdah on the slant back of a drunken giant giraffe.

"Go instantly where?" Fafhrd demanded, somewhat humbly.

"How should I know and why should I tell you if I did? I'm not your wizard. I'm just taking you to Lankhmar by secret ways as a favor to that paunchy, seven-eyed, billion-worded dilettante in sorcery who thinks himself my colleague and has gulled you into taking him as mentor," the harsh voice responded from the hood. Then, relenting somewhat, though growing gruffer, "Overlord's palace, most likely. Now shut up."

The rocking of the hut and also its speed increased. Wind pushed in, flapping the edge of Sheelba's hood. Flashes of moon-dappled marsh shot by.

"Who were those riders after me?" Fafhrd asked, clinging to his wall posts. "Ilthmar brigands? Acolytes of the grisly, scythe-armed lord?"

No reply.

"What *is* it all about?" Fafhrd persisted. "Grand assault by a near numberless yet nameless host on Lankhmar. Nameless black riders. The Mouser deep-buried and woefully shrunk, yet alive. A tin whistle maybe summoning War Cats who are dangerous to the blower. None of it makes sense."

The hut gave a particularly vicious lurch. Sheelba still said not a word. Fafhrd grew seasick and devoted himself to hanging on.

Glipkerio, nerving himself, poked his pansy-wreathed, gold-ringleted head on its long neck through the kitchen door's leather curtains and blinking his weak yellow-irised eyes at the fire's glare, grinned an archly amiable, foolish grin.

Reetha, chained once more by the neck, sat cross-legged in front of the fire, head a-droop. Surrounded by four other maids squatting on their heels, Samanda nodded in her great chair. Yet now, though no noise had been made, her snores broke off, she opened her pig-eyes toward Glipkerio, and said familiarly, "Come in, little overlord, don't stand there like a bashful giraffe. Have the rats got you scared too? Be off to your cots, girls."

Three maids instantly rose. Samanda snatched a long pin from her sphere-dressed hair and lightly jabbed awake the fourth, who had been asleep on her heels.

Silently, except for a single swift-stifled squeal from the pricked one, the four maids bobbed a bow at Glipkerio, two at Samanda, and hurried out like so many wax mannequins. Reetha looked around wearily. Glipkerio wandered about, looking anywhere but at her, his chin a-twitch, his long fingers jittery, twining and untwining.

"The restless bug bite you, little overlord?" Samanda asked him. "Shall I make you a hot poppy-posset? Or would you like to see her whipped?" she asked, jerking a thick thumb toward Reetha. "The inquisitors ordered me not to, but of course if you should command me—"

"Oh, no, no, no, of course not," Glipkerio protested. "But speaking of whips, I've some new ones in my private collection I'd like to show you, dear Samanda, including one reputedly from Far Kiraay coated with rough-ground glass, if only you'd come with me. Also a handsomely embossed six-tined silver bull prod from—"

"Oh, so it's company you want, like all the other scared ones," Samanda told him. "Well, I'd be willing to oblige you, little overlord, but the 'quisitors told me I must keep an eye all night on this wicked girl, who's in league with the rats' leader."

Glipkerio hemmed and hawed, finally said, "Well, you could bring her along, I suppose, if you really have to."

"So I could," Samanda agreed heartily, at last levering her black-dressed bulk from her chair. "We can test your new whips on her."

"Oh, no, no, *no*," Glipkerio once more protested. Then frowning and also writhing his narrow shoulders, he added thoughtfully, "Though there are times when to get the hang of a new instrument of pain one simply must . . ."

". . . simply must," Samanda agreed, unsnapping the silver chain from Reetha's collar and snapping on a short leash. "Lead the way, little overlord."

"Come first to my bedroom," he told her. "I'll go ahead to get my guardsmen out of the way." And he made off at his longest, toga-stretching stride.

"No need to, little overlord, they know all about your habits," Samanda called after him, then jerked Reetha to her feet. "Come, girl!—you're being mightily honored. Be glad I'm not Glipkerio, or you'd be rubbed with cheese and shoved down-cellar for the rats to nibble."

When they finally arrived through empty silk-hung corridors at Glipkerio's bed-chamber, he was standing in mingled agitation and irritation before its open, jewel-studded, thick oaken door, his black toga a-rustle from his nervous jerking.

"There weren't any guardsmen for me to warn off," he complained. "It seems my orders were stupidly misinterpreted, extended farther than I'd intended, and my guardsmen have all gone off with the soldiers and constables to the South Barracks."

"What need you of guardsmen when you have *me* to protect you, little overlord?" Samanda answered boisterously, slapping a truncheon hanging from her belt.

"That's true," he agreed, only a shade doubtfully,

and twitched a large and complex golden key from a fold of his toga. "Now let's lock the girl in here, Samanda, if you please, while we go to inspect my new acquisitions."

"And decide which to use on her?" Samanda asked in her loud coarse voice.

Glipkerio shook his head as if in shocked disapproval, and looking at last at Reetha, said in grave fatherly tones, "No, of course not, it is only that I imagine the poor child would be bored at our expertise."

Yet he couldn't quite keep a sudden eagerness from his tones, nor a furtive gleam from his eyes.

Samanda unsnapped the leash and pushed Reetha inside.

Glipkerio warned her in last-minute apprehension, "Don't touch my night-draught now," pointing at a golden tray on a silver night table. Crystal flagons sat on the tray and also a long-stemmed goblet filled with pale apricot-hued wine.

"Don't touch one thing, or I'll make you beg for death," Samanda amplified, suddenly all unhumorously brutal. "Kneel at the foot of the bed on knees and heels with head bent—servile posture three—and don't move a muscle until we return."

As soon as the thick door was closed and its lock softly thudded shut and the golden key chinkingly withdrawn on the other side, Reetha walked straight to the night table, worked her cheeks a bit, spat into the night-draught, and watched the bubbly scum slowly revolve. Oh if she only had some hairs to drop in it, she yearned fiercely, but there seemed to be no fur or wool in the room and she had been shaved this very morning.

She unstoppered the most tempting of the crystal

flagons and carried it about with her, swigging daintily, as she examined the room, paneled with rare woods from the Eight Cities, and its ever rarer treasures, pausing longest at a heavy golden casket full of cut but unset jewels—amethysts, aquamarines, sapphires, jades, topazes, fire opals, rubies, gimpels, and ice emeralds—which glittered and gleamed like the shards of a shattered rainbow.

She also noted a rack of women's clothes, cut for someone very tall and thin, and—surprising beside these evidences of effeminacy—a rack of browned-iron weapons.

She glanced over several shelves of blown-glass figurines long enough to decide that the most delicate and costly-looking was, almost needless to say, that of a slim girl in boots and scanty jacket wielding a long whip. She flicked it off its shelf, so that it shattered on the polished floor and the whip went to powder.

What could they do to her that they weren't planning to do already?—she asked herself with a tight smile.

She climbed into the bed, where she stretched and writhed luxuriously, enjoying to the full the feel of the fine linen sheets against her barbered limbs, body, and head, and now and again trickling from the crystal flagon a few nectarous drops between her playfully haughty-shaped lips. She'd be damned, she told herself, if she'd drink enough to get dead drunk before the last possible instant. Thereafter Samanda and Glipkerio might find themselves hard-put to torment a limp body and blacked-out mind with any great pleasure to themselves.

XIII

THE MOUSER, reclining on his side in his litter, the tail of one of the fore-rats swaying a respectful arm's length from his head, noted that, without leaving the Fifth Level, they had arrived at a wide corridor stationed with pike-rats stiffly on guard and having thirteen heavily curtained doorways. The first nine curtains were of white and silver, the next of black and gold, the last three of white and gold.

Despite his weariness and grandiose feeling of security, the Mouser had been fairly watchful along the trip, suspecting though not very seriously that Skwee or Lord Null might have him followed—and then there was Hreest to be reckoned with, who might have discovered some clue at the water-privy despite the highly artistic job the Mouser felt he had done. From time to time there had been rats who might have been following his litter, but all these had eventually taken other turns in the mazy corridors. The last to engage his lazy suspicions had been two slim rats clad in black silken cloaks, hoods, masks, and gloves, but these without a glance toward him now disappeared arm-in-arm through the black-and-gold curtains, whispering together in a gossipy way.

His litter stopped at the next doorway, the third from the end. So Skwee and Siss outranked Grig, but he outranked Lord Null. This might be useful to know, though it merely confirmed the impression he had got at the council.

He sat, then stood up with the aid of his staff, rather exaggerating his leg cramp now, and tossed the fore-rat a corn-wreathed silver coin he had selected from Grig's purse. He assumed that tips would be the custom of any species of being whatever, in particular rats. Then without a backward look he hobbled through the heavy curtains, noting in passing that they were woven of fine soft gold wire and braided fine white silk threads. There was a short, dim passageway similarly curtained at the other end. He pushed through the second set of curtains and found himself alone in a cozy-feeling but rather shabby square room with curtained doorways in each of the other three walls and lit by a bronze-caged fire-beetle over each doorway. There were two closed cupboards, a writing desk with stool, many scrolls in silver containers that looked suspiciously like thimbles from the human world, crossed swords and a battle-ax fixed to the dingy walls, and a fireplace in which a single giant coal glowed redly through its coat of white ash. Above the fireplace, or rather brazier-nook, emerged from the wall a bronze-ringed hemisphere about as big as the Mouser's own rat-size head. The hemisphere was yellowish, with a large greenish-brown circle on it, and centered in this circle a black one. With a qualm of horror, the Mouser recognized it as a mummified human eye.

In the center of the room was a pillowed couch

with the high back support of one who does a lot of reading lying down, and beside the couch a sizable low table with nothing on it but three bells, one copper, one silver, and one gold.

Putting his horror out of mind, for it is a singularly useless emotion, the Mouser took up the silver bell and rang it vigorously, deciding to see what taking the middle course would bring.

He had little more time than to decide that the room was that of a crusty bachelor with studious inclinations when there came backing through the curtains in the rear wall a fat old rat in spotless long white smock with a white cap on his head. This one turned and showed his silver snout and bleared eyes, and also the silver tray he was carrying, on which were steaming plates and a large steaming silver jug.

The Mouser pointed curtly at the table. The cook, for so he seemed to be, set the tray there and then came hesitantly toward the Mouser, as if to help him off with his robe. The Mouser waved him away and pointed sternly at the rear doorway. He'd be damned if he'd go to the trouble of lisping in Grig's own home. Besides, servants might have a sharper ear than colleagues for a false voice. The cook bowed bumblingly and departed.

The Mouser settled himself gratefully on the couch, deciding against removing as yet his gloves or boots. Now that he was reclining, the latter bothered him hardly at all. However, he did remove his mask and placed it close by—it was good to get more than a squinty view of things—and set to at Grig's dinner.

The steaming jug turned out to contain mulled wine. It was most soothing to his raw, dry throat and wearied nerves, though excessively aromatic—the single black clove bobbing in the jug was large as a

lime and the cinnamon stick big as one of the parchment scrolls. Then, using Cat's Claw and the two-
tined fork provided, he began cutting up and devouring the steaming cutlets of beef—for his nose told
him it was that and not, for instance, baby. From
another steaming plate he sampled one of the objects
that looked like small sweet potatoes. It turned out to
be a single grain of boiled wheat. Likewise, one of the
yellowish cubes about as big as dice proved a grain of
coarse sugar, while the black balls big as the end
joint of his thumb were caviar. He speared them one
at a time with his fork and munched, alternating this
with mouthfuls of the beef. It was very strange to eat
good tender beef, the fibers of which were thick as his
fingers.

Having consumed the meaty portions of Grig's
dinner and drunk all the mulled wine, the Mouser
resumed his mask and settled back to plot his escape
to Lankhmar Above. But the golden bell kept teasing
his thoughts away from practical matters, so he
reached out and rang it. Yield to curiosity without
giving the mind time to get roiled, was one of his
mottoes.

Hardly had the sweet *chinks* died away when the
heavy curtains of one of the side doors parted and
there appeared a slim straight rat—or ratess, rather,
he judged—dressed in robe, hood, mask, slippers
and gloves all of fine lemon yellow silk.

This one, holding the curtains parted, looked toward him and said softly, "Lord Grig, your mistress
awaits you."

The Mouser's first reaction was one of gratified
conceit. So Grig did have a mistress, and his spur-of-
the-moment answer to Skwee's "Wife?" question at
the council had been a brilliant stroke of intuition.

Whether human-large or rat-small, he could out-smart anyone. He possessed Mouser-mind, un-equaled in the universe.

Then the Mouser stood up and approached the slender, yellow-clad figure. There was something cursedly familiar about her. He wondered if she were the ratess in green he'd seen leading short-leashed the brace of shrews. She had a pride and poise about her.

Using the same stratagem he had with the cook, he silently pointed from her to the doorway that she should precede him. She acquiesced and he followed close behind her down a dim twisty corridor.

And cursedly attractive too, he decided, eyeing her slender silhouette and sniffing her musky perfume. Rather belatedly, he reminded himself that she was a rat and so should waken his extremest repugnance. But was she necessarily a rat? He had been trans-formed in size, why not others? And if this were merely the maid, what would the mistress be? Doubtless lard-fat or hag-hairy, he told himself cynically. Still his excitement grew.

Sparing a moment's thought to orient himself, he discovered that the side door they'd gone out by led toward the black-curtained apartments of Lord Null —presumably—rather than to those of Siss and Skwee.

At last the yellow-clad ratess parted gold-heavy black drapes, then light violet silken ones. The Mouser passed her and found himself staring about through the notched eye-holes of Grig's mask at a large bedroom, beautifully and delicately furnished in many ways, yet the weirdest and perhaps the most frightening he had ever seen.

It was draped and carpeted and ceilinged and up-

holstered all in silver and violet, the latter color the
exact complement of the yellow of his conductress's
gowning. It was lit indirectly from below by narrow
deep tanks of slimy glow-worms big as eels, set
against the walls. Against these tanks were several
vanity tables, each backed by its large silver mirror,
so that the Mouser saw more than one reflection of
his white-robed self and his slim cicerone, who had
just let the silken violet curtains waft together again.
The tabletops were strewn with cosmetics and the
tools of beauty, variously colored elixirs and tiny
cups—all except one, near a second silver-draped
door, which held nothing but two score or so black
and white vials.

But between the vanity tables there hung on silver
chains, close to the walls and brightly lit by the glow-
worm's up-jutting effulgence, large silver cages of
scorpions, spiders, mantises, and suchlike glittering
vermin, all large as puppy dogs or baby kangaroos.
In one spacious cage coiled a Quarmall pocket-viper
huge as a python. These clashed their fangs or
hissed, according to their kind, while one scorpion
angrily clattered its sting across the gleaming bars of
its cage, and the viper darted its trebly forked tongue
between those of its own.

One short wall, however, was bare except for two
pictures tall and wide as doors, the one depicting
against a dusky background a girl and crocodile
amorously intertwined, the other a man and a
leopardess similarly preoccupied.

Almost central in the room was a large bed covered only by a tight-drawn white linen sheet, the
woven threads looking coarse as burlap, yet inviting
nonetheless, and with one fat white pillow.

Lying supine and at ease on this bed, her head

propped against the pillow to survey the Mouser
through the eye-holes of her mask, was a figure somewhat slighter than that of his guide, yet otherwise
identical and identically clad, except that the silk of
her garb was finer still and violet instead of yellow.

"Well met below ground. Sweet greetings, Gray
Mouser," this one called softly in a familiar silvery
voice. Then, looking beyond him, "Sweetest slave,
make our guest comfortable."

Softest footsteps approached. The Mouser turned
a little and saw that his conductress had removed her
yellow mask, revealing the merry yet melancholy-
eyed dark face of Frix. Her black hair this time hung
in two long plaits, braided with fine copper wire.

Without more ado than a smile, she began deftly
to unbutton Grig's long white robe. The Mouser
lifted his arms a little and let himself be undressed as
effortlessly as in a dream, and with even less attention paid the process, for he was most eagerly scanning the violet-masked figure on the bed. He knew to
a certainty who it must be, beyond all contributing
evidence, for the silver dart was throbbing in his temple and the hunger which had haunted him for days
returned redoubled.

The situation was strange almost beyond com-
prehension. Although guessing that Frix and the other must have used an elixir like Sheelba's, the
Mouser could have sworn they were all three human
size, except for the presence of the familiar vermin,
scuttlers and slitherers, so huge.

It was a great relief to have his cramping rat-boots
deftly drawn off, as he lifted first one leg, then the
other. Yet although he submitted so docilely to Frix's
ministrations, he kept hold of his sword Scalpel and
of the belt it hung from and also, on some cloudy

impulse, of Grig's mask. He felt the smaller scabbard empty on the belt and realized with a pang of apprehension that he had left Cat's Claw behind in Grig's apartment along with the latter's ivory staff.

But these worries vanished like the last snowflake in spring when the one on the bed asked cajolingly, "Will you partake of refreshment, dearest guest?" and when he said, "I will most gladly," lifted a violet-gloved hand and ordered, "Dear Frix, fetch sweetmeats and wine."

While Frix busied herself at a far table, the Mouser whispered, his heart a-thump. "Ah, most delectable Hisvet—For I deem you are she?"

"As to that, you must judge for yourself," the tinkling voice responded coquettishly.

"Then I shall call you Hisvet," the Mouser answered boldly, "recognizing you as my queen of queens and princess of princesses. Know, delicious Demoiselle, that ever since our raptures 'neath the closest tree were so rudely broken off by an interruption of Mingols, my mind, nay, my mania has been fixed solely on you."

"That were some small compliment—" the other allowed, lolling back luxuriously, "if I could believe it."

"Believe it you must," the Mouser asserted masterfully, stepping forward. "Know, moreover, that it is my intention that on this occasion our converse not be conducted over Frix's shoulder, dear companion that she is, but at the closest range. I am fixedly desirous of all refreshments, omitting none."

"You cannot think I am Hisvet!" the other countered, starting up in what the Mouser hoped was mock indignation. "Else you would never dare such blasphemy!"

"I dare far more!" the Mouser declared with a soft amorous growl, stepping forward more swiftly. The vermin hanging round about moved angrily, striking against their silver bars and setting their cages a little a-swing, and clashing, clattering, and hissing more. Nevertheless the Mouser, dropping his belt and sword by the edge of the bed and setting a knee thereon, would have thrust himself directly upon Hisvet, had not Frix come bustling up at that moment and set between them on the coarse linen a great silver tray with slim decanters of sweet wine and crystal cups for its drinking and plates of sugary tidbits.

Not entirely to be balked, the Mouser darted his hand across and snatched away the vizard of violet silk from the visage it hid. Violet-gloved hand instantly snatched the mask back from him, but did not replace it, and there confronting him was indeed the slim triangular face of Hisvet, cheeks flushed, red-irised eyes glaring, but pouty lips grinning enough to show the slightly overlarge pearly upper incisors, the whole being framed by silver-blonde hair interwoven like that of Frix, but with even finer wire of silver, into two braids that reached to her waist.

"Nay," she said laughingly, "I see you are most wickedly presumptuous and that I must protect myself." Reaching down on her side of the bed, she procured a long slender-bladed gold-hilted dagger. Waving it playfully at the Mouser, she said, "Now refresh yourself from the cups and plates before you, but have a care of sampling other sweetmeats, dear guest."

The Mouser complied, pouring for himself and Hisvet. He noted from a corner of his eye that Frix,

moving silently in her silken robe, had rolled up
Grig's white boots and gloves in his white hood and
robe and set them on a stool near the floor-to-ceiling
painting of the man and the leopardess and that she
had made as neat a bundle of all the rest of the
Mouser's garb—his own garb, mostly—and set them
on a stool next the first. A most efficient and fore-
sighted maid, he thought, and most devoted to her
mistress—in fact altogether too devoted: he wished
at this moment she would take herself off and leave
him private with Hisvet.

But she showed no sign of so doing, nor Hisvet of
ordering her away, so without more ado the Mouser
began a mild love-play, catching at the violet-gloved
fingers of Hisvet's left hand as they dipped toward
the sweetmeats or plucking at the ribbons and edges
of her violet robe, in the latter case reminding her of
the discrepancy in their degree of undress and suggesting that it be corrected by the subtraction of an
item or two from her outfit. Hisvet in turn would
deftly jab with her dagger at his snatching hand, as
if to pin it to tray or bed, and he would whip it back
barely in time. It was an amusing game, this dance of
hand and needle-sharp dagger—or at least it seemed
amusing to the Mouser, especially after he had
drained a cup or two of fiery colorless wine—and so
when Hisvet asked him how he had come into the
rat-world, he merrily told her the story of Sheelba's
black potion and how he had first thought its effects
a most damnably unfair wizardly joke, but now
blessed them as the greatest good ever done him in
his life—for he twisted the tale somewhat to make it
appear that his sole objective all along had been to
win to her side and bed.

He ended by asking, as he parted two fingers to let

Hisvet's dagger strike between them, "How ever did you and dear Frix guess that I was impersonating Grig?"

She replied, "Most simply, gracious gamesman. We went to fetch my father from the council, for there is still an important journey he, Frix, and I must make tonight. At a distance we heard you speak and I divined your true voice despite your clever lispings. Thereafter we followed you."

"Ah, surely I may hope you love me as dearly, since you trouble to know me so well," the Mouser warbled infatuatedly, slipping hand aside from a cunning slash. "But tell me, divine one, how comes it that you and Frix and your father are able to live and hold great power in the rat-world?"

With her dagger she pointed somewhat languidly toward the vanity table holding the black and white vials, informing him, "My family has used the same potion as Sheelba's for countless centuries, and also the white potion, which restores us at once to human-size. During those same centuries we have interbred with the rats, resulting in divinely beautiful monsters such as I am, but also in monsters most ugly, at least by human standards. Those latter of my family stay always below ground, but the rest of us enjoy the advantages and delights of living in two worlds. The interbreeding has also resulted in many rats with human-like hands and minds. The spreading of civilization to the rats is largely our doing, and we shall rule as chiefs and chieftesses paramount, or even goddesses and gods, when the rats rule men."

This talk of interbreeding and monsters startled the Mouser somewhat and gave him to think, despite his ever more firmly gyved ensorcelment by Hisvet. He recalled Lukeen's old suggestion, made aboard

Squid, that Hisvet concealed a she-rat's body under
her maiden robes and he wondered—somewhat fearfully yet most curiously—just what form Hisvet's
slim body did take. For instance, did she have a tail?
But on the whole he was certain that whatever he
discovered under her violet robe would please him
mightily, since now his infatuation with the grain-
merchant's daughter had grown almost beyond all
bounds.

However, he outwardly showed none of this wondering, but merely asked, as if idly, "So your father
is also Lord Null, and you and he and Frix regularly
travel back and forth between the big and little
worlds?"

"Show him, dear Frix," Hisvet commanded lazily,
lifting slim fingers to mask a yawn, as though the
hand-and-dagger game had begun to bore her.

Frix moved back against the wall until her head
with its natural jet-black sheath and copper-gleam-
ing plaits, for she had thrown back her hood, was
between the cages of the pocket-viper and the most
enraged scorpion. Her dark eyes were a sleep-
walker's, fixed on things infinitely remote. The
scorpion darted his moist white sting between the
bars rat-inches from her ear, the viper's trifid tongue
vibrated angrily against her cheek, while his fangs
struck the silver rounds and dripped venom that
wetted oilily her yellow silken shoulder, but she
seemed to take no note whatever of these matters.
The fingers of her right hand, however, moved along
a row of medallions decorating the glow-worm tank
behind her, and without looking down, she pressed
two at once.

The painting of the girl and crocodile moved swiftly upward, revealing the foot of a dark steep stairway.

"That leads without branchings to my father's and my house," Hisvet explained.

The painting descended. Frix pressed two other medallions and the companion painting of man and leopardess rose, revealing a like stairway.

"While that one ascends directly by way of a golden rathole to the private apartments of whoever is Lankhmar's seeming overlord, now Glipkerio Kistomerces," Hisvet told the Mouser as the second painting slid down into place. "So you see, beloved, our power goes everywhere." And she lifted her dagger and touched it lightly to his throat. The Mouser let it rest there a space before taking its tip between fingers and thumb and moving it aside. Then he as gently caught hold of the tip of one of Hisvet's braids, she offering no resistance, and began to unweave the fine silver wires from the finer silver-blonde hairs.

Frix still stood like a statue between fang and sting, seeming to see things beyond reality.

"Is Frix one of your breed?—combining in some fashion the finest of human and ratly qualities," the Mouser asked quietly, keeping up with the task which, he told himself, would eventually and after an admittedly weary amount of unbraiding, allow him to arrive at his heart's desire.

Hisvet shook her head languourously, laying aside her dagger. "Frix is my dearest slave and almost sister, but not by blood. Indeed she is the dearest slave in all Nehwon, for she is a princess and perchance by now a queen in her own world. While a-travel between worlds, she was ship-wrecked here and beset by demons, from whom my father rescued her, at the price that she serve me forever."

At this, Frix spoke at last, though without moving else but her lips and tongue, not even her eyes to look at them. "Or until, sweetest mistress, I three times save your life at entire peril of my own. That has happened once now, aboard *Squid,* when the dragon would have gobbled you."

"You would never leave me, dear Frix," Hisvet said confidently.

"I love you dearly and serve you faithfully," Frix replied. "Yet all things come to an end, O blessed Demoiselle."

"Then I shall have the Gray Mouser to protect me, and you unneeded," Hisvet countered somewhat pettishly, lifting on an elbow. "Leave us for the nonce, Frix, for I would speak privately with him."

With merriest smile Frix came from between the deadly cages, made a curtsy toward the bed, resumed her yellow mask and swiftly went off through the second unsecret doorway, curtained with filmy silver.

Still lifted on her elbow, Hisvet turned toward the Mouser her slender form and her taper-face alight with beauty. He reached toward her eagerly, but she captured his questing hands in her cool fingers and fondling them asked, or rather stated, her eyes feeding on his, "You will love me forever, will you not, who dared the dark and fearsome tunnels of the rat-world to win me?"

"That will I surely, O Empress of Endless Delights," the Mouser answered fervently, maddened by desire and believing his words to the ends of the universe of his feelings—almost.

"Then I think it proper to relieve you of *this,*" Hisvet said, putting the fingers of her two hands to his temple, "for it would be an offense against myself and my supreme beauty to depend on a charm when I may now wholly depend on *you.*"

And with only the tiniest tweak of pain inflicted,

she deftly squeezed with her fingernails the silver
dart from under the Mouser's skin, as any woman
might squeeze out a blackhead or whitehead from
the visage of her lover. She showed him the dart
gleaming on her palm. He for his part felt no change
in his feelings whatever. He still adored her as divinity—and the fact that previously in his life he had never put any but momentary trust in any divinity whatever seemed of no importance at all, at least at this
moment.

Hisvet laid a cool hand on the Mouser's side, but
her red eyes were no longer languorously misty;
they were sparklingly bright. And when he would
have touched her similarly she prevented him,
saying in most businesslike fashion, "No, no, not
quite yet! First we must plan, my sweet—for you can
serve me in ways which even Frix will not. To begin,
you must slay me my father, who thwarts me and
confines my life unbearably, so that I may be im-
peratrix of all and you my most favored consort.
There will be no end to our powers. Tonight,
Lankhmar! Tomorrow, all Nehwon! Then . . . the
conquest of other universes beyond the waters of
space! The subjugation of the angels and demons of
heaven itself and hell! At first it may be well that you
impersonate my father, as you have Grig—and done
most cleverly, by my own witnessing, pet. You are of
men the most like me in the world for deceptions,
darling. Then—"

She broke off at something she saw in the Mouser's
face. "You will of course obey me in all things?" she
asked sharply, or rather asserted.

"Well . . ." the Mouser began.

The silver drape billowed to the ceiling and Frix
dashed in on silent silken slippers, her yellow robe

and hood flying behind her.

"Your masks! Your masks!" she cried. " 'Ware!
'Ware!" And she whirled over them to their necks an
opaque violet coverlet, hiding Hisvet's violet-robed
form, the Mouser's unclad body, and the tray between them. "Your father comes with armed atten-
dants, lady!" And she knelt by the head of the bed
nearest Hisvet and bowed her yellow-masked head,
assuming a servile posture.

Hardly were the white and violet masks in place
and the silver curtains settled to the floor than the
latter were jerked rudely aside. Hisvin and Skwee appeared, both unmasked, followed by three pike-rats.
Despite the presence of the huge vermin in their
cages, the Mouser found it hard to banish the illusion
that all the rats were actually five feet and more tall.

Hisvin's face grew dusky red as he surveyed the
scene. "Oh, most monstrous!" he cried at Hisvet.
"Shameless filth! Loose with my own colleague!"

"Don't be dramatic, Daddy," Hisvet countered,
while to the Mouser she whispered tersely, "Slay him
now. I'll clear you with Skwee and the rest."

The Mouser, fumbling under the coverlet over the
side of the bed for Scalpel, while presenting a steady
white be-diamonded mask at Hisvin, said blandly,
"Calm yourthelf, counthillor. If your divine daughter
chootheth me above all other ratth and men, ith it
my fault, Hithvin? Or herth either? Love knowth no
ruleth."

"I'll have your head for this, Grig," Hisvin
screeched at him, advancing toward the bed.

"Daddy, you've become a puritanical dodderer,"
Hisvet said sharply, almost primly, "to indulge in
antique tantrums on this night of our great conquest.
Your day is done. I must take your place on the

Council. Tell him so, Skwee. Daddy darling, I think you're just madly jealous of Grig because you're not where he is."

Hisvin screamed, "O dirt that was my daughter!" and snatching with youthful speed a stiletto from his waist, drove it at Hisvet's neck betwixt violet mask and coverlet—except that Frix, lunging suddenly on her knees, swung her open left hand hard between, as one bats a ball.

The needlelike blade drove through her palm to the slim dagger's hilt and was wrenched from Hisvin's grasp.

Still on one knee, the bright blade transfixing her outstretched left palm and dripping red a little, Frix turned toward Hisvin and advancing her other hand graciously, she said in clear, winning tones, "Govern your rage for all our sakes, dear my dear mistress' father. These matters can be composed by quiet reason, surely. You must not quarrel together on this night of all nights."

Hisvin paled and retreated a step, daunted most likely by Frix's preternatural composure, which indeed was enough to send shivers up a man's or even a rat's spine.

The Mouser's fumbling hand closed around Scalpel's hilt. He prepared to spring out and dash back to Grig's apartment, snatching up his bundle of clothes on the way. At some point during the last score or so heartbeats, his great undying love for Hisvet had quietly perished and was now beginning to stink in his nostrils.

But at that instant the violet drapes were torn apart and there rushed from the Mouser's chosen escape route the rat Hreest in his gold-embellished black garb and brandishing rapier and dirk. He was followed by three guardsmen-rats in green uniforms, each with a like naked sword. The Mouser recognized the dirk Hreest held—it was his own Cat's Claw.

Frix moved swiftly behind the head of the bed to the post she'd earlier taken between viper and scorpion cage, the stiletto still transfixing her left hand like a great pin. The Mouser heard her murmur rapidly, "The plot thickens. Enter armed rats at all portals. A climax nears."

Hreest came to a sudden halt and cried ringingly at Skwee and Hisvin, "The dismembered remains of Councillor Grig have been discovered lodged against the Fifth Level sewer's exit-grill! The human spy is impersonating him in Grig's own clothes!"

Not at the moment, except for mask, the Mouser thought, and making one last effort cried out, "Nonthenthe! Thithe ith midthummer madneth! I am Grig! It wath thome other white rat got tho foully thlain!"

Holding up Cat's Claw and eyeing the Mouser, Hreest continued, "I discovered this dagger of human device in Grig's apartment. The spy is clearly here."

"Kill him in the bed," Skwee commanded harshly, but the Mouser, anticipating a little the inevitable, had rolled out from under his sheets and now took up guard position naked, the white mask cast aside, Scalpel gleaming long and deadly in his right hand, while his left, in lieu of his dirk, held his belt and Scalpel's limp scabbard, both doubled.

With a weird laugh Hreest lunged at him, rapier a-flicker, while Skwee drew sword and came leaping across the foot of the bed, his boot crunching glass against tray beneath the coverlet.

Hreest got a bind on Scalpel, carrying both long swords out to the side, and stepping in close stabbed with Cat's Claw. The Mouser struck his own dirk aside with his doubled belt and drove his left shoulder into Hreest's chest, slamming him back against two of his green-uniformed sword-rats, who were thereby forced to give ground too.

At almost the same instant the Mouser parried high to the side with Scalpel, deflecting Skwee's rapier when its point was inches from his neck. Then swiftly changing fronts, he fenced a moment with Skwee, beat the rat's blade aside, and lunged strongly. The white-clad rat was already in retreat across the foot of the bed, from the head of which Hisvet, now unmasked, watched critically, albeit a little sulkily, but the Mouser's point nevertheless reached Skwee's sword-wrist and pinked it halfway through.

By this time the third green-clad rat, a giant relatively seven feet tall, who had to duck through the doorway, came lunging fiercely, though a little slowly. Meanwhile Hreest was picking himself up from the floor, while Skwee dropped his dagger and switched his rapier to his unwounded hand.

The Mouser parried the giant's lunge, a hair's-breadth from his naked chest, and riposted. The giant counter-parried in time, but the Mouser dropped Scalpel's tip under the other's blade and continuing his riposte, skewered him through the heart.

The giant's jaw gaped, showing his great incisors. His eyes filmed. Even his fur seemed to dull. His weapons dropped from his nerveless hands and he stood dead on his feet a moment before starting to fall. In that moment the Mouser, squatting a little on his right leg, kicked out forcefully with his left. His

heel took the giant in the breastbone, pushing his
corpse off Scalpel and sending it careening back
against Hreest and his two green-clad sword-
rats.

One of the pike-rats leveled his weapon for a run at
the Mouser, but at that moment Skwee commanded
loudly, "No more single attacks! Form we a circle
around him!"

The others were swift to obey, but in that brief
pause Frix dropped open the silver-barred door that
was one end of the scorpion's cage, and despite her
dagger-transfixed hand lifted the cage and heaved it
sharply, sending its fearsome occupant flying to land
on the foot of the bed, where it jigged about, big by
comparison as a large cat, clashing its claws, rattling
its chelicerae, and menacing with its sting over its
head.

Most of the rats directed their weapons at it.
Snatching up her dagger, Hisvet crouched at the opposite corner from it, preparing to defend herself
from her pet. Hisvin dodged in back of Skwee.

At the same time Frix dropped her good hand to
the medallions on the glow-worm tank. The painting
of man and leopardess rose. The Mouser didn't need
the prompting of her wild smile and over-bright eyes.
Snatching up the gray bundle of his clothes, he
dashed up the dark steep stairs three at a time.
Something hissed past his head and struck with a
zing the riser of a stone step above and clattered
down. It was Hisvet's long dagger and it had struck
point-first. The stairway grew dark and he began
taking its steps only two at a time, crouching low as
he could and peering wide-eyed ahead. Faintly he
heard Skwee's shrill command, "After him!"

* * *

Frix with a grimace drew Hisvin's stiletto from her palm, lightly kissed the bleeding wound, and with a curtsy presented the weapon to its owner.

The bedroom was empty save for those two and Hisvet, who was drawing her violet robe around her, and Skwee, who was knotting with spade teeth and good hand a bandage round his injured wrist.

Pierced by a dozen thrusts and oozing dark blood on the violet carpet, the scorpion still writhed on its back, its walking legs and great claws a-tremble, its sting sliding a little back and forth.

Hreest, the two green sword-rats, and the three pike-rats had gone in pursuit of the Mouser and the clatter of their boots up the steep stairs had died away.

Frowning darkly, Hisvin said to Hisvet, "I still should slay you."

"Oh Daddy dear, you don't understand at all what happened," Hisvet said tremulously. "The Gray Mouser forced me at sword's point. It was a rape. And at sword's point under the coverlet he compelled me to say those dreadful things to you. You saw I did my best to kill him at the end."

"Pah!" Hisvin spat, turning half aside.

"*She's* the one should be slain," Skwee asserted, indicating Frix. "She worked the spy's escape."

"Most true, oh mighty councillor," Frix agreed. "Else he would have killed at least half of you, and your brains are greatly needed—in fact, indispensable, are they not?—to direct tonight's grand assault on Lankhmar Above?" She held out her red-dripping palm to Hisvet and said softly, "That's twice, dear mistress."

"For that you shall be rewarded," Hisvet said, setting her lips primly. "And for helping the spy escape
—and not preventing my rape!—you shall be
whipped until you can no longer scream—tomorrow."

"Right joyfully, milady—tomorrow," Frix responded with a return of something of her merry
tones. "But tonight there is work must be done. At
Glipkerio's palace in the Blue Audience Chamber.
Work for all three of us. And at once, I believe,
milord," she added deferentially, turning to Hisvin.

"That's true," Hisvin said with a start. He
scowled back and forth between his daughter and her
maid three times, then with a shrug, said, "Come."

"How can you trust them?" Skwee demanded.

"I must," Hisvin said. "They're needful if I am
properly to control Glipkerio. Meanwhile your place
is that of supreme command, at the council table.
Siss will be needing you. Come!" he repeated to the
two girls. Frix worked the medallions. The second
painting rose. They went all three up the stairs.

Skwee paced the bed-chamber alone, head bowed
in angry thought, automatically overstepping the
corpse of the giant sword-rat and circling the still-
writhing scorpion. When he at last stopped and lifted
his gaze, it was to rest it on the vanity table bearing
the black and white bottles of the size-change magic.
He approached that table with the gait of a sleep-
walker or one who walks through water. For a space
he played aimlessly with the vials, rolling them this
way and that. Then he said aloud to himself, "Oh
why is it that one can be wise and command a vast
host and strive unceasingly and reason with diamond
brilliance, and still be low as a silverfish, blind as a
cutworm? The obvious is in front of our toothy
muzzles and we never see it—because we rats have

accepted our littleness, hypnotized ourselves with our dwarfishness, our incapacity, and our inability to burst from our cramping prison-tunnels, to leap from the shallow but deadly jail-rut, whose low walls lead us only to the stinking rubbish heap or narrow burial crypt."

He lifted his ice-blue eyes and glared coldly at his silver-furred image in the silver mirror. "For all your greatness, Skwee," he told himself, "you have thought small all your rat's life. Now for once, Skwee, think big!" And with that fierce self-command, he picked up one of the white vials and pouched it, hesitated, swept all the white vials into his pouch, hesitated again, then with a shrug and a sardonic grimace swept the black vials after them and hurried from the room.

On its back on the violet carpet, the scorpion still vibrated its legs feebly.

XIV

Fafhrd swiftly climbed, by the low moonlight, the high Marsh Wall of Lankhmar at the point to which Sheelba had delivered him, a good bowshot south of the Marsh Gate. "At the gate you might run into your black pursuers," Sheelba had told him. Fafhrd had doubted it. True, the black riders had been moving like a storm wind, but Sheelba's hut had raced across the sea-grass like a low-scudding pocket hurricane; surely he had arrived ahead of them. Yet he had put up no argument. Wizards were above all else persuasive salesmen, whether they flooded you off your feet with words, like Ningauble, or manipulated you with meaningful silences, like Sheelba. For the swamp wizard had otherwise maintained his cranky quiet throughout the entire rocking, pitching, swift-skidding trip, from which Fafhrd's stomach was still queasy.

He found plenty of good holds for hand and foot in the ancient wall. Climbing it was truly child's play to one who had scaled in his youth Obelisk Polaris in the frosty Mountains of the Giants. He was far more concerned with what he might meet at the top of the wall, where he would be briefly helpless against a foe footed above him.

But more than all else—and increasingly so—he was puzzled by the darkness and silence with which the city was wrapped. Where was the battle-din; where were the flames? Or if Lankhmar had already been subdued, which despite Ningauble's optimism seemed most likely from the fifty-to-one odds against her, where were the screams of the tortured, the shrieks of the raped, and all the gleeful clatter and shout of the victors?

He reached the wall's top and suddenly drew himself up and vaulted through a wide embrasure down onto the wide parapet, ready to draw Graywand and his ax. But the parapet was empty as far as he could see in either direction.

Wall Street below was dark, and empty too as far as he could tell. Cash Street, stretching west and flooded with pale moonlight from behind him, was visibly bare of figures. While the silence was even more marked than when he'd been climbing. It seemed to fill the great, walled city, like water brimming a cup.

Fafhrd felt spooked. Had the conquerors of Lankhmar already departed?—carrying off all its treasure and inhabitants in some unimaginably huge fleet or caravan? Had they shut up themselves and their gagged victims in the silent houses for some rite of mass torture in darkness? Was it a demon, not human army which had beset the city and vanished its inhabitants? Had the very earth gaped for victor and vanquished alike and then shut again? Or was Ningauble's whole tale wizardly flimflam?—yet even

that least unlikely explanation still left unexplained
the city's ghostly desolation.

Or was there a fierce battle going on under his eyes
at this very moment, and he by some spell of
Ningauble or Sheelba unable to see, hear, or even
scent it?—until, perchance, he had fulfilled the geas
of the bells which Ningauble had laid on him.

He still did not like the idea of his bells-mission.
His imagination pictured the Gods *of* Lankhmar resting in their brown mummy-wrappings and their
rotted black togas, their bright black eyes peeping
from between resin-impregnated bandages and their
deadly black staves of office beside them, waiting another call from the city that forgot yet feared them
and which they in turn hated yet guarded. Waking
with naked hand a clutch of spiders in a hole in
desert rocks seemed wiser than waking such. Yet a
geas was a geas and must be fulfilled.

He hurried down the nearest dark stone stairs
three steps at a time and headed west on Cash Street,
which paralleled Crafts Street a block to the south.
He half imagined he brushed unseen figures. Crossing curvy Cheap Street, dark and untenanted as the
others, he thought he heard a murmuring and chant-
ing from the north, so faint that it must come from at
least as far away as the Street of Gods. But he held to
his predetermined course, which was to follow Cash
Street to Nun Street, then three blocks north to the
accursed bell-tower.

Whore Street, which was even more twisty than
Cheap Street, looked tenantless too, but he was hardly half a block beyond it when he heard the tramp of
boots and the clink of armor behind him. Ducking

into the narrow shadows, he watched a double squad of guardsmen cross hurriedly through the moonlight, going south on Whore Street in the direction of the South Barracks. They were crowded close together, watched every way, and carried their weapons at the ready, despite the apparent absence of foe. This seemed to confirm Fafhrd's notion of an army of invisibles. Feeling more spooked than ever, he continued rapidly on his way.

And now he began to note, here and there, light leaking out from around the edges of a shuttered upper window. These dim-drawn oblongs only increased his feeling of supernatural dread. Anything, he told himself, would be better than this locked-in silence, now broken only by the faint echoing tread of his own boots on the moonlit cobbles. And at the end of his trip: mummies!

Somewhere, faintly, muffled, eleven o'clock knelled. Then of a sudden, crossing narrow, black-brimming Silver Street, he heard a multitudinous pattering, like rain—save that the stars were bright overhead except for the moon's dimming of them, and he felt no drops. He began to run.

Aboard *Squid*, the kitten, as if he had received a call which he might not disregard despite all dreads, made the long leap from the scuppers to the docks, clawed his way up onto the latter and hurried off into the dark, his black hair on end and his eyes emerald bright with fear and danger-readiness.

Glipkerio and Samanda sat in his Whip Room, reminiscing and getting a tipsy glow on, to put them in the right mood for Reetha's thrashing. The fat palace mistress had swilled tankards of dark wine of Tovilyis until her black wool dress was soaked with sweat and salty beads stood on each hair of her ghostly black moustache. While her overlord sipped violet wine of Kiraay, which she had fetched from the upper pantry when no butler or page answered the ring of the silver and even the brazen summoning-bell. She'd said, "They're scared to stir since your guardsmen went off. I'll welt them properly—but only when you've had your special fun, little master."

Now, for the nonce neglecting all the rare and begemmed instruments of pain around them and blessedly forgetting the rodent menace to Lankhmar, their thoughts had returned to simpler and happier days. Glipkerio, his pansy wreath awry and somewhat wilted, was saying with a tittering eagerness, "Do you recall when I brought you my first kitten to throw in the kitchen fire?"

"Do I?" Samanda retorted with affectionate scorn. "Why, little master, I remember when you brought me your first fly, to show me how neatly you could pluck off his wings and legs. You were only a toddler, but already skinny-tall."

"Yes, but about that kitten," Glipkerio persisted, violet wine dribbling down his chin as he took a hasty and tremble-handed swallow. "It was black with blue eyes newly unfilmed. Radomix was trying to stop me—he lived at the palace then—but you sent him away bawling."

"I did indeed," Samanda concurred. "The cotton-hearted brat! And I remember how the kitten screamed and frizzled, and how you cried afterwards because you hadn't him to throw in again. To divert your mind and cheer you, I stripped and whipped an apprentice maid as skinny-tall as yourself and with long blonde braids. That was before you got your thing about hairs"—she wiped her moustache —"and had all the girls and boys shaved. I thought it was time you graduated to manlier pleasures, and sure enough you showed your excitement in no uncertain fashion!" And with a whoop of laughter she reached across and thumbed him indelicately.

Excited by this tickling and his thoughts, Lankhmar's overlord stood up cypress-tall-and-black in his toga, though no cypress ever twitched as he did, except perhaps in an earthquake or under most potent witchcraft. "Come," he cried. "Eleven's struck. We've barely time before I must haste me to the Blue Audience Chamber to meet with Hisvin and save the city."

"Right," Samanda affirmed, levering herself up with her brawny forearms pulling at her knees and then pushing the pinching armchair off her large rear. "Which whips was it you'd picked now for the naughty and traitorous minx?"

"None, none," Glipkerio cried with impatient glee. "In the end that well-oiled old black dog-whip hanging from your belt always seems best. Hurry we, dear Samanda, hurry!"

Reetha shot up in crispy-linened bed as she heard hinges creak. Shaking nightmares from her smooth-shaven head, she fumbled frantically about for the bottle whose draining would bring her protective oblivion.

She put it to her lips, but paused a moment before upending it. The door still hadn't opened and the

creaking had been strangely tiny and shrill. Glancing
over the edge of the bed, she saw that another door
not quite a foot high had opened outward at floor
level in the seamless-seeming wood paneling.
Through it there stepped swiftly and silently, ducking his head a trifle, a well-formed and leanly
muscular little man, carrying in one hand a gray
bundle and in the other what seemed to be a long toy
sword as naked as himself.

He closed the door behind him, so that it once
more seemed not to be there, and gazed about pierc-
ingly.

"Gray Mouser!" Reetha yelled, springing from
bed and throwing herself down on her knees beside
him. "You've come back to me!"

He winced, lifting his burdened tiny hands to his
ears.

"Reetha," he begged, "don't shout like that again.
It blasts my brain." He spoke slowly and as deep-
pitched as he could, but to her his voice was shrill
and rapid, though intelligible.

"I'm sorry," she whispered contritely, restraining
the impulse to pick him up and cuddle him to her
bosom.

"You'd better be," he told her brusquely. "Now
find something heavy and put it against this door.
There's those coming after, whom you wouldn't
want to meet. Quick about it, girl!"

She didn't stir from her knees, but eagerly suggested, "Why not work your magic and make yourself big again?"

"I haven't the stuff to work that magic," he told
her exasperatedly. "I had a chance at a vial of it and

like any other sex-besotted fool didn't think to swipe it. Now jump to it, Reetha!"

Suddenly realizing the strength of her bargaining position, she merely leaned closer to him and smiling archly though lovingly, asked, "With what doll-tiny bitch have you been consorting now? No, you needn't answer that, but before I stir me to help you, you must give me six hairs from your darling head. I have good reason for my request."

The Mouser started to argue insanely with her, then thought better of it and snicked off with Scalpel a small switch of his locks and laid them in her huge, crisscross furrowed, gleaming palm, where they were fine as baby hairs, though slightly longer and darker than most.

She stood up briskly, marched to the night table, and dropped them in Glipkerio's night draught. Then dusting off her hands above the goblet, she looked around. The most suitable object she could see for the Mouser's purpose was the golden casket of unset jewels. She lugged it into place against the small door, taking the Mouser's word as to where the small door exactly was.

"That should hold them for a bit," he said, greedily noting for future reference the rainbow gems bigger than his fists, "but 'twere best you also fetch—"

Dropping to her knees, she asked somewhat wistfully, "Aren't you ever going to be big again?"

"Don't boom the floor! Yes, of course! In an hour or less, if I can trust my tricksy, treacherous wizard. Now, Reetha, while I dress me, please fetch—"

A key chinked dulcetly and a bolt thudded softly in its channel. The Mouser felt himself whirled through

the air by and with Reetha onto the soft springy
white bed, and a white translucent sheet whirled over
them.

He heard the door open.

At that moment a hand on his head pressed him
firmly down into a squat and as he was about to pro-
test, Reetha whispered—it was a growl like light surf
—"Don't make a bump in the sheet. Whatever hap-
pens, hold still and hide for your dear life's sake."

A voice like battle trumpets blared then, making
the Mouser glad of what shielding the sheet gave his
ears. "The nasty girl's crawled in my bed! Oh, the
disgust of it! I feel faint. Wine! Ah! *Aaarrrggghhh!*"
There came ear-shaking chokings, spewings, and
spittings, and then the battle trumpets again, somewhat muffled, as if stuffed with flannel, though even
more enraged: "The filthy and demonic slut has put
hairs in my drink! Oh whip her, Samanda, until
she's everywhere welted like a bamboo screen! Lash
her until she licks my feet and kisses each toe for
mercy!"

Then another voice, this one like a dozen huge ket-
tledrums, thundering through the sheet and pounding the Mouser's tinied goldleaf-thin eardrums.
"That will I, little master. Nor heed you, if you ask I
desist. Come out of there, girl, or must I whip you
out?"

Reetha scrambled toward the head of the bed,
away from that voice. The Mouser followed
crouching after her, though the mattress heaved like
a white-decked ship in a storm, the sheet figuring as
an almost deck-low ceiling of fog. Then suddenly
that fog was whirled away, as if by a supernal wind,
and there glared down the gigantic double red-and-

black sun of Samanda's face, inflamed by liquor and anger, and of her globe-dressed, pin-transfixed black hair. And the sun had a black tail—Samanda's raised whip.

The Mouser bounded toward her across the disordered bed, brandishing Scalpel and still lugging under his other arm the gray bundle of his clothes.

The whip, which had been aimed at Reetha, changed direction and came whistling toward him. He sprang straight up with all his strength and it passed just under his naked feet like a black dragon's tail, the whistling abruptly lowering in pitch. By good luck keeping his footing as he came down, he leaped again toward Samanda, stabbed her with Scalpel in her black-wool-draped huge kneecap, and sprang down to the parquet floor.

Like a browned-iron thunderbolt, a great ax-head bit into the wood close by him, jarring him to his teeth. Glipkerio had snatched a light battle-ax from his weapon-rack with surprising speed and wielded it with unlikely accuracy.

The Mouser darted under the bed, raced across that—to him—low-ceilinged dark wide portico, emerged on the other side and doubled swiftly back around the foot of the bed to slash at the back of Glipkerio's ankle.

But this ham-stringing stroke failed when Glipkerio turned around. Samanda, limping just a little, came to her overlord's side. Gigantic ax and whip were again lifted at the Mouser.

With a rather happy hysterical scream that almost ruined the Mouser's eardrums for good, Reetha hurled her crystal wine-flagon. It passed close between Samanda's and Glipkerio's heads, hitting neither of them, but staying their strokes at the Mouser.

All this while, unnoticed in the racket and turmoil, the golden jewel-box had been moving away, jolt by tiny jolt, from the wall. Now the door behind it was open wide enough for a rat to get through, and Hreest emerged followed by his armed band—three masked sword-rats in all, the other two green-uni-formed, and three naked-faced pike-rats in browned-iron helmets and mail.

Utterly terrified by this eruption, Glipkerio raced from the room, followed only less slowly by Saman-da, whose heavy treadings shook the wooden floor like earthquake shocks.

Mad for battle and also greatly relieved to face foes his own size, the Mouser went on guard, using his clothes bundle as a sort of shield and crying out fear-somely, "Come and be killed, Hreest!"

But at that instant he felt himself snatched up with stomach-wrenching speed to Reetha's breasts.

"Put me down! Put me down!" he yelled, still in a battle-rage, but futilely, for the drunken girl carried him reelingly out the door and slammed it behind her—once more the Mouser's eardrums were as-saulted—slammed it on a rat-pike.

Samanda and Glipkerio were running toward a distant, wide, blue curtain, but Reetha ran the other way, toward the kitchen and the servants' quarters, and the Mouser was perforce carried with her—his gray bundle bouncing about, his pin-sword useless, and despite his shrill protests and tears of wrath.

The rats everywhere launched their grand assault on Lankhmar Above a half hour before midnight, striking chiefly by way of golden ratholes. There were a few premature sorties, as on Silver Street, and elsewhere a few delays, as at ratholes discovered and blocked by humans at the last moment, but on the whole the attack was simultaneous.

First to emerge from Lankhmar Below were wild troops of four-foot goers, a fierce riderless cavalry, savage rats from the stinking tunnels and warrens under the slums of Lankhmar, rodents knowing few if any civilized amenities and speaking at most a pidgin-Lankhmarese helped out with chitters and squeals. Some fought only with tooth and claw like the veriest primitives. Among them went berserkers and special-mission groups.

Then came the assassins and the incendiaries with their torches, resins, and oils—for the weapon of fire, hitherto unused, was part of the grand plan, even though the rats' upper-level tunnels were menaced thereby. It was calculated that victory would be gained swiftly enough for the humans to be enforced to put out the blazes.

Finally came the armed and armored rats, all going biped except for those packing extra missiles and parts of light-artillery pieces to be assembled above ground.

Previous forays had been made almost entirely through ratholes in cellars and ground floors and by way of street-drains and the like. But tonight's grand assault was delivered whenever possible through ratholes on upper floors and through rat-ways that emerged in attics, surprising the humans in the supposedly safe chambers in which they had shut themselves and driving them in panic into the streets.

It was turn-about from previous nights and days,

when the rats had risen in black waves and streams.
Now they dropped like a black indoor rain and
leaked in rat-big gushes from walls thought sound,
bringing turmoil and terror. Here and there, chiefly
under eaves, flames began to flicker.

The rats emerged inside almost every temple and
cultish hovel lining the Street of the Gods, driving out
the worshippers until that wide avenue was milling
with humans too terrified to dare the dark side
streets or create more than a few pockets of organized
resistance.

In the high-windowed assembly hall of the South
Barracks, Olegnya Mingolsbane loudly sputter-
quavered to a weary audience which following custom had left their weapons outside—the soldiers of
Lankhmar had been known to use them on irritating
or merely boresome speakers. As he perorated, "You
who have fought the black behemoth and leviathan,
you who have stood firm against Mingol and
Mirphian, you who have broken the spear-squares of
King Krimaxius and routed his fortressed elephants,
that *you* should be daunted by dirty vermin—" eight
large ratholes opened high in the back wall and from
these sinister orifices a masked battery of crossbow
artillery launched their whirring missiles at the aged
and impassioned general. Five struck home, one
down his gullet, and gargling horridly he fell from
the rostrum.

Then the fire of the crossbows was turned on the
startled yet lethargic audience, some of whom had
been applauding Olegnya's demise as if it had been
a carnival turn. From other high ratholes actual fire
was tossed down in the forms of white phosphorus
and flaming, oil-soaked, resin-hearted bundles of
rags, while from various low golden ratholes, noxious

vapors brewed in the sewers were bellows-driven.

Groups of soldiers and constables broke for the doors and found them barred from the outside—one of the most striking achievements of the special-missions groups, made possible by Lankhmar having things arranged so that she could massacre her own soldiers in times of mutiny. With smuggled weapons and those of officers, a counter-fire was turned on the ratholes, but they were difficult targets and for the most part the men of war milled about as helplessly as the worshipers in the Street of the Gods, coughing and crying out, more troubled for the present by the stinking vapors and the choking fumes of little flames here and there than by the larger fire-danger.

Meanwhile the black kitten was flattening himself on top of a cask in the granaries area while a party of armed rats trooped by. The small beast shivered with fear, yet was drawn on deeper and deeper into the city by a mysterious urging which he did not understand, yet could not ignore.

Hisvin's house had in its top floor a small room, the door and window shutters of which were all tightly barred from the inside so that a witness, if there could have been one, would have wondered how this barring had been accomplished in such fashion as to leave the room empty.

A single thick, blue-burning candle, which had somewhat fouled the air, revealed no furniture whatsoever in the room. It showed six wide, shallow basins that were part of the tiled floor. Three of these basins were filled with a thick pinkish liquid across which ever and anon a slow quivering ran. Each pink pool had a border of black dust with which it did not commingle. Along one wall were shelves of small vials, the white ones near the floor, the black ones higher.

A tiny door opened at floor level. Hisvin, Hisvet, and Frix filed silently out. Each took a white vial and walked to a pink pool and then unhesitatingly down into it. The dark dust and pinkish liquid slowed but did not stop their steps. It moved out in sluggish ripples from their knees. Soon each stood thigh-deep at a pool's center. Then each drained his vial.

For a long instant there was no change, only the ripples intersecting and dying by the candle's feeble gleam.

Then each figure began to grow while soon the pools were visibly diminished. In a dozen heartbeats they were empty of liquid and dust alike, while in them Hisvin, Hisvet, and Frix stood human-high, dry-shod, and clad all in black.

Hisvin unbarred a window opening on the Street of the Gods, threw wide the shutters, drew a deep breath, stooped to peer out briefly and cautiously, then turned him crouching to the girls.

"It has begun," he said somberly. "Haste we now to the Blue Audience Chamber. Time presses. I will alert our Mingols to assemble and follow us." He scuttled past them to the door. "Come!"

Fafhrd drew himself up onto the roof of the temple of the Gods *of* Lankhmar and paused for a backward and downward look before tackling the belfry, although so far this climb had been easier even than that of the city's wall.

He wanted to know what all the screaming was about.

Across the street were several dark houses, first

among them Hisvin's, while beyond them rose
Glipkerio's Rainbow Palace with its moonlit, pastel-
hued minarets, tallest of them the blue, like a troup
of tall, slender dancing girls behind a phalanx of
black-robed squat priests.

Immediately below him was the temple's unroofed
yet dark front porch and low, wide steps leading up
to it from the street. Fafhrd had not even tried the
verdigrised, copper-bound, worm-eaten doors below
him. He had had no mind to go stumbling around
hunting for a stairs in the inner dark and dust, where
his groping hands might touch mummy-wrapped,
black-togaed forms which might not lie still like other
dead earth, but stir with crotchety limitless anger,
like ancient yet not quite senile kings who did not
relish their sleep disturbed at midnight. On both
counts, an outside climb had seemed healthier and
likewise the awakening of the Gods *of* Lankhmar, if
they were to be wakened, better by a distant bell
than by a touch on a skeletal shoulder wrapped in
crumbling linen or on a bony foot.

When Fafhrd had begun his short climb, the Street
of the Gods had been empty at this end, though from
the open doors of its gorgeous temples—the temples
of the Gods *in* Lankhmar—had spilled yellow light
and come the mournful sound of many litanies,
mixed with the sharper accents of impromptu prayers and beseechings.

But now the street was churning with white-faced
folk, while others were still rushing screaming from
temple doorways. Fafhrd still couldn't see what they
were running from, and once more he thought of an
army of invisibles—after all, he had only to imagine
Ghouls with invisible bones—but then he noted that

most of the shriekers and churners were looking
downward toward their feet and the cobbles. He rec-
ollected the eerie pattering which had sent him running away from Silver Street. He remembered what
Ningauble had asserted about the huge numbers and
hidden source of the army besieging Lankhmar. And
he recalled that *Clam* had been sunk and *Squid* captured by rats working chiefly alone. A wild suspicion
swiftly bloomed in him.

Meanwhile some of the temple refugees had
thrown themselves to their knees in front of the dingy
fane on which he stood, and were bumping their
heads on the cobbles and lower steps and uttering
frenzied petitions for aid. As usual, Lankhmar was
appealing to her own grim, private gods only in a
moment of direst need, when all else failed. While a
bold few directly below Fafhrd had mounted the
dark porch and were beating on and dragging at the
ancient portals.

There came a loud creaking and groaning and a
sound of rending. For a moment Fafhrd thought that
those below him, having broken in, were going to
rush inside. But then he saw them hurrying back
down the steps in attitudes of dread and prostrating
themselves like the others.

The great doors had opened until there was a
hand's breadth between them. Then through that
narrow gap there issued from the temple a torchlit
procession of tiny figures which advanced and
ranged themselves along the forward edge of the
porch.

They were two score or so of large rats walking
erect and wearing black togas. Four of them carried
lance-tall torches flaming brightly white-blue at their
tips. The others each carried something that Fafhrd,

staring down eagle-eyed, could not quite discern—a little black staff? There were three whites among them, the rest black.

A hush fell on the Street of the Gods, as if at some secret signal the humans' tormentors had ceased their persecutions.

The black-togaed rats cried out shrilly in unison, so that even Fafhrd heard them clearly, "We have slain your gods, O Lankhmarts! We are your gods now, O folk of Lankhmar. Submit yourselves to our worldly brothers and you will not be harmed. Hark to their commands. Your gods are dead, O Lankhmarts! We are your gods!"

The humans who had abased themselves continued to do so and to bump their heads. Others of the crowd imitated them.

Fafhrd thought for a moment of seeking something to hurl down on that dreadful little black-clad line which had cowed humanity. But the nasty notion came to him that if the Mouser had been reduced to a fraction of himself and able to live far under the deepest cellar, what could it mean but that the Mouser had been transformed into a rat by wicked magic, Hisvin's most likely? In slaying any rat, he might slay his comrade.

He decided to stick to Ningauble's instructions. He began to climb the belfry with great reaches and pulls of his long arms and doublings and straightenings of his still longer legs.

The black kitten, coming around a far corner of the same temple, bugged his little eyes at the horrid tableaux of black-togaed rats. He was tempted to flee, yet moved never a muscle, as a soldier who knows he had a duty to perform, though he has forgotten or not yet learned the nature of that duty.

XV

GLIPKERIO SAT FIDGETING on the edge of his seashell-shaped couch of gold. His light battle-ax lay forgot on the blue floor beside him. From a low table he took up a delicate silver wand of authority tipped with a bronze starfish—it was one of several dozen lying there—and sought to play with it nervously. But he was too nervous for that. Within moments it shot out of his hands and clattered musically on the blue floor-tiles a dozen feet away. He knotted his wand-long fingers together tightly, and rocked in agitation.

The Blue Audience Chamber was lit only by a few guttering, soot-runneled candles. The central curtains had been raised, but this doubling of the room's length only added to its gloom. The stairway going up into the blue minaret was a spiral of shadows. Beyond the dark archways leading to the porch, the great gray spindle balancing atop the copper chute gleamed mysteriously in the moonlight. A narrow silver ladder led up to its manhole, which stood open.

The candles cast on the blue-tiled inner wall several monstrous shadows of a bulbous figure seeming to bear two heads, the one atop the other. It was made by Samanda, who stood watching Glipkerio with stolid intentness, as one watches a lunatic up to tricks.

Finally Glipkerio, whose own gaze never ceased to twitch about at floor level, especially at the foot of blue curtains masking arched blue doorways, began to mumble, softly at first, then louder and louder, "I can't stand it any more. Armed rats loose in the palace. Guardsmen gone. Hairs in my throat. That horrid girl. That indecent hairy jumping jack with the Mouser's face. No butler or maid to answer my bell. Not even a page to trim the candles. And Hisvin hasn't come. Hisvin's not coming! I've no one. All's lost! *I can't stand it. I'm leaving! World, adieu! Nehwon, goodbye! I seek a happier universe!*"

And with that warning, he dashed toward the porch—a streak of black toga from which a lone pansy petal fluttered down.

Samanda, clumping after him heavily, caught him before he could climb the silver ladder, largely because he couldn't get his hands unknotted to grip the rungs. She grasped him round with a huge arm and led him back toward the audience couch, meanwhile straightening and unslipping his fingers for him and saying, "Now, now, no boat trips tonight, little master. It's on dry land we stay, your own dear palace. Only think: tomorrow, when this nonsense is past, we'll have such lovely whippings. Meanwhile to guard you, pet, you've me, who am worth a regiment. Stick to Samanda!"

As if taking her at her literal word, Glipkerio, who

had been confusedly pulling away, suddenly threw his arms around her neck and almost managed to seat himself upon her great belly.

A blue curtain had billowed wide, but it was only Glipkerio's niece Elakeria in a gray silk dress that threatened momently to burst at the seams. The plump and lascivious girl had grown fatter than ever the past few days from stuffing herself with sweets to assuage her grief at her mother's broken neck and the crucifixion of her pet marmoset, and even more to still her fears for herself. But at the moment a weak anger seemed to be doing the work of honey and sugar.

"Uncle!" she cried. "You must do something at once! The guardsmen are gone. Neither my maid nor page answered my bell, and when I went to fetch them, I found that insolent Reetha—wasn't she to be whipped?—inciting all the pages to revolt against you, or do something equally violent. And in the crook of her left arm sat a living gray-clad doll waving a cruel little sword—surely it was he who crucified Kwe-Kwe!—urging further enormities. I stole away unseen."

"Revolt, eh?" Samanda growled, setting Glipkerio aside and unsnapping whip and truncheon from her belt. "Elakeria, look out for Uncle here. You know, boat trips," she added in a hoarse whisper, tapping her temple significantly. "Meanwhile I'll give those naked sluts and minions a counter-revolution they'll not forget."

"Don't leave me!" Glipkerio implored, throwing himself at her neck and lap again. "Now that Hisvin's forgot me, you're my only protection."

A clock struck the quarter hour. Blue drapes parted and Hisvin came in with measured steps instead of his customary scuttling. "For good or ill, I come upon my instant," he said. He wore his black cap and toga and over the latter a belt from which hung ink-pot, quill-case, and a pouch of scrolls. Hisvet and Frix came close after him, in sober silken black robes and stoles. The blue drapes closed behind them. All three black-framed faces were grave.

Hisvan paced toward Glipkerio, who somewhat shamed into composure by the orderly behavior of the newcomers was standing beanpole tall on his own two gold-sandaled feet, had adjusted a little the disordered folds of his toga, and straightened around his golden ringlets the string of limp vegetable matter which was all that was left of his pansy wreath.

"Oh most glorious overlord," Hisvin intoned solemnly, "I bring you the worst news"—Glipkerio paled and began again to shake—"and the best." Glipkerio recovered somewhat. "The worst first. The star whose coming made the heavens right has winked out, like a candle puffed on by a black demon, its fires extinguished by the black swells of the ocean of the sky. In short, she's sunk without a trace and so I cannot speak my spell against the rats. Furthermore, it is my sad duty to inform you that the rats have already, for all practical purposes, conquered Lankhmar. All your soldiery is being decimated in the South Barracks. All the temples have been invaded and the very Gods *of* Lankhmar slain without warning in their dry, spicy beds. The rats only pause, out of a certain courtesy which I will explain, before capturing your palace over your head."

"Then all's lost," Glipkerio quavered chalk-pale and turning his head added peevishly, "I *told* you so,

Samanda! Naught remains for me but the last
voyage. World, adieu! Nehwon, farewell! I seek a
happier—"

But this time his lunge toward the porch was
stopped at once by his plump niece and stout palace
mistress, hemming him close on either side.

"Now hear the best," Hisvin continued in livelier
accents. "At great personal peril I have put myself in
touch with the rats. It transpires that they have an
excellent civilization, finer in many respects than
man's—in fact, they have been secretly guiding the
interests and growth of man for some time—oh 'tis a
cozy, sweet civilization these wise rodents enjoy and
'twill delight your sense of fitness when you know it
better! At all events the rats, now loving me well—
ah, what rare diplomacies I've worked for you, dear
master!—have entrusted me with their surrender
terms, which are unexpectedly generous!"

He snatched from his pouch one of the scrolls in it,
and saying, "I'll summarize," read: ". . . hostilities
to cease at once . . . by Glipkerio's command transmitted by his agents bearing his wands of authority
. . . Fires to be extinguished and damage to
Lankhmar repaired by Lankhmarts under direction
of . . . et cetera. Damage to ratly tunnels, arcades,
pleasances, privies, and other rooms to be repaired
by humans. 'Suitably reduced in size' should go in
there. All soldiers disarmed, bound, confined . . . and
so forth. All cats, dogs, ferrets, and other vermin . . .
well, naturally. All ships and all Lankhmarts aboard
. . . that's clear enough. Ah, here's the spot! Listen
now. Thereafter each Lankhmart to go about his customary business, free in all his actions and
possessions—*free*, you hear that?—subject only to the

commands of his personal rat or rats, who shall crouch upon his shoulder or otherwise dispose themselves on or within his clothing, as they shall see fit, and share his bed. But *your* rats," he went on swiftly, pointing to Glipkerio, who had gone very pale and whose body and limbs had begun again their twitchings and his features their tics, *"your* rats shall, out of deference to your high position, not be rats at all—but rather my daughter Hisvet and, temporarily, her maid Frix, who shall attend you day and night, watch and watch, granting your every wish on the trifling condition that you obey their every command. What could be fairer, my dear master?"

But Glipkerio had already gone once more into his, "World, adieu! Nehwon, farewell! I seek a—" meanwhile straining toward the porch and convulsing up and down in his efforts to be free of Samanda's and Elakeria's restraining arms. Of a sudden, however, he stopped still, cried, "Of course I'll sign!" and grabbed for the parchment. Hisvin eagerly led him to his audience couch and the table, meanwhile readying his writing equipment.

But here a difficulty developed. Glipkerio was shaking so that he could hardly hold pen, let alone write. His first effort with the quill sent a comet's tail of inkdrops across the clothing of those around him and Hisvin's leathery face. All efforts to guide his hand, first by gentleness, then by main force, failed.

Hisvin snapped his fingers in desperate impatience, then pointed a sudden finger at his daughter. She produced a flute from her black silken robe and began to pipe a sweet yet drowsy melody. Samanda and Elakeria held Glipkerio face down on his couch, the one at his shoulders, the other at his ankles, while

Frix, kneeling with one knee on the small of his back began with her fingertips to stroke his spine from skull to tail in time to Hisvet's music, favoring her left hand with its bandaged palm.

Glipkerio continued to convulse upward at regular intervals, but gradually the violence of these earthquakes of the body decreased and Frix was able to transfer some of her rhythmic strokings to his flailing arms.

Hisvin, hard a-pace and snapping his fingers again, his shadows marching like those of giant rats moving confusedly and size-changingly against each other across the blue tiles, demanded suddenly on noting the wands of authority, "Where are your pages you promised to have here?"

Glipkerio responded dully, "In their quarters. In revolt. You stole my guards who would have controlled them. Where are your Mingols?"

Hisvin stopped dead in his pacing and frowned. His gaze went questioningly toward the unmoving blue door-drapes through which he had entered.

Fafhrd, breathing a little heavily, drew himself up into one of the belfry's eight windows and sat on its sill and scanned the bells.

There were eight in all and all large: five of bronze, three of browned-iron, coated with the sea-pale vertigris and earth-dark rust of eons. Any ropes had rotted away, centuries ago for all he knew. Below them was dark emptiness spanned by four narrow flat-topped stone arches. He tried one of them with his foot. It held.

He set the smallest bell, a bronze one, swinging. There was no sound except for a dismal creaking.

He first peered, then felt up inside the bell. The

clapper was gone, its supporting link rusted away.

All the other bells' clappers. were likewise gone, presumably fallen to the bottom of the tower.

He prepared to use his ax to beat out the alarum, but then he saw one of the fallen clappers lying on a stone arch.

He lifted it with both hands, like a somewhat ponderous club, and moving about recklessly on the arches, struck each bell in turn. Rust showered him from the iron ones.

Their massed clangor sounded louder than mountainside thunder when lightning strikes from a cloud close by. The bells were the least musical Fafhrd had ever heard. Some made swelling beats together, which periodically tortured the ear. They must have been shaped and cast by a master of discord. The brazen bells shrieked, clanged, clashed, roared, twanged, jangled, and screamingly wrangled. The iron bells groaned rusty-throated, sobbed like leviathan, throbbed as the heart of universal death, and rolled like a black swell striking a smooth rock coast. They exactly suited the Gods *of* Lankhmar, from what Fafhrd had heard of the latter.

The metallic uproar began to fade somewhat and he realized that he was becoming deafened. Nevertheless he kept on until he had struck each bell three times. Then he peered out the window by which he had entered.

His first impression was that half the human crowd was looking straight at *him*. Then he realized it must be the noise of the bells which had turned upward those moonlit faces.

There were many more kneelers before the temple now. Other Lankhmarts were pouring up the Street of the Gods from the east, as if being driven.

The erect, black-togaed rats still stood in the same tiny line below him, auraed by grim authority despite their size, and now they were flanked by two squads of armored rats, each bearing a small weapon which puzzled Fafhrd, straining his eyes, until he recalled the tiny crossbows which had been used aboard *Squid*.

The reverberations of the bells had died away, or sunk too low for his deafened ears to note, but then he began to hear, faintly at first, murmurings and cries of hopeless horror from below.

Gazing across the crowd again, he saw black rats climbing unresisting up some of the kneeling figures, while many of the others already had something black squatting on their right shoulders.

There came from directly below a creaking and groaning and rending. The ancient doors of the temple of the Gods *of* Lankhmar were thrust wide open.

The white faces that had been gazing upward now stared at the porch.

The black-togaed rats and their soldiery faced around.

There strode four abreast from the wide-open doorway a company of fearfully thin brown figures, black-togaed too. Each bore a black staff. The brown was of three sorts: aged linen mummy-banding, brittle parchment-like skin stretched tight over naught but skeleton, and naked old brown bones themselves.

The crossbow-rats loosed a volley. The skeletal brown striders came on without pause. The black-togaed rats stood their ground, squeaking imperiously. Another useless volley from the tiny crossbows. Then, like so many rapiers, black staffs thrust out. Each rat they touched shriveled where he stood, nor moved again. Other rats came scurrying in from the crowd and were similarly slain. The brown company advanced at an even pace, like doom on the march.

There were screams then and the human crowd before the temple began to melt, racing down side streets and even dashing back into the temples from which they had fled. Predictably, the folk of Lankhmar were more afraid of their own gods come to their rescue than of their foes.

Himself somewhat aghast at what his ringing had roused, Fafhrd climbed down the belfry, telling himself that he must dodge the eerie battle below and seek out the Mouser in Glipkerio's vast palace.

At the corner of the temple's foot, the black kitten became aware of the climber high above, recognized him as the huge man he had scratched and loved, and realized that the force holding him here had something to do with that man.

The Gray Mouser loped purposefully out of the palace kitchen and up a corridor leading toward the royal dwelling quarters. Though still tiny, he was at last dressed. Beside him strode Reetha, armed with a long and needle-pointed skewer for broiling cutlets in a row. Close behind them marched a disorderly-ranked host of pages armed with cleavers and mallets, and maids with knives and toasting forks.

The Mouser had insisted that Reetha not carry him on this foray and the girl had let him have his way. And truly it made him feel more manly again to be going on his own two feet and from time to time swishing Scalpel menacingly through the air.

Still, he had to admit, he would feel a lot better were he his rightful size again, and Fafhrd at his side. Sheelba had told him the effects of the black potion would last for nine hours. He had drunk it a few minutes at most past three. So he should regain his true size a little after midnight, if Sheelba had not lied.

He glanced up at Reetha, more huge than any giantess and bearing a gleaming steel weapon tall as a catboat's mast, and felt further reassured.

"Onward!" he squeaked to his naked army, though he tried to pitch his voice as low as possible. "Onward to save Lankhmar and her overlord from the rats!"

Fafhrd dropped the last few feet to the temple's roof and faced around. The situation below had altered considerably.

The human folk were gone—that is, the living human folk.

The skeletal brown striders had all emerged through the door below and were marching west down the Street of the Gods—a procession of ugly ghosts, except these wraiths were opaque and their bony feet clicked harshly on the cobbles. The moonlit porch, steps, and flagstones behind them were blackly freckled with dead rats.

But the striders were moving more slowly now and were surrounded by shadows blacker than the moon could throw—a veritable sea of black rats lapping the striders and being augmented faster from all sides than the deadly staves could strike them down.

From two areas ahead, to either side of the Street of the Gods, flaming darts came arching and struck in the foreranks of the striders. These missiles, unlike the crossbow darts, took effect. Wherever they struck, old linen and resin-impregnated skin began to flicker and flame. The striders came to a halt, ceased slaying rats, and devoted themselves to pluck-

ing out the flaming darts sticking in them and beating out the flames on their persons.

Another wave of rats came racing down the Street
of the Gods from the Marsh Gate end, and behind
them on three great horses three riders leaning low in
their saddles and sword-slashing at the small beasts.
The horses and the cloaks and hoods of the riders
were inky black. Fafhrd, who thought himself in-
capable of more shivers, felt another. It was as if
Death itself, in three persons, had entered the scene.

The rodent fire-artillery, slewed partly around, let
off at the black riders a few flaming darts which
missed.

In return the black riders charged hoof-stamping
and sword-slashing into the two artillery areas. Then
they faced toward the brown skeletal striders, several
of whom still smoldered and flickered, and doffed
their black hoods and mantles.

Fafhrd's face broke into a grin that would have
seemed most inappropriate to one knowing he feared
an apparition of Death, but not knowing his experiences of the last few days.

Seated on the three black horses were three tall
skeletons gleaming white in the moonlight, and with
a lover's certainty he recognized the first as being
Kreeshkra's.

She might, of course, be seeking him out to slay
him for his faithlessness. Nevertheless, as almost any
other lover in like circumstances—though seldom,
true, near the midst of a natural-supernatural battle
—he grinned a rather egotistic grin.

He lost not a moment in beginning his descent.

Meanwhile Kreeshkra, for it was indeed she, was
thinking as she gazed at the Gods of Lankhmar, *Well,
I suppose brown bones are better than none at all. Still, they*

*seem a poor fire risk. Ho, here come more rats! What a filthy
city! And where oh where is my abominable Mud Man?*

The black kitten mewed anxiously at the temple's
foot where he awaited Fafhrd's arrival.

Glipkerio, calm as a cushion now, completely
soothed by Frix's massage and Hisvet's piping, was
halfway through signing his name, forming the letters more ornately and surely than he ever had in his
life, when the blue drapes in the largest archway
were torn down and there pressed into the chamber
on silent naked feet the Mouser's and Reetha's
forces.

Glipkerio gave a great twitch, upsetting the ink
bottle on the parchment of the surrender terms, and
sending his quill winging off like an arrow.

Hisvin, Hisvet, and even Samanda backed away
from him toward the porch, daunted at least momentarily by the newcomers—and indeed there was
something dire about that naked, shaven youthful
army be-weaponed with kitchen tools, their eyes
wild, their lips a-snarl or pressed tightly together.
Hisvin had been expecting his Mingols at last and so
got a double shock.

Elakeria hurried after them, crying, "They've
come to slay us all! It's the revolution!"

Frix held her ground, smiling excitedly.

The Mouser raced across the blue-tiled floor,
sprang up on Glipkerio's couch and balanced himself
on its golden back. Reetha followed rapidly and
stood beside him, menacing around with her skewer.

Unmindful that Glipkerio was flinching away, pale
yellow eyes peering affrightedly from a coarse fabric
of crisscrossed fingers, the Mouser squeaked loudly,
"Oh mighty overlord, no revolution this! Instead, we

have come to save you from your enemies! That one"
—he pointed at Hisvin—"is in league with the rats.
Indeed, he is by blood more rat than man. Under his
toga you'll find a tail. I saw him in the tunnels below,
member of the Rat Council of Thirteen, plotting
your overthrow. It is he—"

Meanwhile Samanda had been regaining her
courage. Now she charged her underlings like a black
rhinoceros, her globe-shaped, pin-skewered coiffure
more than enough horn. Laying about with her black
whip, she roared fearsomely, "Revolt, will you? On
your knees, scullions and sluts! Say your prayers!"

Taken by surprise and readily falling back into an
ingrained habit, their fiery hopes quenched by familiar abuse, the naked slim figures flinched away from
her to either side.

Reetha, however, grew pink with anger. Forgetting the Mouser and all else but her rage, envenomed by many injuries, she ran after Samanda,
crying to her fellow-slaves, "Up, and at her, you cowards! We're fifty to one against her!" And with that
she thrust out mightily with her skewer and jabbed
Samanda from behind.

The palace mistress leaped ponderously forward,
her keys and chains swinging wildly from her black
leather belt. She lashed the last maids out of her way
and pounded off at a thumping run toward the servants' quarters.

Reetha cried over shoulder, "After her, all—before
she rouses the cooks and barbers to her aid!" and
was off in sprinting pursuit.

The maids and pages hardly hesitated at all.
Reetha had refired their hot hatreds as readily as
Samanda had quenched them. To play heroes and
heroines rescuing Lankhmar was moonshine. To

have vengeance on their old tormenter was blazing sunlight. They all raced after Reetha.

The Mouser, still balancing on the fluted golden back of Glipkerio's couch and mounting his dramatic oration, realized somewhat belatedly that he had lost his army and was still only doll size. Hisvin and Hisvet, drawing long knives from under their black togas, rapidly circled between him and the doorway through which his forces had fled. Hisvin looked vicious and Hisvet unpleasantly like her father—the Mouser had never before noted the striking family resemblance. They began to close in.

To his left Elakeria snatched up a handful of the wands of office and raised them threateningly. To the Mouser, even those flimsy rods were huge as pikes.

To his right Glipkerio, still cringing away, reached down surreptitiously for his light battle-ax. Evidently the Mouser's loyal squeaks had gone unheard, or not been believed.

The Mouser wondered which way to jump.

Behind him Frix murmured softly, though to the Mouser's ears still somewhat boomingly, "Exit kitchen tyrant pursued by pages unclad and maids in a state of nature, leaving our hero beset by an ogre and two—or is it three?—ogresses."

XVI

FAFHRD, ALTHOUGH HE came down the temple's wall fast, found the battle once more considerably changed when he reached the bottom.

The Gods *of* Lankhmar, though not exactly in panicky rout, were withdrawing toward the open door of their temple, thrusting their staves from time to time at the horde of rats which still beset them. Wisps of smoke still trailed from a few of them—ghostly moonlit pennons. They were coughing, or more likely cursing and it sounded like coughs. Their brown skull-faces were dire—the expression of elders defeated and trying to cloak their impotent, gibbering rage with dignity.

Fafhrd moved rapidly out of their way.

Kreeshkra and her two male Ghouls were slashing and stabbing from their saddles at another flood of rats in front of Hisvin's house, while their black horses crunched rats under their hooves.

Fafhrd made toward them, but at that moment there was a rush of rats at him and he had to unsheathe Graywand. Using the great sword as a scythe, he cleared a space around him with three strokes, then started again toward the Ghouls.

The doors of Hisvin's house burst open and there fled out down the short steps a crowd of Mingol slaves. Their faces grimaced with terror, but even more striking was the fact that they were thin almost beyond emaciation. Their once-tight black liveries hung loosely on them. Their hands were skeletal. Their faces were skulls covered with yellow skin.

Three groups of skeletons: brown, ivory and yellow—*It is a prodigy of prodigies,* Fafhrd thought, *the beginning of a dark spectrum of bones.*

Behind the Mingols and driving them, not so much to kill them as to get them out of the way, came a company of crouchy but stalwart masked men, some wearing armor, all brandishing weapons—swords and crossbows. There was something horribly familiar about their scuttling, hobble-legged gait. Then came some with pikes and helmets, but without masks. The faces, or muzzles rather, were those of rats. All the newcomers, masked or nakedly furfaced, made for the three Ghoulish riders.

Fafhrd sprang forward, Graywand singing about his head, unmindful of the new surge of ordinary rats coming against him—and came to a skidding halt.

The man-sized and man-armed rats were still pouring from Hisvin's house. Hero or no, he couldn't kill *that* many of them.

At that instant he felt claws sink into his leg. He raised his crook-fingered big left hand to sweep away from him whatever now attacked him . . . and saw climbing his thigh the black kitten from *Squid.*

That scatterbrain mustn't be in this dread battle, he thought . . . and opened his empty pouch to thrust in the kitten . . . and saw gleaming dully at its bottom the tin whistle . . . and realized that here was a metal straw to cling to.

He snatched it out and set it to his lips and blew it.

When one taps with idle finger a toy drum, one does not expect a peal of thunder. Fafhrd gasped and almost swallowed the whistle. Then he made to hurl it away from him. Instead he set it to his lips once more, put his hands to his ears, for some reason closed his eyes tight, and once more blew it.

Once again the horrendous noise went shuddering up toward the moon and down the shadowed streets of Lankhmar.

Imagine the scream of a leopard, the snarl of a tiger, and the roaring of a lion commingled, and one will have some faint suggestion of the sound the tin whistle produced.

Everywhere the little rats held still in their hordes. The skeletal Mingols paused in their shaking, staggering flight. The big armed rats, masked or helmeted, halted in their attack upon the Ghouls. Even the Ghouls and their horses held still. The fur on the black kitten fluffed out as it still clung to Fafhrd's crouching thigh, and its green eyes became enormous.

Then the awesome sound had died away, a distant bell was tolling midnight, and all the battlers fell to action again.

But black shapes were forming in the moonlight around Fafhrd. Shapes that were at first no more than shadows with a sheen to them. Then darker, like translucent polished black horn. Then solid and velvet black, their pads resting on the moonlit flagstones. They had the slender, long-legged forms of cheetahs, but the mass of tigers or lions. They stood almost as high at the shoulder as horses. Their somewhat small and prick-eared heads swayed slow-ly, as did their long tails. Their fangs were like needles of faintly green ice. Their eyes, which were like frozen emeralds, stared all twenty-six at Fafhrd —for there were thirteen of the beasts.

Then Fafhrd realized that they were staring not at his head but at his waist.

The black kitten there gave a shrill, wailing cry that was at once a young cat's first battle call and also a greeting.

With a screaming, snarling roar, like thirteen of the tin whistles blown at once, the War Cats bounded outward. With preternatural agility, the black kitten leaped after a group of four of them.

The small rats fled toward walls and gutters and doors—wherever holes might be. The Mingols threw themselves down. The half-splintered doors of the temple of the Gods *of* Lankhmar could be heard to screech shut rather rapidly.

The four War Cats to whom the kitten had at-tached himself raced toward the man-size rats com-ing from Hisvin's house. Two of the Ghouls had been struck from their saddles by pikes or swords. The third—it was Kreeshkra—parried a blow from a rapier, then kicked her horse into a gallop past Hisvin's house toward the Rainbow Palace. The two riderless black horses followed her.

Fafhrd prepared to follow her, but at that instant a black parrot swooped down in front of him, beating its wings, and a small skinny boy with a puckered scar under his left eye was tugging at his waist.

"Mouser-Mouser!" the parrot squawked. "Danger-danger! Blue-Blue-Blue Blue Audience Chamber!"

"Same message, big man," the urchin rasped with a grin.

So Fafhrd, running around the battle of armed rats and War Cats—a whirling melee of silvery swords and flashing claws, of cold green and hot red eyes—set out after Kreeshkra anyhow, since she had been going in the same direction.

Long pikes struck down a War Cat, but the kitten sprang like a shining black comet at the face of the foremost of the giant rodent pike-wielders as the other three War Cats closed in beside him.

The Gray Mouser lightly dropped off the back of the golden couch the instant Hisvin and Hisvet got within stabbing distance. Then, since they were both coming around the couch, he ran under it and from thence under the low table. During his short passage through the open, Glipkerio's ax crashed on the tiles to one side of him, while Elakeria's bundle of wands smashed clatteringly down on the other. He paused under the center of the table, plotting his next action.

Glipkerio darted prudently away, leaving his ax where he had let go of it from the sting of the blow. Plump Elakeria, however, slipped and fell with the force of her clumsy thwack and for the moment both her sprawled form and the ax were quite close to the Mouser.

Then—well, one moment the table was a roof a comfortable rat's-span or so above the Mouser's head. The next moment he had, without moving, bumped his head on it and very shortly afterward somehow overturned it to one side without touching it with his hands and despite the fact that he had sat down rather hard on the floor.

While Elakeria was no longer an obese wanton bulging out a gray dress, but a slender nymph totally unclad. And the head of Glipkerio's ax, which Scalpel's slim blade now touched, had shrunk to a ragged sliver of metal, as if eaten away by invisible acid.

The Mouser realized that he had regained his original size, even as Sheelba had foretold. The thought flashed through his mind that, since nothing can come of nothing, the atomies shed from Scalpel in the cellar had now been made up from those in the ax-head, while to replace his flesh and clothing he had stolen somewhat of that of Elakeria. She certainly had benefited from the transaction, he decided.

But this was not the time for metaphysics or for moralizing, he told himself. He scrambled to his feet and advanced on his shrunken-seeming tormenters, menacing with Scalpel.

"Drop your weapons!" he commanded.

Neither Glipkerio, Elakeria, or Frix held any. Hisvet let go of her long dagger at once, probably recalling that the Mouser knew she had some skill in hurling it. But Hisvin, foaming now with rage and frustration, held onto his. The Mouser advanced Scalpel flickeringly toward his scrawny throat.

"Call off your rats, Lord Null," he ordered, "or you die!"

"Shan't!" Hisvin spat at him, stabbing futilely at Scalpel. Then, reason returning to him a little, he added, "And even if I wished to, I couldn't!"

The Mouser, knowing from his session at the Council of Thirteen that this was the truth, hesitated.

Elakeria, seeing her nakedness, snatched a light coverlet from the golden couch and huddled it around her, then immediately drew it aside again to admire her slender new body.

Frix continued to smile excitedly but somehow composedly, as if all this were a play and she its audience.

Glipkerio, although seeking to firm himself by tightly embracing a spirally fluted pillar between candlelit chamber and moonlit porch, clearly had the grand, rather than merely the petty twitches again. His narrow face, between its periodic convulsions, was a study in consternation and nervous exhaustion.

Hisvet called out, "Gray lover, kill the old fool my father! Slay Glip and the rest too, unless you desire Frix as a concubine. Then rule all Lankhmar Above and Below with my willingest aid. You've won the game, dear one. I confess myself beaten. I'll be your humblest slave-girl, my only hope that some day I'll be your most favorite too."

And so ringingly sincere was her voice and so dulcet-sweet in making its promises, that despite his experiences of her treacheries and cruelties and despite the cold murderousness of some of her words, the Mouser was truly tempted. He looked toward her —her expression was that of a gambler playing for the highest stakes—and in that instant Hisvin lunged.

The Mouser beat the dagger aside and retreated a double step, cursing only himself for the wavering of his attention. Hisvin continued to lunge desperately, only desisting when Scalpel pricked his throat swollen with curses.

"Keep your promise and show your courage," Hisvet cried to the Mouser. "Kill him!"

Hisvin began to gabble his curses at her too.

The Mouser was never afterwards quite certain as to what he would have done next, for the nearest blue curtains were jerked away to either side and there stood Skwee and Hreest, both man-size, both unmasked and with rapiers drawn, both of lordly, cool, assured, and dire mien—the white and the black of rat aristocracy.

Without a word Skwee advanced a pace and pointed his sword at the Mouser. Hreest copied him so swiftly it was impossible to be sure it was a copy. The two green-uniformed sword-rats moved out from behind them and went on guard to either side. From behind *them,* the three pike-rats, man-size like the rest, moved out still farther on the flank, two toward the far end of the room, one toward the golden couch, beside which Hisvet now stood near Frix.

His hand clutching his scrawny throat, Hisvin mastered his astonishment and pointing at his daughter, croaked commandingly, "Kill her too!"

The lone pike-rat obediently leveled his weapon and ran with it. As the great wavy blade passed close by her, Frix cast herself at the weapon, hugging its pole. The blade missed Hisvet by a finger's breadth and Frix fell. The pike-rat jerked back his weapon and raised it to skewer Frix to the floor, but, "Stop!" Skwee cried. "Kill none—as yet—except the one in gray. All now, advance!"

The pike-rat obediently swiveled round, re-leveling his weapon at the Mouser.

Frix picked herself up and casually murmuring in Hisvet's ear, "That's three times, dear mistress," turned to watch the rest of the drama.

The Mouser thought of diving off the porch, but instead broke for the far end of the room. It was perhaps a mistake. The two pike-rats were at the far

door ahead of him, while the sword-rats at his heels
gave him no time to feint around the pike-blades, kill
the pike-rats and get around them. He dodged behind a heavy table and turning abruptly, managed to
wound lightly in the thigh a green-uniformed rat who
had run a bit ahead of the rest. But that rat dodged
back and the Mouser found himself faced by four
rapiers and two pikes—and just conceivably by
death too, he had to admit to himself as he noted the
sureness with which Skwee was directing and controlling the attack. So—slash, jump, slash, thrust,
parry, kick the table—he must attack Skwee—thrust,
parry, riposte, counter-riposte, retreat—but Skwee
had anticipated that, so—slash, jump, thrust, jump,
jump again, bump the wall, thrust—whatever he was
going to do, he'd have to do it very soon!

A rat's head, detached from its rat, spun across the
edge of his field of vision and he heard a happy, familiar shout.

Fafhrd had just entered the room, beheaded from
behind the third pike-rat, who had been acting as a
sort of reserve, and was rushing the others from behind.

At Skwee's swift signal, the lesser sword-rats and
the two remaining pike-rats turned. The latter were
slow in shifting their long weapons. Fafhrd beheaded
the blade of one pike and then its owner, parried the
second pike and thrust home through the throat of
the rat wielding it, then met the attack of the two
lesser sword-rats, while Skwee and Hreest redoubled
their assault on the Mouser. Their snarl-twisted
bristles, snarl-bared incisors, long flat furry faces and
huge eyes blue and black were almost as daunting as
their swift swords, while Fafhrd found equal menace
in his pair.

At Fafhrd's entry, Glipkerio had said very softly to himself, "No, I cannot bear it longer," run out onto the porch and up the silver ladder, and sprung down through the manhole of the spindle-shaped gray vehicle. His weight overbalanced it, so that it slowly nosed down in the copper chute. He called out, somewhat more loudly, "World, adieu! Nehwon, goodbye! I go to seek a happier universe. Oh, you'll regret me, Lankhmar! Weep, oh City!" Then the gray vehicle was sliding down the chute, faster and faster. He dropped inside and jerked shut the hatch after him. With a small, sullen splash the vehicle vanished beneath the dark, moon-fretted waters.

Only Elakeria and Frix, whose eyes and ears missed nothing, saw Glipkerio go or heard his valedictory.

With a sudden concerted effort Skwee and Hreest rammed the table, across which they'd been fencing, against the Mouser, to pin him to the wall. Barely in time, he sprang atop it, dodged Skwee's thrust, parried Hreest's, and on a lucky riposte sent Scalpel's tip into Hreest's right eye and brain, whipping his sword out just soon enough to parry Skwee's next thrust.

Skwee retreated a double step. By virtue of the almost panoramic vision of his wide-spaced blue eyes, he noted that Fafhrd was finishing off the second of his two sword-rats, beating through by brute force the parries of their lighter swords, and himself suffering only a few scratches and minor pricks in the process.

Skwee turned and ran. The Mouser leaped from the table after him. Midway down the room something was falling in blue folds from the ceiling. Hisvet, midway along the wall, had slashed with her dagger the cords supporting the curtains that could divide the room in two. Skwee ran a-crouch under them, but the Mouser almost ran into them, dodging swiftly back as Skwee's rapier thrust through the heavy fabric inches from his throat.

Moments later the Mouser and Fafhrd located the central split in the drapes and suddenly parted them with the tips of their swords, closely a-watch for another rapier-thrust or even a thrown dagger.

Instead they saw Hisvin, Hisvet, and Skwee standing in front of the audience couch in attitudes of defiance, but grown small as children—if that can be said of a rat. The Mouser started toward them, but before he was halfway there, they became small as rats and swiftly tumbled down a tile-size trapdoor. Skwee, who went last, turned for one more angry chitter at the Mouser, one more shake of toy-size rapier, before he pulled the tile shut over his head.

The Mouser cursed, then burst into laughter. Fafhrd joined him, but his eyes were warily on Frix, still standing human-size behind the couch. Nor did he miss Elakeria on the couch, peering with one affrighted eye from under the coverlet while also thrusting out, inadvertently or no, one slender leg.

Still laughing wildly, the Mouser reeled over to Fafhrd, threw an arm up around his shoulders, and pummeled him playfully in the chest, demanding, "Why did you have to turn up, you great lout? I was about to die heroically, or else slay in mass combat the seven greatest sword-rats in Lankhmar Below! You're a scene-stealer!"

Eyes still on Frix, Fafhrd roughed the Mouser's chin affectionately with his fist, then gave him an elbow-dig sharp enough to take half his breath away and stop his laughter. "Three of them were only

pikemen, or pike-rats, as I suppose you call them,"
he corrected, then complained gruffly, "I gallop two
nights and a day—halfway around the Inner Sea—to
save your undersized hide. And do so! Only to be
told I'm an actor."

The Mouser gasped out, still with a snickering
whoop, "You don't know how undersized! Halfway
around the Inner Sea, you say . . . and nevertheless
time your entrance perfectly! Why, you're the
greatest actor of them all!" He dropped to his knees
in front of the tile that had served as trapdoor and
said in tones compounded equally of philosophy, humor, and hysteria, "While I must lose—forever, I
suppose—the greatest love of my life." He rapped the
tile—it sounded very solid—and thrusting down his
face called out softly, "Yoo-hoo! Hisvet!" Fafhrd
jerked him to his feet.

Frix raised a hand. The Mouser looked at her,
while Fafhrd had never taken his eyes off her.

"Here, little man, catch!" Smiling, she called to
the Mouser and tossed him a small black vial, which
he caught and goggled at foolishly. "Use it if you are
ever again so silly as to wish to seek out my late mistress. I have no need of it. I have worked out my
bondage in this world. I have done the diabolic Demoiselle her three services. I am free!"

As she said that last word, her eyes lit up like
lamps. She threw back her black hood and took a
breath so deep it seemed almost to lift her from the
floor. Her eyes fixed on infinity. Her dark hair lifted
on her head. Lightning crackled in her hair, formed
itself in a blue nimbus, and streamed like a blue
cloak down her body, over and through her black silk
dress.

She turned and ran swiftly out onto the porch,

Fafhrd and the Mouser after her. Glowing still more bluely and crying, "Free! Free! *Free!* Back to Arilia! Back to the World of Air," she dove off the edge.

She did not seem to enter the waves, but skimmed just along their crests like a small, faint blue comet and then mounting toward the sky, higher and higher, became a faint blue star and vanished.

"Where is Arilia?" the Mouser asked.

"I thought this was the World of Air," Fafhrd mused.

XVII

THE RATS all over Lankhmar, after suffering huge
losses, dove back everywhere into their holes and
pulled tight shut the doors of such as had them. This
happened also in the rooms of pink pools in the third
floor of Hisvin's house, where the War Cats had
driven back the last of the rats who had gained their
human size by drinking the white vials there and at
the expense of the flesh of Hisvin's Mingols. Now
they guzzled the black vials even more eagerly, to escape back into their tunnels.

The rats also suffered total defeat in the South
Barracks, where the War Cats ravaged after clawing
and crashing open the doors with preternatural
strength.

Their work done, the War Cats regathered at the
place where Fafhrd had summoned them and there
faded away even as they had earlier materialized.
They were still thirteen, although they had lost one
of their company, for the black kitten faded away
with them, comporting himself like an apprentice
member of their company. It was ever afterwards believed, by most Lankhmarts, that the War Cats and

the white skeletons as well had been summoned by the Gods *of* Lankhmar, whose reputation for horrid powers and dire activities was thereby bolstered, despite some guilty recollections of their temporary defeat by the rats.

By twos and threes and sixes, the people of Lankhmar emerged from their places of hiding, learned that the Rat Plague was over, and wept, prayed, and rejoiced. Gentle Radomix Kistomerces-Null was plucked from his retreat in the slums and with his seventeen cats carried in triumph to the Rainbow Palace.

Glipkerio, his leaden craft tightly collapsed around him by weight of water, until it had become a second leaden skin molded to his form—truly a handsome coffin—continued to sink in the Lankhmar Deep, but whether to reach a solid bottom, or only a balancing place between world bubbles in the waters of infinity, who may say?

The Gray Mouser recovered Cat's Claw from Hreest's belt, marveling somewhat that all the rat-corpses were yet human size. Likely enough death froze all magics.

Fafhrd noted with distaste the three pools of pink slime in front of the gold audience couch and looked for something to throw over them. Elakeria coyly clutched her coverlet around her. He dragged from a corner a colorful rug that was a duke's ransom and made that do.

There was the noise of hooves on tiles. In the high, wide archway from which the drapes had been torn there appeared Kreeshkra, still on horseback and leading the other two Ghoulish mounts, empty saddled. Fafhrd swung the skeleton girl down and embraced her heartily, somewhat to the Mouser's and Elakeria's shock, but soon said, "Dearest love, I think it best you put on again your black cloak and hood. Your naked bones are to me the acme of beauty, but here come others they may disturb."

"Already ashamed of me, aren't you? Oh, you dirty-minded puritanical Mud Folk!" Kreeshkra commented with a sour laugh, yet complied, while the rainbows in her eye sockets twinkled.

The others Fafhrd had referred to consisted of the councillors, soldiers, and various relatives of the late overlord, including the gentle Radomix Kistomerces-Null and his seventeen cats, each now carried and cosseted by some noble hoping to gain favor from Lankhmar's most likely next overlord.

Not all the new arrivals were so commonplace. One, heralded by more hoof-cloppings on tile, was Fafhrd's Mingol mare, her tether bitten through. She stopped by Fafhrd and glared her bloodshot eyes at him, as if to say, "I am not so easily got rid of. Why did you cheat me of a battle?"

Kreeshkra patted the grim beast's nose and observed to Fafhrd, "You are clearly a man who awakens deep loyalty in others. I trust you have the same quality yourself."

"Never doubt me, dearest," Fafhrd answered with fond sincerity.

Also among the newcomers and returners was Reetha, looking suavely happy as a cat who has licked cream, or a panther some even more vital fluid, and naked as ever except for three broad black leather loops around her waist. She threw her arms about the Mouser. "You're big again!" she rejoiced. "And you beat them all!"

The Mouser accepted her embrace, though he purposely put on a dissatisfied face and said sourly, "You were a big help!—you and your naked army, deserting me when I most needed help. I suppose you finished off Samanda?"

"Indeed we did!" Reetha smirked like a sated leopardess. "What a sizzling she made! Look, doll, her belt of office *does* go three times round my waist. Oh yes, we cornered her in the kitchen and brought her down. Each of us took a pin from her hair. Then—"

"Spare me the details, darling," the Mouser cut her short. "This night for nine hours I've been a rat, with all of a rat's nasty feelings, and that's quite long enough. Come with me, pet; there's something we must attend to ere the crowd gets too thick."

When they returned after a short space, the Mouser was carrying a box wrapped in his cloak, while Reetha wore a violet robe, around which was still triply looped, however, Samanda's belt. And the crowd had thickened indeed. Radomix Kistomerces-no-longer-Null had already been informally vested with Lankhmar's overlordship and was sitting somewhat bemused on the golden seashell audience couch along with his seventeen cats and also a smiling Elakeria, who had wrapped her coverlet like a sari around her sylphlike figure.

The Mouser drew Fafhrd aside. "That's quite a girl you've got," he remarked, rather inadequately, of Kreeshkra.

"Yes, isn't she," Fafhrd agreed blandly.

"You should have seen mine," the Mouser boasted. "I don't mean Reetha there, I mean my *weird* one. She had—"

"Don't let Kreeshkra hear you use that word,"

Fafhrd warned sharply though *sub voce*.

"Well, anyhow, whenever I want to see her again," the Mouser continued conspiratorially, "I have only to swallow the contents of this black vial and—"

"I'll take charge of that," Reetha announced crisply, snatching it out of his hand from behind him. She glanced at it, then expertly pitched it through a window into the Inner Sea.

The Mouser started a glare at her which turned into an ingratiating smile.

Flapping her black robe to cool her, Kreeshkra came up behind Fafhrd. "Introduce me to your friends, dear," she directed.

Meanwhile around the golden couch was an ever-thickening press of courtiers, nobles, councillors, and officers. New titles were being awarded by the dozen to all first-comers. Sentences of perpetual banishment and confiscation of property were being laid on Hisvin and all others absent, guilty or guiltless. Reports were coming in of the successful fighting of all fires in the city and the complete vanishment of rats from its streets. Plans were being laid for the complete extirpation from under the city of the entire rat-metropolis of Lankhmar Below—subtle and complex plans which did not sound to the Mouser entirely practical. It was becoming clear that under the saintly Radomix Kistomerces, Lankhmar would more than ever be ruled by foolish fantasy and shameless greed. At moments like these it was easy to understand why the Gods *of* Lankhmar were so furiously exasperated by their city.

Various lukewarm thanks were extended to the Mouser and Fafhrd, although most of the newcomers seemed not at all clear as to what part the two heroes had played in conquering the rats, despite Elakeria's repeated accounts of the final fighting and of Glipkerio's sea-plunge. Soon, clearly, seeds would be planted against the Mouser and Fafhrd in Radomix's saintly-vague mind, and their bright heroic roles imperceptibly darkened to blackest villainy.

At the same time it became evident that the new court was disturbed by the restless tramping of the four ominous war-horses, three Ghoulish and one Mingol, and that the presence of an animated skeleton was becoming more and more disquieting, for Kreeshkra continued to wear her black robe and hood like a loose garment. Fafhrd and the Mouser looked at one another, and then at Kreeshkra and Reetha, and they realized that there was agreement between them. The Northerner mounted the Mingol mare, and the Mouser and Reetha the two leftover Ghoulish horses, and they all four made their way out of the Rainbow Palace as quietly as is possible when hooves clop on tile.

Thereafter there swiftly grew in Lankhmar a new legend of the Gray Mouser and Fafhrd: how as rat-small midget and bell-tower-tall giant they had saved Lankhmar from the rats, but at the price of being personally summoned and escorted to the Afterworld by Death himself, for the black-robed ivory skeleton was remembered as male, which would doubtless have irked Kreeshkra greatly.

However, as next morning the four rode under the fading stars toward the paling east along the twisty causeway across the Great Salt Marsh, they were all merry enough in their own fashions. They had commandeered three donkeys and laden them with the box of jewels the Mouser had abstracted from Glipkerio's bed-chamber and with food and drink for a long journey, though exactly where that journey would lead they had not yet agreed. Fafhrd argued for a trip to his beloved Cold Waste, with a long stop-over on the way at the City of Ghouls. The Mouser was equally enthusiastic for the Eastern Lands, slyly pointing out to Reetha what an ideal place it would be for sunbathing unclad.

Yanking up her violet robe to make herself more comfortable, Reetha nodded her agreement. "Clothes are so itchy," she said. "I can hardly bear them. I like to ride bareback—my back, not the horse's. While hair is even itchier—I can feel mine growing. You will have to shave me every day, dear," she added to the Mouser.

He agreed to take on that chore, but added, "However, I can't concur with you altogether, sweet. Besides protecting from brambles and dust, clothes give one a certain dignity."

Reetha retorted tartly, "I think there's far more dignity in the naked body."

"Pish, girl," Kreeshkra told her, "what can compare with the dignity of naked bones?" But glancing toward Fafhrd's red beard and red, curled chest, she added, "However, there is something to be said for hair."

A magnificent new illustrated novel by the author of RINGWORLD and co-author of LUCIFER'S HAMMER!

$4.95 *Cover illustration by Boris*

Here is a science-fantasy novel such as only Larry Niven could create. And to make this magical tale even more so, it is stunningly and profusely illustrated with black and white drawings by Esteban Maroto in this special over-sized (6" x 9") edition.

 Ace Science Fiction